Bountiful Bridge
www.bountifulbridge.com

Acknowledgments

This book is dedicated to my family. Without them, I would not be where I am today. This is a journey of creativity; my creative energy blossoms through them. May my daughters always believe in their dreams as I have. Follow your heart, always be true to yourself, and magic will happen in your life.
My life's journey has led me to this moment to be able to write this book. At times, it was something that I never thought I would do. Friends and family knew otherwise and helped support this dream to come true.
Thank you, friends, for believing in me.
To my Ava. You have helped me, inspired me, pushed me, and supported me. For that, I am eternally grateful. I love you with my whole heart.
To my readers - I always look at books as a moment of escape but also to immerse myself in a different life or journey. So, thank you for trusting me and going on this journey with me. It means more than you will ever know.
For my muse with the opal eyes - only you and I know if you are real. The true joy in writing this story is that you vividly came to life in this book. Therefore, you will forever live in my heart.
To Kyra and Gina, for hearing me, believing in me, and driving me forward. You are my forever people.

Happy Reading.

FROM THE AUTHOR

There isn't always a clear path to love and happiness. A person's journey to find this sometimes occurs through trial and error but eventually finds its way. Much involves genuinely wanting to be happy and figuring out how to get there. This can be enriched by sharing that journey with someone that sees what you see, loves how you love, and appreciates taking that journey with you.

This book attempts to encompass a story of just that, along with discovering happiness, individually and with someone. I hope you draw inspiration to pave your own path toward love and happiness.

Be a reflection of light and love in a world that sometimes does not see or appreciate its beauty.

Illuminate love where darkness and hate sometimes prevail. Journeys have highs and lows, yet one cannot truly be appreciated without the other.

"There comes a point in your life when you need to stop reading other people's books and write your own."

- Albert Einstein

PROLOGUE

WINTER WAVES

"Through the gray, love always finds its way."

Emma stood at the edge of the sand, leaning over the vast sea of water. Her head lifted toward the gray sky as if wishing the ocean waves would gently wash away her unease. It was an especially chilly day on the Oregon coast. Perhaps it was the change in the weather, but she felt it reflected the sadness she was immersed in.

She knew it wouldn't be easy, but she had returned to say goodbye. That was what she was determined to do. How could she possibly make it through the next several days, weeks, or years? Her constant solace of strength had passed away three days before, and her heart hadn't been the same.

She took gentle deep breaths in hopes that the scents and smells of the west coast would calm her and make it all ok.

"Deep breaths. Slow, deep breaths. One moment at a time. That's what she would want you to do." She slowly repeated as she silently pushed back the tears and looked up to the sky.

Only the gentle tug of the leash in her left hand offered the touch of comfort that she so desperately needed right now. Brayley had a way of making her feel a sense of calm.

He stood along the sand, staring off into the distance. Something about the gray, windy days along the ocean gave him energy and inspiration. It was good that Jake had barked his way into a walk earlier. They both needed the break. The water made ideas flow, and that was just what he needed.

As he stood along the shore, he turned to his left, and could it be?

She moved away years ago after he had left for the military, although he always thought she'd stay. He couldn't tear his eyes away from her.

The tall, slim figure in the distance was wrapped in a long black coat, a dark gray wool scarf blowing in the breeze that intermixed gently with her flowing auburn hair.

On top of her head was a fur Pom-Pom beanie hat. He warmly recalled that she could never pass up a good knit hat. The memory made him gently smile.

Perhaps it was the fresh air jarring his memory, and it wasn't whom he thought. Yet just as soon as he felt it wasn't her, he looked a little closer. Was it her? Could it be the only one that's ever made his heart beat this quick or make him smile this big?

Miles slowly walked towards her, trying to be cautious about approaching someone who may be a stranger, but Jake had another agenda.

Before he knew what was happening, the dog started barking loudly and incessantly, running quicker than Miles could keep up. The quicker he tried to run, the faster Jake pulled him forward.

Miles suddenly face-planted in the sand, letting go of the leash, allowing Jake to run free toward the dog sitting next to the woman in the distance. Cautiousness fled like the ocean wind.

Miles quickly popped to his feet and tried to run after Jake, who was animatedly trying to play with his new dog friend he saw on the beach. As he approached, still unsure of who this woman was, it was with one single sound that he knew it was her. He could hear her laugh. It was a sound that he would recognize anywhere.

He stopped a few feet away and asked, "Is it you?"

Emma's laughter stopped. Hurt flashed in her eyes momentarily and was almost immediately replaced with a tinge of sadness.

"Yes, it is me. Is it you?" she said with a slow smile.

"I didn't realize you were in town."

More sadness entered her eyes as she said earnestly, "I just got back. Grammy finally passed. I didn't make it in time. And...I guess it doesn't matter now."

He felt a jolt of sadness for her. How did he not know that Grammy had passed? He knew she wasn't doing well, but it didn't occur to him that the stoic, strong, lively woman living in the Glass House would not live forever.

"Emma, I am so very sorry. I didn't know she passed away. I guess I've been a little distracted with, well, everything. Listen, do you need anything?"

A lump rose in her throat, and she instinctually touched the scar on her neck. *Of course*, she thought, *I need you. Stop, Emma. Don't go down that path. You get hurt every time.*

So, she stood a little straighter, a little stiffer to guard her heart, as she had so many times before.

She looked at him and lightly said, "No, I'll be fine. Thank you. The funeral arrangements are pretty set. You know how Grammy was. She made sure everything was always in place. Her funeral is no different."

Instantly, she was jolted forward by the dogs tugging at their leashes, playfully wrestling in the sand. She bumped straight into Miles's chest. Emma reached forward and gently but awkwardly touched his chest to steady herself. For a moment, she missed touching him.

Simultaneously, they both yelled, " Jake!" They caught each other's eye with an amused look that mirrored their thoughts. They always had a way of saying and doing the same things simultaneously. It had been that way from the beginning.

Some things never change.

CHAPTER 1

THE BEGINNING

" Love knows no age, space, or time. It only knows the heart it finds."

The excitement of the first away football game in the fall of 1998 was like an electric current running through the high school. The rival teams were set to meet on Friday night, and everyone was excited to go. It was the game of the year.

The students constantly planned whom to ride with and where they would meet. There were two popular pizza places in town, so it was a 50/50 shot of where the groups_would meet.

Emma was still relatively new to this high school. She and her mom had officially moved back to town at the beginning of Emma's senior year.

She felt relieved when Isabelle Price, one of the more popular girls in her class, invited her to ride with some classmates. Izzy, as she liked to be called, told Emma to meet the group at Rinaldo's Italian Pizza after school.

It took more than a bit of convincing for her mother to feel comfortable with everyone riding together to the away game. Emma's mom liked to keep tabs on everything she did, much like Grammy. She often thought that all of their questions were annoying. Yet, she also understood that they loved her and wanted her to be safe. Caroline said this to her daughter as they pulled into Rinaldo's parking lot.

"Mom, we will be fine. This game happens every year. We aren't going that far away. I'll be home before you know it."

"I just wish you could tell me when you got there and when you were coming home," said Caroline. She loved her daughter so much. The roads to the next town were curvy, and no stranger to black ice around dusk and at night. "Just make sure that whoever is driving pays attention to the road and not the chatter in the car."

"Ok, Mom, I get it. We will be careful. Now, can I have $10 for pizza? I'm starving!" And with that, Emma grabbed the cash from her mother's hand and bounded out of the car before she could say anything else. As she closed the door to her mother's reminder of "I love you! Be safe!" she turned around, smiled, waved, and quickly ran into the restaurant.

Rinaldo's was bustling with kids eating and chatting inside before the caravan left for the game. It was hard to spot Izzy initially because of the number of people there. Just as she tried to squeeze past a large group in the waiting area, Emma accidentally bumped into a tall guy with sandy brown hair. "Oh, sorry! Just trying to get through!" she said to the stranger's back. She then heard a smooth, calm voice say, "Well, you can bump into me anytime."

Emma looked up and was met with the most gorgeous blue eyes and bright smile she had ever seen. The feeling she had was so strong that it startled her a little. She stammered for a moment before saying, "Oh, yeah, well, sorry, anyway. Just looking for my friend." then quickly squeezed past as she finally saw Izzy in the distance.

"Emma, over here! We just ordered. Come on! I saved you a spot!" Izzy was standing on a chair in the far left corner of the restaurant. As Emma made her way over, she began to think, *Who was that guy with the gorgeous blue eyes, and why was her heart beating so hard in her chest? Whatever,* she thought flippantly. She was starving.

"Are you ok?" Izzy said, "You look a bit flush." *Great,* Emma thought, *my face is red.* How embarrassing, which of course, only made her flush more. "Seriously, are you ok? Why are you so flustered?" Izzy remarked as Emma sat down. She took a second to adjust her backpack behind her chair, hoping to slow her heartbeat a bit. "Oh, nothing. It is so warm in here with all of these people! I'm glad you ordered already because I am starving! Plus, mom was rambling about being safe and paying attention to the road, blah, blah, blah."

"Ok, I just thought you were flush from running into the gorgeous Mr. Miles Woods." said Izzy. *Wait, what? Who was this guy,* Emma thought.

"Well, no. Who? Why haven't I heard of this person before now?" Emma quickly replied.

"Oh, so he did grab your attention! Just like every other girl in town!" laughed Izzy. "He's the big brother of one of the cheerleaders, so he's going to watch the game and make sure she stays in check! Miles graduated last year. He works at the local wood mill for now, but I guess he's headed off to the Navy sooner or later. All the girls have eyes for him, and he's left a few broken hearts around here. Guess you gotta watch those blue eyes!"

Emma thought *I'd love to stare at those eyes all day. Stop! Oh my gosh! Great, now I'm blushing again.*

"Seriously, Emma. I've never seen you like this!" Izzy said with another giggle. With that, their pizza arrived, and they gobbled it up before hitting the road.

Everyone in the restaurant seemed to head into the parking lot at the same time, so Emma followed right along as the crowd filed out. She was so distracted by her literal run-in with Miles that she didn't ask Izzy whom they were riding with.

As it turned out, Izzy had talked to Nate about riding in his car, so they walked toward his sporty black sedan and began to get in the back.

"Hey, Izzy, want to ride up front with me?" Nate said suddenly.

"No, I'm good. Gotta keep my girl, Emma, in check, ya know?" Izzy quickly responded and gave me a side-eye to support her comment.

"Yeah, I need my Izzy to keep me in line!" giggled Emma as they climbed into the back seat.

Nate and his friend, Jon, sat up front, and before Emma realized what was happening, someone was pushing her into the middle of the back seat. A shrill voice yelled, "Room for one more? Let's go!"

Emma looked to her left to see a gorgeous waft of blonde hair shaking side to side. It was Jennifer, one of the more popular girls in school. She had always seemed friendly enough, so Emma thought nothing of it. As she slid over and tried to adjust herself in the small back seat, she felt Izzy grab her hand. She looked over and noticed that Izzy was giving her a look that said, *Oh, great.* Not knowing what that meant and having no way of getting the scoop from Izzy, she just slightly shrugged, scooted over, and tried to start a conversation with Jennifer. Izzy slumped to the right side of the car seat as if she were giving up.

As they took off down the road, it wasn't long before Emma realized why Izzy had given her the strange look earlier. Jennifer would not stop talking, laughing, and grabbing Nate's seat as he drove, and she was constantly pushing Emma out of the way to reach up to adjust the radio station. *This is going to get old fast,* Emma thought.

Emma also noticed that Nate had a bit of a lead foot, and when Jennifer grabbed his shoulders or adjusted the radio station again, he took his eyes off the road.

They continued on the curvy roads that led inland towards Nettleton, where the game would be played. It was about 45 minutes inland from Heceta Beach, with only a thick covering of pine trees in between the two towns.

The sun and the temperatures were falling fast since it was late autumn. When that happens, black ice can form unexpectedly, especially in the wooded areas they were driving through.

Aside from a few cabins or trailers scattered here and there, it was a dense forest. The road was only two lanes with no highway lights, so it was common for animals, mainly deer, to run out onto the road, especially around dusk.

The timing was perfect for a mama deer and her young to intercept Nate's speeding car suddenly. In his confidence to race past everyone, he had taken the lead in the caravan. No vehicles were ahead of him when the deer family trotted onto the narrow, curvy road. Jennifer again reached over Emma toward the front console to turn up the volume to hear her favorite Journey song.

Nate looked down in amusement, wishing she was reaching into his lap instead of the volume button. The quick shift of his eyes was enough to narrowly miss the deer trotting onto the curved road.

Emma suddenly screamed, "Look out, Nate!"

He veered to the right, barely missing the last baby deer running across the road. Hitting the brakes a little too hard, the car hit black ice and suddenly spun out of control—one, two, then three rotational spins. Jennifer was thrown forward, violently hitting her head on the dashboard and finally landing in Jon's lap. Nate fought valiantly to regain control of his black sedan as the deer dashed to the other side of the road. Before anyone knew what was happening, the car landed in a ditch and slammed into a sturdy pine tree.

What in the hell just happened was Emma's first thought as she lifted herself off of Izzy. She quickly looked ahead and into the front seat. Nate looked stunned but aware of what happened. Jennifer was not so gracefully splayed out onto Jon's lap, knocked out cold, with the slightest bit of blood beginning to ooze from her forehead. *What in the holy hell? Emma* was stunned. *Mama was right. Now what?*

"Um, is everyone ok back there?" Nate said with the heaviness of someone that knew he had done wrong.

He hesitantly turned to see Emma and Izzy's surprised, scared faces. "Yeah. I think we are ok." Emma said as she slowly leaned forward to gain her bearings. "Izzy, are you ok?"

"Yeah. I'm ok. Just a little shaky. I don't think I'm hurt. Is Jennifer ok?" Izzy said with a little more bravery than she honestly felt.

And with that, Jennifer was conscious. "What in the hell just happened! Nate, what were you thinking? Oh my God! Is that blood on my forehead? That is totally going to ruin my makeup! Jon, seriously, are you trying to hold my hand right now? Ewe! Let go! Does anyone have, like, a tissue or something to get this blood? Oh my God! It's, like, going to leave a scar. I am ruined!"

Her rambling didn't stop; it made Emma and Izzy's heads spin all the more.

Until there was a gentle knock on the back driver's side window. "Hello? Are you guys ok? Holy shit, that was crazy! Seriously, are you guys ok?"

Still trying to gain her bearings, Emma looked to her left to see who stood outside her window. She had a hard time sitting up to see who was standing outside. She lifted her body off of Izzy to see who was there.

Just as she peered out the back passenger window, she was met with one gorgeous blue eye. *What? Really? Who's eyes are that blue? Oh, ok. Play it cool,* Emma thought.

Of course. It was Miles.

CHAPTER 2

LET THE GAMES BEGIN

" Games of the Heart are never easily won, perhaps because, in the end, everyone loses."

Emma stared out the window, trying to think of something to say. Suddenly, Miles' whole face peered into the window, looking directly into Emma's eyes. Simultaneously, they both said, "Is it you?"

They both looked surprised and then started to laugh at the irony.

"Miles, oh, thank goodness. Can you help us get out of here?" Izzy said a little too loudly from behind as she pushed Emma toward the rear car door. Since the sedan had landed in a ditch, they leaned severely to the right and downward. Gravity pulled them back and made opening the door to climb out a challenge.

Emma grabbed the handle with her hand but had to force the door open by pushing it hard with her foot. She slid forward to get her left leg to reach the ground for more balance. Suddenly, she could feel the door's weight lifting off her right leg. She stumbled as both of her feet hit the dirt.

As she tried to avoid falling headfirst into the ditch, she felt a strong arm around her waist, catching her as she almost fell. She looked up, and there were those blue eyes again.

Miles peered down at her, smiling, and said, "We really have to stop bumping into each other." Oh, there was that out-of-control heartbeat again. *Stop, Emma. Say something. Anything.*

"Well, that's quite a line." she stammered. *Ugh. Embarrassing*, she thought.

Miles laughed at her response, saying, "Well, it seems you keep bumping into me. I don't even know your name. Or should I call you "It's Me?""

Emma laughed, "No, of course. I'm Em-" Izzy was pushing on the car door behind them and started yelling, "Emma, Miles, are you going to get me outta here?"

They quickly looked toward Izzy and reached to help pull her to her feet. She started to thank them when Jennifer suddenly started pushing Izzy from behind.

Her blond hair seemed to explode from the car, just like her words. "Help me out of here. I'm bleeding. Actually bleeding, y'all. Please, can someone just help me? Jon keeps trying to hold my hand. I was stuck in the front seat. Did I mention that I'm bleeding, and it's getting on my sweater? Oh, damn it! That's going to stain..."

And on and on went her chatter, even when the three of them hoisted her out of the car and onto the roadside. She never stopped talking.

The girls watched Miles climb back into the ditch to help give Nate and Jon a hand out of the car. Nate got a better view of the damage outside the vehicle. He was not happy, and it showed.

Nate suddenly started yelling, "God damn it! My dad is gonna kill me! How the hell am I going to get this out of here? Oh, man! Look at the dent on the backside. Damn, deer. And fucking Jennifer! Couldn't stop messing with the radio!"

His anger rose within him so quickly that he kicked the other side of the car, leaving another small dent. "Fuck!" he screamed.

The girls watched them while Jon and Miles stood beside him as Nate ranted about his wrecked car. Miles knew he needed to try and calm him down. He said, "Dude, it's ok. No one got hurt. We can try and get this out of here. I'll go get my truck."

He turned to go up the bank and heard the sirens in the distance. The police were on their way, so there was no need for Miles to stick around.

Jogging quickly back down the hill, Miles called out to the guys below, "The cops are on pulling up now. Their rig can pull you out, so you'll be fine. See you guys at the game?"

The other two guys nodded in agreement while Jon tried to get Nate to calm down a bit more before the police got to them.

As Miles climbed back up to the roadside, he thought about asking Izzy and his new friend Emma to ride with him to the game. The new girl intrigued him, and he wanted to talk to her more.

Yet, they were nowhere in sight when he stepped onto the pavement.

Looking off in the distance, a few small crowds of people had gathered near Miles's dark blue truck.

Since Nate was leading the caravan when he lost control, most of the other cars had pulled off onto the side of the road to see if they could help.

The scene was chaotic as more police cars, an ambulance, and a tow truck arrived. The bright lights from the service vehicles lit up the road and pine trees like Independence Day.

He spotted Jennifer in the first group of kids, babbling about her part in the drama and still asking for tissues. She eventually got into the ambulance to get her forehead checked.

As an officer stepped off to the side, Miles finally spotted the ladies talking to a different cop. It was chilly and dark, so the officer had the girls sit in the police car to take their statements.

Miles still wanted to see if Emma and Izzy were attending the game.

Nate and Jon finally climbed up to the roadside and talked with the tow truck driver about recovering his car. Nate still looked pretty upset, and although quiet, Jon appeared to be a little shaky. This made Miles wonder if any of them would make it to the game.

An officer appeared as Miles approached his truck and began addressing the gathered groups.

The tall officer spoke sternly, "If you weren't in the wrecked car, please return to your vehicles and be on your way. Follow me if you haven't given me your statement. Otherwise, please leave the scene so we can wrap this up."

Everyone scattered pretty quickly, and Miles didn't want to cause any trouble. Not sure he would see the girls again, he climbed into his truck.

"What up, brother? Everyone good?" said Big Reggie.

There was a reason why everyone called Reginald Jones by the name of Big Reggie. The boy was big, not too bright, and although not a man of many words, somehow always became the life of the party.

Big Reggie had decided to wait in the car when he and Miles came across the accident. He knew the police would be arriving soon and didn't want to draw any attention to himself or, more importantly, the 12-pack of beer he had stowed at his feet. That boy loved beer and hardly went anywhere without it.

Miles started the truck and leaned forward slightly to look into his side-view mirror. The line of cars slowly moving up behind him seemed endless, so he sat back to wait for the traffic to clear.

"Yeah, everyone is good. Nate's pissed, but only because his dad will give him hell about wrecking his car. Jenny wouldn't shut up." replied Miles.

Big Reggie giggled and said, "Does she ever?" as he tilted his open beer to his mouth and took a giant swig.

"Are we headed to the game?" said Big Reggie. Still watching the line of cars pass him from behind, Miles took a pinch of snuff from his container and said, "Yeah. I have got to keep Linds under control." He, of course, was referring to his little sister, Lindsey.

She was the youngest of the three and the wildest. And that was saying a lot considering how much trouble the Woods boys always seemed to get themselves into. She was the only girl, the baby. Beautiful, blonde, and too smart for her own good. Miles was not about to have her get into any trouble. She was less than a year away from her high school graduation, and he would ensure she made it.

Big Reggie took another swig of beer and asked about the girls in the car with Nate and Jon. At this point, they were back on the road and headed to the game. Miles leaned back and thought about how to play this, not wanting to let on that he had his eye on someone new.

"Oh, it was Izzy, Jennifer, and the new girl. What's her name?" Miles paused and tried to appear like he was thinking about her name. Of course, he knew it, but he had to play it cool. "Oh, yeah, Emily. No. Emma." he muttered. Big Reggie gave him a side-eye as he finished the last of his beer. "Gotcha." was all he said back.

As they drove the last twenty minutes to the football field, they continued with small talk while Big Reggie downed another beer. Miles couldn't get Emma out of his head the whole time he drove. She was stunningly beautiful to him, and he just wanted to kiss her.

They pulled into the high school stadium parking lot, which was already packed, and found a spot near a faraway tree line. Miles slowly backed his truck in, turned off the engine, and grabbed a beer.

Big Reggie grinned and said, "About time you start to try to catch up. Let's down a few and then head in."

They snickered at knowing they were breaking the rules by drinking before a high school game. As they clinked their beer bottles together and gave them a good chug, a cop car appeared at the front of the parking lot.

Miles watched curiously as the car slowed and stopped at the game's main entrance. Big Reggie was busy amusing himself by burping the alphabet, even though he seemed to forget a few of the letters. Miles continued to keep a direct eye on the patrol car.

After a few minutes, a tall, slender policeman got out and walked around to the passenger side. He opened the car door, and slowly, Izzy and Emma emerged. Miles felt a little flutter in his stomach when he saw Emma. She had made it to the game!

He quickly downed the rest of his beer, told Big Reggie to do the same, and tossed his empty bottle into the woods behind the truck. Miles said, "Let's go, man. The game's gonna start!"

Big Reggie lumbered out of the truck and belched ridiculously loud while he tossed his beer bottles into the brush.

"All right, man, don't get your panties in a twist. Let's go!" he said jovially as they walked toward the entrance.

Big Reggie had to double-step to catch up with Miles. That boy was on a mission to get into the game. The admission line was long, which made Miles impatient. He wanted nothing more than to see Emma again.

"I knew I should have had Linds get me tickets ahead of time." Miles said under his breath.

Big Reggie laughed and said, "Boy, you should have had yourself another beer because you are being a tight ass about this line. Just chill, dude."

Miles looked annoyed at his friend but tried to play it cool as they inched their way inside. With sarcasm dripping from his voice, Miles shuffled forward, looked over his shoulder at Big Reg, and said, "Listen, if there is one person who knows about asses, it is me."

And with that, he bumped right into Emma's backside.

"Um, excuse me?" she purred.

Miles was startled that he had bumped into this gorgeous girl once again. He sputtered before thinking about what he was saying, "Is it you? Oh, yeah... Well, I do know about asses."

He was trying to recover from what he said to his friend, but instead, he fucked it up. *Damn it*, he thought. His face was turning a funny shade of pink, which Emma found very amusing.

She waited a moment to see if he would say anything else, but he thought better of it.

"Well, I may not know that much about asses, but I sure can spot an asshole when I see one," Emma responded, and just as quickly, she sauntered off to find Izzy.

What the hell was that? is precisely what Emma and Miles thought as they both turned and walked off in separate directions.

Big Reggie giggled as he put his arm around Miles while they walked off to the sidelines.

Emma was left flustered, and it showed as she rejoined Izzy.

"Are you ok?" Izzy was curious as she had noticed that Miles and Emma seemed to have some conversation, but she didn't think it went well. Emma tried to shake off the questions in her head quickly, but she couldn't stop thinking of Miles. It showed. At least to Izzy, and she wasn't about to let it go.

She looked inquisitively at Emma and said, "Do you have a thing for Miles?" in a tone almost like school kids chanting "K-I-S-S-I-N-G."

This bothered Emma even more, and she was trying not to let it show. She shook her head and answered, "No, of course not. I don't even know him. Well, other than the fact that he likes asses."

Izzy's eyes grew wide as she intriguingly said, "What? Tell me more!"

The girls giggled and linked arm-in-arm as Emma relayed her funny interaction with Miles. She decided to blow off her odd feelings and enjoy the game. So, they joined the others in the bleachers and cheered on the team.

Heceta Beach ended up beating Nettleton 45-3. It was embarrassing, but the students loved it! The cheers were loud, and the excitement was incredible. Spirits were high as everyone began heading to the parking lot.

The ladies were so into cheering on the team that they never thought to ask someone for a ride home. They temporarily forgot that the friendly officer offered to bring them to the game. They discussed whom they would ride with as they headed into the parking lot.

"Well, I'd rather stay with you since I don't know that many people yet," Emma said to Izzy as Big Reggie stumbled past.

Izzy was thinking and talking at the same time since she was noticing how quickly the parking lot was clearing out. She was trying to figure out who had enough seats left in their car so that they could both ride together.

She looked at Emma with slightly worried eyes and said, "Gosh, I'm sorry, Emma. I should have been thinking about how to get home earlier. Don't worry. We'll find a ride."

Big Reggie picked up on their conversation and proceeded to edge his way closer to the pretty girl with brown hair. Emma could smell the beer on his breath and casually stepped to the side. He didn't notice and offered assistance by saying, " You know, Miles and I came over together. It'll be a tight squeeze in his truck, but ya'll can hitch a ride with us. But ya gotta be willing to hold my beer when I tell ya."

Emma looked over at Izzy as if to say, *"You've got to be kidding me,"* but Izzy didn't notice.

"Are you sure? Where's Miles?" Izzy asked. Emma was not thrilled, but then again, what choice did they have as they saw the almost empty parking lot?

"He's in the pisser. That boy can't hold his beer." Big Reggie said with a giggle and a little belch under his breath. He was in the presence of ladies, after all.

Miles sauntered out of the bathroom with his hands casually tucked into the front pockets of his jeans. Izzy and Emma looked at him as he walked over in his white T-shirt, black leather jacket, and slightly too-tight jeans.

What was it about a guy that dressed like a rebel? Don't know, but girls love it, Emma thought.

Miles was more than pleased to see that the two prettiest girls in the place were finally hanging out with him and Big Reg.

He smiled, looked at Emma, and said, "You still on asshole duty or what?"

The girls laughed, and Izzy stepped in to answer quickly. "Oh, it's always easy to spot one of those. What we need is a ride back to town. Mind if we catch a ride with you and Big Reg?"

Well, that was the best news that Miles had heard all night. He could hopefully redeem himself and get to know Emma better. He started walking into the parking lot, knowing the group would follow him, and casually responded, "I guess so. I am headed back that way. Let's go."

As they arrived back at the truck, Emma quickly realized that the words "tight squeeze" put it lightly.

How were they all going to fit? It was like Miles could read her mind because he started explaining where everyone could sit without Emma saying a word.

"I'll just pull the cooler in the back, adjust the jump seat, and your skinny little ass can fit right back there." he said with that ornery smile she was quickly starting to like more and more.

She smiled back and sarcastically said, "Oh, so you *have* been checking out my ass."

He continued to smile but decided to hold his tongue as he pushed the truck's front seat forward to pull out the cooler. He tossed it in the back of the truck.

Big Reggie must have heard the sound of the beer bottles rattling in the cooler because he was at the back of the truck, popping open the cooler and passing out the cold beverages before anyone could say anything.

He explained that the caravan back to town would be slow, so they might as well hang around for a few minutes and have a beer.

So, Miles let down the truck's back gate, and the girls sat on the edge while the guys wandered along the edge of the woods.

They all had beers to sip on, but Emma could tell Miles barely drank his. That made her feel better since he was the driver.

They all chatted for quite a while, and as they talked, Miles found himself leaning on the outside of the truck but close to Emma. Her back mainly was towards him, and in the dark, it was hard for her to notice that he kept staring at her.

He thought she was beautiful. Her face and lips enticed him, and he loved her long auburn hair.

As she told a story, a gentle breeze blew and pushed delicate wisps of hair into her face. Without even thinking, he reached across and lightly lifted the hair away so she could finish talking.

His fine touch surprised her and sent a shock through her system. The feeling took her breath away, so she subtly tried to control herself by telling her story as normally as possible.

Emma wondered if anyone had noticed her reaction because she felt like she had been hit with a lightning bolt. Miles had seen her response and was shocked to realize he had felt the same thing.

He wanted to touch her again, so in the dark, with the shadow of Emma blocking the view from everyone else, he gently reached down and rested his hand on her shoulder. As his hand lay there, he couldn't help but play with a few strands of her hair. It felt so soft and light. It also felt a little dangerous to touch her without anyone else knowing. It was like their little secret.

As the four of them continued chatting, Emma finally regained the courage to turn around and look at Miles. His hand on her shoulder was warm and comforting.

When he looked down at her, he could see in her eyes that she welcomed his gentle touch. They were drawn to each other without even knowing much about one another. It was a surreal feeling for the two. It was something that they couldn't explain, but it felt good, almost natural.

Before they knew it, an hour or more had passed, and they needed to get on the road. The girls had finished their beers and had wandered into the woods to pee before they left.

It was dark, but their chatter and giggles let the guys know where they were. Big Reggie grabbed two more beers from the cooler, shut the truck's tailgate, and started walking toward the passenger side to get in.

Miles called out to him, "Gotta piss. Start the engine, and I'll be back in two." Big Reg stepped back and caught the keys Miles had tossed in his direction.

He laughed again as he got in the car and said, "Boy, you have got to learn how to hold your piss!"

So as not to startle the girls, Miles gently whistled as he walked into the woods. It signaled that he was there but far enough away not to freak them out.

He was zipping up his fly when he felt a pair of soft, gentle hands reach around his waist from behind. *She feels so good*; he thought as she hugged him close.

As the dark figure swiftly moved before him and wrapped her arms around his neck, he leaned down to kiss her. She didn't hesitate, and soon they were passionately kissing.

A rustling of the leaves in the woods suddenly caught Miles's attention, followed by a voice saying, "Izzy, where did you go? You can't leave a girl with her pants down."

She was giggling, but as soon as Emma was close enough to see what was happening, she stopped.

Izzy and Miles were embracing, and she could see Izzy leaning into Miles's chest. Emma was confused about what she saw but felt she had interrupted them.

Embarrassed, she started to walk back to the truck quickly. She could see the taillights in the distance since Reg had started the truck. She needed to get away from them.

Her thoughts began to race again. *Does he just see which girl will kiss him first?* She had been warned that he was a player but didn't think it would happen this fast. At this point, she just wanted to go home.

Miles pushed Izzy's hands away as soon as he saw Emma head back to the truck. He was pissed and confused. He could have sworn those hands and kisses were Emma. That's who he wanted it to be.

What was Izzy thinking? This is precisely what he asked her as they stood in the woods. Izzy laughed, walked towards the truck, and explained quickly, "Oh, come on, Miles. You know you've always wanted to kiss me. Now let's hit the road!"

When they got to the truck, Emma was sitting in the jump seat behind the driver's side, looking sullen and tired. Izzy bounded into the middle of the front seat and grabbed a beer from Big Reg. She smiled back at Emma as she twisted the cap off the beer. "Want one, sweetie?" she said to Emma.

Miles was in the driver's seat, looking in the rearview mirror at Emma. Their eyes met in the mirror, and they stared back at each other as Emma responded, "No, I'm good. Let's just get home. It's been quite a night."

CHAPTER 3

HISTORY

" Always bound to repeat itself."

Miles pulled up to the house and adjusted the front seat to let Emma out of the back. He kept looking over his shoulder at her home and couldn't help but ask, "Is this your house? I thought this is where The Raymonds lived."

Emma was anxious to get inside and leave this night behind, so she nonchalantly responded, "Yeah, it is. They're my grandparents. My mom and I live here with Grammy now. Look, thanks for the lift home. I gotta go."

He could sense her frustration, and it bothered him. He didn't want her to go in yet, so he quickly said, "Emma, it was really nice to meet you tonight, and it was no problem with bringing you home. Would you ever want to hang out sometime?"

She couldn't believe what she was hearing. Did he not remember that she discovered him kissing her best friend a little more than an hour ago?

She stumbled over her words as she responded, "Um, yeah, nice to meet you, too. I'm sure we'll see each other around. It's a small town. Ok, good night."

She peered into the truck and said, "Good night, Iz. I'll talk to you tomorrow. Big Reg, well, it was a pleasure."

She couldn't help but smile at the sweet, drunk, big guy. He leaned forward, and an unexpected belch escaped his mouth, "Oops. Uh, yeah, good to meet you, too. See ya later."

Emma turned and briskly walked down the path to the front door, opened it, and went inside without looking back. She didn't realize that Miles just stood and watched her until she closed the door. He didn't know how, but he wanted to see her again.

Grammy and Mom were sitting in the living room when Emma walked in. Her mom stood up as soon as the front door opened.

She couldn't help herself because she had been so worried, "Emma, there you are. It was so late, and we were beyond worried. Why didn't you just come home after the car accident? Where have you been? How did you get home? It's been hours."

Grammy could sense that Emma was a bit overwhelmed, so she quickly interjected, "Caroline, she's home safe now, so just give her a minute. Emma, get settled, and we will meet you in the kitchen to discuss this."

Emma dropped her jacket and purse at the front door, kicked off her shoes, and decided to get this over with. She'd had enough for one night and just wanted to go to bed.

As all three walked into the kitchen, it was impossible not to notice the clear moonlight shining in through the wall of windows that faced the ocean.

Grammy glanced up and said to no one in particular, "That view will never cease to amaze me. Pete knew what he was doing when he built this house."

Caroline was busy putting the kettle on the stove for tea. Emma said, "You're right, Grammy. It sure is a gorgeous view. Look at the moon. It's so close. You can almost touch it."

Her mom turned around, crossed her arms, and leaned against the counter. She was ready to talk about what happened with Emma and was not at all interested in the moonlight view.

Her voice was curt and robust as she began, "Emma, I was worried about you going to the game in the first place. When Jenny's mom called to let me know about the accident, I was stunned that I hadn't heard from you. Where did you go? Are you ok?"

"Mom, slow down. I'm fine. I know you were worried, but I didn't think Jenny's mom would call you right away. Since Izzy and I were ok, we still wanted to go to the game. We gave our side of the story to the policeman, and then he offered to drive us the rest of the way to the game." Emma explained.

She continued, "We had so much fun at the game that we forgot to figure out how we would get home. Two guys from Heceta Beach offered to give us a ride back. They wanted to let the traffic die down a bit before we got on the road, so we just hung out in the parking lot for a while. Mom, it was fine. Look, I'm good as new." She twirled around the kitchen and stopped just in front of her mother to take the cup of tea from her hands.

Grammy found this amusing, but her mom was not done with her lecture.

Caroline looked at her daughter with a bit of amusement, but there was still worry in her voice as she spoke, "You know how much I love you. I worry when I'm not with you, which made me concerned when Jenny's mom called. We've already lost your dad, and now, Gramps. I can't handle anymore."

This gave Emma a giant twinge of guilt in the pit of her stomach. She hadn't meant to worry her mother. She felt selfish because she focused only on going to the game and not calling her family. After what happened between Izzy and Miles, she felt ridiculous and guilty.

She looked at her mom over the top of her teacup as she took a sip.

Her mother had the same auburn hair and a full smile. Her eyes shined bright green when she was upset, and with the brightness of the moonlight coming in, they almost looked like they were glowing cat eyes.

She knew how her mom felt about losing her husband and her father so close together.

Emma spoke softly, "Mom, I am so sorry. I wasn't thinking about how much you may have worried. I should have called you when I got to the game. I promise that I won't let something like this happen again."

She set her teacup on the kitchen counter and leaned into her mother's shoulder. She wrapped her arms around Caroline's waist and continued, "I'm sorry. But, can you just be thankful that I'm ok and we won the game?"

Emma looked up with her big brown eyes and smiled like she did she was younger.

Her mother could never resist her sweet daughter's smile, so she said, "Ok, but next time, I better find out from you and not some chatty girl's mom. You know, her mom can talk even more than Jenny can?"

And they all laughed at that comment, knowing it must have been a lengthy phone call.

Emma suddenly felt exhausted and said goodnight to Grammy and her mom. She turned to head to her room and noticed Grammy staring out the window, looking towards the moonlight. She knew Grammy must be thinking of Grandpa, which saddened her.

Now, those were two people that loved each other. They still do.

Emma awoke the next day to the sound of her phone ringing. Sleepily, she answered, " Hello? And this better be good, Izzy." She opened one eye when she heard her friend laugh on the other end of the line.

Izzy responded, "Hello, darling. Of course, it's good. Don't I always have the best information for you?"

Emma slowly sat up in bed, knowing there was no chance of returning to sleep.

She said, "Well, yes, you do. So what is this information that I must know?"

Izzy hoped that Emma would be willing to go with her, so she launched into what she knew, "Well, rumor has it that there is going to be a huge bonfire up in the Heceta Dunes tonight. We have to get up there early, before nightfall, so we can figure out where everyone will be. My parents are out of town this weekend, so we can take the four-wheelers to the dunes. Do you think your mom will let you stay the night with me? That way, there's no curfew."

It sounded like so much fun to Emma. She loved four-wheeling in the Dunes last summer, although she hadn't ever been at night.

Her mom was so upset and worried about the trip to the game that she didn't want to push it.

Izzy was still waiting for an answer, and Emma heard her say, "Hello, Em? Are you there? Did you fall back asleep? Girl, come on! We have got to go tonight!"

Maybe if Emma spent most of the day with her mom and Grammy today, they would let her stay the night at her friend's. She said that to Izzy, and they decided to chat later.

Emma crawled out of bed and went to the kitchen for breakfast, where she found Grammy cooking. She walked in and said brightly, "Good morning, Gram! Where's mom? And what are you making? It smells so good!"

Grammy looked over her shoulder from the stove and responded, "Good morning, sweetheart. Your mom went into town for a bit, and I am whipping up some French Toast and eggs. Would you like some?" Suddenly, Emma realized that she was starving and immediately said so.

Grammy brought up last night's discussion as they sat down to breakfast. She watched Emma inhale her breakfast as she took small sips of coffee.

So many times, Rosie was surprised at how much her little Emma reminded her of how she was when she was younger. Watching her now was no different.

Emma could feel Grammy watching her, so she stopped mid-bite and mumbled, "What?"

This made Rosie smile, and she quietly said, "Oh, nothing. You just remind me so much of myself at times."

It was the perfect time to bring it up, so Rosie decided to ask about last night.

She chose her words carefully and said, "So, did anything else happen last night? Other than the car accident?"

She immediately noticed that her granddaughter was turning a brilliant shade of pink, and that was all she needed to know. Emma had met someone special.

Rosie watched as Emma chewed her bite slowly, trying to figure out what she would say.

Finally, her granddaughter spoke. "Well, I did make some new friends, if that is what you're asking—no big deal. Izzy ended up kissing the cute guy." Emma said a little too quickly and nonchalantly.

"You know that I have been around the block once or twice. You don't have to hide anything from me. Do you like this 'cute guy'?" Grammy asked.

Emma was slightly surprised at the forward question but decided to be honest.

She took a sip of orange juice and dabbed her mouth with her napkin before responding, "I mean, he's cute, yeah. Maybe he liked me too, but then he ended up kissing Izzy, so maybe not. It was just weird. And then he was so curious about our house when they dropped me off. Whatever. I hear he likes to date around anyway, so I'm sure he would never be interested in me. Although, I couldn't figure out why he kept looking at the house."

Rosa gently set down her coffee cup and said, "What did you say this boy's name was?"

It was a small town where you knew almost everyone. Since Emma was still new to Heceta Beach, there was no way she would know who was who.

Emma looked at her Grammy and replied, "Miles. Miles Woods, I think. I just met him yesterday. He has a sister in my grade who's a cheerleader."

Rosie became very interested all of a sudden. She and Peter knew the Woods family quite well.

Before Peter passed, the two families had a long-standing business rivalry. The Woods family used to be the only successful architectural firm in town.

Peter worked for them when he was young but then decided to go out on his own. This didn't sit well with the Woods family, primarily after Peter built The Glass House.

Emma suddenly became aware of Grammy's interest in who this new person could be. She watched as her grandmother shifted in her chair and took another sip of her coffee.

She inquired about her Grammy's interest and asked, "Why are you curious about whom I met last night?"

Rosie took an extra-long sip of her coffee and said, "Well, Heceta Beach is a small town, and it's good to know whom you spend time with."

And with that, Emma didn't ask any more questions. After all, she was a teenager with an agenda and wanted to see if she could get Grammy to help convince her mom that it was okay to let her spend the night at Izzy's.

She stood up from the table to take her dish to the sink, asking, "Do you know when Mom will be back?"

Her Grammy seemed lost in thought for a moment, and then she heard her say, "I'm sure it won't be too long. Why do you ask?"

This was the opportunity that Emma was hoping for, and she took it. She walked back over to her Grammy and said, "Well, Izzy invited me to stay the night at her house, and I was hoping to head over this afternoon. Do you think Mom will be ok with that?"

Rosie didn't think it would be a big deal and said as much. She knew Izzy's parents well since they were around the same age as Caroline. They all went to school together and still chatted in town when they saw each other.

However, after last night's shenanigans, Rosie thought Emma should ask Caroline directly. This didn't make her granddaughter happy at all. So, it was no surprise when Emma started with why it would be a good idea to spend the night at Izzy's.

After five straight minutes of listening to the reasoning from her teenage granddaughter, she finally relented.

Rosie took a deep breath, knowing that she would have to answer Caroline, and said, "Fine. Go get your things, and I'll drop you off on my way to the grocery. But just remember that I will have to put up with *your* mother if she's not happy with this." Of course, this was said with a grin that was shared between the two of them.

Rosie and Emma loved each other dearly. It seemed that they were two peas in a pod.

Emma hugged her grandmother tightly and said, "Oh, thank you, Grammy! I'm so excited. It's going to be a fun girl's night! Thank you! Love you! Ok, going to pack now!"

Before Grammy could change her mind, Emma bounded down the hall to her room to call Izzy and pack her bag.

This left Rosie alone again with her thoughts. She cleared the table, cleaned the dishes, and in a few moments, found herself staring out of one of the vast windows that looked out onto the ocean. Soon, she was flooded with a mixture of memories from the past.

———————————————————

Young Rosa couldn't remember a time when she wasn't looking at the ocean. She was born on the Pacific Northwest coast, and she loved it. Yes, she may have traveled here and there, but her heart always belonged to this place.

She met Peter when they were in high school. She was the Prom Queen, initially dreaming of life beyond Heceta Beach. He was a rebel with an eye for the ladies. Well, until he met Rosie. She stole his heart, and he never asked for it back. They may have had a little heartbreak after high school because Rosie was determined to go off to college. Yet, their hearts always remained connected.

Peter had a love for architecture almost as strong as his love for Rosie. After trying for a year to let her find herself at college, he soon joined her and began studying architecture at the same university. As they learned and grew from education, so did their love. He proposed to his beloved Rosie on the evening of their college graduation.

They moved back to Heceta Beach and were married the following summer. Peter also decided to take an entry-level position with Woods Architecture. By the time their daughter, Caroline, was ready for elementary school, he had decided to try and open his own architecture firm.

He had secretly been working on his first big project since he proposed to Rosie. The project was to build the Glass House.

It was the house that he had dreamed of building for her. When they were too young and too naive even to recognize the true love between them, they would sneak to this very place. At the time, it was an ocean-battered wooden framework of some shanty that someone had started to build and never finished. There was no glass, only open areas separated by several staircases that climbed higher and higher.

Their favorite spot was at the very top. When the moon was at its peak and shining bright, it appeared to be almost daylight with a sheer covering of stars and ocean waves. It was magical.

They would kiss and hold each other tight. Eventually, when she was ready, Peter would make love to Rosie under the moonlight at the Glass House and relish in her beauty. Looking at her, he always imagined that she illuminated everything around him.

As Rosie thought about their adventure, she smiled with a small tear in her eye as she recalled what he would say to her, or anyone that would listen, for that matter.

Pete would brag that Rosie's love was so bright that it would bounce off of him and illuminate the world, so only a glasshouse would do for their kind of love.

And that's how the beauty that was the Glass House came to be.

CHAPTER 4

THE BONFIRE

"There is such a similarity between fire and love. Both are bright, hot, and oh, how they can burn."

Emma was looking forward to going to the bonfire that night. It was the first big party she would attend since officially moving back to Heceta Beach.

She packed her bag quickly before Grammy had time to change her mind or if her mom would return earlier than expected.

As luck would have it, they made it out of the house before Caroline returned. Perhaps it was her age or that she had already raised a daughter, but Rosie didn't ask many questions about the where and why of her teenage granddaughter's plans for the evening.

She trusted that she would do the right thing. Deep down, Rosie was so confident in the similarity between her young self and Emma that she didn't worry as much. Rosie had always been wise beyond her years, and Emma was no different.

They pulled up to Izzy's house, but not before they saw Emma's friend bounding out of the house with joy, with her bright eyes and strawberry blonde hair flowing behind her.

Grammy smiled at the ease and innocence of such a simple time for the two friends. She put the car in park just long enough for Emma to lean over to give her a quick kiss goodbye and grab her overnight bag from the backseat.

The two girls raced up the steps to drop Emma's things off before packing a cooler of snacks and wine coolers to take to the Dunes.

At this point, it was late afternoon, and the sun would be setting soon. They needed to head to the Dunes right away to see where the party would be. Dressed in jeans, t-shirts, and hoodies tied around their waists, they looked like the epitome of a "Coastie" chick.

Izzy had taught Emma everything she needed to know about four-wheelers. They had spent the summer learning how to speed down the curvy roads and down-shift gears on the sandy incline to get to the top of the dunes.

Helmets were a must, and getting stuck in the sand was par for the course when crossing the vast desert that led to the Pacific Ocean. The girls quickly became experts in helping each other out of their sand ditches, and it was always worth it.

The view from the top of the Heceta Dune was breathtaking. Emma could only imagine what it was like at night, knowing it would be the second night of a full moon.

They quickly attached the cooler to Izzy's four-wheeler, adjusted their helmets, and then they were off.

The road into Heceta Dunes was about five or six miles long, with various turn-offs for parking and restrooms. Since Izzy's property backed into the park grounds, they had a shortcut into the main dunes. This cut down about two miles or so from the usual route.

The sun quickly lowered when they reached the first of the three major dunes. They weren't concerned about finding their way to the party since once they hit the peak of the first dune, there was a caravan of four-wheelers, 4x4 trucks, and dirt bikes all headed in the same direction.

Some would veer off to attempt some crazy trick in the sand to show off, but most were trying to get to the third peak before sunset.

This was part of the unique adventure of the Oregon dunes. You could take the curvy paved road to the third dune, but why would you when you could race each other through a cloud of sand, exhaust, and spinning tires, along with squeals of delight?

Emma and Izzy rode side-by-side for most of the ride. As they were cresting the second mound of sand and making their way down, a dark blue truck appeared out of nowhere and seemed to be following them a little too close.

Izzy took the lead, with Emma close behind, while the truck moved sharply to the left. They were suddenly neck in neck with the truck, leaving them more than a little curious to see who it was.

Emma throttled her engine and zipped up quickly to the right of Izzy's ATV. She flipped up the visor of her helmet while moving a little closer to Izzy's vehicle. With a wink and a nod, the two girls knew exactly what to do next - they would show their friends in the 4x4 truck what they could do.

The girls momentarily let the truck pass them by, but not by much. Emma went to the truck's left, while Izzy went to the right. Izzy gave her rig a full throttle and zipped past the truck effortlessly.

Emma waited just a moment longer and then did the same thing. With both four-wheelers so close to the truck and with that much speed, they left the truck in a heavy cloud of sand. At this point, they were racing up the third dune, knowing that their stop would likely be at the top or just beyond.

The four-wheelers quickly passed the truck, zipping back and forth in front of the slower, heavier-moving vehicle. The girls had succeeded in successfully "dusting" their mysterious followers. They thoroughly enjoyed the adventure.

When the dark blue truck made its way to the bonfire location, the girls were dismounting their rigs and taking off their helmets. Smiling and giggling, there was no doubt that they had enjoyed their ride. As Emma ran over to Izzy to help grab the cooler, she looked over her shoulder to watch the approaching truck.

She was more than a little amused to see the driver. It was Miles.

The sun was lowering and hitting his windshield at just the right angle so she could see the blue of his eyes radiating through the glass. She wanted to return a smile to him but knew she had to play it cool. After all, he had kissed her best friend last night.

She took one last look in his direction as she and Izzy carried the cooler over to the fire pit and noticed that Big Reggie was with Miles.

Well, at least she knew the big guy would offer some entertainment while Izzy and Miles went off and kissed some more. *Why did that bother her? She didn't even know the guy.*

The thought was quickly forgotten when Emma took a good look around and realized the view of the ocean that was before her. There were lots of kids that she recognized from school unloading their coolers and wood for the fire. Yet, she couldn't help but think, *How are they not just as mesmerized by this view as I am?*

Many often wonder at the beauty of the Pacific Northwest coastline, but until you see it, you genuinely have no idea of the view's impact on a person. This was the feeling that Emma was having as she and Izzy dropped their cooler in their spot on the dune.

The fall sun was setting among a few hazy, longline clouds and reflected off of a mostly calm ocean. The colors were a mix of red, orange, pink, and violet. In front of her was the most gorgeous canvas she had ever seen. The captivating image of these glorious colors reflecting off the water was almost too much for one person to take in. Emma was transfixed.

Izzy had run off to help the others with the bonfire, so Emma was left alone in this open area to wonder at the stunning view. She stood for several minutes, watching the sun's light show as it slowly set beneath the water.

She was about to head to the bonfire when she heard a gentle voice behind her.

Miles had been watching her from a distance. When he realized she was one of the two daredevils on the ATVs, he kept his eye on her.

He loved watching her because she seemed to appreciate the beauty of her surroundings. So many locals took these sights for granted, so he loved it when someone intently watched the ocean and sky shows.

He came up behind her and stood, perhaps, a little too close and said, "There's only one thing more beautiful than an Oregon sunset. It's an Oregon sunrise." His soft voice talking in her ear sent shivers through her.

Damn it, she thought, *why does he do that to me?* He liked her friend, not her, so why was he here now, ruining her moment of bliss as she watched the sunset?

She stepped to the side, turned slightly from her colorful view, and said, "Thanks for the advice. I'll have to try it sometime. I need a drink."

And with that, she flipped open the cooler to grab a wine cooler, shut the lid, and sauntered off to the bonfire, where the group had begun to gather.

Miles knew that she was pissed that he had kissed Izzy. Hell, he was still pissed about it too. He kicked up some sand alongside the cooler as she walked away and stormed off to grab a beer with Big Reggie.

The sun dropped quickly, and so did the temperature. Everyone donned their sweatshirts and jackets as they moved closer to the bonfire.

There were probably 40 people that made their way to the party, and it was in full swing by the time true nightfall hit.

Izzy and Emma stayed close together while chatting with friends from school. The wine coolers and beers were refreshing next to the dry heat of the enormous fire built in the sand.

While the gorgeous colors of the sunset had faded, the bonfire's flames took center stage, adding a hypnotizing effect.

The flames started at the base of the firewood in a blueish-purple haze, yet as the fire grew higher and higher, the shades would pop from red to orange to bright yellow and then disappear in a cloud of grayish smoke. The pop of the fire was both soothing and startling at times when a piece of wood fell or shattered from the heat.

Someone had begun playing music from their 4x4 truck, so the mood was a mix of festive and chill. A few people that were either warm from the heat of the fire or too drunk to notice the cold started climbing higher up on the peak and sliding down the hill of sand on their cooler lids.

Emma occasionally looked back as she heard a squeal of delight from the people on the dune. Yet, she chose to remain close to the fire, happy to stare into its transfixing glow and sip on her wine cooler.

Izzy had made her way over to another group of friends. She told Emma earlier in the evening that she had her eyes set on Andy, a very handsome football player who had just broken up with his girlfriend a week or so ago.

This made Emma confused about why Iz had kissed Miles if she was interested in Andy but let the question pass. The girls had avoided talking about Emma discovering Izzy kissing Miles.

Watching Izzy through the flames of the bonfire, she could see that her friend was trying to move in on Andy tonight.

She kept leaning into his arm, laughing at anything he said, and gazing up at him with looks that said she wanted to be kissed.

Emma was so focused on what was happening that she hadn't noticed Miles walking up beside her. She felt a little nudge on her arm and looked to her right.

There he was, his face lit up by the flames, with one hand holding a beer and the other casually placed in his jeans pocket. *Why was this so cute?* Emma thought. She felt herself smile as she looked up into his face.

He seemed pleased she was smiling and hadn't yet stormed off again.

He took a chance and asked her, "Is that a smile I see on your face?" Emma's smile couldn't help but get bigger, and she said, "It happens every once in a while."

She decided to keep the banter light and let go of the awkwardness of last night.

Perhaps Miles had changed his mind about being interested in her. It happens, and it wasn't like they were on a date. They had just met.

She continued the conversation and asked, "So, do you come to these bonfires a lot?"

Miles smiled back at her and replied, "I came to a lot more of these when I was still in high school. My mom's out of town this weekend, so I'm on Lindsey patrol." He nodded toward the sandhill just in time to see Lindsay jump on a cooler lid with some guy and slide down the dune.

She let out a squeal of delight and then jumped in the guy's arms as soon as they hit the bottom. This made Emma smile, and she said, "Well, it looks like she's having fun. What's the big deal?"

Miles rolled his eyes while he sipped his beer and then responded, "She has a habit of flirting with the boys, and she loves beer almost as much as I do. She tends to get into trouble when you put those two things together. If mom comes back to drama with her only daughter, it'll be my ass on the line."

Emma was amused by this and laughed at the visual of Miles's mom kicking his ass. She thought he might get back to his sister, but when she mentioned that, he quickly said, "Oh no. I try to keep my distance and only intervene as needed. Luckily, I have a few of my guys around who know to keep an eye on Linds."

He liked watching Emma smile, and it was even more impressive with the glow of the fire. The reflection of the flames made her eye color change to deep gold, and he loved it.

He hesitated and said, "Look, I'd like to talk to you more, but I really gotta piss. Mind if we meet up in a few?"

This made Emma giggle more as she remembered the jokes that Big Reggie kept making last night.

She responded, "As a matter of fact, I have to go too. I've never been to the dunes at night before. Where do you go to pee around here?"

This amused Miles, and instead of making her squat out in the open, away from the party, he offered to take her to the park restrooms. He said they could take his truck. He explained that he knew a shortcut to the closest rest area in the park, and they'd be back in a flash.

She agreed, and they set off for his truck. Izzy caught her eye and looked curiously at Emma, so she called out, "I gotta pee! Be back in a few!" Not realizing that the whole group had heard, she immediately felt embarrassed.

They climbed into Miles's truck, and he mumbled, "Smooth move, Exlax." as he started the engine. Emma playfully hit him in the arm and said, "Oh, stop." which was quickly followed with, "I guess I didn't realize I would be saying that to everyone!"

She covered her forehead with her hand in more embarrassment. This made Miles laugh as she was only more attractive to him now.

As they made their way down the dune, although bumpy, Miles tried to make the ride as smooth as possible, knowing they both had to pee. They were relieved when the sand finally leveled out and eventually became a paved road.

In two short turns, they arrived in a dark parking lot with only one light on the side of the restrooms. Since the parking lot was empty, he could pull right up to the sidewalk entry. He parked the truck and reached across Emma's lap to open the glove compartment.

His arm brushed her leg as he searched for what he was looking for, and she honestly didn't mind.

He pulled a flashlight out of the compartment and slammed it shut. He handed the flashlight to her and reached under his seat to pull out another one. Miles explained, "No lights are in the bathroom, so you'll need this. Don't drop it in the shitter because once it's gone, it's gone."

This indicated that these were true park toilets—an open gate to stinky heaven. Emma almost decided to hold it, but her bladder was telling her otherwise. She quickly turned the flashlight on and off before jumping out of the truck to head in. She looked back and said, "Ok. Thanks. Be back in a minute."

Emma finished up quicker than Miles, so she quickly jumped back into the front of the truck to warm up. She saw him come out, walk around the back of the truck to grab two beers and climb in.

After he closed the door, he handed her a beer and said, "Drink up! We gotta keep the system flowing." She giggled and took a drink of the cold beer.

She thought he would have started driving back by now, so she was surprised to look over and see Miles staring back at her so intently.

She asked softly, "Is everything ok?" It looked as though he wanted to say something but was hesitating.

She said to him, "It's ok. I don't bite. What's up?"

Miles gently smiled at her words and decided to explain, "You know, I didn't mean to kiss Izzy last night. I thought it was you. It was dark, and she came up behind me. I was so surprised and knowing that we, well, I thought we had a bit of a connection at the truck...I thought for sure it was you. I-I wanted it to be you. Not Izzy. She pissed me off, and I shoved her away as soon as I realized it was her. What was she thinking?"

Initially, Emma didn't know what to say. She was trying to see if he was telling the truth. When she looked into his beautiful blue eyes, she knew he was being honest with her.

She thought momentarily and then said, "Honestly, it surprised me too. That was the last thing I thought I would discover walking through the woods. I thought that I misread everything that had happened up until that point. I mean, I don't care if you do like her. I didn't pick up on that last night, so I felt stupid when I saw you two."

Miles could see that Emma was questioning what she felt yesterday, and he wanted to reassure her.

He quickly said, "I promise you didn't misread anything that happened when we were hanging by the truck. Emma, I think you're amazing, and I don't even really know you. You're beautiful, have a great ass, and have gorgeous eyes."

She was shocked at what he was saying. At her young age and with the bit of dating experience she had so far, she had never had someone say such nice things to her.

She would have left out the "ass" part, but at least he was honest with her.

She decided to be just as honest with him, so she started to say, "That was really nice. I've never had someone say those things to me, so it's surprising. When you touched my shoulder last night, I thought I felt a lightning bolt in my stomach. I can't believe I'm saying this, but..." Miles leaned in and kissed her before she knew what was happening.

It was a tender, loving kiss that felt warm, caring, and delicious. Emma kissed him back, and soon the tenderness in their kiss was replaced with passion.

Their hearts were racing, and Miles pulled her closer to him. The heat from just the two of them was more than just emotional because the windows were soon fogged over. They couldn't stop, and neither wanted the kissing to end.

She touched his face with her left hand, still holding her beer in her right. Miles opened his eyes just enough to notice this. He rolled down his window, grabbed both beer bottles, and threw them aimlessly into the parking lot. When they both heard the crash of the glass, they laughed but went right back to kissing.

Soon, Miles was leaning heavily into Emma. He wanted to touch her but didn't know if it was too soon. She smiled through their kiss, looked into his eyes, gently took his hand, and placed it on her chest. She wanted him to touch her. She wanted more of him than she had ever wanted anyone else.

His kisses made her feel breathless, so she was dying to know what his touch felt like on her skin. Miles gently slid his hand under her shirt, searching for her breasts. She leaned into him and gasped through their endless kiss as he finally touched her.

He maneuvered around her bra and lovingly fondled her breasts until he found what she liked. He slid his other hand under her shirt and cradled her back. As they continued to kiss, learning each other's mouths and tongues, he swiftly lifted her onto his lap. She willingly straddled him and took off her sweatshirt. He didn't mind at all when she did this.

They made out with each other for a long time. Emma finally caught herself when they reached for each other's jean zippers.

She pulled back and breathlessly said, "This is too soon. We don't even know each other. What are we doing?" Miles was startled out of his sexual haze.

She had entranced him with her kisses, and he was having difficulty coming back down from this high. He looked at her and she slid back onto the seat.

She grabbed her sweatshirt and started to put it back on while saying, "I'm sorry. That was great. Amazing actually, but we don't even know each other. It's too soon for anything more. I'm sorry." As much as he hated to admit it, she was right.

He would have persisted with any other girl, but Emma was different. He even surprised himself when he said, "You're right. Too soon. I get it. But, damn, you're hot. And a great kisser."

He took a deep breath, readjusted himself in the driver's seat, and reached for her hand. They were both still a little breathless from their moment of passion. Emma's hair was damp along her forehead, and she wished her heartbeat would slow down just a little.

She took his hand in hers, smiled back at him, and said, "Back at ya, babe."

Oh, how he loved that she had said that. It made him so happy, and he didn't quite know why.

He decided not to tell her yet, so he responded, "I need a beer. You want one?"

She needed to cool down too, so she said, "Yes, I do!"

He popped out of the truck to grab two more beers from the back cooler.

As he did, he let out a "Woo-hoo!" as loudly as he could. This at once surprised her and made her happy. She was still laughing as he got back into the truck.

He handed her an open beer, leaned over, and gently kissed her. The smile in his eyes told her more than she needed to know, but then he leaned back and quietly said, "Back at ya, babe."

He shifted the truck into gear and they headed back to the bonfire, with both of them smiling the entire time.

Miles realized they were gone for a long time as they drove back to the party. Knowing how quickly people would begin to talk, he explained to Emma what he would do. He handed her his beer to shift the truck into a lower gear as they hit the steepest part of the dune's crest.

He told her the plan, "Once we start to come over this hill, I'm going to switch off the headlights, throw the truck in neutral, and we're going to use the weight of the truck to slowly slide our way down to the rest of the trucks. No engine, no attention. Got it?"

Emma shook her head in agreement. Miles accelerated one last time as they crested the dune, hit the lights, shifted into neutral, and, as promised, they slid down the sand. It felt as if they were gliding on ice. It was eerily silent but cool at the same time.

Emma reached over and took Miles's hand. They smiled at each other. At the very end, Miles cut the wheel to slow them down without brake lights, and they landed almost silently into an angled makeshift parking place.

Before exiting the truck's cabin, they leaned in and kissed each other. Without needing to explain to each other, they walked away separately so as not to raise suspicions with anyone at the party.

They didn't realize Big Reg and Izzy had seen Miles's truck come down the hill. They also saw their kiss before rejoining the party. Big Reg thought it was cool, even for his drunk ass. But Izzy was pissed.

Instead of letting her frustration show, Izzy ran over to Emma as she walked back to the group by the bonfire and yelled, "Well, there you are, Emma! I thought you were never coming back. Did you and Miles get lost in the dunes?"

Everyone casually looked over as Miles headed off in the opposite direction. He was out of earshot, so it was Emma left to deal with the loud interaction. She dashed up to Izzy and tried to say under her breath, "Don't yell that. I'm trying not to draw attention. It's no big deal."

They continued walking quickly, and suddenly Emma realized Izzy was very drunk.

She slowed down, looped her arm through Izzy's, and said, "Are you drunk? How much have you had to drink in the last hour?"

This did not make Iz any happier. She pulled her arm out of Emma's, stepped back dramatically, and with slurred speech said, "Who do you think you are? My mother? I thought she took the weekend off, Mom! I can drink as much as I want. And stop trying to change the subject. Emma and Miles sitting in a truck, K-I-S-S-I-N-G!"

This was embarrassing them both. Emma's mind was racing to try and figure out how to get them both out of there. They had ridden up separately on ATVs, and there was no way that Izzy could handle driving hers back to the house. She didn't think Izzy was sober enough to hold onto Emma if they rode together. This was turning out to be quite a drunk disaster.

Just as Emma struggled to help a stumbling Izzy back towards the 4-wheelers, she heard Andy call out, "Hey! Need some help? I told her not to take that last shot. Damn, Izzy, you're ripped."

As Andy grabbed Izzy's other arm to help Emma walk her through the sand, she leaned into Andy's arm a little heavier.

Through bleary eyes, she looked up and repeatedly told him how cute, sweet, and kind he was. Andy thought her eyes were crossing at one point, and he was right. She suddenly slowed down her pace, leaned back a little too far, and fell into the sand.

As they turned back to help her, Izzy leaned over on her side and began throwing up. A lot. Both Andy and Emma said, "Ugh. Ewe." at the same time and backed up.

They suddenly noticed that people were watching, so they moved in a little closer and stepped as much to the side as possible to block the view of the others. She would be mortified tomorrow, so they might as well protect her as much as they could.

Miles came over to see if he could help when he realized Izzy was puking. He kind of smiled and said, "Ooh. She is not going to feel good in the morning. Come on. Let's get her up and home."

Emma was grateful for his offer and said, "Thanks, but we rode up separately on the ATVs. I don't know how I'm going to get her home."

Miles didn't hesitate in offering to put Izzy in his truck so that Emma and Andy could drive the 4-wheelers back to Izzy's house. With the plan in place, Miles ran off to get his truck to load Izzy into it while Andy and Emma stayed put with Iz. *What an ending to the night*, thought Emma, *Again*.

Soon, Miles was back with his truck and, along with Andy, hoisted Izzy into the front passenger seat. Emma was busily trying to reattach their cooler to her ATV so that she could lead the way back to Izzy's house. It was dark, and she had never taken the route back at night.

Just as she thought this, it was as if Miles had been reading her mind. He slowly crept forward in his truck, rolled down the window, and said, "I'm pretty familiar with the back way to Izzy's house. I'll take the lead so you and Andy can follow my taillights." She was thankful for the offer and quickly nodded in agreement.

It didn't take long for their little caravan to return to Izzy's house. There was a long staircase up to the main level, so Andy and Miles had to carry Izzy up the steps into the house.

Emma quickly unloaded the cooler and headed inside. By the time she entered the living room, Izzy was passed out on the couch. Andy was looking for a bucket and towel in case she had to throw up again.

Emma was starting to think that Andy liked Izzy a lot. You'd have to if you were willing to look for a puke bucket for a girl.

This thought made Emma smile a little, and Miles quickly noticed. They had moved into the kitchen so Emma could get

Izzy a glass of water. She was going to need to rehydrate when she woke up.

Miles stood close to Emma as she filled the glass and quietly said, "What is making you smile?" She couldn't help but grin wider as she said, "Oh, a couple of things."

Andy had just walked into the kitchen and felt like he was walking in on something private.

He stayed in the doorway to the living room and said, "Hey, I'll take the water for Iz and just crash on the couch in case she needs something."

Emma was about to say she could take care of it, but Miles spoke out quicker, "That would be great. I'm sure she'll appreciate the company. Thanks, man."

And with that, they were left alone. Together, standing close to each other in the kitchen. All alone. It was like a magnet pulling them together, and they couldn't stop it.

As much as Miles was willing to help Izzy, he had only Emma on his mind the entire time. There was part of him that thought he was crazy, and the other part just couldn't help but want to be near her, touching her, kissing her, talking to her.

He wanted Emma and only Emma. Miles was honest enough with himself to know, through dating his share of girls, that this felt different. He felt it in his soul. He felt - in love, which was the part that made him feel crazy because he had just met her.

For a moment, they both had enough clarity to keep their emotions in check.

Emma looked over at Miles, "Thank you for helping us. I had no idea how I was going to get her back home by myself. She is so wasted."

He nodded in understanding, "My mom has gone on a few drunken benders in my lifetime, so I have had quite a bit of experience with this type of situation."

This simultaneously touched and bothered Emma. She had to think for a moment as to what to say. Finally, she spoke from the heart as she gently reached for his hand, "I'm sorry that you have had to deal with that."

Her compassion touched him, which was a new feeling for him. Miles thought that maybe this girl was different from the others. Perhaps that's why he felt so strongly about her so quickly. This did more than intrigue him.

Passion overtook any reasoning that would momentarily enter his mind, and if he could see into Emma's mind, she was instantly thinking the same.

Their eyes locked while standing under the harsh, bright lights of Izzy's kitchen. They wanted to escape and be completely alone.

Miles gently but firmly pulled Emma into his arms and kissed her with such emotion that it could only mean one thing.

Without hesitation, she started walking toward the other end of the house. She knew a guest bedroom was just beyond the kitchen and dining room so that no one would interrupt them.

Part of him wanted to stop, but the longing within him just wanted Emma. They reached the guest room door and looked at each other as if to say, "Are you sure?"

Neither said no, so Emma opened the door and turned on a low-lit lamp as Miles softly closed the door. He turned to face her and looked at her with longing eyes, while she met him with the same gaze. She took his hand and led him to the bed, then turned to give him a tender kiss.

He tenderly slid his arms around her waist and let his hands travel inside her shirt while pulling her closer.

It was almost as if he couldn't get close enough. He needed her. He needed to be inside her. He needed to feel everything about her. He was entranced.

Slowly, they pulled away just enough so he could lift her shirt above her head to remove it. Miles kept searching for a signal in her eyes to stop, but each time he met her eyes, they reflected nothing but love and pure wanting. Had he finally met his match?

Emma felt breathless and swore that she had temporarily lost her hearing from only being able to hear her heartbeat. She had never felt something so strong and never wanted anything more. She almost felt like she was floating or in love. Yet, it couldn't be love. She had only met this guy, but the feelings were so intense that she couldn't stop. There was no doubt that she did not want to stop.

Miles's hands gently held her face as they continued to kiss passionately. He then let his hands slowly travel over her neck and shoulders, feeling every part of her for the first time as if trying to memorize it. He then slid his hands over her breasts, gentle at first and then with a firmer touch over her nipples as she began to gasp at his touch. He paused long enough to let a little smile show as they continued to kiss.

He could feel how she wanted him, and it drove him crazy. With one hand still on her breast, he let his other hand graze down her side. Then with one gentle finger, he let it run along the waistline of her jeans, almost taunting her. She was breathless and wanted more of his touch, so she moved in with her body to feel his wanting against hers.

He lazily unbuttoned her jeans and unzipped them even more slowly. She was ready to burst with anticipation as he finally took both hands and slid off her pants. They were both still standing as he bent over to help her with her jeans. When he came back up, she leaned forward slightly to meet his gaze. Her eyes were mischievous yet loving. She would show him what loving torture he had bestowed upon her.

She gently removed his shirt and then sat down on the edge of the bed. He was standing before her. He was more gorgeous without his shirt than she had even imagined. Emma lifted her arm and traced the length of his chest, slowly, ever so slowly, until she reached the top of his jeans.

He looked down at her with such passion that she unexpectedly gasped again. As he leaned down to start kissing her again, she pushed him back up so she could unbutton his jeans. Just before she undid the last of his zipper, she cupped him between one of her hands and leaned her head into his chest.

With her other hand, she slid it behind him and grabbed his behind to push it towards her. As she did so, she looked up and said, "Nice ass." and then just as abruptly pulled down his jeans. He was shocked but in a very good way.

She took him in her mouth, languishing every part of him. This time, it was Miles that was breathless. She knew how and just where to touch him. If he didn't do something immediately, he would lose complete control.

With one more gasp and a gentle hand, he lifted her chin to look up at him. As she gazed upward, he leaned down to kiss her and she pulled him closer.

Together they lay back on the bed, slowly removing whatever clothing remained on each of them.

Once they were naked, Miles pulled himself away just long enough to admire Emma's beauty. He reached over and turned off the lamp as she settled back into the bed. The shades weren't completely drawn, so they had the light of the moon shining in.

Emma lovingly reached up to Miles to pull him closer to her, but then he stopped. He leaned down and gently kissed her lips, looking into her glowing golden-brown eyes.

She met his gaze, thoroughly mesmerized by his opal blue eyes staring back at her. She wanted him more than she ever thought she could want anyone. Her hips rose to meet his in anticipation of what was to be.

Gently, he smiled at her and then continued to kiss the entire length of her body. Hovering over her breasts, to the brink of gasping torture, he languidly slid his tongue down the length of her torso while letting his hands wander to her waist and between her legs. He could tell with just one touch how much she wanted him, but he wanted all of her. That made it luxuriously torturous for them both.

He touched her in a way that no other man had. She had only been with one other guy and had only let a few below the belt a few times.

This was different. He knew how to move his fingers, and it was glorious. He was touching her and kissing her breasts at the same time when she exploded for the first time. He stopped to look up at her once with a look of accomplishment.

She smiled back, but not before pushing him back and then flipping him over on the bed. She straddled him with humor and passion, languishing him with the same hot kisses and tongue he explored her with moments ago. Emma again took him in her mouth, expertly moving to his rhythm until he thought he might explode.

With one swift move, he lifted her up and back on the mattress to finally enter her. She gasped at first and then quickly found his same motion as their eyes met once again. It was amazing, and their movements felt natural, like they had done this a thousand times before.

At once, they both felt the same shiver up their spine and into their heads as they came together and then lay spent, entirely breathless and satisfied.

Miles gently rolled to his side, pulling Emma with him, as he was still inside her, but he didn't want to yet separate from her. He pulled her closer, gently running his fingers up her back, and said, "I know this is unbelievable, but I think I love you."

CHAPTER 5

THE FIRST DATE

" Its own kind of adventure."

Emma looked closely at Miles, trying to figure out if she had heard him correctly. They had made love in a way that had blown her mind but *in love*? Really? She didn't know what to say.

She rolled back to lay beside him and look at him closer. Her heart was still racing, and while she had felt immense feelings, was it love? How could she be sure? She hadn't ever been in love before.

With the moonlight still shining over them, she leaned down to kiss him delicately. Finally, she smiled and responded, "Oh, I bet you say that to all the girls."

"Emma, I'm not kidding. I've never felt this way before. I know it seems ridiculous, but I think I love you."

From the look on Emma's face, Miles quickly realized that he may have said too much too soon. He decided not to press it anymore, so he hugged and kissed her again. She relaxed a bit from his touch and nuzzled into his chest. They both felt exhausted as they stretched out on the bed. Miles wondered if he should go, so he asked her, "Is it ok if I stay, or do you want me to go?"

At first, still thinking of his comments just a few moments ago, she thought he should go. Yet, she loved physically being with him. She was surprised at how natural it felt to lay there with him. Emma looked up at him lovingly and said, "No, please stay. I like being here with you." This was a relief for Miles to hear.

He felt a little better since she said she wanted him to stay. They lay close together, gently closing their eyes, when Miles said quietly, "I at least owe you a proper date. What are you doing tomorrow afternoon?"

She smiled sleepily and didn't even open her eyes when she responded, "Going on a date with you."

As they drifted off to sleep together, they had no idea that Izzy had made her way down the hall, slowly opened the door to the guest room, and heard the last of their conversation.

She was so pissed that they were together. She had been eyeing Miles for so long and thought she had a shot after the football game. She liked Emma but was extremely jealous of her lying there with him.

Izzy was still really drunk and thought she would throw up again, so she quietly closed the door and sprinted for the bathroom.

The next morning, Emma had woken up a few moments before Miles, and she lay there staring up at the ceiling at first and then rolled over to admire how sweet he looked while he was sleeping. She was trying to determine if she was in love with Miles since he was willing to share that with her.

It still surprised her and, honestly, scared her a bit. Were they too young to be in love? She had just turned 18 two months ago and thought he was probably 18 or 19. *Oh my gosh,* she thought, *I don't even know how old he is!*

Lost in her thoughts, she didn't notice that Miles had begun to stir. Without opening his eyes, he slowly grinned and pulled her closer as he said, "Are you watching me sleep, beautiful lady?"

She smiled back, leaned closer into his chest, and replied, "Perhaps. Good morning. How'd you sleep?" They were both so content to lay there all day, but then he remembered that he had promised her a date.

He looked down at her, kissed her head, and answered, "I slept great. I had the perfect sleeping partner."

Miles was suddenly excited to start the day, so he sat up in bed, looking for his clothes. Emma hadn't yet recalled that they were going on their first date and started having second thoughts about their night together.

She suddenly felt very naked herself and also began getting dressed.

She was also trying to think of something to say to not feel so awkward when Miles filled the silence with, "I'm looking forward to spending today with you. Do you mind if I drop you off at home for a bit, and then I can come by and pick you up this afternoon?"

Then Emma remembered the date.

This quickly eased her fears, but she still felt a little uneasy about their lovemaking. She truly wasn't that kind of girl.

She smiled gently and said, "That sounds like a great plan." Then she hesitated before saying her next thoughts, "Um, Miles, just so you know. I don't normally just jump in bed with guys. Last night was great, but…"

He quickly picked up on her morning-after guilt, "Emma, I get it. I loved being with you last night. I should hope that it shows what a connection we have. I don't think anything other than how much I loved being in bed with you. Now, should we go see what Izzy is up to?" He wanted to say he loved her again but didn't want to spook her.

His words were a relief for her to hear. As they walked toward the door, Miles stepped closer to Emma to give her one small kiss before leaving the room. He felt so happy.

They entered the living room, which was still really dark, and for a moment, they didn't think anyone was in there until they saw someone stir beneath a blanket on the far couch. It was Andy. He had stayed the night to make sure that Izzy was all right. Emma thought this was very sweet and kind.

Izzy was sprawled out on the other couch and was sound asleep for another moment until she felt that other people were in the room.

She opened one eye just enough to see the figures of Miles and Emma. She groaned loudly as she tried to lift her head, which felt like it weighed a thousand pounds. To her dismay, her stomach was beginning to churn again.

She laid her head back down and said, "Nice to see that the little lovebirds have emerged."

Miles and Emma looked at each other, smiling but with a little awkward unease.

Again, Izzy began talking with her eyes closed, "I'm just kidding. Did you two even get any sleep?" There was a little sarcastic giggle that escaped her, even though she had the worst hangover of her young life.

Andy said, "Well, at least they were having a good time. Man, Iz, you know how to hurl. And next time, listen to me when I tell you not to take another shot."

Izzy searched around for a loose pillow and chucked it over in the direction of Andy, not even coming close to him since she couldn't open her eyes.

She groaned and said, "I understand what you mean because I do have one hell of a hangover, but please don't treat me like a kid. You aren't my dad."

Emma lightly walked over to the kitchen to get Izzy some water and searched for a Gatorade to help her rehydrate.

She returned to the living room and set everything down next to her friend. She felt like she should stay but was looking forward to the rest of the day and wanted to leave.

Emma leaned close and kissed Izzy on the forehead before saying, "We're gonna go. Call me when you're feeling better. Your parents will be home soon, so make sure you drink up and try to eat something. You'll give it away that you had a little too much fun if they find you like this."

Izzy laughed a little, still with her eyes closed, and said, "Thanks, babe. I got this. Talk to you later, lovebirds." She then rolled over to go back to sleep.

Andy walked out with the other two, knowing she would be ok now.

The sun was up, and although it was freezing outside, it would be a gorgeous day. The three of them piled into Miles's truck, with Emma in the middle so that they could take Andy back to his truck at the dunes.

Miles dropped Emma off at her house. Once again, she caught him looking intently at the house's structure.

She gazed up, wondering what fascinated him, so she asked, "Everything ok? You seem to have a serious interest in my house."

He looked distracted but not in a bad way when he answered, "I have always admired this house. It's a bit of a sore subject with my family since this was the first build that your Grandpa did after he left our company. My gramps didn't want him to leave because he knew how talented he was. Long story, I guess. Anyway, I'll pick you up in about two hours. Is that good for you?"

Emma was getting more excited about their date, and she couldn't help but smile when she responded, "Sure, that's great. Can I bring anything?"

Miles simply said, "Nope, but wear jeans and bring a jacket. I can handle everything else."

She was curious about what he had planned yet decided to just roll with it and called over her shoulder as she walked towards the door, "Ok, see you soon!"

Emma was surprised that the house was totally quiet when she came in. She called out to her mom and Grammy but received no response.

The sun shone brightly through the windows, and she thought they were on the beach for a leisurely Sunday walk.

She walked over to the patio doors off the living room to see if she could see them in the distance but no luck.

The beach was full of families and couples with their dogs, enjoying the rare sunshine on the coast. It motivated her to go on their date, so she grabbed a quick bite to eat and hurriedly began getting ready.

The time seemed to pass quickly, and before she knew it, she thought Miles would be arriving any moment. She decided to go out front to wait for him since it was such a beautiful afternoon.

Grammy's house was impressive, and Emma found herself admiring the front seating area as she walked out. Settled in an Adirondack chair, she leaned back and enjoyed the bright sun warming her face.

Her mom's voice brought her attention back to the present as Caroline called out, "Well, there you are! I've missed seeing you this weekend."

Emma looked out into the distance and saw her mom and Grammy headed down the walk.

She smiled and said, "Hi! I've missed you both too. Although Grammy made me a mean breakfast yesterday morning."

She stood up and gave them a warm hug and a peck on their cheeks. Her mom smiled back and agreed, "Oh, she does know how to make a fantastic breakfast. Do you want to come in and join us for some lunch? We went for a walk on the beach, and now we're starving."

Grammy could tell by the look on Emma's face that she had other plans. She looked delighted, and her granddaughter confirmed those exact thoughts when she began to tell them about her date, "I'm not sure where we are going, but it's such a beautiful afternoon, I am hoping it's somewhere outside."

Caroline and Rosa gave each other knowing smiles before Grammy said, "Well, do we get to meet this gentleman today?"

Just as she finished her sentence, they all turned around at the sound of the roar of a motorcycle engine.

A black, sleek, shiny Harley-Davidson slowly pulled up in front of their home. The driver wore jeans, black boots, a leather jacket, and a black helmet with a visor covering their entire face in darkness.

Emma didn't know that Miles had a motorcycle, so she slowly walked forward as the engine was turned off and the rider got off the bike.

She hesitantly said, "Is it you? Miles?"

He laughed at the memory of her saying that the other night on the way to the football game and casually said, "It is. Is it you?" as he coyly lifted the visor to reveal his gorgeous eyes.

She could tell that he was smiling, and she melted inside. Her mom and Grammy had followed her up the sidewalk to meet her new friend.

Emma turned around and introduced them, "Miles, this is my mom, Caroline, and my Grammy Rosa, but everyone likes to call her Rosie. Mom and Grammy, this is Miles Woods."

He extended his hand to them both to shake, and they did so warmly. Grammy was the first to speak, "Hello, Miles. Nice to meet you. Are you related to Sarah Woods?"

She knew that he was her son but wanted to be polite. Miles shook his head as he finished removing his helmet, "I am her son. One of two, we also have my younger sister, who is in Emma's class. That's how we met. Well, we went to the same football game the other night."

Caroline watched him closely and thought that he resembled his father so much it was almost startling.

It took her a moment to say, "Nice to meet you, Miles. I'm sure you know this, but you look so much like your father."

He nodded again and said, "Yes, I've been told that often. I'm also following in his footsteps and heading into the Navy next year."

Emma was also learning this information for the first time. Caroline nodded and replied, "Yes, I do recall that he went into the Navy shortly after high school. So, what are you two up to today?"

Her daughter leaned into Miles and looked up, anticipating his response. He grinned again and said, "Well, it's a bit of a surprise, but I thought we would start with a ride up the coast to enjoy this gorgeous day. What time should I have Emma back?"

Grammy was happy to see that he was such a gentleman, but Caroline was a little nervous about the trip on the motorcycle. She explained that Emma had never ridden before, but Miles reassured her that he had ridden for at least four years and was very used to having passengers.

He also let her know that he was a careful rider. Emma then responded, "Mom, we will be fine. Now, go enjoy your lunch with Grammy, and stop worrying."

Rosie was also quick to speak up this time, "She'll be fine. Let them go and have a bit of fun on this wonderful afternoon."

She looped her arm through her daughter's and led her back to the house as she sang out, "Have fun, you two, and be back before dinner time!" The couple giggled at this, and Miles led Emma to his motorcycle.

"Sorry that I didn't know it was you when you pulled up. You should have warned me that you would be riding a bike." Emma said as Miles gently and expertly put a helmet on her head and adjusted the chin straps.

He leaned in and lightly kissed her on the nose, which she loved, and he replied, "I can't give away all of my secrets. I wanted this to be part of the surprise."

Emma felt not only comfortable with Miles, but she loved feeling so protected. She animatedly said, "Then let's get started with the rest of these surprises!"

He slid onto the bike and started the motor before motioning for her to get behind him. He pointed to where her feet should go and then turned around to say, "Hold on to me and just let the movement of the bike guide you. Other than that, just enjoy the ride."

She was already enjoying herself and quickly responded, "Kind of like last night, huh?"

Oh, how Miles loved that response, and he smiled broadly underneath his helmet. He turned forward, and they slowly pulled away from her house.

Here's the thing about the Oregon coast - it's known for its rainy, cloudy days, but when the sun shines, these days are nothing short of magical. The ocean gleams almost a tropical blue-green with white caps as the waves roll in. The coastal roads are very curvy and mostly nestled within green hillsides full of lush pine trees. In some spots during the rainy season, pops of blooming color will shine through the green forests. This contrast against the ocean blue is nothing short of stunning.

Emma was taking this in as they drove out of Heceta Beach and further up the coast. They passed park entrances and lookout points that were overflowing with people. While riding, Miles reached back and took Emma's hand, encouraging her to wrap her arms around him as they rode on. That was nothing short of magical on its own.

She hadn't remembered being this happy to be with someone. He felt the same.

They rode the twisting coastal Highway 101 for about half an hour before Miles turned off onto a hilly dirt road. This wasn't what Emma had expected, so she assumed this was the next surprise.

She held on a little tighter to him as he skillfully maneuvered the bumpy road. They continued for about ten minutes, mostly surrounded by tall pine trees. It was cooler along this path since the sun completely shaded it.

The scent of the forest was enticing, almost soothing, as it mixed with the fragrance of the ocean. Just when Emma was going to ask where they were going, the bike rounded a bend and crested out onto a clear landing that faced the vast sea of water shimmering in the distance.

The view took her breath away, and she gazed at the pops of color before them. The scents in the air mixed with the view of the majestic rock formation standing at full attention in the ocean, along with the birds flying overhead, singing their praises to the sun and the sea, were almost too much to take in at once.

Miles turned off the motorcycle's engine and popped off the bike to assist Emma. He lifted the storage compartment hidden underneath their seats and leg rests as she stood on the ground, gazing at everything around her.

From there, he pulled out a blanket and a paper grocery bag of goodies. She was very impressed and even more intrigued. He seemed so full of energy and excitement.

After he secured their helmets to the bike, he pulled her forward to a trail that seemed to lead to the sky.

"Come on, Em!" is all she heard as he took her hand and led the way. Just when she thought the view couldn't get any better, they took a short walk down a slightly worn path through some taller grass along the hillside facing the ocean.

It was steep, so they couldn't walk that fast, but in a matter of moments, after keeping a closer eye on her footing, Emma looked up at her surroundings.

It was nothing short of spectacular. It was the same tranquil blue of the ocean with the birds flying overhead, yet now, it just seemed to reach farther toward the endless sky. The sea birds seemed to be circling one of the humongous rocks in the water to find a place to land. There was so much to take in from this peak view.

Emma and Miles were now in the midst of a small field of bright pinkish-red flower bushes that were also sprinkled with vibrant purple-blooming plants.

He found just the spot he was looking for before laying the blanket down. He knelt while setting his bag of goodies on the ground. Once again, he easily reached for her hand to come to sit with him, which she willingly did. *How in the world had he found this little piece of heaven?*

Emma didn't need to say a word because it was almost like he was again reading her mind.

He started speaking calmly, "You know, a lot of people think I spend my time just looking for the next girl to take out, and for a brief time, that was true. But after the last girl, I realized I needed a break. I love riding and try to get out on my bike every chance I get. The weather here can be so unpredictable, and one day, I was out on my bike when it started to rain that misty rain where it's hard to keep my helmet visor clean, so I randomly turned onto this dirt road. I sat under the pines for quite a while, but then I just got bored. I was halfway up this hill, so I decided to hike the rest of the way. When I got up here, I swear I thought I found heaven. Even on a gross, cloudy day, this place is impressive. When the clouds and the fog roll in, sometimes those rocks shoot out of the mist like their ghost ships or something. By the worn trails, someone else must come up here, but I've never seen anyone else."

Emma was hanging on every word he was telling her, both amazed that he had read her mind and by the way he shared how he found this amazing secret spot.

Miles had unpacked the grocery bag while he told her about this place. She was warm from the sun's intensity but also suddenly very hungry.

Her eyes were happy as she responded, "Miles, this is simply amazing. Every view is breathtaking, and I love how you just happened to stumble across this place. It is like it was meant to be a place for you to come and enjoy. Thanks for bringing me here."

He was assembling his special picnic lunch but stopped what he was doing when she thanked him. It touched him that she would say that. Gently, he pulled her close and kissed her before saying, "There's another surprise I'm dying to give you, lovely lady, but first we must eat."

A glimmer of lust and amusement crossed his eyes, and she loved it. She gave him a quick peck back and said, "Yes, let's eat!"

She wanted him just as much and was distracted the whole time they ate.

It must have been the view combined with the sensual way they were eating their food with their fingers, the heat of the sun, and the attraction between them.

Miles had chosen a mix of charcuterie, fresh grapes, lightly salted pecans, and dried cranberries. Somehow, the bottled water and small bottles of Coke had stayed cold on the ride to their secluded spot. They were refreshing, almost intoxicating, along with everything else.

They talked easily as they ate and admired their surroundings. Having such a clear, warm day so late in the season was unusual, but they were taking full advantage. Both Emma and Miles kept thinking about how easy it was to talk with each other. They shared things about their lives that they didn't discuss with anyone. At the same time, they were trying to figure out why they would share such personal things.

Emma talked about the grief she and her family had been going through since losing her Grandpa and father so close together.

This prompted Miles to talk about the passing of his grandparents and then how his dad had just decided to walk away from everything shortly after. It left his mom in quite an awkward position, but she was strong and determined to take care of her family and the Woods business until her boys could take over. It was too early to tell what young Lindsay would do after high school.

They must have talked for at least two hours and leisurely lay in the sun while they ate. Since they were up so much higher and slightly more protected by the tall grass, the wind wasn't as strong, but the sun was way more intense. Emma was glad she wore layers as she removed her jacket and button-down shirt from the sun's intense heat.

As they talked, Miles was distracted by this beautiful lady before him in jeans and a sheer tank top. She had long since kicked off her boots and socks to try and stay cool.

He admired her as she talked. He intently watched how her facial expressions changed with the part of the story she was sharing.

She easily leaned back on one arm but quickly sat up and used animated hand gestures to get her point across. The sun hit her hair and the color of her eyes just right, and it appeared as if she were glowing.

He was entranced and distracted by her beauty. So much so that he leaned in to kiss her, not letting her finish the last of her sentence. He wanted her again, in this beautiful place. He loved that she was so easy to talk to, kiss, and touch. He wanted her so badly.

Emma felt this passion within Miles. She had been talking more than usual to try and fill the dynamic tension between them since they sat down.

With all of her words, she kept thinking of how much she wanted him again. Her mind drifted back to their night of lovemaking, and she impatiently wanted to feel that again.

When he finally leaned in and kissed her, she didn't resist. She felt relief that he wanted her as much as she wanted him.

She leaned up just enough to help him remove his shirt. He was tugging at her tank top, which easily slipped around her waist. She wasn't wearing a bra, and Miles gasped with passionate surprise this time. He loved her breasts, and this only made him more intoxicated with passion for Emma.

He leaned back so that she lay on the blanket before him. His hands slid from her waist up to her breasts, gently fondling them while he kissed her mouth and teased her with his tongue. He could tell she wanted him again, but he would enjoy this moment of surprise a little longer.

He lay on his side and admired her beauty with a sweet smile. At first, she looked at him to question why he had pulled away, but she quickly realized it was only to admire her body.

She reached for his hand and brought it back to her chest, showing him how to touch her. He thought he would go wild with pleasure for her, so he leaned close to her ear and whispered, "Do you know how much you drive me wild? This is all I have wanted to do since we woke up this morning."

He lazily traced a finger from her breasts to her jeans, circled her belly button, and reached between her legs to pleasure her.

This made Emma just as insane with passion, so she looked back at him with the same desire and said, "Back at ya, babe." Then with one swift move, she pushed forward to roll Miles onto his back and straddle him.

She pressed herself against him, feeling how rock-hard he was for her, and she grinned while taking both of his hands and putting them on either side of his head. She pressed herself against him while slowly sliding her body upward against his.

He could do little while she was on top of him, but he wasn't fighting it. She continued to glide upward until they were face-to-face. Emma leaned down, kissing him with such passion that they both thought they would lose control.

Then, she pulled away and glided her body up higher until her breasts were inches from his mouth. She looked down, smiling while teasing him by bringing her breasts closer to his mouth and then pulling away. This was driving him crazy, and she loved every minute of it.

She would let him tease her breasts with his mouth, then spontaneously pull away just enough that he would have to lean up to try to kiss her breasts again. She was driving him wild.

She felt he was close to the brink, so she slowly slid down and pressed her body against his while kissing him passionately. All at once, he flipped her over on her back just long enough to undo his pants. They were both on fire, clearly ready to explode.

Miles slid into Emma gently at first and then rocked fiercely within her while never breaking her gaze. He was hovering just above her while she kept leaning up to kiss him, only to have him pull his face up just out of her reach.

This drove her insane with passion, and he knew it. When they were both close to losing control, he leaned against her ear again and said, "Two can play at that game."

He grabbed both hands, looked down into her eyes, and thrust into her hard and deep. They came together, and both thought they had seen stars, even amid the bright sunlight.

Miles slowly slid to the side of Emma and looked down at this amazing girl. They were both still breathless, hot, and fully satisfied.

No words were needed when the passion was this strong. So, he rested his hand on her belly and slowly let a finger travel up to where her heart was still beating out of control.

She gazed at him in amazement, thinking of the wonderful things they could do to each other. She had never felt this intensely with anyone else.

Could she be falling in love with him so quickly? Could she have met her person? Was she crazy?

She needed to just breathe and get her heartbeat to slow down. Feeling so shaky from their lovemaking was new to her. Emma took a deep breath, smiled, and finally said, "That was amazing. Must be the ocean air."

He gazed at her with love in his eyes and a mischievous twinkle and said, "Must be."

He leaned down and kissed her slowly, languidly, and so lovingly that she thought she might burst again. He loved it, and when he pulled back from their kiss, she saw by the look in his eyes that he loved making her feel this way.

The sun was beginning to fade behind the rocks in front of them, so they knew their date was coming to an end. They lay there holding each other as long as they could before slowly packing their things to head back to Heceta Beach.

Their ride back to The Glass House was quiet but pleasant. Very few words were spoken on their trip back.

Emma leaned in closely to Miles as he drove her back home. They were peaceful, fulfilled, and dare Emma to think it, in love.

They were happy.

CHAPTER 6

LOVE'S HOLIDAY

"Everything just stops, and it's bliss."

The next day, Emma was surprised when Izzy didn't show up for school. She was worried that she had drunk too much. It was only a few weeks before the holiday break, so everyone's motivation for learning was low.

Emma was distracted most of the day, wondering if Izzy was ok and thinking about her new relationship with Miles. She kept catching herself smiling and daydreaming about more adventures with him.

At the end of the school day, she decided to swing by Izzy's house to make sure that she was feeling better. She had picked up some Gatorade and her favorite snacks in case Iz was still recovering from the bonfire.

Emma was a little intrigued when she pulled into her friend's driveway and saw a moving trailer attached to her dad's truck.

She parked her car behind it and headed up the front stairs to open the door. It was already open, so she felt comfortable walking in, but it still felt a little odd.

Hesitantly, she yelled out, "Hi, Iz! It's Emma! I missed you at school today. Where are you, girlie?"

There were moving boxes scattered around the front living room and into the kitchen as she walked through. Emma was curious as Izzy hadn't mentioned anything about moving.

The door to Izzy's room was cracked as she gently pushed it open. Her mom was standing over Izzy as Emma walked in. It was easy to tell that she had stumbled upon an intense conversation, so she quickly said, "I'm sorry to interrupt. I just thought I would stop by and see if Izzy was ok. I missed you at school today. Should I just call you later?"

Izzy's mom walked towards Emma and gave her a warm look, and responded by saying, "Oh, no. I think your timing is perfect, Emma. It's good to see you, sweetie. I'll leave you two alone to chat." and she closed Izzy's bedroom door behind her.

Looking at her friend's face, she could tell something was seriously wrong. Emma walked over, sat beside Izzy, and asked, "What's up? Is everything ok? I got worried when you didn't show up for school today. Are you still hung over?"

Izzy looked at her and leaned into Emmy's side for comfort as she explained, "Oh, I wish it was just a hangover. My mom and dad are getting a divorce. Dad is moving to Portland, and I'm not sure what we will do yet."

Izzy was crying, and Emma felt horrible for her friend. "Oh, Iz, I am so sorry. But they just went away for the weekend. What happened?"

Izzy shrugged and continued, "I don't know. Maybe something was up before they left, but Mom seemed so happy about getting away for a few days. Mom didn't see it coming. Dad travels to Portland a lot for work, and apparently, he's met someone else. Like, what the fuck, Em! How could he do this to us?"

She leaned in, and Emma wrapped her arms around her to console her. After letting Izzy cry, she gently pushed her hair out of her friend's eyes and said quietly, "I'm so sorry that this is happening. It's a lot to take in. Is your mom ok? Where's your dad?"

Thinking of her father right now made Izzy angry, and she expressed it in her words, "I don't care where he is. He is determined to leave, so I can't wait until he is good and gone. He's a bastard for leaving us. Good riddance."

And then, she began to cry harder. Emma could feel the pain in her friend's heart and just held her close while she cried.

It reminded her of when her father had passed away. She felt a mixture of indescribable pain, anger, and love. It was strange to feel then, and she began to feel it again now.

They sat like that for what felt like hours until Izzy finally pulled away slightly and looked up at Emma. She was calmer and began thinking about what happened over the weekend besides her parents breaking up.

She looked at Emma mischievously and finally asked what was happening with Miles. Emma felt a little awkward talking about this with Izzy because of what she was going through and because they both knew that Izzy had kissed Miles just a few days before.

She thought carefully and then responded, "We are getting to know each other. We were both surprised about how attracted we were to each other. It's kind of nice to get to know him more. He took me on a picnic yesterday. No big deal."

Emma took a moment before she said more, "Izzy, this is kind of weird. I saw you and Miles kissing in the woods the night of the game. Do you like him?"

The look that crossed Izzy's face was at once confused and blank. Emma couldn't tell what her friend was thinking.

Truthfully, Izzy was jealous, but with everything happening with her parents, she felt like she couldn't go there right now. She'd get Miles all to herself at some point, but right now, she didn't know when.

"Oh, that. Em, I was drunk and had no idea what I was doing. It was a little mindless fun. I barely know him," Izzy explained.

Emma didn't know what to think about Izzy's response, but she had no reason not to believe her.

After a longer-than-usual silence, Izzy smiled and joked, "Plus, with the noise I heard coming from the guest room, I'd say you know each other pretty well."

Both girls giggled, and Emma playfully hit Izzy over the head with a pillow. It felt good for both girls to laugh after the mixture of emotions from the last few days.

Emma felt relieved that Izzy was being lighthearted about her new relationship with Miles. She had no idea where it was headed, but she was glad that Iz wasn't upset with her about it. They hugged each other gently and continued gossiping about what Izzy had missed at school that day.

The next few weeks leading up to the holiday break flew by. Miles and Emma fell into an easy routine of talking on the phone daily, hanging out at local parties, or sneaking away for a date or two. The more they learned about each other, the more their attraction grew.

Izzy was still having a hard time adjusting to her parents separating, but she was so relieved to have Emma there to support her. They were practically inseparable at school and talked on the phone as much as possible.

Izzy didn't like spending much time at home since her mom was in a total funk once her dad officially moved out. Even if Emma and Miles were on a date, it was common for Izzy to spend the weekends at Emma's house. She seemed to get along great with Caroline and Grammy, so Emma didn't mind.

As Christmas approached, Izzy became more emotional and uneasy. She shared this with Emma on the last day before the holiday break. "What am I going to do? The last thing I want to do is to go to Portland to see my dad. He's such a bastard." Izzy complained as she leaned against the locker next to Emma's.

She had been dreading this time away from school, and now that it was here, she did nothing but complain about it.

Emma still felt the utmost sympathy for what Izzy and her mom were going through and spent plenty of hours talking her through what she was feeling.

This time, she focused on the positive and reminded Izzy about the fun evening they had planned that night.

Emma closed her locker and gently touched Izzy's arm in support, "I know it sucks, but let's just focus on tonight. It will be fun not to worry about school for the next few weeks.

Are we still meeting in town for the tree lighting? Andy is so excited to come with us."

The reminder of what they had planned for the evening made Izzy smile. She was looking forward to their double date to go to the tree lighting in town.

She finally smiled and said, "Yes, I am looking forward to tonight. Thanks for distracting me away from another one of my rage fests. What would I do without you?"

They all met at the center of town, with plans to go back to Emma's house after they had their fill of the Holiday Festival.

Miles and Emma were getting along great, and their relationship was starting to grow. Andy and Izzy enjoyed each other's company a lot more, and he was a good distraction for her.

The foursome walked towards the large tree that had been set up just past the shops, restaurants, and bars that lined the blocks through the center of town.

There was something so magical about the holidays. The people of Heceta Beach went all out with their lights and decorations. The coolest part of this night was the parade of boats that motored down the river just after the tree lighting.

Anyone who wanted to participate could decorate their boats festively and slowly float down the river toward the ocean. It was cold but a tradition everyone loved, so many people joined the event.

They were all in high spirits for the first time in quite a while. Most of the town, including their classmates, were there, and it was fun to chat, sing carols, and enjoy the festivities.

Caroline owned a small bakery in the center of town, where Emma spent many days baking. So after a while, they went there to warm up and grab some snacks before heading to the official tree lighting and boat parade.

Emma's mom always had a passion for baking, especially around Christmastime. Her shop gleamed with holiday spirit, with a little Christmas village in the front window decorated with sugar cookie snowflakes hanging over the cookie town and gingerbread people filling the village.

There was even a little train that ran around the holiday display. It delighted the little ones and gave a sense of nostalgia to the grown-ups that passed by.

When you entered the shop, it was easy to know that there were baked goodies to be savored. This was a special place to visit in their small town, with doughnuts, cookies, cakes, savory loaves of bread, and freshly brewed coffee and teas.

It was a very special place for Emma. She dreamed of attending culinary baking school and learning to create amazingly decadent treats. She hadn't decided whether to move away or expand on what her mom had already built in Heceta Beach. Yet one thing was certain: Emma loved baking and saw this as part of her future.

Festive holiday music filled the bakery as they all walked in. Due to the winter season and the tree-lighting festival, the shop was open later than usual.

It was always busy during this time, so it was worth it. Caroline came from the back kitchen when she heard the door open and smiled when she saw her daughter and her friends.

She warmly welcomed them and said, "Help yourself to anything. It's frigid tonight, so who wants coffee or hot cocoa?"

Once everyone told her what they wanted, she set off to get their drinks and a platter of sweet treats for them to snack on. They settled into a table and were glad to finally sit down after endless walking.

As they chatted easily, Miles noticed the large gingerbread village display behind the counter, "That is amazing! Who did all of that? Your mom?"

Emma finished her sip of hot cocoa and then answered, "Well, it was a team effort between all three of us. It's one of our favorite things to do just after Thanksgiving."

Miles was intrigued, "Really? I've never built a gingerbread house before. Sounds sweet."

And they all laughed at his cheesy joke, followed by Emma's suggestion that they have a gingerbread house decorating contest over the holidays. They all agreed and then set off for the rest of the evening's activities.

It was pretty cold that night, so it was easy for the two couples to walk arm in arm and snuggle close for warmth.

They joined a larger group of people near the tree to listen to the mayor's speech, the school carolers, and finally, the tree lighting.

Shortly after, everyone wandered to the docks and walkway near the water to watch the boat parade. Every year, the boat decorations got more and more creatively festive. It always ended with a large boat lit up like Santa's sleigh, followed by a beautiful fireworks display across the water.

This year was no different, and everyone's holiday spirits were high. During the fireworks finale, Miles and Emma pulled away from their romantic kiss long enough to see Izzy and Andy in a warm embrace, clearly enjoying their evening together.

The rest of the days leading up to Christmas flew by. Emma helped her mom at the busy bakery and then spent her evenings with her favorite foursome.

The night before Christmas Eve, she noticed that Izzy wasn't in as high of spirits as she had been since the Tree Lighting festival.

When Emma asked why, Iz was quick to share what was bothering her, "I have to go and spend Christmas Day with my dad in Portland. I just don't understand why he can't come here. It's what we've always done, so why does he have to change Christmas too?"

Emma wasn't sure how to respond and then said, "Maybe it's just too hard for him to come back here so soon. I'm sure he's having a hard time, too, Iz."

Her friend did not like this answer and snapped back, "Why are you defending him? He's the one that decided to leave. He's the one that broke up our family. And now, I'm expected to go there and pretend that I'm happy to be with him instead of at home like we're used to?"

Emma knew she had struck a nerve with Izzy and immediately apologized, "Iz, I'm sorry. I shouldn't have said that. I was just trying to help you understand why he doesn't want to come back here for Christmas."

Izzy was still upset when she snapped again, "I don't care how he feels. I'm still pissed that he is going through with the divorce. My mom is a mess, and now I have to leave her on Christmas."

Emma reached over and hugged her friend. She hated that she was going through this. It was almost harder than losing someone like Emma had lost her father and grandfather. Almost.

Sometimes the grief from being unable to be with them hurt her more than she thought she could bear. Yet, she always came through it somehow. Friends like Izzy and now Miles had helped.

Emma shared this with Izzy now, hoping she would understand that even though she was hurting, you somehow came through it, almost like riding a wave.

They walked over to one of the large windows of the Glass House to view the water as the sun was setting. The reflection of the water made the waves almost glow.

As they looked out onto the water, Emma tried to explain what she had learned by watching the ocean. She looked out onto the shoreline and spoke quietly, "The waves are quite calm, but no matter the intensity, they never stop rolling in. Kind of like grief and sadness."

She looked over at Izzy, who was looking at her friend intently, so she continued, "At times, we can ride the top of the wave and think that we will make it through easily to the shore. Other times, the wave is too big or strong, overtaking us, and we tumble. Either way, each wave eventually makes it to shore, so we have to choose how we ride the wave."

This explanation brought tears to both of their eyes. Both girls realized that they were grieving in their own way and were glad to have each other.

As the sun set over the waves, they put their arms around each other. Emma and Izzy were thankful to have each other to navigate what they were going through.

Eventually, they returned to their evening, but without saying anything to each other, they knew that the moment at the window had brought them closer. And they were both thankful for this.

On Christmas Eve morning, Izzy left to go to her house to pack for Portland. She wasn't happy, but she wasn't as angry as she was before she and Emma talked. They promised to call each other the next day to wish each other a "Merry Christmas."

Emma spent the first part of Christmas Day quietly with her mom and Grammy. They had a lovely morning, but it was still a hard day since it was the first without Pete and Graham. Everyone was in good spirits, but there was also a sense of sadness.

When Miles arrived later in the day, Emma was happy to see him and also more than a little relieved to have someone else there to lift their spirits.

Grammy had fixed a fantastic holiday dinner, with everyone pitching in to help here and there. They exchanged gifts, walked on the beach for a bit, and then stuffed themselves with dinner and sweet treats Caroline had made especially for the day.

The foursome had just settled in front of the fireplace to play a board game when there was an urgent knock on the door.

Caroline went to the door to answer it, and just as she opened the entry door, Izzy came barreling past her.

Her eyes, raging with anger and pain, were set straight on Miles. Before anyone could say anything, Izzy walked over to him and yelled, "You, asshole! Why didn't you tell me that your mother was fucking my father?"

CHAPTER 7

EVERYTHING CHANGES

"The only constant is change."

The whole room was stunned into an uncomfortable silence for what seemed like an eternity.

Finally, Rosie spoke up in a clear, strong voice. "Isabelle, I understand you are upset, but this is no way to begin a conversation. Now, it's clear that you have found something upsetting, so let's discuss this. Please have a seat."

Izzy wasn't used to this kind of direct order, so she slowly lowered herself onto the couch across from Emma and Miles.

As she sat down, her angry, accusing eyes never left his. She was shaking with adrenaline and fury as she spent the last few hours in the car seething over what she had just discovered.

She wanted to lash out at someone for breaking her family apart, and Miles seemed to be the perfect target.

More silence filled the room as they were all lost in their thoughts about what was happening. Miles was shocked, along with Emma. Rosie was trying to figure out how to proceed calmly, and Caroline was lost in her memories of a similar situation so many years ago.

How could this be happening again? I thought cheating and heartbreak were only caused by Wood's men, not the women. Guess I was wrong. Graham and I survived our cheating drama. What is going on here? How could Sarah do this to Izzy's family? I knew I should have warned Emma about what the Woods family can do to fragile hearts.

Caroline stopped her thoughts long enough to hear her mother speaking again. "…it's hard when you find out that someone you love has found someone new. Izzy, this whole situation will not be easy, and we are here for you no matter what. But you have to realize that yelling is not a solution. Take a deep breath, and then let's talk."

Izzy was still leering at Miles, making him very uncomfortable. He knew his mother had begun seeing someone new, but he didn't realize it was Izzy's father.

He tried to explain this to her, but it was met with more irate anger.

She rolled her eyes and exclaimed, "That's bullshit. This is your mother we are talking about. How could you possibly not know that she was sleeping with my father? This is going to kill my mother. And then, they dared to act like today would be the perfect day to share their 'love' with me. It makes me want to puke."

Izzy burst into tears as she covered her face with her hands. Emma immediately got up and went to her friend to try and console her, but Izzy pushed her away in jealous anger, "Did you know about this? You two are such lovebirds. Did you just laugh at how funny it is that you found love, and now my dad is hooking up with your mom? You both love this, don't you?"

Emma's heart was breaking for her friend and honestly didn't know what to do.

At this point, Caroline stepped in, "Izzy, that's not true. You are hurting right now, but taking this out on your closest friend will not help."

She turned to face her daughter, "Emma, Miles, did you know about any of this?"

They both simultaneously shook their heads, saying, "No." Both of them were wary of speaking, knowing that Izzy was so angry and emotional.

As Izzy continued to cry, Miles stood up to leave. It had been a long day, and he felt like being there made this worse. He walked towards Izzy, but she stopped him immediately, "Don't you dare come near me. You and your family have done enough."

Miles looked at Emma for help in what to say next, as he was at a loss for words.

He finally spoke directly to Emma, "I'm so sorry that this is how the night has to end, but I think it's best if I go. I swear that I didn't know this was going on."

He looked over at Izzy, who was still crying into her hands, "Iz, I'm so sorry. I will talk to my mom, but please believe me when I say I didn't know." He walked slowly to the door, and Emma followed.

She took his hand, lifted it to her lips, and kissed it gently. He looked her in the eyes and whispered, "I swear that I didn't know."

Emma just shook her head up and down, signifying that she agreed and believed him. They gave each other a loving hug, and Miles left.

As Emma walked back into the living room, she grabbed some tissues for Izzy. Grammy and her mom had taken seats across from Izzy, trying to give her some space.

Emma walked over to her friend and quietly sat down while handing her the tissues.

Softly, Emma began, "Iz, I'm so sorry about all this. It's heartbreaking, and I can't even begin to understand half of what you must be feeling. But I promise you I didn't know anything about what was happening. And, well, I know that you may not like it, but I believe that Miles didn't know either. It sounds like his mom has been gone a lot lately, which now we know why. That means he probably hasn't had much time to talk to her, and she probably didn't want him to know right now."

These words just made Izzy cry even harder. Emma was at a loss as to what to do, so she looked over at her mom and Grandma. They both had tears in their eyes.

Rosie spoke up again after a few moments, "Izzy, it's ok to cry. Lord knows plenty of tears have been shed in this house over the years. We are here for you."

No one knew if any words were helping Izzy because she lay there on the couch for a long time crying. She finally let Emma put her arm around her and willingly accepted a blanket that Rosie had laid on her.

The fire was dying down in the fireplace, and it was very late. Emma continued to sit with Izzy all night while Grammy and her mom went off to bed. They knew the girls would be fine if they left them alone.

Finally, the exhaustion of the long emotional day took over Izzy, and she fell asleep before too long.

Emma sat there for a long time and just watched her sleep before finally settling on the other couch for the night. She was truly worried about her friend.

The following day, the sun shone brightly through the large windows overlooking the ocean. Izzy pulled the blanket over her head, trying to shut out the day that had just begun.

Emma padded off into the kitchen to make tea for both of them. As she entered, she was surprised to see her mom standing there sipping her coffee, looking off into the distance.

Caroline had been up for hours, which showed in her tired eyes. Emma recognized that her mother looked worried and thought she should ask.

Warmly, she began with, "Good morning, Mom. How are you? Have you been awake long?"

Caroline looked slightly distracted but was happy to see her daughter. "Good morning, sweetie. I'm ok. I think we should all talk when Izzy wakes up. I've been thinking about things since last night, and it's sometimes good to share past experiences when someone is hurting as much as she is right now."

For some reason, this wasn't the response that Emma was expecting. She was about to ask her mom to explain, and they heard Izzy stirring in the living room.

Emma checked on her while her mom finished getting the tea ready. Not that Emma was going to mention it, but Izzy looked awful. Unsure of the response that she was going to get, she gently said, "Good morning, Iz. Did you get some sleep?"

"A little, I suppose. Emma, thanks for letting me stay here. You didn't have to sleep on the couch."

Emma was relieved that Izzy seemed a bit calmer after last night.

She began, "I wanted to be here for you in case you needed anything. Mom is getting some tea for us and said she wanted to talk. I hope that's ok."

Izzy seemed a little surprised, like Emma was, but shook her head in agreement.

Caroline and Grammy came in together, carrying tea and toast for everyone.

The sun was shining on them, offering a warm, comforting glow.

When they were all settled, Caroline took a deep breath before speaking. "You know, this house is built out of love. It's so much more than the wood and glass that hold it together. Mom and Daddy ensured that whoever came here was loved and cared for. Izzy, you are no different. We love you like our own family, and we are so sorry that you are hurting like this. We have also had our share of pain and hurt. Much like what you are going through now."

Emma and Izzy looked at each other in shock. What was she talking about? They also looked at Grammy for direction, but she looked down at her cup of tea.

Caroline continued, "You see, I once was in a situation where I was caught between two men I cared for deeply. It was one of the hardest decisions that I ever had to make because I knew that I was going to hurt someone."

"Mom," Emma interjected, "what are you talking about?"

"Let me finish, sweetie. This is something that I have never shared with you before. Izzy, you know what a small town this is. I was raised here with your family and the Woods family. It's also how I met Graham."

She couldn't help but smile as she mentioned his name. "When Graham and I started dating, I had already been seeing Warren, Miles's father."

She glanced over at Emma as she continued to share. "Warren was lovely, such a gentleman. Of course, Mom and Daddy liked him because of their history with the Woods family, so he seemed like a good fit to be my boyfriend. But then, I met Graham. He was charming, polite, and oh-so-handsome. I was smitten from the start." She again smiled at recalling the first time she saw her husband.

"I made a mistake. I started seeing Graham while I was dating Warren. Looking back, I didn't want to hurt anyone because I cared for them both. I wasn't trying to keep my attraction to Graham a secret, but that's what I ended up doing for quite a while. Eventually, Mom and Daddy found out. I'll spare you the details, but they forced me to decide. I don't think I ever cried that much, well, until I lost your father."

She said this last part while looking at Emma with eyes full of love. Emma knew how much her parents adored each other. She only dreamed of that kind of love in her life.

"So, in the end, I chose Graham. It was the best decision I ever made. We truly loved each other, and we were happy together. And, of course, we had our lovely Emma. But besides that, I hurt Warren tremendously. As you know, he left town, but I don't think he ever forgave me. Since I hurt him by letting him go, he made sure to hurt me with his words. Whenever I saw him in town, there was always a dirty look or a snide remark. I can't prove it, but there were rumors about me for a long time. They were mean, awful rumors, and I have always wondered if he started them. Even though it was the main reason we left town for all those years, in the end, it doesn't matter. What's done is done. I decided to follow my heart, and in doing so, I broke Warren's heart. Thankfully, no children were involved, so that's where the story is a little different from yours, Izzy."

At this point, Caroline got up and sat on the other side of Izzy. She gently took her hand and looked her in the eyes.

"You will get through this, my love. I'm so sorry that your dad is causing you so much pain. I can assure you that he is hurting too. Break-ups are never easy, and I'm sure divorce with kids is even harder. I know it will take some time, but try, just try to be a little understanding of what he may be going through. He probably feels like he has lost his daughter."

Izzy's eyes filled with tears, "He has lost his daughter. And his wife. I don't want to see him ever again."

"Oh, sweetie, you may feel like that now, but he is your dad. He will love you through anything that you may feel. Give it some time. And we're here if you need to cry or yell or whatever you need," Caroline said as tears filled her eyes.

It was emotional for her to share this, bringing back so many memories. "Why don't you girls get dressed and go for a walk on the beach? The sun and fresh air will do you some good."

"Before you do, there is something that I would like to say," Grammy interjected. They all looked up at her, a little startled since she had been silent during this conversation.

"Love is a complicated thing. It's constantly changing. Just when you understand one side of it, something changes your view of love. Not all of it is bad, but it can be challenging. I don't know what happened with your father and Sarah, Izzy, but I do know that he loves you. I've watched him grow up to be a very fine man. This is the hurtful side of love that you are seeing now, but it is possible for good to come from this."

Izzy smiled slightly at Grammy, but the tears began to flow more as she stumbled to say, "Thank you, Grammy. And thank you, mama Caroline. I'm sorry for how I acted last night."

"No need to apologize, dear." Grammy said, "We have all been there. And don't ever let anyone dampen that fire of yours." With that last statement, they all softly laughed.

Emma and Izzy changed their clothes, grabbed jackets, and headed out onto the beach while the other two cleaned the kitchen. Within moments of the girls leaving, the phone began to ring, and Caroline answered, "Hello?"

It was Miles. "Good morning, Mrs. Foster. Did everyone sleep well?"

"I believe we all did, Miles. How are you?" Caroline replied kindly.

"To be honest, I didn't sleep very well. I was going to tell Emma the same thing when I talked to her, but since my mom is in Portland, I haven't been able to get ahold of her." Miles sounded stressed.

"Well, I'm sure she will be back soon. Listen, Emma and Izzy are out for a walk on the beach. Would you like to come by for lunch?"

He hesitantly replied, "Are you sure? I think Izzy was pretty worked up last night, so I'm not sure that is a good idea."

"Miles, this is my home, and I am inviting you to lunch. The more distance you put between friends, the harder it is to recover. Come on over when you're ready. It looks like a great day to have lunch by the big windows."

She referred to the large eating area just off the kitchen, between the formal dining and living rooms. This area had a high-pitched ceiling with huge windows that allowed for gorgeous ocean views.

On a clear day, you could see Heceta Lighthouse in the distance. This room held a comfortable but substantial table for dining. She liked to refer to this area as the Morning Room, but they almost always enjoyed lunch here, especially on winter days like today.

The sun naturally warmed the room, and the chairs were so cozy that no one ever wanted to leave the table quickly.

When Emma and Izzy returned from their walk, they immediately smelled freshly baked bread. Caroline loved baking almost everything, but the bread was her go-to when she wanted to let off a little steam. The kneading of the dough was always her version of a punching bag.

They came into the kitchen and found her gathering ingredients for lunch and noticed not one but two loaves of freshly baked bread cooling on the counter. "Were we gone that long, Mother? You literally punched out two loaves of bread?" Emma said laughingly.

"Very funny, dear Emma. I had some dough already in the fridge, so yes, I suppose I did take full advantage of baking this morning." her mother replied. "By the way, Miles called while you were out, and I invited him for lunch."

They both looked at Izzy, curious about her response. She looked back and said, "What? I'm not happy with him, but we can all at least eat together." She then walked off toward Emma's room to freshen up.

Caroline and Emma worked in the kitchen for a while before discussing Miles coming over. "Mom, I'm not sure if this is a good idea. I don't know what Miles has said to his mom yet. We haven't talked about this."

"It will be fine, Emma. When I spoke with him earlier, he seemed stressed, and I thought having him over might help. He hasn't talked to his mom yet since she is still out of town." Caroline said as she busied herself with the lunch dishes. "I'll make sure that you two have a chance to talk without Izzy. You both should clear the air between you. And Emma, be careful. The Woods men have a way of breaking our hearts."

This took Emma back for a moment, "What do you mean? You said that you broke up with his dad. Did I miss something?"

"Just because I was the one that broke up with Warren doesn't mean that I didn't care for him or that he couldn't hurt my feelings. I took the lighter side of explaining things this morning. Some day I may want to share more, but for right now, just be careful. I don't want my baby girl's heart to get broken like mine." And with that, Caroline walked into the Morning Room to set the table.

About an hour later, Miles arrived for lunch. They all sat down and ate while bantering lightly about the weather, the delicious food, and what to do for New Year's Eve.

Everyone was on their best behavior, especially Izzy, which was a relief.

After they ate, Izzy announced that she was still tired and wanted to lie down in Emma's room. Grammy and Caroline excused themselves to clean up the dishes, giving Miles and Emma a chance to chat.

As they all left the room, Emma reached for Miles's hand and immediately felt calmer. He looked over at her, leaned in, and kissed her lightly. It felt like an eternity since he had kissed her lips, and he suddenly realized how much he had missed her.

"Before last night's debacle, I enjoyed spending Christmas with you." he said kindly.

This made her smile, and she agreed. "I know it didn't end well, but we all enjoyed having you. I didn't know how things would be without Dad or Gramps here this year."

"Well, apparently, fireworks were in order. I thought that was more of a New Year's Eve thing." he joked as they laughed.

"Miles, have you talked with your mom? What do you know?" she asked him curiously.

He shook his head as he explained, " I knew that she was going away for a few days, and she didn't leave a number where I could reach her. Normally, she calls, but she hasn't yet. I guess I'll have to wait until she returns or calls. Believe me. I want to find out what the hell is going on."

Emma nodded in agreement as he continued, "I hope you know that I had no idea this was going on. I would have told you, or especially Izzy. This has got to be so hard for her. She hates me for it, but I swear, I didn't know anything until last night."

"I believe you, Miles. It is hard on her. Not only is she hurting, but she's mad as hell. She will have to deal with her parents at some point, but she should at least wait until she is calmer." she said.

They talked a while longer and then decided to go outside and walk on the beach.

Hand in hand, they went out onto the balcony just off the living room and down the stairs to the walkway that led to the sand.

Before Emma realized what was happening, Miles pulled her close and led her underneath the upper balcony. It was semi-private under there, and Miles wanted to kiss her without anyone around.

He slowly backed her up against one of the wood posts that supported the porch, kissing her longingly. She realized she had missed his kisses and welcomed his touch with a mixture of love and lust.

They enjoyed each other's kisses and a little more for several minutes before Emma moved away slightly.

"As much as I love this, we should talk a little more. Want to walk for a bit?" she said to him as she reached up and touched his cheek.

"Lady, you drive me crazy, and I want nothing more than to make love to you right now, but yes, let's walk and talk. I need to cool down. It's all your fault." he joked as he lightly touched her behind while she led the way to the beach.

There were lots of people on the beach enjoying the sunshine that day. It was refreshing to feel the sun on their face, even in the cold winter air. So, the couple walked for a bit before continuing their conversation.

They eventually came upon a log that had washed up on shore, so they used this as a place to sit and talk.

"My mom was up early this morning, and so she talked with Izzy and me about last night." Emma began.

"She likes her and wants to comfort Iz. I don't think her mom is in a good place to be able to do that right now. She is just as angry and hurt as Izzy." she explained.

"So, my mom sat down with us today and tried to advise her about her dad and how he may be hurting too. Iz wasn't too keen on this, so my mom drew on her experience as an example. Miles, did you know that my mom dated your

dad?" Emma looked closely at him while he thought about
how to answer.

"Yes," Miles said, "I did. My mom told me when I let her
know about us. Em, my mom tried to warn me about you,
and I know it's not true. She doesn't even know you, and it
pisses me off that she compares you to what happened with
my dad and Caroline years ago."

Upon hearing this, Emma was a little mad, "Why didn't
you tell me this before, Miles?"

"I didn't want to upset you. When I met you, I fell in love
with you for who *you* are, not for who our parents are or
what happened to them in the past. Maybe I should have said
something to you, but I just didn't think it was worth it. My
mom wasn't even around when they dated, so she only
knows what my dad told her." he explained.

Emma responded slowly, "My mom does. She mentioned
that she thought that he was angry and hurt. She wonders if
he started some rumors that she had to deal with after they
broke up. I'm sure that's why she didn't mind that we moved
away for a few years. Miles, I like being with you. Does your
mom hate me? I don't want to cause a problem between you
and your mom."

Miles looked at her with nothing but love in his eyes as he
pulled her closer and gently brushed her hair from her face.

"Emma, I know this scares you, but I love you. You. Not
your mom or my dad or my angry mom. See, she still hasn't
gotten over the fact that my dad left us, either. Which is so
confusing to me because of how much he hurt her. How can
she be with someone that left his family to be with her? It
doesn't make any sense to me. So, I don't think she hates you,
but even if she does, remember how I feel about you. That's
all that matters—you and me. No one can feel what we feel

for each other. I know you haven't said it, but I can feel that you love me. What happens with everyone else won't change that."

The power of his words took her breath away. She leaned into Miles and kissed him so passionately that they almost fell off the log.

This made them giggle in between their kisses and only made them hold each other closer. They sat and kissed for a while and then quietly looked out at the ocean's rolling waves.

To the two of them, this was heaven. The wind mixed with the ocean air while they held each other was more than they ever needed. They were content and, dare Emma to think it, in love.

As they made their way back to the Glass House in the late afternoon, they were playfully struck with each other. They chased each other along with the waves, laughing and enjoying the last few moments of the warm sun.

Finally, they walked a little closer inland so their pants could dry a bit before heading inside. With time on their side during this holiday week, they were in no rush to get back, so they wrapped their arms around each other and slowly walked back.

Izzy had been on the balcony for quite some time trying to collect her thoughts because she knew she would have to face her mother soon.

As she gazed along the beach, she watched Emma and Miles intently. She was extremely jealous of their ease with each other and even more so of their passion.

It made her mad. Really mad. She also didn't believe that Miles didn't know what was going on with her dad and his mom. How could he not know? Was he blind?

As angry as she was, she knew she couldn't let it show. Emma was her best friend, and she was thankful for the love and care that her family had shown her.

Miles wouldn't be around for long because he was a player. He was always moving on to the next girl, quicker than the last.

Izzy decided she would be there for Emma when he broke her heart, and then they would get back at Miles and her dad for hurting them.

Izzy knew that in the end, she would seek revenge on those that had hurt her and her mother. She just needed to figure out how.

CHAPTER 8

NEW YEAR, NEW ADVENTURE

" Happy New Year. Really?"

Emma was relieved and happy to see that Izzy was in better spirits when they returned to the house. It seemed that a little more sleep did help her.

They decided to hang out at the house that evening and pick up where they left off with the board games by the fire. Once the sun had set, the temperature dropped outside, and so they were perfectly happy to sit by the fire. Izzy even asked if she could invite Andy over for the fun.

Caroline and Rosie were also happy that the foursome seemed to have found their way and let them be after they all had dinner together.

Andy was a little more forward with hugging and kissing Izzy that night, and Emma wondered what Izzy had shared with him. They seemed to be getting closer, and that made Emma happy that Iz had someone to support her.

Sitting by the fire and chatting while playing games, they decided that the Glass House would be the perfect place to spend New Year's Eve. Little did the girls know that Andy and Miles had a special evening surprise for everyone.

Over the next several days, Izzy had her ups and downs. She eventually went home for a night or two but inevitably ended up back at the Glass House with Emma because her mom's pain was too much for her to bear.

They spent their days on the beach, playing games and enjoying their free time. Miles and Emma were able to go out on a few dates, but they mostly spent their time together at the house. Caroline and Rosie were happy to have the kids there, too.

Soon New Year's Eve was upon them, and they had all decided that it would be best for everyone to stay the night at Emma's since it would likely be a late night. Everyone was in high spirits and excited to start a new year.

The girls decorated the house's interior and added little white lights to the outdoor patio. The evening's sunset was a gorgeous backdrop against a relatively calm sea, rare for December.

Grammy and Caroline cooked most of the wonderful dinner, but everyone pitched in. The guys handled grilling steaks, and the ladies each made a side dish.

Yet, the highlight of the evening was a magnificent black and white 3-tiered cake with gold flecks and tiny streamers set on top to resemble fireworks.

Emma's mom had made this at the bakery as a surprise for their little party. It added just the right amount of excitement to the evening.

Festive music played in the background as everyone floated from the beach to the patio to the warm fire inside.

Miles and Andy lit a bonfire on the beach, and the fantastic foursome headed there after dinner. Grammy and Caroline were content to sit by the fire inside the Glass House.

Bundled in sweaters and scarves, they put chairs by the bonfire and settled in to celebrate. How wonderful it was to be surrounded by your favorite people on the beach beside a fire. This is what Emma was thinking of when she heard a familiar drunken "Hello" call out from a distance.

She started giggling as she recognized this voice as Big Reggie, followed by his date for the evening, Annie. She was a classmate of Miles and Reg's that had always had a soft spot for the big guy.

As they approached, they all noticed that they had a cooler packed with beverages to celebrate the new year.

"Got room for two more?" Big Reg said as they planted his ever-present cooler in the sand beside the bonfire.

Of course, they were all happy to have them, and the boys quickly found two more chairs for their new guests.

Beers and champagne quickly emerged from the cooler for whoever decided to partake. Soon, it was a beach party, and they were all having a great time.

For only tonight, Grammy and Caroline decided to look the other way on the drinking. They were right there and could handle it if anyone had too much to drink. At least they had the foresight to make sure everyone was staying with them for the night.

Just before midnight, Big Reg had asked Miles and Andy to walk with him down the beach. The girls had so much fun chatting that they overlooked the time.

Before they knew what was happening, they heard the guys call out in the dark, "HAPPY NEW YEAR!"

The girls laughed but jumped up in surprise when a colorful bouquet of fireworks lit up the sky just down the beach.

Rosie and Caroline had run out onto the deck to see what the noise was about and were stopped in their tracks when they saw the beauty before them.

The fireworks lasted for a good ten minutes. During the grand finale, the boys had a moment to return to the bonfire to officially kiss their girls and welcome the start of the new year. It truly was a magnificent start to a memorable year.

Giggles and chatter abounded from the beach as the older two ladies wandered back inside to their glowing fire. The three couples were happy and warm on the beach.

By 3 am, Caroline could no longer keep her eyes open, so she checked one last time on the group before heading off to bed. Grammy had gone to bed soon after midnight.

She had set up sleeping bags and extra blankets in the living room for everyone. She knew this was going to be a late night for all.

Eventually, the cold got the better of the group, and they headed inside for extra warmth. Since the adults had gone to bed, Big Reg snuck in a few drinks for a nightcap. They had all played several rounds of Gin Rummy before. One by one, everyone lost steam and fell asleep.

By 5 am, it was only Emma and Miles left awake. They had discovered they were quite competitive with card games and played until the ultimate death. Even though they debated who had won the final round, they decided to call a truce when they realized that everyone around them was fast asleep.

The light of dawn was barely legible to the human eye, but Miles knew the sunrise would be amazing. He looked at Emma and suggested they go to the beach to enjoy the first sunrise of the new year. She loved the idea.

They grabbed a few blankets and pillows and headed out to the beach while the others slept. Tiny embers of the bonfire they had lit were still burning, so they had a bit of light to find their way in the dark.

Once they were settled on the sand, wrapped in their blankets, away from everyone, it didn't take long for the two to find each other. Their slow, magical kisses soon burned with the same intensity as the bonfire they had sat beside earlier in the night.

There, in the sand, covered by blankets and early morning darkness, they stripped away each other's clothes. Miles had learned what Emma liked and satisfied her needs while she moaned quietly with pleasure.

He drove her wild, and she was always surprised by how he made her feel. It was more than the magnificent feelings that he gave her with his lips and hands. When he entered her, it was like nothing she could describe.

They moved in the same motion as the waves meeting the shoreline. Slow and steady at first and then with a deeper, headier pace until they could no longer fight the intense ecstasy of their lovemaking.

This time, she was sure. This time, she knew what she was feeling. He didn't rush her, and she adored him even more for his patience.

Just as the sun slowly rose above the Glass House, offering the first few rays of the new day, Miles and Emma came together as intensely as they ever had.

Fearlessly, Emma reached for Miles's face so he could see hers. As she barely caught her breath from their lovemaking, she looked him in the eyes and whispered, "I love you."

The words he longed to hear touched him more than he thought they would. He whispered back to Emma, "I know. I love you too. I knew that we loved each other from the moment we met." Emma kissed him and knew that he was right.

Wrapped in their blankets, they sat quietly together and watched the sunrise. Although it rose behind them, the light on the ocean was colorful and soothing. Miles leaned down and whispered again in Emma's ear, "I told you that the only thing better than an Oregon sunset is an Oregon sunrise." She couldn't remember being happier than she was at this very moment.

They managed to pull themselves away from each other and head inside before the others woke up. They were exhausted but energized from their time together.

As they crept back inside the house, they smiled at each other. In love and excited about their secret way of celebrating.

Soon, they were snuggled together on the floor and fell fast asleep.

A few hours later, everyone was awake and ready for breakfast. It was a great beginning. Everyone was happy being together. Finally.

As the morning wore on, storm clouds rolled in over the ocean. Soon, sheets of cold rain fell on the beach and hit the panes of glass like a steady drumbeat.

It was the perfect day to stay by the fire, but everyone needed to return home. Slowly, they all gathered up their things to leave since the holiday bliss was quickly coming to an end.

The others had just left, and Emma was giving Miles another hug and kiss goodbye when the phone rang.

Caroline called out from the kitchen, "Miles, it's your mom!" He walked to the phone and talked in hush tones for several minutes. Emma could tell that he was upset, and he confirmed this once he finally hung up the phone.

He walked toward her, taking her hand to lead her back into the living room. With a worried look, he began, "We need to talk."

CHAPTER 9

ALL IS LOST

"Can you recover from a heartbreak?"

At first, Miles was at a loss for words about how to begin. Emma looked panicked and beyond worried. Was someone hurt? Or worse? What was happening?

He didn't let go of her hand while he began talking, "My mom just got back from Portland. I haven't had a chance to talk with her about Izzy's dad, but I promise I will. She checked our messages when she got home, and there was a call from the Navy. I signed up months ago, and I have been waiting to go to basic training. Emma, I leave in three months."

Emma was still processing everything that he had said. At first, she was relieved that someone wasn't hurt or an accident hadn't happened. Then she thought of the situation with his mom and Izzy's dad. Feelings of sadness mixed with dread washed over her. She didn't think this would be easy for Miles or Izzy.

As she thought a little more about Miles leaving for the Navy, she didn't realize it was a big deal. So, she gently smiled and said, "Well, that's good, right? It's what you want to do. I'm happy for you."

He smiled back, loving her for her strength and support. "Yes, I am happy to finally know when I am going to training. Em, I did this before I met you. I'm sad because it means I'll be gone for a long time. Like, at least four years. I don't know where I'll be stationed or what the final plan will be. But. I." He took a deep breath before he continued, "Emma, I won't be coming back here for a long time."

She looked at him intently, and the smile on her face gently faded as tears filled her eyes. Now she understood what he was saying. Emma pulled her hand away from Miles's.

He stood up and began pacing around the room, walking to the windows and then back to her, who was still sitting motionless on the couch.

A lump of emotion had risen in his throat. *Damn it,* he thought, *I don't want to hurt her. I never meant to hurt her. Why did we have to find each other right now? Why now?*

Miles returned to stand at the large windows to stare as the angry ocean waves crashed into the shore and the cold, hard rain continued to pound against the glass.

He wanted to be swallowed up by the waves and carried out to sea instead of breaking her heart.

He stood motionless as he continued to explain, "It wouldn't be fair to you if I didn't let you go. This doesn't mean that I don't love you. I love you more than you will ever know and don't want to lose you. But you have your

Senior year and your first years of college in front of you. I can't expect you to be tied down to me during that time and, even worse, not be able to see me. When I signed up for the Navy, I was free. I wasn't attached to anyone, so I did what I thought was best. I want to see the world, learn more about different types of architecture, and, most importantly, serve my country. I can't back out. But please know that I don't want to hurt you."

Silence. She said nothing. He finally turned around to see if she was still in the room.

She was still there, staring at the same dark and angry water. Her eyes were glazed over with pain and tears. Every once in a while, a single tear would gently fall down her cheek. She didn't care to brush it away. Her heart had been broken into a million pieces.

Why did the people, *the men* that she loved, always get taken away from her? Just moments before, she had been so happy and in love with Miles. Now, her heart had been crushed by the same person she had just professed her love to.

Why? Why was this happening? Why did she let herself fall? Of course, it was too easy. Nothing this good is ever this easy.

"Emma, are you ok? Have you heard anything that I have said?" Miles asked cautiously.

She was motionless except for a tear or two that would fall occasionally. He was worried.

"Emma, should I get your mom? Are you ok?" he asked again, but this time with a strained voice.

Miles slowly walked over and sat down beside her. He touched her shoulder and leaned into her, resting his head against hers.

His loving touch always felt so good to her. This time, it was the one thing that caused her emotions to break. She leaned into him, and he wrapped his arms around her as she cried.

They sat like this for quite a while as she continued to let the tears flow. Both of their hearts were breaking. It did seem unfair to them that a situation like this would pull them apart. They loved each other so intensely. Why couldn't they be together?

No words needed to be spoken as they held each other, and Emma continued to cry, for they both knew what each was feeling. It was a mixture of anger, sadness, and immense heartbreak.

Finally, Emma sat up straighter and pulled herself away from Miles. She wiped her tears, cleared her throat, and, as best she could, said, "You should probably go now. I'm sure your mom is expecting you home, and you need to talk to her."

He tried to interject, "Emma, it's ok. I am not in any hurry to get home. My mom can wait. I want to make sure you are…" Emma was quick not to let him finish his sentence.

Mustering strength that she wasn't even sure she had, she replied, "No, you should go. It's best for both of us."

Miles knew when to stop and nodded in agreement. Emma walked him to the door, and they stood in the hallway for a long time, hugging each other.

How had everything changed so quickly? Just a few hours ago, she told him she loved him, and now she had to let him go. It was cruel.

Miles kissed the top of her head and then pulled back slowly to say, "I'm not leaving tomorrow. We still have a little time together. This isn't goodbye right now. I just wanted to be honest with you right away."

Tears once again began to fill Emma's eyes. She nodded and sadly said, "I know. I need some time to think about all of this. Maybe we should stop now. Three months from now, it will be even harder to say goodbye."

He hugged her closer and said, "Yes, but it is three more months that I get to spend with you. Emma, I love you. That didn't change. I'm just trying to be fair to us both."

She moved out of his embrace, slowly opened the front door, and replied, "I know. But it still hurts, and I don't know how much more hurt I can handle."

This broke his heart to hear. He didn't want to hurt her. Miles had no choice now but to leave her, so he slowly walked out.

As soon as he cleared the door, she closed it behind him, leaned against the wall in the foyer, and sank to the floor in tears.

Grammy and Caroline had been listening quietly from the kitchen. They let Emma cry for a bit and then went to the foyer to get their girl.

She needed them now more than ever. Their hearts broke for her, but they knew she would be ok.

Tenderly, they helped her onto her feet and led her back into the living room, where they sat with her as she cried. Her tears were just as heavy and wet as the rain that continued to batter the Glass House. It seemed so fitting for her misery.

He sat in his truck in her driveway for quite a while, debating whether to go back in. Tears filled his eyes, knowing that this heartbreak was different from any other relationship he had with a girl.

It didn't help that his mother had been so callous on the phone. She almost enjoyed telling him that he had been called into the Navy. She didn't want him to be with Emma, which pissed him off.

Eventually, he began his drive home in the pouring rain. He knew his Mom would be waiting to talk to him as soon as he entered the door. She never allowed him to breathe when she was in this kind of mood. He didn't know if anyone else would be home, and it didn't matter. When Sarah wanted a confrontation, she made sure it happened.

They had a long driveway leading to a private clearing between gorgeous tall pine trees. His dad loved this spot because it was off the beaten path. The house was solid pine with an elegant yet rustic Craftsman-style porch entry.

The Woods family had spent plenty of days enjoying the porch swing and climbing on the posts that lined the front of the house. Miles never understood how his dad could walk away from a home that he loved so much.

Of course, Miles also didn't know what it was like to be married to Sarah.

She was tiny but tough. Growing up with older brothers, she had to be. They weren't going to go easy on her just because she was a girl. She was attractive, spunky, had a quick wit, and liked a good, strong drink a little more than she probably should have.

Men had nothing on her. She had broken more hearts than she could count. Married and divorced twice, she always tried to protect her heart, and her defensiveness showed it.

She certainly didn't care what others said about her. Sarah would date whom she wanted when she wanted and leave them behind just as quickly when it suited her.

Her passion was her kids. She loved her three children fiercely. That was always very clear.

No one would ever be good enough for them. So, when she found out about Emma, she quickly figured out how to stop it.

Luckily, she didn't have to do much. She was thrilled when she learned that Miles had finally been called to the Navy. That would put a stop to him dating that bitch's daughter.

She was referring to Caroline, of course. Oh, how she hated that woman. She believed that Caroline was the reason her marriage to Warren didn't work out.

He couldn't get over her, which made Sarah extremely jealous and even angrier. So angry that it finally drove Warren straight out of town and out of their lives.

She heard Miles pull into the driveway, and as usual, she was waiting for him as soon as he opened the door. Sarah was more anxious than usual to talk to her son because of what was happening in her love life and his.

He came in and found her in the kitchen cooking dinner. He kissed her cheek and said, "Hey, Mom. Whatcha making for dinner?"

Miles could tell from the aroma as soon as he entered the house, but he attempted to strike up a pleasant conversation in preparation for what he knew was coming from his mom.

She smiled, "Hello, there, my second favorite son. I'm making lasagna. Perfect for this cold, rainy night."

Sarah always liked making Miles's favorite dish, especially when she wanted to talk to him.

"Mom, why do you always insist on calling me your 'second favorite son'?" Miles said with a little grin.

She continued to put together the dish and slyly remarked, "Because you are my second-born son and my favorite. But I'll never admit the last part, especially around your brother. Come sit with me while the lasagna bakes."

As they walked toward the living room, she stopped at the bar cart to pour herself a bourbon. This was always her drink of choice. Straight, no ice. That was for weak drinkers.

Miles settled onto the couch across from her favorite chair and tried to prepare himself for the conversation that was to come.

Their dog, Wolf, was asleep in front of the fire, making him realize how exhausted he was. Not only did he not get enough sleep last night, but his emotions were raw.

Sarah did not pick up on any of this as she settled into her chair, took a sip of her drink, and started in on Miles. "So, did you drop her like a lead balloon, or will you string her along for a while?"

This comment pissed him off. "Mom, why do you have to say things like that? I really like Emma. She's not just some chick I'm going to toss to the side because I'm leaving."

This confused Sarah, and she didn't like what she was hearing.

She fired back, "What do you mean? I thought we decided that you would break up with that girl when you left for the Navy. Miles, don't be silly. You are way too young to be tied down to some high-schooler while you are away growing up in the real world. You're smarter than that."

She took a big gulp of her bourbon and awaited his response.

"It's not that easy. I mean, I told her we can't stay together, but it's hard when you care about someone. I won't be mean to her just because I'm leaving." He said as he rubbed the side of his head in frustration.

Smiling sarcastically and swirling what was left of her drink, she tried to drive home her point, "Sometimes, if the girl is clingy, you have to be mean. Keep that in mind if you're going to continue to hang on to this one. I say, just dump her. Like ripping off a bandaid."

Miles was getting pissed, "Mom, I'm not like you. Yeah, I've dated but found someone special this time. You haven't even met her, so how do you know?"

Sarah snapped back at him, "Oh, believe me, I know her mother, and that's all I ever need to know. If she is anything like Caroline, she'll wrap you around her little finger and then break you in two. Little evil bitch."

She looked directly at Miles when she said that last part and kind of felt bad at the harshness of her words.

"That was uncalled for, Mom. I know how you feel about Caroline, but you don't know what you're talking about. You don't know Emma or her mom. You only know what Dad told you, so it's unfair."

Sarah laughed cynically, "I know all I need to know. I no longer have a husband because he couldn't handle living in the same town as his *lost love*. She knew she was twisting the knife in his heart for years. Then she got married, and it broke him. Cheers to breaking his heart and mine!" She raised her glass to no one and took another swig of bourbon.

Miles wondered if he could handle much more of this conversation, so he changed the topic.

"You've moved on. As I understand it, with Izzy's dad, why do you care? What is going on anyway? Why didn't you tell me?" he asked pointedly.

She stood up and began pacing in front of the fireplace with her drink dangling in her hand, which made the dog wake up. "I don't think that I owe you any explanation. We are both grown adults and can make our own decisions."

"Well, if you haven't noticed, he does have a daughter, and she is more than a little pissed about your relationship. How long has this been going on?" he pressed.

"It doesn't matter. And, why all the questions, son?" she asked.

He was getting more frustrated by the second at his mother's nonchalance about dating Izzy's dad. "Because I don't like getting caught in the middle of something I know nothing about. Izzy screamed at me because you were with her dad on Christmas. How did you not think that she would be mad?"

Sarah was getting irritated, too, "She's practically an adult. I'm sure she knew that her parents weren't happy. That's another bitch for you, Izzy's mom. She's always mopey and complaining about her husband all the time. That's how you lose them, and then they become mine."

Her defenses were up, and Miles knew that she didn't mean everything she was saying.

"Mom, I realize that you aren't happy about me dating Emma. I also know that you don't hate everyone, especially Izzy. It just would have been nice to have a head's up about what was going on. I was just as confused as everyone else when Izzy started yelling at me. You're my mom, and I can't very well defend you if I don't know what's going on." he practically shouted at her.

This calmed Sarah down a bit. She liked when her sons protected her. They did what Warren never had, which was to protect and defend her. He just ran off when he couldn't hack it anymore.

He left her with everything - the kids, the house, the business. Why wouldn't she be an angry woman? None of this was her fault.

"Well, I suppose you're right about that part." she began, "But I'm not going to let you talk me out of this new relationship. It's fun, and since he's still technically married, no strings are attached."

Miles shook his head in disagreement as he said, "Yes, there are strings attached. His daughter, for one thing. Mom, are you just toying with this guy, or do you like him? If it's just fun, break it off. Don't hurt other people."

Her anger was back when she heard that comment, so she said, "Oh, I see. Are you saying people can hurt me and break up my marriage, but I can't do the same thing? Doesn't seem fair to me. I will keep seeing him if I want, and Izzy can just deal with it. Same for you. If she has questions, have her come to me then, all right?"

She took a long swig of her drink, emptied the glass, and then walked to the kitchen.

"Mom, I love you, and I know you love me. Can we not hurt each other over the people that we are dating? It's not worth it." Miles said quietly.

He didn't want to fight with his mother about either topic anymore.

Wolf came over and sat by Miles to be petted. It helped calm everyone in the room a little bit.

Sarah heaved a heavy sigh and said, "No, it's not worth fighting about. And yes, dear son, I do love you. I don't know what's going on with Izzy's dad yet. I like him, and we have fun. If it becomes anything more than that, I will tell you. Please don't string that girl along. Talk about not being fair to either of you. Now, go set the table. It's time for lasagna."

CHAPTER 10

THE LONG GOODBYE

" Goodbye, my love. Now what?"

The sky is so dark and filled with gray clouds. The wind howls and makes the waves crash violently into the beach. Rain pelts her in the head with cold, hard droplets. She looks up at the sky as if to say, "Why now?" She drops her head to look out into the distance, but it's difficult to see clearly with the storm rolling in.

Suddenly a large ship appears in the distance. Its beacon shone brightly onto land. Emma feels elated to see the boat, and suddenly she is in the water, swimming toward it. She must get there, but the waves are so strong. At one point, she's pulled under by the weight of the water crashing in on her. Quickly, she finds her way to the surface, only to be pulled under again. This time she pushes hard against the waves and shoots straight out of the water. Emma is flying through the air, higher and higher, until she is just over the top of the ship. She looks down to see if she can navigate her landing.

Suddenly, her dad is standing on the side of the ship, waving his hands overhead and screaming her name. The wind blows hard, and she can't seem to make herself come down from the air. She tries to push down, but the wind is working against her.

As she keeps her eyes on her dad, she screams back at him, and then Miles appears beside him. She needs to get to them both. Miles is yelling something, but she can't quite hear what he is saying.

Emma uses all her strength to try and fly down closer and closer to the ship. Every time she thinks she is close enough to land beside them, the wind carries her further out, away from them. She has to circle like a hawk scouting where to land to catch its prey.

As she bears down one more time, she sees a group of men pushing something heavy along the ship's floor. It is moving towards her father and Miles. It's a silver and white rectangle, and they seem to be pushing it with all their might.

She catches another blast of wind that carries her further away once again. Emma is screaming at the top of her lungs because she desperately wants to land on that ship.

She swoops in closer, pushing against the wind with all her might. The silver and white rectangle has now turned into a bed. It's her grandfather in his hospital bed. The men are trying to bring her grandfather closer to her. How can this be? How are all three men together on this ship? She has to reach them.

In the distance, a giant wave is rolling closer to the ship. All the men are shouting at her now, but she can't understand what they are saying. She has to land now!

This time she almost touches the deck of the ship. They are shouting her name and something else she can't understand.

Something sharp violently hits her head, and she is sent tumbling into the water. She can't reach the surface. She paddles vehemently to try and come up for air.

Emma is being pulled down into the water.

She can't breathe, and where did everyone go?

———————————

The sun shined brightly through her bedroom window as she sat up in bed with a jolt, catching her breath as her eyes shot wide open.

It was a dream.

Or a nightmare.

It was so real that it took Emma a moment to realize she was shaking. She needs them. She needs her father, her grandfather, and Miles. She's lost without them.

At this realization, she started to cry again. She misses everyone so much. Her grief is like a never-ending wave of emotion and sadness constantly overwhelming her.

She suddenly realized that she could still see Miles, so she immediately picked up the phone to call him. When the line picked up, the voice at the other end wasn't his.

It was Sarah, and she was not happy to hear that Emma called to speak with Miles.

"If I see him, I will try to remember to tell him that you called." Sarah bluntly said to Emma and then abruptly hung up on her.

Just as Emma was trying to figure out where to find Miles, her mother softly knocked on her bedroom door.

"Sweetie, Miles is here to see you. Are you ok with that? I wasn't sure how you were feeling after yesterday." her mom said quietly.

Caroline saw the answer when she looked into her daughter's eyes. *Oh, yes, she is happy that Miles is there to see her.*

"I just called his house, and his mom said he wasn't there. She did not seem happy that I called." Emma responded absentmindedly.

Under her breath, Caroline muttered, "That woman is never happy unless it's her child or someone she's sleeping with."

"What was that, Mom?" Emma asked.

Her daughter's words quickly brought Caroline back into the moment, and she quickly brushed off her emotions. It wouldn't do any good to stoop to Sarah's level of anger.

She quickly responded, "Nothing, sweetie, go ahead and get ready. You don't want to keep him waiting long."

Emma quickly dressed and then hastily bounded into the living room. Driven by her anticipation of seeing Miles, a smile immediately spread across her face when they saw one another.

He was so nervous about coming over unannounced after the way things ended the day before. Yet he had to try to talk with her again. And now that he saw the love in her eyes, he was relieved.

"I hope you don't mind that I just came over," he said shyly.

In Emma's head, she wanted to jump into his arms and stay there forever. Somehow she found the self-control to respond, "No, not at all. I just tried to call you, but your mom said you weren't there."

A slight annoyance crossed Miles's eyes, but he said nothing. Instead, he suggested that they take a walk along the beach.

It was still a dark, rainy day, but they were used to it during winter on the Oregon coast. As they grabbed their rain jackets and scarves, both were surprised by how relieved they were to be with each other again.

Although it had only been hours since they talked, the dynamic of their relationship had shifted drastically. Yet it was apparent that there was still an abundance of love between them.

The wind and misty rain whipped around them, keeping them from looking up often as they walked quietly along the sand.

He took her hand reassuringly, and with that single touch, she felt the warm familiarity she had expected from Miles.

Eventually, they stopped and sat on a weather-worn log that had washed up on the shore. He put his arm around her, and she leaned in for extra protection from the constant, cold breeze.

She rested her hand on his chest and looked at him for a warm kiss. Even in the short time that they had been together, he never could resist kissing her.

Finally, he pulled away and said, "You know I don't want to leave you, Emma. I'm just trying to do what's best for both of us. The last thing I want to do is hurt you. I promise you that. This is just something that I am committed to doing for many reasons. It's a commitment I made before I fell in love with you."

Emma's eyes filled with emotion as she began to think of that sad day that would be here before they knew it. She whispered back to him, "I know. I can feel that you don't want to hurt me, and I trust that it's true. But it does hurt. It hurts so much."

She continued to explain, as she sat up to look at him while they talked, "I had a horrible dream last night. You were on a ship with my dad and my grandfather. I wanted to get to all of you, but the wind carried me farther away every time I got close. I was crying and screaming, but I couldn't get to any of you."

Tears flowed as she said, "I woke up scared and wanting more than anything just to see you. When you came over, it was a relief that I can't quite describe. Miles, I don't want to lose you. I just told you yesterday how much I love you, and now we can't be together. It's like a sad joke."

As she described her dream, her face reflected her sadness. Miles's heart ached for her pain. He felt helpless that he couldn't do anything about it.

His mother added another element of angst to the situation by pushing him to separate from Emma. Instead of feeling sad, he was suddenly feeling angry.

In frustration, he quickly stood up and began pacing up and down the sand. His thoughts were racing, so he needed to move just as quickly. This confused Emma because he wasn't saying anything and had inadvertently pushed her away as he stood up. This made her more emotional, which made her cry harder.

"I… I just need some time to think, Emma. Maybe this is too much, and we *should* just end things now before they get harder. I don't know. I love you, but I can't stand seeing you like this. Damn it!" He kicked at the sand in his anger.

Suddenly, the sadness in Emma instantly switched to anger, too. She jumped up and walked toward Miles as he continued to stomp back and forth. The rain started coming down harder as if to meet their equal frustration. They both blinked away the wet raindrops as they began yelling at each other.

Emma screamed through the heavy rain, "Why would you not stop and think about the fact that you signed up for the Navy before asking me out? Did you think I was just some girl that you could kiss and then toss aside? What were you thinking?"

Miles yelled back, just as angry, "I don't know, Emma. I guess I wasn't thinking! I was focused on you. Loving you. Kissing you and just wanting to be with you. I was selfish, ok? I was mesmerized by you, and that turned into loving you. I didn't mean for this to happen. It just…happened. I was a selfish jerk, ok. I'm sorry!"

She met his anger with a forceful response, "You should be sorry! You made me love you, and now I have to say goodbye to you! What part of this is fair? To either of us? We love each other, but we can't be with each other! I hate this! I lose every man I love. My dad. My Grandpa. And now you."

With that last part of her rant, she sank to her knees into the sand, crying for the three men that she loved more than anything—mourning the thought of losing another important man in her life. Scorning the idea that she didn't get to be with Miles for very long yet knowing she loved him with the depths of her soul. This was so cruel.

Miles had stopped pacing with the mention of everything that Emma had lost. Tears had stung his eyes and mixed with the raindrops pelting his face. He dropped onto the sand beside her and held her close as she cried. He felt awful and so very selfish. He reprimanded himself in his head for hurting her more.

"I'm so very sorry, Emma. This is not what love is supposed to be. I never meant to hurt you. You've been through enough with your family. I feel awful. Like I should leave you alone. But I love you. Look at me. I love you and want to be with you more than anything."

He kissed her before she had a chance to respond. The flame of their love combusted in a passionate kiss. Rain fell harder onto them repeatedly, but it didn't interrupt their kisses. Eventually, Emma began to shiver with cold and a little from her emotions, so she pulled away.

In the distance was a rocky cove that provided a bit of shelter from the cold, windy rain, so they ran over to hover inside it. They sat quietly and watched the rain pour down for a few moments before their lips found each other again.

The cove wasn't very big, so their body heat quickly warmed them. Their attraction to each other was once again undeniable. Hungrily, they unzipped each other's jackets, and Miles's hands made their way inside Emma's sweater to her aching breasts.

He took off his jacket and laid it down on the sand for them. She leaned back and shimmied her pants to her ankles as he did the same. They joined together in an instant, almost aggressive passion, each feeling so many different emotions.

The roughness of their touch was not hurtful but rather aggressive *because* they were hurting. It was as if, with each touch, they were trying to push away the pain that they were feeling.

As Miles entered her abruptly, he leaned heavily on top of her and kissed her with a hunger that she met with the same fierceness. Their lovemaking was intense and raw, like their emotions.

Afterward, they lay beside each other, spent and out of breath, still reeling from their actions and thoughts.

What was to become of their love? No one knew the answer.

For now, they were comforted by being together for the time that they had. Goodbye was inevitable. It was the in-between that was still unchartered.

The next few months flew by, yet all the while, it was as if Miles and Emma were orchestrating a delicate dance with their emotions. They knew they loved each other and wanted to be together, but going their separate ways was bound to happen.

Their fun times during these weeks were overshadowed by a cloud of knowing that they would have to say goodbye. So, they focused on the positive. They spent as much time as they could together, going on dates and motorcycle rides when the weather allowed.

Miles also continued to deal delicately with his mother, who wanted nothing more than for him to break up with Emma.

Every chance she had, she constantly reminded him of this, and it was driving him crazy. Luckily, she was spending more and more time in Portland with Izzy's dad, John, so he did get an occasional break from her nagging.

Izzy and Andy turned into quite the item, and the four loved their double dates. They often joked about Emma becoming the third wheel after Miles left, but they all were aware of the pain that would come when that happened.

Since Emma's mom and Grammy knew the emotional rollercoaster that love can be, they tried to limit their advice and stay quiet while Emma continued to see Miles.

They decided they would be there when she fell and hold her up when she hurt. That's what family does, and she would eventually be stronger because of the pain. That's how they each had survived the loss of their great loves.

The final few days before Miles's departure appeared with the heaviness that one would expect. Caroline and Grammy decided to visit Eugene, a second larger city outside Heceta Beach. They wanted to give the couple their space to say goodbye.

Miles decided to stay with Emma at the Glass House two days before he was to leave. He felt like they needed the warm embrace of her home.

During their time together, they loved to lay on the couches in the great room and look up at the walls and ceiling to follow the shadows and streams of light that came in from the large windows. It was, at times, mesmerizing.

Miles truly appreciated the design details that Emma's grandfather, Pete, had put into the home. He was inspired, while slightly intimidated, by the architectural details of this house.

He had been lying with his head in Emma's lap as she was reading that afternoon when she caught a glimpse of this fascination in his eyes. So, she gently lifted his hand to her lips to kiss it and said, "Penny for your thoughts."

It took him a moment to realize she was talking to him, and was slightly embarrassed by his distraction. "Well, if I'm being honest, I'm thinking about this house, specifically this room. I'm sorry that I never had a chance to get to know your grandpa. He truly knew what he was doing when he designed this home."

Emma was touched by Miles's honesty and explained, "He loved my grandmother so much. When they were younger, this was one of their favorite spots on the coast, and he always promised to build a home for her here. This house lived in his mind long before it was ever built. I guess he had time to think through the details. I love this house because it's all about them and their love for each other. It's kind of magical if you think about it."

This was what Miles loved about Emma. She saw so much more than what someone else would see.

Instead of wood, glass, and concrete, she saw the passionate story behind this house. She could see the story behind so many different things in life. To him, she was amazing and brought so many things to life through her eyes.

Miles smiled up at her as he continued to lay there, "I know it's only been an hour or so, but I love you. I love that you see so much more than everyone else. You have this ability to make everything more beautiful."

She giggled out of embarrassment since she wasn't used to someone telling her these things, "Oh, Miles, are you trying to get into my pants again?"

With that response, he laughed out loud and pulled her closer, "Always. And don't forget it. I will always try to get into your pants."

Soon after, they willingly took off their pants and made love in the gently fading sunlight of the day. This was an easy love. Relaxed, fun, and yet intense and natural.

Their connection was something that most people spend their entire lives looking for, yet because it happened so early in life for them, they had not realized how rare it was.

The next couple of days were much of the same. They spent time together being lighthearted and happy and having fun dates with Izzy and Andy.

Their last days together were spent on the beach, riding the dunes, and plenty of time making the most of loving each other.

When the final night came, an inevitable heaviness filled their time together.

It was almost a two-hour drive to the airport the next day. Izzy and Andy had agreed to ride along, more as a support for Emma and because they had all grown quite close these last couple of months.

Sarah was not pleased with this decision, but in the end, she agreed, hopeful that this would be the end of Miles's relationship with Emma.

Since the next day was planned, the couple chose to spend their last night alone. Emma cooked a simple dinner, and Miles built a bonfire on the beach outside the Glass House. It was just how they wanted to spend their last night together.

A few days prior, Big Reg had surprised Miles with a wild going-away party full of beer and shenanigans. It was a well-deserved final hurrah for the good friends and many others.

This night, however, was more emotional and intimate. After dinner, they wandered down to the bonfire with glasses of wine and sat quietly.

The ocean waves were loud yet soothing at the same time. It was almost as if the water knew they needed something to help drown out their aching sadness.

Miles had found a stick and began drawing different patterns in the sand as if wishing for a Zen moment to calm his anxiety about leaving.

He finally said, "In a dream world, I could sit here with you like this forever and be blissfully happy."

Emma smiled as she heard this because, at that moment, she was having a similar thought.

Instead, she responded, "Well, it doesn't take too much to entertain you, does it, Mr. Woods?"

He laughed at her sarcasm and pulled her close for a hug and a kiss, then explained, "What I mean is that I am happy at this moment. It's nothing grand or fancy, but I don't know. I guess it means that I'm just happy with you."

Emma kissed him back, this time more seriously, and said, "I couldn't agree more."

They sat in the sand, leaning into each other for a little longer, staring into the fire, and listening to the endless waves rolling into the shore.

"Miles, do you think it's crazy that we fell in love so soon? I mean, we are young. Does everyone feel this way?" Emma said as she gazed into the glow of the fire's embers, almost as if she were in a trance.

He peered down at her, initially unsure how to respond.

Finally, he thoughtfully said, "I don't know. The only thing I know for sure is that this feels different from anyone I have ever dated. I don't know what being young has to do with love. Maybe when you know, you just know."

She thought about this for a while and then said, "Then am I done looking? Is it you? Are you my one person? How do I know for sure? How do you know I'm the one for you, too?"

They both continued to stare into the fire and think about each other's words. Neither of them had an answer. They honestly didn't know.

Miles thought fleetingly about how happy his mother would be to know that they were questioning the realness of their love.

Sarah would say it wasn't real. That there's no way they could find their person so young in life. She would say they would end up hating each other if they got married so young. She believed that love equaled hurt, and she wanted nothing to do with hurt.

He wasn't sure he felt the same way. He didn't know much about love, but he knew what he felt for Emma. And right now, at this moment, that was enough for him. More than enough for him.

"Em, it's getting chilly. Let's go inside," he said suddenly. They stood up, and she collected their things as he doused the fire with sand to put it out safely.

She thought about how abruptly he stopped the conversation as they did this. She questioned why he had done that but thought better of mentioning it right then.

When they got back inside, he lovingly took her by the hand and led her back to her bedroom. He closed the door behind them and slowly took her in his arms.

As he quietly spoke, he gently began to disrobe her. Warm kisses followed after each piece of her clothing was removed. She was completely entranced by his actions and words.

"My lovely Emma," he began as his fingertips grazed her cheek and down her neck. Whisper-light kisses followed where his fingers had just been.

"I cannot answer all the questions you asked on the beach." His hands were now wrapped around her waist, sliding her sweatshirt above her head. He let the shirt drop to the floor as his hands quickly found their way to her belly and then her breasts.

"I'm not ignoring you. I promise," he said as he met her eyes with a lustful gaze. He cupped her breasts and then kissed them delicately at first and then teasingly. He knew how much she liked this and smiled as she gasped at his touch.

"I will, however, tell you what I know to be true." His fingers were now toying with the top of her jeans, tickling her belly ever so softly and driving her crazy

Instead of undoing her jeans, he slowly walked behind her and whispered in her ear, "I love you, sweet Emma. I want you, and I can't imagine I'll ever stop."

He then brought his arms around her front and pressed her backside into him. She could feel how much he wanted her, which was beginning to drive her wild. But he held her steady and close as he finally undid her jeans and slid his hand inside her. He knew exactly how and where to touch her. He could feel with his fingers how much she yearned for him.

Miles breathed heavily into her ear, licking and gently biting her earlobe and continuing down her neck. Emma couldn't help herself as she swiftly turned around to kiss him on the lips and began to unbutton his shirt.

He let her take off his shirt but continued to pleasure her with his hands at the same time. Soon, she was standing before him, completely naked.

Now it was he that was now entranced by her. To Miles, she was stunning perfection.

He took her by the hand once again and laid her on the bed. She watched with loving, lustful eyes as he took off his clothes and lay beside her.

Once again, his hands found their way between her legs, pleasuring her in ways she never knew. Just when she thought she would explode, he stopped and rolled over on top of her. He kissed her breasts while pressing himself into her while not yet entering her. She was moaning with sweet pleasure as he moved his mouth from her breasts to her abdomen and then down further to her sweet spot.

It was warm and wet from his touch. He began to explore the same area with his mouth as she moved her hips along with his motion. He was driving her wild, and he loved it. He moved his lips and tongue in a quick, circular motion, darting in and out of her, faster and faster.

Her hips met this motion, and she began breathing just as quickly. Emma was surprised at the natural rhythm that her body was moving and didn't want it to stop.

She could feel every part of her body tingling with want but not wanting his mouth to move from her. She reached down and grabbed his head as the pleasure built within her. Suddenly, she shuddered with ecstasy brought from the motions of his mouth. He let her enjoy this moment before rising above her and then easily entering her.

She was still high on her own pleasure as he rocked slowly back and forth inside her. Their eyes were now locked on each other, knowing they were on the brink of doing what they knew they could do so well together.

As they were ready to succumb to their pleasure, their hands found each other. Miles pulled their hands above her head. He rose just above her, eyes open, so he could see her face at just the right moment.

As they came together in a way neither of them had ever felt before, Miles said, "You, Emma, are what I know. You will be with me forever, no matter where I am. I love you."

Tears stung her eyes as the flood of emotions from their lovemaking overwhelmed her. "You will always be with me, too. I didn't know this could happen so soon. I love you, Miles."

They didn't sleep much at all that night. They lay together, talking, laughing, and making love again. It was as if they were trying to memorize each other so they wouldn't forget.

They didn't know when or if they would see each other again. Yet, one thing was for sure. They knew that these feelings would never quite go away.

Just before dawn, as Emma was dozing a bit, Miles motioned to her to wake up. "Come on, sleepyhead. We can't miss the sunrise." With her eyes still closed, she smiled at hearing his words.

They dressed quickly and walked hand in hand out onto the deck of the Glass House. The sun was rising in the east behind them, but the reflection of the sunrise on the water was the most vivid mix of colors they had ever remembered seeing on the ocean.

It was peaceful and energizing at the same time. They held each other close and embraced for as long as possible.

Izzy and Andy arrived to take Miles to the airport an hour later. Emma had a lump in her throat from the moment they knocked on the door.

The time had come to say goodbye, and everyone was feeling it.

The first part of the drive was a bit jovial as they all exchanged stories about the last couple of days. It was more of a forced conversation to fill the void of what they knew was coming, but it was comforting.

The road to the small airport was not very wide. It was a long, slightly hilly two-lane road.

As Andy made the final turn onto Airport Drive, they all fell quiet, so Izzy turned up the radio. The melody of "If You

Leave" by OMD blared through the speakers as Andy picked up speed and headed down the long road.

Miles reached over, taking Emma's hand as they sat in the backseat. Their eyes met, and it was all she could do not to burst into tears.

Within moments, which seemed like seconds, they arrived at the Departure gate. Andy and Izzy jumped out of the car to grab Miles's bags and give them a moment to say goodbye.

They sat silently for a long moment, and then Emma spoke first, "I know you don't want to hurt me and that you love me. I also know that you are doing what is right, which makes me love you more. I love that you believe in doing the right thing for me and you by letting me go. But I also want you to know I'll never completely let you go. You stole my heart, and I'm not sure that I want you to give it back. So, I want you to go fulfill your dreams because that's why I love you. When you love someone, you want what is best for them. I am letting you go because I love you."

She couldn't believe she said all that without bursting into tears, but she did. She did so because her love for Miles was stronger than her sadness.

He looked at her with amazement and adoration as he took a breath and said, "You amaze me. I'm not sure why we met and fell in love right now, but I am so happy that we did. In this short time, you have given me more love than I ever imagined. I also don't want to let you go, but I have to. It's best for both of us. It doesn't change the love I have for you. It just has to be this way. You will be with me forever too, Emma. I love you so much."

And with those last words, he had to stop. He was too full of emotion and didn't want to make a rash decision not to leave. He was so very tempted, but he knew deep down that he had to go.

They slowly climbed out of the car, holding hands, not wanting to let go. Izzy and Andy made silly jokes to try and make the moment lighter. In the end, they got choked up when they said their goodbyes to Miles.

At last, Emma stepped onto the sidewalk leading to the airport so that she was almost as tall as Miles. She pulled him close into her for one last long hug and said, "Come here, sailor. Kiss me."

He smiled, kissed her, and dramatically leaned her backward so that her head almost touched the sidewalk. This made them both giggle and reminded them of what fun they had with each other.

They were going to be ok. Or at least that's what it felt like at that moment. The three friends stood on the sidewalk for as long as they could see him as they watched him walk away. They stayed and lingered longer than they should have, but it was so hard to just leave.

Suddenly, Emma was shaky with emotion. She slid into the backseat and eventually crumpled into a ball of tears as Andy slowly pulled away from the airport.

It was a long, emotional drive home which exhausted Emma. When she walked into the house, she was met with warm hugs from her mom and Grammy, but she didn't cry. Her tears were all spent during the long drive back from the airport.

She slowly walked into the kitchen for something to drink. As she went to open the fridge, she noticed a letter addressed to her with a return address from New York.

Her life was about to change forever.

CHAPTER 11

LEAVE OR STAY

" There are no exact directions in life. Only choices."

For as long as Emma could remember, she loved baking. Her mother and grandmother constantly created delicious new versions of their favorite recipes. Cookies, cakes, and loaves of bread were always readily available because of someone's baking inspiration.

The smells mixed with the warmth of the kitchen, along with the creativity of each recipe, were things that Emma would genuinely crave.

When she was very young, she would help with whatever they were making. She would scoop, measure, pour, and mix. In her teens, she began baking traditional items like cookies and small pastries on the weekends. Soon, most of her summer days were spent at her mother's bakery, Caroline's.

For her mom, it took several years and loads of encouragement from her husband, but she leaped to open her first bakery ten years into their marriage. This was something that Caroline had never truly envisioned. Still, after years of making cakes and cookies for friends and family, she finally admitted that there was something delicious about her baking.

What took a couple of centuries for her mother to realize only took Emma a few years to recognize. She also had a passion for baking.

It energized her. Inspired her and gave her a sense of purpose. Baking helped her through the loss of her grandfather and her dad. There's something about kneading and pounding out bread dough that can heal what tears sometimes cannot do.

Similarly, baking was helping her now that Miles was gone. She needed an outlet to either think about how she was feeling. Or sometimes to completely forget about her heartbreak.

Emma also really enjoyed seeing people's reactions to her decadent treats. She loved experimenting to see what worked and didn't, pushing her forward. She rarely got negative feedback, but she always welcomed constructive criticism. It only stood to make her a better baker.

Before Miles, she had been so focused on going to culinary school to specialize in baking & pastries. She wanted to learn from the best because she envisioned always offering her best creations.

Yet, after her relationship with Miles, her heart ached like nothing she had ever experienced. Sometimes, she thought she would never recover, and anything beyond Miles wasn't inspiring her. She felt a sadness stronger than death.

She was officially heartbroken, and it showed. So, when the acceptance letter arrived, the joy she had once envisioned had been replaced with confusion and a lackluster feeling of dread.

Emma was so in love with Miles that she couldn't see anything else. She wanted everything to stay the same. She wanted Miles to stay here with her forever. The feeling of love that she felt for him had completely overwhelmed her, and she mourned the loss of it. How could this be happening? She just wanted him back.

When Emma had discovered the letter, Grammy had been watching her from a distance, feeling the mixture of emotions emanating from her. After a few moments, she moved from the doorway into the kitchen and slowly leaned on Emma's arm.

With a deep, heady sigh escaping her, Emma leaned her head down on Grammy's.

Quietly, Rosie began to speak. "You know, this is probably the best thing that could have happened to you."

Swiftly, Emma lifted her head and turned to look at her grandmother. How could she be thinking that, let alone saying such a thing? "Grammy, what are you talking about? This is just confusing me more," she said as she let the open letter fall to the kitchen table.

"I am trying to tell you that this opportunity could be really good for you. You need to be looking forward and not stuck on the sadness you are feeling now. Believe me. I know." Grammy said.

Emma immediately knew what she was talking about. She felt a simultaneous feeling of guilt mixed with tremendous sadness. Of course, Grammy knew how she was feeling.

Every day, she realized that the love of her life was gone. Truly gone.

Yet Grammy wasn't trying to make her feel guilty about the reminder of her loss. She was trying to help Emma see that moving forward was the only choice. That's what life and love are about.

Emma listened intently as her grandmother explained her experience of trying to get through life without Pete. Rosie loved her husband more than her own life. There were days early on when she didn't think that she would make it another day without him. The first few days, even hours, without him filled her with unimaginable dread.

Slowly the days passed, along with the never-ending waves of grief. Yet, each morning, she would awaken and try to begin the day positively. At first, there was nothing, absolutely nothing, to be optimistic about. She struggled to find a new routine, but it inevitably happened.

The days weren't filled with joy. There were days when she had to think about when she had last smiled. Her daily reflections began to reveal that she was moving forward. It wasn't willingly. It just was.

Rosie quickly realized that no matter how she spent her days, she was still here, and time was passing by. Quite often, she would think she wanted time to stop or return to when Pete was still here, but reality told her that couldn't happen.

So, what was she to do? First, she always thought of Emma and Caroline. The sun shined brightest when she focused on them. She was also able to forget or release her grief through baking.

It was the one thing that she knew was her own. If she was reminded of Pete when baking, it became a solace and outlet for her sadness.

She would pound the bread dough in anger and frustration that he was gone. Though most times, when the loaf was taken from the oven, she felt a sense of accomplishment and an odd sense of peace. Soon, she was able to make it through another day.

As days weeks, and months ticked along, she began to find a new path. It wasn't full of the love and joy that she had when her husband was still with her, but she began to realize that she was ok. Family and baking helped her through this time.

Emma thought about what Rosie was telling her. She had no idea that her grandmother struggled as she had. It wasn't a surprise that she had grieved the passing of her husband, but she had no idea the depth of her sadness.

Soon, Emma began to understand better what she needed to do. Miles was still alive and well in the world. He was living his life, fulfilling his dreams. He did what he had planned, no matter how he felt about her. So, why wasn't she doing the same?

She hugged Grammy with such emotion that it surprised the elder, which unexpectedly brought tears to her eyes.

Emma then stood up with a confidence that had been missing lately. "Grammy," she said, "your words were what I have been feeling. Why should I let my dreams pass me by when Miles is pursuing his? I'm going to do this. I'm going to New York."

Away from the Glass House

CHAPTER 12

NEW YORK, NEW EMMA

" My, how she shines bright."

She enters the bar with a slight nod of her head as she walks swiftly to the end seat closest to the jukebox. He knows what she needs and has a glass of Pinot Grigio with one sidecar of whisky on ice before she settles in. Emma takes a deep breath as the music of the Counting Crows fills the almost empty room with the ramblings of "Round Here."

She takes a generous sip of the whiskey on the rocks before looking up and saying, "How ya doing today, Sam?"

He meanders over, knowing she will sit quietly. First, sipping on her whiskey, then as the songs continue to play, she will relax and go to that place in her head.

Some nights she's lively and talkative.

Other times, she stares off into the distance as the music plays while she sips her odd combination of liquor and wine.

Sam often thinks she's chasing something, yet other times, he imagines she's pushing something away.

In reality, she is just trying to hold on. Hold on to her future, her past, and the drink in her hand.

Emma has embraced living in New York City for the past four years. The intoxicating vibe and energy can be felt everywhere. No drink is really needed.

Some days, she walks endlessly, thinking, observing, and absorbing the mystical world that NYC can capture in anyone's heart. Sometimes she feels like it's home, but then she is reminded that home is nothing like this.

Emma worked hard at culinary school during the week and various restaurant jobs in the evening and on the weekends. She was endlessly perfecting her baking skills, knowing that one day, she would be able to make it on her own. She's patient and dedicated to learning all there is to know about the world of patisserie.

However, in the quiet of the night, while the occasional car horn blares and sirens cut through the traffic noise, she allows her mind to wander back to the Glass House.

Her home is filled with the sweet smells of baking, family, and comfort. A place that she has loved for as long as she can remember. But also a place where her heart was severely broken.

The next song begins to play, and "Black" by Pearl Jam fills the bar and her heart. He just left.

Sure, there were letters filled with love and words of longing in the beginning, but soon the letters became fewer and far between. What were once many pages of feelings and thoughts quickly dwindled to a single short update, hastily written, then reduced to the occasional postcard. Eventually, the communication just stopped.

He was truly letting go. Her emotions bounced back and forth like a ping-pong ball on a table. She was happy he was experiencing all he had dreamed of, yet pissed that he missed her. He constantly told her so in his letters.

What did it matter in the end? He was gone. First, he shipped off to boot camp and then out at sea. Months would go by with no word or contact. She filled her days with her own experiences, but the nighttime was so hard.

She stumbled upon Sam's Place in the West Village soon after she found her apartment. It was kind of like the little bar on 'Cheers,' where everyone quickly knew your name.

Well, the regulars, anyway. There was always an influx of tourists during the summer and occasional weekends, but it was mostly filled with folks from the neighborhood.

Her place was a sparse, small unit on a tidy side street. A 'killer find' as she had been told repeatedly by her New York friends.

Thank goodness for roommates that helped with the outrageous rent, but also for their friendship.

They were strangers at first. Emma was cautious, but then, she realized the magic of New York. Bringing together unlikely people, initially to survive the city jungle but eventually to become lifelong friends.

Gemma moved to the city from London. What was to be a summer of fun "across the pond" turned into a multi-year stay to get over a nasty breakup from a bloke that was a complete "arse." She was lively, quick to tell anyone off, and an absolute dream of a roommate.

Kiera was quiet, focused on her career, and determined not to have to go back to New Jersey. She worked at a smaller marketing agency since college and dreamed of having her own business someday. She was learning the ropes, and co-workers viewed her as one of the hardest-working team members.

There was no doubt that Kiera was a rising star in her field. Until then, the three girls survived growing into adulthood in NYC together.

The apartment was initially Kiera's. She loved the place and knew the town better than most born and raised New Yorkers. She placed an ad for two roommates and was soon inundated with requests.

She was picky about whom she wanted to share her place with. They didn't have to be friends, but no men, no weirdos, and they had to be ok with sharing one very tiny bathroom. It was New York, after all.

Quickly, she chose Gemma and Emma (yes, note the irony of their rhyming names) as her roommates. The friendships didn't take long to blossom.

At first, she thought she had made the wrong choice with Gemma. She was vivacious, loud, and livened up any room she entered. Quiet didn't seem to be in Gemma's vocabulary at any time of day.

But Emma was different. She kept to herself a lot while also carrying around a little sadness just below the surface all the time.

Kiera knew that she was from a small town out west. Who knows what odd things go on out there? Being from the east coast, wherever Emma came from was too close to California for her taste. It was a true wonder as to why the girl always looked sad.

Compared to Gemma, she was happy to have at least one quiet and reserved roommate.

Always dressed with impeccable taste and, more often than not, in heels that were way too high for NYC streets, Gemma was all about living and getting the most out of life.

She was just what Emma and Kiera needed. *Why are they always so serious?* she often thought at the beginning of their friendship.

She did like that they watched her, however. Gemma loved being the center of attention, whether through the eyes of handsome men or women. She would take the stares and smiles any way she could get them.

It was partly why her bloke in London finally let her go. He often complained about her fashion and said it was sad that she always had to live her life based on other people's opinions.

He frequently asked her why she couldn't be more reserved like other London girls.

That should have been enough of a sign for her, but he had her heart, so she put up with his limiting thoughts and opinions.

She only took his break-up seriously when she found him in bed with one of her lifelong friends. She cried for days in bed, and her parents were genuinely concerned. After a week of sulking, she arose from her room with her many bags packed and a plan to escape to New York City.

While her family thought it would be a short, fleeting phase of rebellion and heartbreak, it soon turned into a new way of life for Gemma. Maybe getting her heart shattered was the best thing to ever happen to her.

She had no clue that New York would capture her attention as much as it had. She was working at an up-and-coming fashion house on the Lower East Side and loving what she was learning. She was willing to try anything on and had no boundaries for daring and colorful fashion. The designers loved her energy and willingness to learn.

She may be fetching coffee and making copies now, but soon she wanted to learn how to make the fashions that she loved to wear. But make them more spectacular. She often thought Harry, her ex from England, would be appalled.

So, here they were. Three very different, lovely girls taking over their own little space in New York City.

Looking back over the last few years, they all had to smile at just how different each was from one another.

Reserved and almost painfully shy Kiera, allowing vibrant and loud Gemma into her apartment with her suitcases, boxes, and trunks of fashion. Clothes, shoes, and make-up seemed to trail behind her on move-in day.

Gemma had no interest in cooking, as that was what take-out menus were for. Yet, clothing and accessories ruled her life and her space. She would soon invest in clothing racks since her tiny bedroom closet could only hold a third of what she owned.

Seeing the number of things that Gemma couldn't live without was genuinely amusing. Upon seeing the amount of what she was bringing in, Kiera politely but firmly declared that space was limited in the bathroom, so Gemma must keep her beauty products at bay and confine most to her room. She couldn't help but wonder what she was getting herself into.

As Emma began to move in, she had two very large suitcases, a few boxes, and a well-equipped trunk packed full of baking supplies. This truly intrigued Kiera.

If there was one ironic thing that she had in common with Gemma, it was knowing how to order take-out. What was to become of their small, under-used kitchen?

She watched from the doorway as Emma searched for the perfect place to put her baking supplies in cupboards and drawers.

On the other hand, Emma was surprised at Kiera's lack of cooking utensils and essentials. She worked swiftly but spoke quietly as she unpacked her tools, "Do you cook much?" she asked.

Kiera was so taken by all of the odd gadgets coming out of Emma's trunk that she didn't answer right away. "Oh, sorry, I am completely intrigued by what you are unpacking. No, I'm not one to cook. More of a strategic thinker that's a whiz at ordering pizza and Chinese food." They both smiled at her comment.

"Well, I was raised learning how to bake and cook. It's why I'm here, so do you mind if I make the most of the kitchen space?" Emma asked.

"No, of course not. This is the least used space, and from what Gemma is bringing in, I don't think she'll be in here much, either." Kiera said with amusement.

And with that, Gemma's bright voice came from behind Kiera in the doorway, "Now, that is not true. There is nothing like fresh cucumbers and cold eye cream from the fridge to help with a hangover. Speaking of which, where's the wine?"

They all couldn't help but laugh at this response and spent the rest of the evening sipping wine, getting to know each other, and, of course, ordering take-out.

CHAPTER 13

NICE TO MEET YOU

" Sometimes big things happen when you least expect it."

Sam was a little surprised when Emma asked for a second whiskey, especially on a Tuesday night. He didn't ask why and served her the drink.

As a lifelong bartender and owner, he had learned when to talk and when not to. He also knew when it was time for the guest to go or at least switch to water.

He had gotten to know Emma quite well over the years. She made damn good bread, and her Christmas cookies were the one thing he looked forward to during the holidays. Sam was a loner, and that time of year didn't sit well with him.

However, she knew how to bake, and even for a big Grinch like him, it brought about a little Christmas cheer.

She baked to push back the guilt about not going home for the holidays. At the same time, he was relieved to have someone else not so excited about Santa and his reindeer.

Emma was just so busy these days with school and work. There was not enough time to make the long trek back to the coast. It made her sad not to be home with Grammy and her mom for the holidays. *They* were the holidays to her.

Here she was, slightly more depressed and sadder than usual about not going home again, so she ordered another drink.

As she took a small sip of her bourbon, a sexy male voice came from behind her, "Hi. I've been watching you from a distance, and well, I'm nervous to ask, but would you mind if I joined you?"

She was about to turn around and respond curtly, but then she saw him.

Dark, neat-cut hair with a chiseled jawline and the most gorgeous hazel eyes she had ever seen. Emma was all at once flustered and nervous.

Could he be talking to her? Not that this was a hotbed for NYC women, but really? He was just too good-looking for her.

"Um, really?" she began to say.

He cut her off, "Oh, I'm sorry. I was hesitant to come over. I'll leave you alone."

"No, no. That's not what I meant. I just think you are too handsome to be talking to me." she stammered.

"What? What did you say?" he asked, confused.

"I mean, of course, please sit down if you want." she finally managed to say.

She took another small sip of her drink. All she could focus on was how to calm down. She hadn't felt this way since, well, whatever. She thought, *Focus on who is sitting in front of you, Emma.*

He sat down and waved a hand to Sam for a drink. As they waited, he gently extended his hand to introduce himself to Emma, "Hi, there. I'm Maxwell. It's a pleasure to meet you."

She smiled as she took his hand and responded, "Hi, I'm Emma. Nice to meet you."

As Sam brought Maxwell his drink, he couldn't help but smile and wonder what the night would bring for the two new friends.

Maybe it was the whisky or the loneliness that Emma was feeling, but it had been a long time since a conversation had been this easy with someone.

Sure, she had been on dates here and there, but no one ever made her want to pursue more. She was so focused on school and work, plus she enjoyed time with her roommates. They helped her forget what she wanted to avoid and taught her that there was more to life than a big house on the ocean.

However, Maxwell was interesting. He told great stories, all while looking Emma in the eyes. She saw and felt what he was explaining.

She was intrigued by him. So much so that she couldn't believe how late it was. She mentioned the same to him, and he eloquently asked to walk her out.

Emma began questioning how she wanted the night to end as they walked to the door. Before she could decide, they were outside and standing on the sidewalk. She needed to go right, and he mentioned that he needed to go left. It was chilly outside, and a few light snow flurries had begun to fall.

Maybe it was nerves, and perhaps it was the cold, but Emma had begun to shiver. Maxwell stood intimately close, and she thought he would bring her in for a hug. Instead, he lightly took her hand and kissed it while looking right into her eyes.

He then said, "Emma, it was a true pleasure spending the evening with you, and I hope to do so again soon. Have a good evening." And with that, he let her hand go and walked off into the cold winter night.

She stood there in the night, surrounded by the soft snow, staring after Maxwell. *What in the hell was that?* she thought to herself. All at once, she was both confused and intrigued.

A strong flutter filled her stomach when he kissed her hand. That was new. As she watched him walk away, she wondered when she would see him again.

She slowly turned to begin the short walk to her apartment. They didn't exchange phone numbers, so he had no direct way to contact her. But maybe he preferred it that way. Perhaps he wasn't as into her as she thought.

Emma entered the door to her apartment to find the living room cluttered with Gemma's clothing once again. Nestled in the corner of the couch, she spotted Kiera finishing a bowl of something and intently reading a book.

"Hey," she grunted without lifting her eyes from the page. When Kiera is into a book, she is completely engrossed.

And tonight, Emma didn't mind since she was lost in her thoughts about Maxwell and their evening discussion. So, she quickly responded, "Hey." as she walked to her room and closed the door.

That was so unexpected. Her mind started to swirl over what she said, how she said it. *Was she being stupid?*

Her mind instantly filled with doubts about his interest in her. Suddenly, her thoughts stopped to focus on one thing. She liked this guy. A slow, cautious smile came across her face. Perhaps it's time to start something new.

The next evening, Emma made a beeline for Sam's. She sat at the bar with her glass of wine, pensively tapping her finger against the long grain of wood that held her drink.

Her foot bobbed up and down nervously as she checked the door every few moments. Her mind had been focused on Maxwell all day, hoping she would see him again today. She had no other way to get ahold of him, yet she found herself wanting to see him again.

Emma waited an hour or so and finally gave up on seeing him that night. Doubts crept into her head, and she wondered if she had misread the gentle, sweet kiss that he left on her hand. She began to think that he must be a lovely gentleman that knows how to grab the attention of many women.

Sam noticed the pensive look on Emma's face and wandered over to see if she would like another drink. She had gone from tapping her fingers on the bar to twirling the stem of her wine glass.

"You know how to release the flavor of any wine, but if you twirl that glass any faster, you may end up wearing it," he said with a teasing smile.

"Sorry, Sam. Just a little distracted tonight," she replied while casually glancing once again at the main door.

"I've seen him in here a few times, but I wouldn't say he's a regular. Maybe he'll stop in tomorrow or over the weekend. Another glass of white for you?" Sam asked.

Emma was a little taken aback that her friend knew or thought he knew who she was looking for, so she tried to play it off with innocence. "Why, I have no idea whom you are referring to. Yes, I will have one more glass, and then off I go."

She watched as Sam slowly walked over to grab a bottle of wine and then back to fill her glass. "So, can I ask if you enjoyed your evening last night, or is that too much?" he asked as he refilled her glass.

Before she could help it, a smile crept into her eyes and quickly spread to her lips as she quietly replied, "I think it was ok. It's not like we exchanged numbers or anything, so who knows if anything will come of it."

And, of course, her face flushed and turned bright red as she said this. This amused Sam as he walked away to help someone else at the bar. "Gotcha." is all he said with a smile. *She likes him*, he amusingly thought.

She smiled to herself as she sipped her wine. Finally, she started to relax, and her thoughts began to slow down. Maybe it was just a fleeting, interesting conversation with a handsome guy in a bar. It sounds cliché, but perhaps that's all there was to it.

Emma paid her tab, took one last sip of wine, and stood up from her seat to wrap her scarf around her neck and bundle up before heading out.

"Goodnight, Sam. Thanks for the chat." she bellowed over her shoulder as she walked to the door. As she pulled on the handle, she was met with a cold bluster of wind, so she quickly tilted her head down to brace for the chill. With her next step, she walked head first right into him.

CHAPTER 14

BAR FLY

" Well, this could get sticky."

A cold New York City wind will sting your eyes, bite your cheeks and the tip of your nose almost instantly. So it's no surprise that people tend to innately put their heads down in anticipation of that chilled-to-the-bone feeling.

Emma knew to do this as soon as she felt the pull of the gusty wind from opening the door to exit Sam's. She bowed her head and bravely stepped forward to brace for the icy cold. What she didn't expect was to run directly into him.

Before she could raise her head to see whom she had run into, she took a deep breath to brace for the chilly winter air, but she immediately recognized his scent. Could it be?

She quickly raised her head to focus and, all at once stepped back into the bar. It wasn't. Was it? Really?

Emma pointedly asked, "Is it you?"

He couldn't help but laugh softly as he said, "Yes, it's me. Is it you?"

She smiled and immediately leaned into Miles for a deep, welcoming hug.

Her mind was spinning with thoughts of what he was doing here. *How had he found her? Why was he here, especially after so long of not talking to each other?* It had been forever since they had communicated, let alone seen one another.

As usual, he knew what she was thinking and wanted to explain. So, he gently took her by the arm and led her back into the bar. "Come on. I'll buy you a drink and let you know why I'm here," he responded. It never failed to surprise her that he could read her thoughts, or at least it felt like he could read them.

Her face quickly flushed with surprise, and she immediately began to take off the scarf wrapped around her neck. She also removed her gloves and coat as she took the lead and walked Miles back to her favorite seat at the bar.

Sam watched from a distance with bold curiosity as they settled into their seats. Something told him that bourbon on the rocks was precisely what they both would need.

He silently served them both the drinks with a slight wink and a nod at Emma as he walked away. Emma was settled enough to smile softly and say, "Thanks, Sam," as he shuffled off down to the other end of the bar to let them talk.

They both took small sips of their drinks, and then with a deep breath, Miles began to explain how he had found her, "Well, it wasn't that hard since I had your return address from our letters. And as soon as I found out that we would dock in New York, I knew I had to see you."

This made Emma smile, but she was also very confused about the lack of correspondence over the last several months. She missed hearing from him and mentioned this as they continued to sip their whisky and catch up.

He nodded in agreement and sheepishly replied, "I know. I know. I feel horrible about not keeping up with writing you back. Which is crazy because all I've done is think about you. My days were filled with my responsibilities on the ship, and I just didn't take the time to write you. I'm sorry. I really dropped the ball. But I'm here now." Miles smiled at her as he said this.

They had just now noticed that they were holding hands and leaning into each other this whole time.

Emma leaned back while simultaneously pulling her hand away to brush the hair out of her eyes and take another sip of her drink. She was trying to think of what to say next.

"It's not easy to be so far away from you. It never has been. I've been hurting and wondering what is going on with you. Writing didn't seem to help anymore, especially when I didn't hear anything back. I wondered why I should keep telling you what is going on in my life when you won't share with me what is happening in yours. So, I just stopped," she responded, with hurt and love filling her eyes as she stared back at him.

Their eyes locked in full emotion of what the other was feeling.

He could see the ache of missing him in her eyes, which killed him. Miles leaned in and gently reached to touch her cheek. Fire immediately spread throughout her body. She couldn't help but ask herself how he had this kind of power to invoke these feelings in her instantly.

As he touched her cheek, he leaned in and kissed it. She took a quick breath in as he whispered, "I'm sorry. I'm here now, and it's the only place I want to be. With you."

The emotions that she felt in her body also made tears spring to her eyes. She felt that way too. He leaned back, and as he took his hand away from her face, she lovingly wrapped it within her own.

Miles immediately felt loved and at ease, something he had been struggling with since he left home.

Their eyes met again, and they couldn't help but smile at each other. He knew she had forgiven him, so he lifted his glass to her with his other hand and said, "Well, cheers to reconnecting and for your forgiveness."

As they clinked their glasses, she jovially said a short "Cheers" and leaned in to kiss him.

Perhaps it was the warmth of the whiskey, combined with how much she missed him, but what she thought would be a quick kiss turned into a moment of passion and longing that they both welcomed.

Still kissing him, she stood up from her barstool and leaned into Miles, wrapping her arms around his neck as she had done a thousand times before. It was welcoming and natural. There it was. The kiss that they had both thought of, dreamed of for weeks, months, and longer. It was the kiss that connected their hearts and felt like it would forever tie them to one another.

She finally pulled away as a bit of clarity entered her mind. She didn't want to be *that couple* making out in the middle of a bar. What would Sam think? This was totally out of character for her. Emma realized she did need a minute to pull herself together. Breathlessly, she backed up and said she would be back in a moment.

Emma unsteadily walked to the bathroom at the rear of the bar. The alcohol, mixed with the rush of emotions she was feeling, made each step she took a challenge. Feeling shaky, she needed to think for a moment.

This had all happened so fast. One moment she found herself wondering about someone new; the next, her past walked right into her. Literally.

She stared at her reflection in the restroom mirror for a long moment, willing clarity to enter her brain. Yet, she could only think of Miles and that he was here with her.

This was exciting yet gave her a familiar sense of comfort. She wanted to be with Miles. He found her again, and while she didn't quite know what that meant beyond tonight, he was here now.

Emma smiled back at herself in the mirror and felt bold as she admitted this to herself. She wanted all of Miles. With a deep, energizing breath, she was suddenly excited to return to the bar to be with him.

Staring right at him as she made her way back to her stool, she realized that he was chatting with someone. She couldn't quite see who it was, but she knew it was a man whose back was to her. Emma walked up to Miles, and as she put her arm around him, she pivoted slightly so that she could finally see the person's face.

It was Maxwell.

The sheer look of surprise on Emma's face was hard to miss. However, she brilliantly recovered before Miles had time to notice. Rare in and of itself for Miles not to notice Emma's emotions, Maxwell was fully aware of her bewilderment and was amused. Always up for an interesting time, he extended his hand to shake Emma's as Miles introduced them.

All Emma could focus on was the captivating situation of having the two most intriguing men on either side of her. She finally mumbled, "Nice to meet you," as she swiftly removed her hand and reached for her bourbon to take a sip.

The irony of Maxwell shaking the same hand he had lovingly kissed the night before was not lost on her. She really needed a sip of her drink.

Ever appreciative of Sam's spot-on awareness of awkward situations, she welcomed his interruption as the men continued to chat about the Navy.

Sam met Emma's eyes with understanding as she raised her glass to signify that she would have another.

An experienced bartender knows when to fill a drink with no small talk. He sensed her uncomfortable vibe as he slid her a new bourbon. Not wanting to add more drama to this moment, he simply nodded his head toward Emma with a wink of reassurance and walked away.

While this happened, she frantically tried to figure out how to navigate this awkward situation. She tried to think clearly as she nodded her head along with the conversation the other two were having.

Somehow, Maxwell found his way to Miles at the bar. Was he watching from a distance and decided to make his move when she went to the restroom? Was it just a coincidence, or was he trying to create an issue with her? Where was he taking this? What the hell is going on?

Emma was jarred away from her racing thoughts by the sound of Miles's voice. "Emma, what do you think? Should we grab a table so you don't have to stand here?"

It took a moment to register what he was saying to her, but she suddenly came out of her head long enough to agree to move from the bar.

As they settled into their seats, she quickly realized this was an even more awkward situation. Here she sat with two men, both of whom she was very attracted to, on either side of her. *How could this possibly be happening?*

Once again, she was brought back to the conversation around her. Emma was startled to realize that both of them were staring back at her, expecting her to respond.

Yet, she had no idea what she was supposed to say. So, she honestly asked, "I'm sorry. I think I zoned out for a moment. What are you talking about?"

Miles and Maxwell exchanged an amused look while Maxwell piped back, "Well, it's quite important, actually. Would you like to get something to eat? That's the question." Miles reassuringly rested his hand on her shoulder while she laughed uncomfortably about the question.

"Of course. Yes, I think we should eat something, as this whiskey is going right to my brain." she replied tightly.

Maxwell quickly got Sam's attention to order from the menu, as Miles locked eyes with Emma as if to say, *Are you ok?"*

She just shrugged simply as she picked up her glass to take another small sip. She could only think *If you only knew how weird this is for me.*

Surprisingly to her, the three of them fell into a comfortable banter as they awaited the food that Maxwell ordered. Blame it on the drinks, but soon Emma found she was relaxed around them and finally started to enjoy the night a little more. The food was delicious, the conversation seemed to flow, and she couldn't help but think how lucky she was to be among two fascinating, handsome guys.

Emma must have been smiling without realizing it because she suddenly heard Miles ask, "Well, what is with that sly smile?"

She blushed at this question but answered honestly, "As a matter of fact, I was just thinking about how lucky I am to be sitting between the two most handsome men in New York City."

Both men smiled at her flirtatious comment, and unbeknownst to Miles, Maxwell took the opportunity to slide his hand onto Emma's knee underneath the table.

This happened right as Miles took Emma's hand that was resting on the table. She felt a jolt of sexual electricity so strong that it made her physically jump in her seat.

Her thoughts began to race again, but this time about how she felt.

Is it possible to be into two men at once? How hot is it to be in this predicament right now? Are you crazy? This situation is crazy! Get up from the table right now before you lose total control of yourself!

When Emma jumped, it startled both men, and they both pulled back. Maxwell was more than a little amused as he said, "Everything ok?"

Of course, he knew the answer because he had every intention of toying with her just a bit more. He was pretty sure she liked him, but he was also confused about her apparent connection with Navy Boy. He decided not to be jealous but instead to have a little fun.

She shot a look at him as if to say, *Of course, everything is not ok, you hot piece of ass.*

But instead, she quietly mumbled something about needing to use the restroom and jumped up to head to the back of the bar once again.

She stumbled a bit more as she walked away from the table, but this time it was definitely because of what she was feeling and not the drinks.

It took her a few minutes to pull herself together. She was more resolute in staying clear of Maxwell for the rest of the evening. She was still thinking about how to do this as she walked out of the bathroom and back to the guys.

She quickly realized this was a lost worry when she spotted Maxwell standing up to leave. She couldn't help but feel relieved.

Miles and Maxwell were shaking hands and exchanging pleasantries as she walked up.

"Look me up the next time you are in New York. I'm always up for a night out with a Navy guy!" Maxwell exclaimed to Miles as he shook his hand and slapped his other shoulder jovially.

Emma noticed that Miles seemed slightly put off by this comment but still smiled and nodded in agreement with Maxwell. His response triggered her curiosity, but she didn't mention anything.

Then Maxwell turned to Emma and took her hand, yet again. He raised it slowly to his lips while looking her deep in the eyes. He kissed her hand and slowly lowered it back down, as he flirtatiously said, "Emma, it was a true pleasure meeting you. We should plan to do it again soon."

A red flush of embarrassment filled her cheeks, and she stammered to respond with, "It. It…was a… It was nice to meet you, Maxwell."

She abruptly pulled her hand out of his but not without noticing the same sexual jolt of energy that she felt when he kissed her hand. Again.

Miles and Emma sat back at the table as Maxwell headed out into the cold New York evening.

Miles slid Emma's chair closer to him this time, and he instantly put his arms around her to lean in for a kiss. Her heart was still racing from Maxwell kissing her hand, and it began to race even more because she was once again in Miles's arms. She kissed him back, but this time with more passion than he anticipated.

She suddenly didn't feel like sitting at Sam's anymore. She wanted to take Miles home. Immediately.

Emma stood quickly and pulled Miles up with her. She hurriedly grabbed her coat and scarf while she led him to the bar door. She yelled over her shoulder to Sam and said, "Good night, Sam! I'll catch up with you tomorrow!"

With a subtle grin, the wise bartender barely looked up from the bar as he knew Emma was about to have a very memorable night with the handsome man in the Navy uniform.

Emma had never been more thankful for the short walk from Sam's bar to her apartment than she was that night. She was hopeful that her roommates weren't home yet. All she needed was Gemma's loud questions or Kiera's piercing judgmental eyes about bringing someone home. Not that she had done this often, but she didn't need questions or chastising looks. She needed Miles. Now.

They barely hit the door before he pushed her against the wall while stripping her off her coat and purse. Same as always, their magnetic attraction to each other was unstoppable. Miles had been wanting to kiss Emma for months, if not longer. He didn't want to stop now.

She began to giggle between kisses as she reached for his uniform. She couldn't help but wonder if it was wrong to throw Navy clothes on the floor. She'd never done it with a military guy before.

She didn't have to ask because just as quickly as he removed her top, he just as swiftly began to undress. Emma led him to her bedroom before all of their wits were completely lost in passion. She closed the door, and they both fell onto her bed together.

This time Emma took the lead with Miles. She quickly flipped on top so that she was straddling him. He couldn't help but love the surprisingly dominating position that she took. He loved looking up at her and was still astounded that he was back in her bed.

He reached up to touch her breasts, and she gasped as he reached for her. She easily removed her bra, and this time, Miles gasped as he looked at the beauty of Emma's body sitting above him. He had truly missed her. All of her.

Her hair cascaded down her back, and she leaned down to kiss Miles hard on the mouth while his hands moved from her breasts to her back and began to wander down to her waist. She still had her pants on, and he could not wait to remove them. Emma could feel his anticipation, so she stood up long enough to remove the rest of her clothes.

Before getting back onto the bed, she peered down at him. It excited her to see how much he wanted her. She felt free with him. Free to feel sexy and alive. She had missed these feelings so much and wanted to soak in every moment.

She walked to the edge of the bed and lazily let her fingertips follow the line of his belt. She lingered there for a moment before confidently taking him in her hand. She could feel how hard he was for her through his pants, but she didn't quite want to remove them yet, knowing that this was torture for Miles. She also knew he loved seeing her naked before him, empowering her.

She moved her body easily onto his and leaned down to kiss him. Straddling him, her waist began to move in a rhythm against his that only they knew. The passion from their kiss began to grow, and Miles couldn't hold back wanting her any longer.

He quickly and powerfully flipped her onto the bed. Now he was the one to feel emboldened and in control. Miles removed his pants while looking down at Emma with a loving, fiery gaze. He had wanted her for so long. Now it was finally time to make love to her once again.

He entered her with a thrust so deep she could barely contain herself. He felt so good inside of her. The rhythm that their bodies found within each other was nothing short of mind-blowing. They moved in sync, touching, loving, and kissing each other in all the right ways. It didn't take long for their movements to explode into spine-tingling orgasms that seemed to last forever.

Miles finally rolled over onto the bed and pulled Emma closer to him. He didn't want this to end. He didn't want to tell her this was only a short visit. He didn't want to tell her that his time in the Navy was ending and that he had to go home. He didn't want to tell her anything that would make her disappointed in him.

The shadow of Miles's feelings crossed his face, and Emma immediately noticed it. She felt so good after reuniting with him, yet she couldn't help but see something was wrong.

She touched his face and leaned in to give him a light kiss. Emma asked quietly, "A penny for your thoughts? Are you ok?"

He took a deep breath while trying to decide what to say. He chose to stay in this special moment and quietly replied, "I'm great. God, I have missed you. I think you are more beautiful than I remember."

"Seriously, are you ok? Was I ok? I thought maybe something was wrong when I looked at you just now." she responded.

Miles could only smile gently at her words and quickly countered, "You are perfect. How could anything be wrong when I am lying with you in your bed? I am so happy to see you, Emma."

And with that, they chatted easily for a while before realizing that it was almost morning. They lay wrapped in each other's arms as comfortably as they always had.

Somehow, Miles had found his way back to Emma. It was a complete surprise but a wonderful one at that. She was happy, content, and full of love as she drifted to sleep in his arms.

CHAPTER 15

ATYPICAL SITUATION

" Well, that was unexpected."

There's something about the quiet of the morning before anyone stirs. The stillness of a room, before eyes open and senses fully awaken to the awareness of the day ahead. It's beautiful and peaceful.

That is unless you live with two very lively, very intrusive roommates that burst into your room to find you lying naked next to the love of your life.

This is just how Kiera and Gemma found Miles and Emma the next morning.

Gemma entered the room first, singing, "Emma, have we got an idea for you, our lovely baking machine!… Oh, well, what bloody situation do we have here, Kiera!"

She openly let out her loud British laugh while Kiera gasped in horror and loosely covered her eyes as she continued to stare at Miles's bare ass.

Emma was simultaneously mortified and amused by this inopportune situation that her roommates had walked into.

It was a first for her to bring someone home, let alone find them lying spread-eagle in their birthday suits at 7 am.

She swiftly covered Miles up with the sheet with one hand, then dramatically threw a pillow at the girls standing in the doorway.

"What the hell, you two? Ever heard of knocking first?" was all she could conjure up to say. Then they all burst out laughing after taking in the full site.

Kiera finally found a voice to speak with, "Well, we have an interesting proposition for you, but it looks like we may be a little late."

The confused look on Emma's face was enough to let Gemma jump in on the announcement. "What dear Kiera is trying, albeit quite poorly, to say is that we have an opportunity for you to bake to your heart's content. Well, in front of a camera, because we think you would be just smashing at it! Now, get your knickers on and come out onto the couch to talk about it. Boy Toy, over there, can join if he wants, and his knickers can be optional. Hot ass, by the way, sir." And with that, she walked out of Emma's room.

Poor Kiera was left to stand there, still staring at Miles and Emma lying in bed, with her mouth hanging open. It was an overtly awkward situation, but she couldn't stop staring.

Gemma's voice boomed at top volume from down the hall, "Dear lord, Kiera, it's a naked arse. Now let them be so we can chat."

This made everyone jump back to attention, so Kiera scurried out of the room, but not before knocking into the wall while trying to close the door. The back of her head hit the doorframe, leading it to ricochet forward and slam the door as she pulled it shut.

"Sorry. Oh. Ouch. Oh, god. Well, that's embarrassing." is all that she could mutter as she backed clumsily out of the room.

Emma fell back onto the bed, pulling the sheet over her head in a fit of giggles. This made Miles laugh in amusement at the situation, along with the sheer joy of waking up next to Emma. He pulled himself up higher on the bed and casually leaned over to kiss her forehead and then her lips.

It didn't take much to realize that they were very happy to be here with each other. The roommates would have to wait. They had more important physical things to attend to first.

The happy couple eventually made their way into the living room. They found Gemma and Kiera sitting casually on the small couch, sipping coffee and grinning at each other as they entered the room.

Gemma began, "Nice to see you up and dressed." She stood up gingerly to shake Miles's hand. She continued, as she outstretched her hand, "I am the lovely and lively British roommate, Gemma."

Kiera rolled her eyes at this comment and stood up to shake his hand, "And I'm Kiera, the American roommate." She bumped Gemma on the hip as she said this with a giggle.

She then looked over at Emma, who was amusingly watching this interaction. Miles had a grin on his face but hadn't said anything to either of the ladies yet.

"Well, it certainly is entertaining to meet you both." he began, "I'm Miles. Not sure if Emma has ever mentioned me before, but we know each other from back home."

Gemma couldn't let this little comment pass by, so she spouted, "Oh, from what I hear, that's putting it mildly."

And with that, Emma jumped into the conversation, "Ok, you two, that's enough digging for now. What is this emergency that made you bust in on us this morning?"

This triggered Kiera's memory back to the main point of what she wanted to talk with Emma about, "Oh, yeah. Hot pants over here got us distracted."

She said this as she waved a flippant hand toward Miles, who looked surprised at what she said. Ultimately, this made him laugh as Gemma jumped into the conversation to add, "Oh, there were no pants involved with that ass this morning."

Emma was getting embarrassed at this point, "Ladies, seriously, enough with Miles's ass." And this comment made them all laugh a little harder.

Kiera jumped in again to explain, "Ok, back to business. Our newest client at the agency is a baking company called Heather's Bakery. They are pushing us to do something different with their upcoming campaign, so we thought how great it would be to have videos of someone baking their recipes. Enter you. I think you would just be perfect with all of your experience. You're also likable and relatable to everyday people, so what do you think?"

Honestly, Emma didn't know what to think. She had never thought of working in front of a camera, and she hadn't ever taught anyone how to bake. She was still learning through culinary school, so how could she even think of doing this?

Miles could see the surprise and uncertainty on Emma's face. As they always had, they could sense each other's feelings so clearly, so he spoke first.

"This is so new for Emma. She just bakes when the mood strikes her. She hasn't ever taught anyone how to cook or bake before." Emma was shaking her head, agreeing with everything he was saying.

Before she could speak up, Gemma jumped in on the conversation, "But that's what is so great about this concept. She won't be teaching but rather showing what she does in the kitchen. The internet is so new. Who knows what will happen with it? Just shoot some videos they will put on their website for customers to watch, and don't overthink it. It's a great opportunity to do something different, Em."

As Gemma talked, Emma's head spun about what everyone was saying.

Cameras, the internet, and her doing all of this? That was unbelievable. But was it?

Suddenly, Emma was cool with it. Miles could see that her feelings on this had shifted, and he smiled, knowing what she would say.

Emma looked around the room at her friends, and before she could stop herself from overthinking it further, she piped up and said, "Oh, why not. Let's try it to see what happens."

And with that, Emma's life was about to change forever.

CHAPTER 16

FULLY BAKED

" Sometimes you just have to rise to the occasion."

Emma's head spun while everyone began chatting about what would happen next. *What have I just done? I am not ready for all of this. Am I going to be able to do this?*

Once again, Miles noticed that Emma's head was swirling with thoughts. When she got like this, she often overthought things and was very hard on herself. So, he wanted to let her know she was ok.

"Hey there." he quietly whispered in her ear as Gemma and Kiera continued to talk through the details of the first meeting with the brand. She looked at him with unsure but loving eyes and quietly responded, "Am I crazy to be doing this? What are they thinking? I'm not an actor."

He smiled down at her and pulled her into him a little closer as he explained, " I don't think they want an actor. They want someone that knows how to bake and can show other people how to make things on their own. You've shown me a couple of tricks that you have in the kitchen before. Just act like you're doing that."

He could always find a way to get her to see clearer and not overthink. She loved this about him, and at that moment, she was reminded how much she missed him in her day-to-day life.

She smiled easily back at him as she said, "Thanks. I guess I was starting to overthink this a bit. I've missed having you there to understand where I'm coming from." This touched Miles, so he kissed the top of her head reassuringly.

Kiera was admiring their connection from across the room as Gemma was yammering on about how exciting this would be for everyone. Something about how Gemma talked made Kiera think this would involve all three of them.

She finally brought Emma back to the discussion, "Ok, so you're on board with doing this?"

Emma quickly nodded in agreement, but a look of doubt crossed her eyes, and they all picked up on that.

This time, Gemma spoke up, "Look, it's going to be fantastic. You're a natural in the kitchen, and it will be the same way on camera. I'll make sure of it!"

They all laughed at this last comment, with Emma piping up, "Oh, are you my professional representation now?" laughing as she said it.

Her friend looked at her quite seriously this time, "Um. Yes, that would be just fabulous, now, wouldn't it? Leave it to me, darling. You have nothing to worry about. Now, Kiera, we have much to discuss."

And with that, she walked towards the kitchen with a wave of her arm to have their other roommate follow her. Kiera chased after her like a puppy, but she was genuinely excited to have this happen to her career and friends. She had a hunch that they were on to something.

Miles and Emma made their way to the now-empty couch and snuggled beside each other. It was she that broke their comfortable silence. Both were enjoying the quiet after the eventful beginning of their day.

She quietly started talking as she held up their intertwined hands to gaze at them, "Well, I have to say, the last twenty-four hours have not been boring. It's wild to think how life can change so fast."

He brought their clasped hands up to his lips and kissed the back of her hand, "That is very true. Now, how should we spend the rest of the morning?"

He had every intention of taking her back to the bedroom, but the roommates had other plans.

As he nuzzled her neck, both girls bounded back into the living room. Gemma appeared to leap dramatically as she entered and landed right next to them on the sofa, "No time for that, my darlings. We have cooking of our own to do. Now, let's get to it. Miles, you're welcome to join us, but we have to move it."

She said this as she popped onto her feet while pulling Emma along with her. "Let's go! Right now!"

Emma rolled her eyes as she stood up and looked down at Miles, "Well, I guess I'll have to take a rain check for later?"

He laughed back at her and stood up next to her. "I have to get back to the base anyway. Call me later?" Then he kissed her on top of her head.

"Yes, yes, she'll give you a ring when she gets back! Now come on, Emma. We really must go." Gemma piped back.

Suddenly, Emma realized that she had no way of calling him. He quickly wrote down the number to the Navy base, and then he was off.

The girls were a huge ball of excitement as they headed uptown to the agency offices where Kiera worked. As they rode the subway, they fed Emma as much information as possible about Heather's Bakery.

It was even more of a whirlwind of activity when they arrived at the agency. Kiera's team comprised creative, copywriting, consumer research, and the Vice President of Marketing.

This team was seated in a very large boardroom, where Emma suddenly felt overwhelmed.

There was a lot of chatter when the girls entered, and then it completely stopped.

All eyes were on Emma, and she was slightly embarrassed by the attention. She could feel the heat rising in her cheeks as she quickly scanned the room at all the humans staring in her direction.

She felt reassured that Gemma and Kiera were standing beside her, but it would help to see a friendly face.

And then she saw him, sitting at the end of the table, staring at her with his sharp green eyes. It was Maxwell.

As if her mind weren't racing enough already, she couldn't believe he was surprising her yet again in the most unlikely place.

It took all of her mind's focus to pay attention to everyone introducing themselves to her while she continued to stand in the doorway. Her eyes were only focused on him.

Their eyes were locked on each other, and it was impossible for the others not to notice.

Gemma purposely bumped Emma back to reality when she caught on to what everyone else had already seen.

Something was going on between Emma and Maxwell, and it was clear that everyone was more interested in that.

"Emma, take a seat." she whispered quite loudly. This startled her friend back to the moment.

"Oh, yes, of course. Sorry, everyone. I was just taken aback for a moment. It's already been quite a day of surprises for me. Where should I sit?" Emma rambled to the group.

His smooth, effortless voice responds with, "Anywhere you feel comfortable. Nice to see you again, Emma."

She took note of the room and slid into a chair at the far end of the table. It gave her the perfect view of Maxwell but not in an overly obvious way.

Once seated, she spoke quietly and firmly, "Thank you, Maxwell and everyone."

She briefly made eye contact with him and nodded once, saying, "Nice to see you again, as well. Shall we get started?"

With this, she looked to Kiera to begin the meeting before she decided whether or not to crawl under the table.

The roommates sat down beside Emma as the meeting officially started.

Kiera quietly cleared her throat to bring the group to attention before she began, "Thanks to everyone for coming together so quickly. As you all know, Heather's Bakery wants to do something very different and fresh with its brand. What better way to shake up their image than by introducing a young, talented, relatable baker to their core audience? That is why Emma Foster is here. Born and raised in the Pacific Northwest, her small-town, genuine demeanor combined with her excellence in making the kitchen a welcome domain for everyone will open doors to current and new consumers. She is the perfect fit for Heather's Bakery."

The people in the room were all looking at Emma. She felt exposed and very vulnerable at this particular moment.

This was all happening so fast that she barely had time to process the gravity of what her friend was saying. *What does it mean to be the perfect fit for anything?*

Just as she was processing the words, the room erupted in a welcoming clap of adoration and acceptance. Emma could feel the heat rising in her cheeks, and she glanced from person to person.

Finally, her eyes fell upon Maxwell. He subtly smiled at her and gave her a small wink when their eyes met. She wasn't quite sure why, but she instantly felt more at ease by looking at him.

She nodded in appreciation and then quietly began to speak to the group. "As Kiera mentioned, I am a baker. I'm actually a lifelong baker. I grew up watching my mother and grandmother perfect their recipes or, at least, try and try again to make it their version of perfect."

The room quietly laughed at this light comment. She continued, "I feel like baking and culinary skills are in my DNA. I came to New York to refine those skills and have learned so much. While this opportunity with Heather's Bakery is still very new to me, I am very excited to see where we can go together. Well, if you'll have me."

Those last words were spoken with such a quiet shyness. It touched Maxwell, which was something that he wasn't used to feeling at the office.

He began to speak with a booming tone that even surprised him, "Well, Emma, thank you for those remarks.

Kiera and Gemma speak highly of you, and we look forward to seeing what you can do to help Heather's Bakery grow in sales and add a fresh new consumer base."

Emma looked directly at Maxwell as he spoke, her heartbeat increasing with every word. She was worried that the whole group could tell how much she was attracted to him.

She couldn't quite understand why, especially when she was so in love with Miles. Completely distracted by those thoughts, she did not hear another word that Maxwell was saying.

When she finally came down from her infatuated and intrusive thoughts, she realized the meeting had adjourned.

She looked around, slightly startled, as the group filed out of the room. Maxwell was addressing Kiera and Gemma directly when she started paying attention again.

He was firm as he said, "I will walk Emma back to your office, Kiera. I want a moment to officially welcome her to the team and address any questions she may have."

No need to question the boss, so the ladies also filed out of the room, leaving the two of them alone. Maxwell took no time walking up to Emma, leaning into her closely and looking her right in the eye.

She could feel the heat from his body, and it made her blush. Well, that, combined with the intensity with which he looked at her, she was suddenly more than a little warm.

Words spontaneously sprang from her mouth, "Well, fancy meeting you here, Maxwell. How long have you known about this crazy little idea that my roommates came up with?"

He lightly brushed her arm with his hand and smiled gently as he answered, "Well, my dear Emma, I must admit that I have been watching you for quite a while. Yet, it was still a surprise when I finally connected the dots that you were the same Emma Kiera had talked to me about for weeks. A pleasant surprise, of course."

Damn it, she was blushing again. There were questions in that statement that needed to be answered, but he didn't allow the opportunity at that moment.

He just leaned in close to her. So close. Her heart was racing. He immensely turned her on, and she wasn't sure she wanted it to stop. That was ridiculous. She was in love with someone else. And that someone was here, in New York, waiting for her.

She was tempted to kiss him. So very tempted to lean in and give in to what her body was aching for. However, something in her head was telling her to stop.

They were in an office with lots of people, for goodness sake. And she hadn't even officially begun working for the agency or brand or whoever the hell she was going to be working for.

At the same time, her mind was spinning with thoughts of Miles. The man she had been pining over for the last few years was back in her life. Emma had spent endless sleepless nights thinking of where he was and if they would ever see each other again. Something in her heart wouldn't let Miles go. Yet, now…this?

All she knew at this moment was that she was very interested in kissing Maxwell. Emma loved when he looked at her. It made her feel like she was the only one in the room, whether they were at Sam's or standing in this very open, very modern, very professional meeting room. *Damn it.*

As if they were reading each other's minds, they both backed away at the same time. Emma fidgeted for a moment with an invisible speck on her dress while Maxwell decided to gather his things from the table.

When he was done, he finally spoke to her with a professional tone of voice, "I think that you are a great fit for Heather's Bakery. You're going to be the breath of fresh air that is needed. I look forward to working together."

"Thank you, Maxwell. I hope so." Emma said as she walked towards the doorway to meet her friends.

She met his eyes as he graciously opened the door and felt the same craving for him that she had that first night they talked at the bar.

Emma was in trouble. Yet somehow, she didn't mind.

CHAPTER 17

CROSSROADS

" Two paths don't always lead home."

Emma called Miles to let him know she was heading back to the apartment, which left him just enough time to walk over to meet her. They had plans to see the sites. He was visiting New York City, after all.

She was about a block away from her place as she rounded the corner. As she walked, her thoughts drifted back to Maxwell. Her mind had captured his face so perfectly. His dark hair, hazel eyes, and the chiseled features of his face were hard to forget. He had this perfect cupid's bow on his top lip. She couldn't help but think of how much she wanted to devour it with kisses. *Whoa.*

Just as she was thinking of Maxwell, she looked down the busy sidewalk.

Sometimes there were so many people crowded on the same stretch of concrete in New York City that she felt so small and invisible. Often, she would try to look at all of the faces passing her by as if she were searching for a familiar face. At times, doing so made her feel more lonely.

Today was different because as she looked past the people before her, walking quickly to get to wherever they were going, she saw him standing on the corner across the street.

He was leaning casually against the light pole, hands stuffed in the front of his blue jean pockets, looking down slightly.

The late-day sun was peeking through just enough to highlight his sandy blond-brown hair. The light also made his blue eyes dramatically sparkle as he tilted his head up to look for Emma.

He recognized her in the distance, and a small, easy smile crossed his face. She had seen that look so many times before and made her feel like it was only for her. If her intuition was right, he really did love her. It seemed as if he couldn't help but smile every time he saw her.

Emma smiled back as she waited at the red light to cross the busy street to get to him and waved her hand as if he didn't already see her. The traffic seemed to be endless as they stood across from one another, impatiently waiting to kiss each other.

It wasn't lost on them that this was something that they each missed desperately over these last few years apart.

Finally, she reached him and didn't waste a moment before wrapping her arms around his neck to kiss him. Miles took one hand out of his pocket and put it around her waist while the other hand gently grazed her jawline as his lips met hers.

Time stopped, and people disappeared at this moment. It always did when they kissed each other. Typically, it takes a lot to get a city person's attention, so Emma giggled when they began to turn a few heads with their street corner embrace.

She finally pulled away and took his hand as they began to walk towards her apartment while she said, "Well, that's something that doesn't happen here every day."

This time, it was Miles that blushed a little.

When they walked in, they were the only ones in the apartment, and Emma took full advantage of the privacy.

Was it the afternoon of sexual tension with Maxwell or just being here with Miles that made her want to peel off her clothes? She wasn't sure, but she didn't want to figure it out at that particular moment.

Miles loved that she was taking charge and showing him with her body what she wanted.

As they closed her bedroom door, she pushed him down on the bed and then double-checked to ensure her door was locked.

Now was not the time for her nosy roommates to burst in. She had needs that she wanted fulfilled, and there was no one better than Miles to take care of that for her.

He sat on the bed, watching her as she stared back at him. Slowly and seductively, she unbuttoned the front of her dress.

While they gazed directly at each other, she let her arms slide out of her sleeves. Emma let her fingers graze along the edge of her lace bra and gently slid the shoulder strap down her left arm. She knew that he loved watching her undress.

It made her more aroused and confident with her body. She then stepped forward to put one foot on the bed beside Miles. This made her full skirt rise on her thigh, and because she still had on her heels, it made the angle of her leg look sexy as hell. He couldn't help himself, so he glided his hand up her leg. She gasped, and he knew he could let his hand continue to move higher on her body.

She took her hand to grab his neck firmly, bringing his head level with her breasts. His hot breath on her skin made her want him more, so he took full advantage of kissing her breasts while lazily yet expertly running his fingers along her underwear just beneath her skirt.

He placed his other hand on her lower back to support her as he pulled her closer. At first, he let his other fingers gently graze the outside of her lace bikini, but he quickly felt her wetness through the thin material.

So, he gently pushed her underwear to the side and let his fingers glide inside her. Emma leaned easily into his fingers and grabbed his neck a little rougher this time. Her bra was around her waist, and his mouth was devouring her naked breasts. This completely turned her on and quickly exploded within his hands. He smiled, knowing that she was satisfied.

She backed up long enough to push Miles's pants down to his ankles and lift her skirt to sit on his lap. Turnabout was fair play, and she would give back what he had just given her.

Slowly, he entered her as she sat down. They quickly and luxuriously found their rhythm as she rode him while they sat perched on the edge of the bed. Together they found the familiar pleasure of each other, and right before they came together, Miles gently rolled Emma onto her back to look down at her.

She never ceased to amaze him. They smiled easily at each other, comfortable and wonderfully satisfied.

They rolled over onto their backs with their legs dangling down off the edge of the bed. He turned onto his side, propped his head in his hand, and gazed at her. She was still smiling, feeling content, fulfilled, and very loved. He began to laugh, and she looked over at him to question why, "What is that laugh for?"

He was feeling the same way she was and amused by the spontaneous lovemaking. He chuckled, "I was just thinking how awesome it is that you still have your heels on. You always did capture my attention. Sex first, shoes later."

Emma grabbed a pillow above her head to playfully hit him with it. "Well, I never claimed to be boring," she responded. This recharged him, and suddenly, he was on top of her, kissing her with renewed passion. This time, he stood up, lifted her legs one by one, and ever so gently removed her shoes. Next came her dress and then her underwear.

She lay before him, completely naked. He couldn't help but appreciate how lucky he felt to stand here and take in her beauty from head to toe.

They made love again. By the time they pulled themselves away from each other, they suddenly realized how hungry they were. "Shall we head to Sam's for a bite to eat?" she suggested.

They made their way out into the living room to find Gemma and Kiera. Everyone decided that a group dinner was just what they needed. After all, they had a bit of celebrating to do since Emma was officially going to be the new face of Heather's Bakery.

As they entered Sam's, they couldn't help but notice Maxwell sitting at the bar. Gemma invited him to join them at a table for the dinner celebration.

He smiled easily and said, "I can think of no greater reason to drink, eat, and enjoy the company of such a talented team. Dinner is on me."

Emma wasn't sure why, but she seemed to sense that this didn't sit well with Miles but decided to let it go. As the evening wore on, many drinks were consumed, including champagne before and after dinner.

With her friends all together, Emma felt so happy and adored. She couldn't help but cherish this evening. She was with Miles, on the brink of a very intriguing career adventure, and she was in New York City.

Happy couldn't quite describe how wonderful she was feeling, but she knew it had been a long time since she felt this way.

It was Maxwell that was the first one to call it a night. He had paid the tab and told Sam he would take care of whatever anyone else wanted to enjoy for the night.

Gemma was quick to make her escape as well. She had her eye on Maxwell, and this was the perfect opportunity to get some one-on-one time with him.

As Gemma was collecting her things, Maxwell shook Miles's hand, gave a friendly hug to Kiera, and then leaned in to hug Emma. He met her eyes with a soft, seductive look that made her very warm all at once. He hugged her a little longer and more tenderly than he had her friend. Miles immediately noticed.

Maxwell began, "Emma, we are so thrilled you have decided to join the team. You will bring a renewed freshness to the brand many have been craving for quite a long time. It will be a pleasure to work with you."

The tone of his voice was both intriguing, slightly sexy, and powerfully firm. Once again, their eyes met as he pulled away from their embrace.

Miles, on the other hand, wanted to deck him, but there wasn't anything he could do to justify it right now.

Emma giggled a little uncomfortably and mumbled a quiet thank you for dinner. With that, he and Gemma headed towards the door with her hand on his arm, a little too possessively.

The remaining three sat back down at the table to sip their drinks, but the tension was undeniable.

Kiera hadn't noticed it before, but she could see how much Maxwell was attracted to Emma. Yet, she had no clue how her dear friend felt about his apparent interest.

After what seemed to be an endless amount of silence, she felt compelled to leave too. She tipped back the rest of her drink and grabbed her coat.

"Well, I don't want to be the third wheel at this little celebration, so I am going to go. Emma, love, it was wonderful to celebrate with you tonight. I am so thrilled that you decided to take us on. It will be fun working together, you know? Miles, keep our girl safe. I'll see you two later."

And with that, she blew two kisses toward her friends and was out the door. She knew when she needed to make herself scarce.

Emma looked over at Miles while she took another sip of her drink as Kiera left. He had been noticeably quiet during the dinner, but she hadn't had the opportunity to say anything.

"Thank you for coming to dinner tonight. It made it more special to have you here to celebrate with me," she said quietly as she looked at him.

Miles looked at her out of the corner of his eye as he took another sip of his bourbon. One more nightcap on her friend, Maxwell. His irritation was growing as much as he tried to put it aside. He just couldn't get past it.

He responded with just a tinge of bitterness in his voice, "Are you sure about that? Sometimes, I thought you didn't even remember I was here."

She was surprised by his tone and his words. "What are you saying, Miles? Of course, I am happy you are here, especially tonight."

He sarcastically smiled as he drained the last of his glass and set it down a little too harshly on the table.

"Are you sure about that, sweetie? Your friend Maxwell seemed to be captivating almost everyone's attention during the night. And don't think I missed how he hugged you. For god sake, get a room."

He abruptly stood up to leave as Emma peered up at him with an astonished look on her face. She had no idea he felt this way, which made her feel awful.

"Miles, I had no idea that you were this upset. I certainly hadn't planned to have dinner with Maxwell. Please sit down so we can talk about this," she tried to say quietly.

He was irritated, and she wanted to make it go away. She wanted to spend the time they had together happily, not fighting.

He hadn't even told her how long he would be in town. Emma felt like this was about nothing. It was nothing, right?

Honestly, she didn't understand what she felt for Maxwell, so the last thing she wanted to do was fight with Miles about something that was practically non-existent in her eyes.

The last little bit of whiskey was making him feel warm and a little woozy. He needed fresh air and said as much to her. "I should go back to the base anyway," he responded curtly.

Sam was watching from behind the bar, feeling bad for his friend because she was so upset. He had noticed the physical attraction that she had with both Miles and Maxwell.

As Miles walked out into the cold, the bartender wandered over to clear the last few glasses from the table. As he approached, he could see that there were tears in Emma's eyes.

Quietly he said to her, "Sometimes it's hard to choose a path when you find yourself at a crossroads in life. You'll figure it out."

And then he walked away, leaving Emma to wonder what she would do.

CHAPTER 18

BEST OF WHAT'S AROUND

" Life moves fast."

The remainder of the weekend with Miles was spent showing him around the city or in Emma's bed. He called the following day and apologized, blaming the whiskey and jealousy. She was quick to forgive because she wanted to be with him as much as possible.

He was due to leave early that Monday morning, and the Navy ship was headed out to sea indefinitely. That day hung before them like a heavy, gray fog on an endless winter day on the coast. Its dark, gloomy arrival was inevitable, but one could hold out hope that it would take its time making it to shore.

Sunday began as a lazy day filled with warm coffee, and the two of them snuggled under the covers. They were so happy like this.

Emma decided she needed to talk with Miles about where they would go from here. He was leaving, and she was starting a new career path, confusing them both.

"So, when do you need to be back at the base? Today or tomorrow?" she asked quietly. She lazily let her fingers trace his arm that was lovingly wrapped around her shoulders. They were lying in her bed, propped up on pillows, sipping their coffee, naked—their idea of a perfect morning.

He leaned down and kissed her head before he began to speak, "Well, we leave port so early tomorrow, so it makes sense to head back to the ship tonight." They both let out a heavy sigh as he finished his sentence.

Lifting his fingers to her lips, she kissed them lightly and said, "I was hoping you wouldn't say that. Can't you just miss the ship and stay here with me? Forever?"

He laughed at her comment, knowing full well that the same thought had crossed his mind several times.

"Unfortunately, no. That's not how the Navy works. They would send someone to find me and haul my ass back to the ship."

Emma turned slightly inward towards the warmth of his side, looked him in the eye, and said, "Well, at least they would be hauling back the cutest ass I've ever seen."

Just as they began exploring each other's bodies again, Emma's bedroom door burst open. "Oh, come on, you two! Again?" Gemma exclaimed, "Get up! It's time for Boozy Brunch. It's a New York City must-do! Come on, let's go!"

They grumbled and laughed at this interruption but didn't mind.

Sex makes you hungry, and Gemma was right. There truly is nothing like an NYC brunch on a Sunday. So, off they went to a fun little place on Water St. with stunning views of the city and the shoreline.

Even in the early winter, everyone wanted to be near the water to watch the views along the river. Warmed by the cocktails and fantastic food, their morning quickly turned into late afternoon.

Realizing the time, the light-hearted chatter of the group changed to the topic of Miles leaving. Emma took his hand underneath the table and leaned into his shoulder as he reminded everyone that he was heading back to the ship that night.

Always nosy and never shy about asking questions, Gemma was quick to inquire about what would happen between the two lovebirds.

Kiera rolled her eyes at her roommate and quickly interjected, "That is between the two of them. God, Gemma, give them a chance to figure it out."

Emma and Miles smiled at each other knowingly as their two friends bantered back and forth about their apparently, very open relationship.

Gemma was trying to defend her stance by explaining that it was obvious that they all had a vested interest in Emma's love life.

"I mean, it impacts us all. Let's be honest. It's easier to have Miles here to keep her happy. Once he's off sailing off to God knows where, she will be sulking about, pining away for his magical cock."

This shocked everyone at the table. All three simultaneously said, "GEMMA!"

She caught what she had just said out loud and brushed it off, "Oh, come on! It's not like we all don't know what happens in your room. I mean, it's like you two don't know how to come up for air! And if you are sulking around, it will make our jobs that much harder. You can't very well be the new face of Heather's while you're sad and mopey about not getting your favorite dick any time you like."

Emma was shocked. Miles was amused, and Kiera was over it.

"Come on, Gemma. This is why I should have cut you off after that last mimosa. Emma, Miles, and your penis, I apologize on behalf of this plastered Brit. Now, go get yours while you can, and I'll stay with this one to try and sober her up."

The couple was quite amused. The roommates weren't wrong. They did take advantage of each other's bodies every moment they could. And right now was no different.

They looked at each other with loving smiles and stood up to leave. "You don't have to tell me twice," Miles snickered.

Emma playfully hit him on the arm as she stood up, too. "Don't worry. I'll find a way to get them back for this little skit. Girls, thanks for the brunch. We're off to snog. Or shag. Or whatever the British call it."

And with that, they hurried out the door into the cold late afternoon.

Once they reached the apartment, it didn't take long for their clothes to come off. Miles had Emma pressed against the entryway wall the moment the front door closed.

However, their passion was different this time. There was almost a desperation to their lovemaking. They felt like this was the last time they would ever touch each other, especially in this way.

It was as if they were starving and wanting to dissolve into each other forever. It was a weird force of emotions that drove them toward each other.

A trail of pants, sweaters, underthings, and shoes led to Emma's bed. They lay together, holding each other for a long time afterward, languishing in the warmth of each other's bodies.

The weight of Miles's leaving hung in the air, heavy and thick. Neither wanted to mention what was going to happen, but it was there.

Intertwined between the covers, it was Emma who quietly spoke first. "I know you have to leave. I don't want you to, but I know that you have to. What am I going to do without you here?"

Miles didn't respond immediately, "Well, I think you have more than enough to keep you busy. You'll barely know I'm not here." He hugged her tight as he spoke. He had been dreading this part of the day, which had now suddenly arrived.

"That's not true, and you know it." she said and poked him in the side.

He took a deep breath and began, "I have been thinking about this. I can't tell you where we are going or how long I will be gone. I know it will be around six months, but there's no guarantee. That's what makes this so hard. I love you. And, because I love you so much, I can't leave here thinking or expecting you to wait for me. You have to be free to date anybody you're interested in. I mean, I hate the thought of you being with someone else. And don't even get me started about Maxwell. God, just the thought of you spending time with him pisses me off."

They were sitting up in bed looking at each other at this point, and Emma's mind was swirling. She loved Miles, really loved him. How could he think she would just run off and be with someone else because he was on a ship in God knows where? The look on her face said it all.

"Oh, come on, Emma. Do you think I would be ok with you pining away for me when I have no idea when I will see you again? I mean, the next time I'm in the States, there is no way to know if I will land back in New York. I'll probably go home. I don't want you to expect anything from me, and I don't expect anything from you."

She was reeling. This hurt. Again. Just like last time when he left. He was leaving her to be free, but he didn't get that she was never truly free of him, no matter where in the world he was.

"I know. You've said very similar things to me before. And it hurts just as much, if not more, than last time. How can you walk away like this? You say you love me, but then you tell me you have no expectations." She was crying at this point, and seeing that he was causing her pain killed him. Again.

He reached for her and felt her defensively stiffen at his touch. "I say that I have no expectations because I love you so much. I don't want you to hold back from anything in your life. I made a choice, and so did you. They just are very different. I have loved every single moment I have spent with you, even when we fight. But I have to leave while you have your life here. What else are we supposed to do?"

She knew he was right, but damn it, she was pissed at the painful situation it put them in. Emma wanted to be with him. Life just felt right when he was with her. She could feel her heart physically breaking with the realization that they had to say goodbye.

When he reached for her this time, she leaned into him and softly cried. Miles kissed the top of her head, and she lay on his chest and let the tears fall.

"This just isn't fair," she began, "We have loved each other for years, and it always ends with a goodbye. There's nothing like this pain. I hate it."

He got what she was saying, "I completely agree. I don't feel the same when I'm not with you. It's like there's a part of me that is missing. But this is where we are in our lives. I want to say that maybe it won't be forever, but then that gives us false hope that we can't guarantee. I'm sorry."

She could feel how much he loved her as he said those words. They kissed with a passion that was only theirs. This time when they made love, it was just that—made of love.

They knew each other's bodies so well and gave into what made their union. Forget anything like marriage to solidify their connection. Their loving bond made them one, and that is precisely what their lovemaking signified this time.

It was at once happy, loving, and heartbreaking. Something about this physical union was a sad goodbye.

A few hours later, Miles finally climbed out of her bed and got dressed. She just sat there watching him, feeling the lump in her throat rising, knowing another goodbye was only moments away.

After he finished dressing, he sat on the edge of the bed to put on his shoes. She leaned into him and took a deep breath to let the scent of him wash over her. She was trying to memorize everything. The warmth of him, his smell, and his loving presence. It's like he was a ghost that was quickly fading away.

He reached over, wrapped his arms around her, and held her tightly. Miles was trying to do the same thing. "Do you think we would have worked out if we both would have stayed on the coast?"

Her first thought was to answer yes. And then something triggered her to say, "I don't know. This is where we are, and I can't imagine not being here. I don't know, Miles."

As he stood up and looked down at her, still naked and wrapped in a blanket, he smiled and said, " I think we would have made it."

With those words, he put on his dark wool coat. She moved to get up, but he stopped her. He could feel the emotion rising within him, and he didn't want to make it harder than it already was.

"Stay there. I want the image of you laying in that bed so it can live in my mind forever. I love you, Emma. Always have and always will, no matter where I am."

She began to cry again, knowing that this was it. Goodbye. Again.

He came over to her and kissed her with a gentle passion that made her gasp with pure emotion. She touched his face, and he stood up to leave.

"I love you, too, Miles. Always," she whispered. And then he left the room, softly closing the door behind him.

She laid back on her pillows and silently cried. The pain in her heart was more than she could bare. How could she be losing him again?

Miles leaned against her closed bedroom door for a brief moment before walking out. When he walked out, he was surprised to see Gemma and Kiera sitting quietly in the living room. He wiped his eyes and looked over at them.

For once, they were speechless because they knew how hard this was for both Miles and Emma.

A brief moment of hesitancy overtook him, but then he knew better. He had to pick up the pieces of the mess he had made during his service. Emma wouldn't understand that.

"Take care of her. She will be down for a bit, but she'll be ok. See ya, ladies," he said as he walked toward the front door. Then he was gone.

CHAPTER 19

MOVING FORWARD

" One step at a time"

The night that Miles left was hard not only for Emma but for her roommates too. They adored her and hated seeing her in pain.

So, when she finally emerged from her room, they were waiting for her with a bottle of wine, her favorite rom-com movies, and Chinese food. Perfect for a cold Sunday night, especially when one of them was nursing a broken heart.

She was eternally grateful for their friendship and their support. Honestly, the last thing she wanted to do was sit on her couch with them. She wanted to be running through the streets of New York, chasing after Miles so she could beg him not to leave her. But she knew that wasn't the right thing to do.

Something in her head reminded her that she had gotten through their last goodbye and that she would get through it once more.

Thankfully, the next several weeks were a whirlwind filled with non-stop days of meetings, script reviews, recipes, and her best friends.

She would often think that maybe this time, she would be ok. Miles was always in her head, somewhere, but busyness had a way of pushing off the sadness in her heart. Losing him was so painful that she was more than ok with the hectic schedule.

Maxwell had somehow managed to be present but kept his distance. It's almost as if he could sense her heartbreak, and he didn't want to confuse her more. He was very interested in Emma but knew she needed time.

For now, he loved watching her work. She was a master with recipes and making beautiful works of art with food. He had never seen anything like it.

For Emma, the nights were the worst. She could keep her days filled with classes, work, and meetings. Yet, at night, she would lie in the same bed she shared with Miles, aching for his touch and their easy conversations. Sometimes, her feelings were so strong that it felt like he was still there.

Miles hadn't been in contact at all since he left that Sunday night. Days quickly turned into weeks, then months, with no letter or call. She wondered where he was and always prayed that he was safe.

Since she had no relationship with his mother, she had no way of knowing where he was or what he was doing. It was torture. This is what made the nights so challenging.

Emma had always made it a habit to call her mother and grandmother at least once a week. Although more challenging in recent months, she always enjoyed their conversations, and of course, they loved hearing about her big-city adventures.

She never mentioned that she saw Miles. Why would she? They didn't have a committed future together, and she had no idea where he was.

Grammy was the first to talk with her that week, "Emma, how are you? How is it going with the baking?"

She didn't know what else to call it and was slightly confused that anyone would be interested in watching someone else bake. It was just odd to her.

"Grammy, it is going well. I'm not completely used to the cameras, but it's getting better. How are you?"

Her grandmother was a little slow to respond, but when she did, what she said surprised Emma.

Rosie began, "Oh, well, your mother keeps an eye on me more than ever. I had a chance to walk along the beach today. Pete was there, and we had the nicest conversation. I have missed walking on the beach with him. He walked me home, and then when it was time for dinner, he was gone. I suppose he had an errand to run."

Emma was confused. Her grandmother was referencing Pete, her grandfather, who had died years ago. "Grandma, who was with you today on the beach? Did you say it was Grandpa?"

When Rosie spoke again, there was an agitation in her voice that wasn't normal, "Yes, dear, why wouldn't your grandfather walk me home? He always walked with me on the beach, so why would today be any different."

This concerned Emma, but she didn't push. She just asked to speak with her mom, gave her love to Rosie, and then said goodbye.

Caroline took the phone from her mother and nonchalantly began to speak to her daughter, "Hello, Emma. How are you?"

"Um, Mom, is everything ok with Grammy? She said Grandpa Pete walked her back to the house during her beach walk today. That can't be right. What is going on?"

There was a long silence on the other end of the line, and Emma was quickly growing concerned with what was happening with her beautiful, strong grandmother.

"Well, sweetie, of course, Grandpa didn't walk her home. It, um, well, ok. It was Miles."

CHAPTER 20

WHIPLASH

" WTF."

What in the actual fuck is going on?

That's all that Emma could think of as she continued to talk with her mom. She had been so distracted with working on the Heather's Bakery project that it was hard to keep up with what was happening at home.

Grammy had suffered a mild stroke about a month ago. Overall, she was fine, but it was now impacting her thoughts. She had a hard time separating reality from her imagination. If you asked her, Grandpa Pete walked her home from the beach.

Yet, it was Miles. He was supposed to be somewhere in the middle of the ocean on a Navy ship, *not* at home. She was pissed that he didn't tell her. It was also knowing that he and her other favorite people were in the same place that she wasn't made her ache to be at the Glass House.

Her mind was once again racing. They were on good terms when he left. She was heartbroken, but that was no reason not to tell her he was going home soon.

Did he really leave on the ship, or did he just hop on a plane to Oregon? Why was he there, and most of all, why wouldn't he tell her? He could have stayed with her in New York. She didn't understand enough about military service. Could he just leave? She didn't think that was possible. He couldn't be physically hurt and on medical leave if he could walk down the beach, let alone take care of Grammy.

Her mom was explaining the latest with her bakery, Grammy, and random information about their day-to-day lives. At that moment, Emma had no interest, and it showed.

"Mom, what did you say? Miles walked Grammy home? How is that possible? He's away in the Navy." she interrupted.

Caroline seemed surprised by her daughter not knowing that Miles was home.

"He said he had talked with you, so I assumed you knew. I, well, I don't know the exact reason that he is home, but it was just so nice of him to walk her back. I was getting worried because she was gone for so long. I should have gone with her, but you know how stubborn Grammy can be…."

"Mom, he said that he talked to me? When? What else did he have to say?" Emma was beyond confused.

"Emma, you seem upset. Why? Did something happen with you two? Yes, he said that he saw you in New York and that you seemed very happy there. I knew you were happy, of course, with all of these exciting videos you are making," her mom rambled.

"Mom, really, what did he say about being home? I didn't know he would be there," Emma said hurriedly.

Her mother was very curious as to her reaction but knew when she shouldn't push. "He said that he was home for now, that he saw you in New York, and then we talked about Grammy. That's it. That's all I know, sweetie."

Emma finished the conversation with her mom, feeling upset, confused, and overwhelmingly homesick. She sat on her bed for a long time after they hung up.

She was deep in thought when Kiera came in to check on her. They planned to go to dinner for a mini-celebration for the first video series.

"Hi. Wow, you don't look like someone that is going to be a huge video star. You should be glowing, and yet you look like someone just died. They didn't, did they?" Kiera asked.

Emma kept staring into space for a moment longer before she spoke, "No, nothing like that. Well, my grandmother still isn't doing that well. She is getting confused a lot, and she said the strangest thing to me just now."

Kiera was intrigued, "What did she say?"

Emma looked at her dear friend and explained that Grammy had walked on the beach with her grandfather, who had passed away quite a while ago. "And then my mom told me something even more startling. It wasn't Grandpa. It was Miles. He's home. He didn't even fucking tell me. Why would he not tell me that he was going home?"

They both paused to think about why Miles wouldn't be open with Emma about leaving the Navy. He made it seem like he was going on some secret mission.

Kiera spoke first, "I don't know him well enough to understand why he wouldn't explain what was going on. Can you call him? Do you have his number?"

Emma had no idea how to reach him other than his mother. "Ugh. I only have his mother's number, and I am not her favorite, to say the least."

At this point, Gemma came in and bounded onto Emma's bed, as a Labrador would do. "What is bloody going on in here? Why aren't you dressed, Emma? We need to go! I need a drink. Or three. Come on, get going."

Her words made the other two smile. There was nothing that Emma could do about Miles right now. He was three thousand miles away and apparently a million miles away from her in his heart. She had no choice but to push this out of her mind for now.

The threesome went to dinner at a new trendy place several blocks from their apartment, so Emma let Gemma know what had happened on the phone earlier.

They ended up at Sam's for a few after-dinner cocktails. Sam was serving them another round when Maxwell entered the bar.

He immediately saw them and hesitated briefly before joining the ladies at their table.

"You all look very lovely this evening. Celebrating Emma's big success with the videos, I assume?" he said.

For some reason, the direct comments toward Emma made her blush. It wasn't just her efforts. The other two were working just as hard to pull this campaign together.

Emma looked at Maxwell and said, "We are celebrating each other. It's not just me that made the videos happen, Maxwell. It's a team effort."

The three girls smiled at each other and clinked their glasses for a "Cheers!"

Maxwell smiled at this and responded, "Well, let me get myself a drink. Then I will be sure to celebrate the work of all three of you. May I join you, or shall I scurry over to the bar and leave you be?"

Gemma spoke up this time, "Oh, it's always the more, the merrier. You better hurry and catch up, though. We've been here for a while." She then headed to the jukebox to tee up a few of her favorite songs so the real party could begin.

After ordering a bottle of champagne and four glasses, Maxwell headed back to the table. As he approached, he couldn't help but notice that Emma was lost in thought.

She was sitting in her chair, twirling her empty wine glass and staring off into space. Certainly not the look of a girl that had accomplished so much in the last few months.

He smiled, set down the glasses and bottle, then wistfully spoke, "Penny for your thoughts, lovely lady."

At first, she didn't notice him or his words. Then something brought her back to the present. "Oh, Maxwell. I'm sorry. Gosh, I must be getting tired."

"No time for tired. I just brought over this full bottle of bubbly, and I believe Gemma is about to get this party going."

They all heard the unmistakable sounds of "Joy and Pain" by Rob Bass blaring through Sam's less-than-average bar speakers as if on cue.

Gemma began dancing back to the table while Kiera jumped out of her chair as if it were on fire. Maxwell grabbed the champagne and very dramatically opened the bottle, letting the cork fly over Emma's head and lightly spraying her with the mist. She couldn't help but laugh at the scene. It didn't take long for her to join the dance party.

Maxwell filled the glasses as the girls used the wobbly wooden chairs to climb onto the table and began to dance. He handed them each a glass and then awkwardly danced along with his feet firmly planted on the ground.

Had it been any other group in the bar, Sam would have stopped the impromptu table dance, but he had long since thought of these women as "his girls." They deserved more than a little fun, so why not let them dance on the table for a song or two?

Two songs turned into three, while Maxwell kept their champagne glasses full and his eyes on any other guy that tried to approach.

His main attraction was toward Emma, but he felt a little protective over the other two.

He knew that Gemma would take him to bed at a moment's notice, but he wasn't interested. He liked her, but not that way.

Kiera was a gem of an employee and as a person. He truly liked her and respected her work ethic, intelligence, and newfound friendship.

Then there was Emma. He watched her with loving yet lustful eyes as she danced with her friends. Oh, how he had imagined kissing her, loving every inch of her body, and connecting with her. He was really into her. He tried to keep it subtle on the outside, but if she only knew how he wanted her.

She had no idea that to Maxwell, she was amazing. He thought her to be intelligent, beautiful, creative, and very talented.

Unbeknownst to her, she resonated with sexuality that drove him crazy. He watched her closely. The sway of her hips with the beat of the music, the way she suggestively raised her arms over her head, and the sly smile that crossed her lips as she let go and just danced.

Emma needed this moment of freedom. She needed to push away the anger mixed with her ache for Miles. This momentarily faded as she moved to the music, combined with the bubbles of champagne shading her emotional brain.

As she danced, she was keenly aware that Maxwell was watching, and she liked it. Exactly why was still unclear to her intoxicated state, but it turned her on for now. She was curious about this man.

The alcohol quickly got to her, and she knew she needed to get down before she became too dizzy. She looked down, and Maxwell was right there to take her hand to help her to the floor. Their hands stayed connected briefly, making them glance at each other with a subtle, flirtatious look.

The other girls decided to stop dancing on the table, too, so always the gentleman, Maxwell, helped them down as well. They settled into their chairs, happy, drunk, and a little too giggly.

They had made up their version of Truth or Dare. They were calling it "Bubbles or Burst." Tell the truth or drink. They made the questions up as they went along, and the discussion quickly became very colorful.

Gemma was very aware that Maxwell was attracted to Emma. She had made a move on him weeks ago and was startled to figure out that his attraction to Emma was much more than she had initially thought. Tonight, she took full advantage of this little nugget of knowledge.

It was her turn to ask the question, and she directed it to Emma, "Lovely Emma, Bubbles or Burst. Will you kiss Maxwell or take a sip?"

Emma could feel the heat rising in her cheeks, unsure if it was from the wine or the question. Her mind knew the real truth. Drinking be damned, she wanted to kiss him, but Miles was still so fresh in her head. And her heart.

Yet Emma was feeling flirty and confident, so instead of just rebuffing the offer to kiss him, she made her move.

They were already sitting next to each other at the table, so it was easy for her to lean in slowly and seductively toward Maxwell. Their eyes met, and there was no doubt that there was a mutual attraction.

Emma leaned in closer and closer. Their lips ever so slightly grazed each other. They could feel the heat from each other's breath, pausing just a moment to make sure it was what she was choosing to do.

Yet suddenly and swiftly, she had already reached for her glass and brought it to her lips to take a drink, never breaking eye contact with Maxwell. He was both taken aback and highly turned on. As was she.

An uncomfortable quiet settled around the table briefly before Emma and Maxwell began giggling. This led the other two to fall into a fit of laughter, knowing that it was a sly move on Emma's behalf.

They continued the game until the bottle and their glasses were empty. The night was coming to a close, so they gathered their things and walked outside. Gemma and Kiera walked ahead, singing, arm in arm, and giggling at some random joke as the other two lagged behind.

Maxwell and Emma were just about to cross the intersection to her apartment when he suddenly looped his arm through hers and pulled her to the side. Before she knew what was happening, he had her pressed against the brick wall of the corner building. As surprised as she was by this move, she liked feeling the warmth and heaviness of his body pressed against hers.

Once again, she could feel the warmth of his breath against hers, mainly in contrast to the chilly night air.

He gazed deeply into her eyes before he began to speak. "Do you know how long I have wanted to kiss you? I mean, really kiss you, Emma?"

She couldn't find her voice to speak, overtaken by an immense feeling of passion, so she only shook her head from side to side to say "No."

"It has been a very, very, very long time. I was so jealous when that glass touched your lips tonight instead of touching my lips." And then, every so gently, he kissed her.

She had visions of butterflies lightly touching her mouth as he continued to kiss her. Then it became more passionate. The intensity was new to her, and dare she think that she actually saw stars in her eyes as she gave into his kiss. It was beyond amazing. It was mesmerizing.

Just as quickly as the kiss began, it was over. She was breathless as he lifted his body away from hers, grabbed her hand, and continued walking across the street into the night.

The next morning, instead of waking up with a hangover, Emma awoke with her head spinning about Miles. It was driving her crazy that he was home and had yet to reach out to tell her.

Did she think about the amazing kiss with Maxwell? Of course, she did, which aroused her more than expected.

However, she pushed away those thoughts because she could only focus on Miles.

After letting the thoughts swirl in her head for way too long, she decided to pick up the phone. It was still early on the West Coast, but she was determined to talk to him.

The only place she knew to call was his mother's house. It was a chance she was willing to take.

The line rang several times before a sleepy, raspy female voice answered the call, "Hello?"

"Hi. Could I speak with Miles, please?" Emma said quietly.

"Who is this?" the voice suddenly sounded much more alert and more accusatory than curious.

It was Miles's mother. Emma would know that voice anywhere.

She took a deep breath before she responded, " Mrs. Woods, this is Emma. Is Miles there?"

His mother sarcastically laughed into the phone, "Oh, he's stayin' with me, but he's not here. No, the last time I saw him was at the bar last night. I think he was headed out with his arm around that girl, you know, your friend. What's her name? Izzy? Yeah, that's it. They looked pretty into each other, too, if you know what I mean."

Sarah may have been sound asleep, but she was wide awake now and wanted to make Emma disappear. She had gotten to know Izzy over the last few years since they worked at the same bar. Izzy had convinced her that Emma had stolen Miles away from her in high school, and Sarah would not let that happen again.

Emma stammered back, "Oh, ok. So, he's not there now?"

"Did you hear me, girl? He's not here. He's with that chick, Izzy." Sarah cackled.

Tears stung Emma's eyes. She didn't know if Sarah was lying or if it was the truth. Miles hadn't called her. He made sure that she knew that they were open to seeing other people. Maybe this was his plan all along.

Once again, the thoughts in her head began to swirl, and she couldn't figure out what the hell was going on.

She finally spoke, "Ok. Could you tell him that I called?"

Sarah laughed again, "I can do what I want when I want. If he hasn't called you, what makes you think I can make him? He's with the other girl now. Just leave him be."

And with that, she hung up on Emma.

CHAPTER 21

THE BEST AND WORST DAY

"You can live a lifetime in just a day."

She cried. Cried like her soul was going to break into a million little pieces and then just fade away into the wind. Her heart was broken once again. She didn't know much about Miles, but what she knew was enough to leave her devastated.

Was the week they spent together just a dream? No, it was very real. For some reason, he made sure to let her know that he wanted her to be free. All the while knowing he was going home. Not just go home to his mama but home to Izzy.

She hadn't talked to Izzy much since moving to New York. Emma knew from a few updates from her mom that Izzy wasn't doing well.

Her former best friend tried attending college in Eugene but ended up partying too much and flunked out of school. So, the last she knew of Izzy was that she was working at one of the local bars with Miles's mom.

Emma couldn't help but think those two women were quite a pair to be reckoned with in a small town bar. They both liked to drink, loved men, and loved drama even more.

And now, Miles was hooking up with Izzy, who was supposed to be her best friend. Well, not anymore, and not really for a long time, but still. Friendship was friendship. Although not according to Izzy.

After spending over an hour lying on her bed, sobbing, Emma pulled together and decided to just forget about it.

Today was going to be a good day. She was determined to make it a great day, knowing everything she had been working toward over the last few months.

Tonight was the Launch Party for the new Heather's Bakery campaign. As heartbroken as she was, Emma wouldn't let it get in the way of this celebration. So, she dried her tears, took another deep breath, and walked out into the living room to join her roommates.

She didn't have the energy to tell them about Miles and Izzy. There was no need to say anything because they were more interested in the fact that she kissed Maxwell.

Kiera, surprisingly, was the first to mention it, "So, let the cat out of the bag. How was the kiss with Maxwell?" She couldn't help but giggle her way through the question.

This made Emma smile, and then Gemma was all over it, "Yes, give us the details. I've been dying to kiss that man for ages. What's it like? Did you get all tingly in the toes?"

While she said all this, Gemma had bounded over to her friend's side of the couch. She was not going to let Emma out of her sight until she knew everything!

Emma rolled her eyes and laughed, "It was fine. It was good. It was a kiss, Gem."

Her roommates laughed at this response. Kiera jumped in, "You are holding back on us, love. Really. How was it?"

This time, Emma genuinely smiled when she thought about how Maxwell made her feel last night when he finally kissed her.

"It was pretty amazing. He surprised me because he had had other opportunities to kiss me, and he never did. So, I didn't think he would do it. Maybe it was the champagne?" she explained.

All the girls squealed and laughed, two of them envious and the other surprised at how excited she was to think again about the kiss.

For the rest of the day, they planned their outfits, did their makeup, gossiped, and got ready for their party. Emma didn't have a chance to dwell on anything related to Miles, and when he did pop into her head, she pushed it away. She didn't want to hurt today. She wanted to celebrate.

The party was being held at the very swanky Tavern On The Green.

Their whole team was going to be there, including Maxwell, the executive team from Heather's Bakery, and the production people that helped put this campaign together. Lots of people, lots of food, and lots of cocktails. That should do the trick for a broken heart, Emma thought as they left for the restaurant.

Tavern On The Green is an iconic restaurant located in Central Park. Any time of year, the gardens and surrounding area are simply stunning.

Heavy snow had fallen earlier in the day, and the grounds were blanketed. White twinkle lights hung from the trees, making the snow glisten in the night. It was truly magical to see.

They entered through the side into a tent set up for the event. Inside, blue and white lights hung from green palm-like trees, with a glittering chandelier as the visual centerpiece of the room. It almost felt angelic.

Emma chose to wear a form-fitting silver sparkly dress with spaghetti straps. Since it was cold, she wore a white faux fur wrap draped around her shoulders. Her dark hair fell in loose soft waves, with one side pulled up with a crystal clip. She kept her makeup simple except for a bold slick of red lipstick. It wasn't planned, but she looked like she was a part of the room's elegant decor. She was a shining star that night.

Kiera was dressed in a black velvet sleeveless dress with a high turtleneck. She wore her light brown hair pulled back in an elegant chignon. Her only bit of sparkle was a simple round diamond pendant that she wore around her neck. Against the deep black of her dress, it sparkled in the wintry light of the room.

Gemma went for a bold look, as was her signature. She wore a sleeveless garnet red sequined dress with a deep v-cut down the front that almost hit her belly button. Her blond hair was styled straight and gleamed against the shine of her dress. She also opted for the same bold shade of red for her lips.

The trio looked stunning and added even more glamour to an already beautiful room. Maxwell found himself temporarily speechless when he saw them walk into the party. He had a drink attendant follow him to the ladies, and he promptly served them all a glass of champagne.

"Cheers to another fabulous evening celebrating three very lovely ladies," he said elegantly.

Gemma laughed, "Oh, Maxwell, now you're trying to charm all three of us? Down, boy."

This made everyone laugh, but they all said "Cheers!" and toasted to what was sure to be a glamorous evening.

They made their way to their table, which included all four of them. Heather, the bakery's owner, and CEO, and her husband, Jonathan, also joined them.

The room quickly filled with others that they knew as the cocktail reception soon came to an end. They all gathered at their table for dinner.

The tables somehow glowed due to strategically placed lights, while mirrors on the table reflected the white candles and the flower arrangements. It made everything on the table appear to be magically floating.

It was the most elegant dinner event Emma had ever attended. It was a far cry from her small-town dinners. She laughed at that thought, knowing how hurt she felt that morning.

Maxwell noticed her smile and gently took her hand under the table, so no one else would see. "I love your smile. You should do it more often."

She slowly leaned into him and quietly responded, "Well, maybe you should give me a few more reasons to smile." They caught each other's eye, and both felt a strong jolt of attraction between them.

Heather and Jonathan had just sat down, and after polite introductions to her husband, she said, "Maxwell, how long have you and Emma been together?"

This completely startled them both, and it was visually apparent as they slowly moved away from each other.

Maxwell was the first to speak, "We've been friends for several months now, but we aren't together."

Emma jumped in, "Yes, we are just friends. That's funny you should say that. Why would you think we are together?"

Heather met their words with immediate apologies, "I'm so sorry. It was just the way you two were looking at each other tonight. I guess I misread your body language. I'm so embarrassed."

Jonathan quickly took her hand and reassured her it was ok, mentioning that he had thought the same thing.

They all laughed it off, but it gave Maxwell and Emma pause to cool their attraction, at least while they were at the dinner.

After they ate, there were several speeches about the new campaign. People from Heather's Bakery and the agency talked about the exciting new direction the brand was taking their consumers.

Soon, it was time to reveal the videos that Emma had made. She was so nervous and felt a small drop of sweat slide down her back as she sat and listened. *What if these videos failed? What if her recipes didn't work? What if everyone thought that she was a complete idiot?*

Although they hadn't spoken since the conversation with Heather and Jonathan, Maxwell could tell Emma was beginning to feel tense.

The tablecloth covered their hands, so he felt it was ok to reach for her hand. She took it and immediately felt more at ease. He could see her shoulders soften a bit, and she looked more relaxed.

The agency shared three full-length videos featuring Emma and her recipes. The demonstrations would eventually be edited down into shorter lengths, but the audience would see these short films in their entirety tonight.

It took about an hour to get through all the videos, which seemed like an eternity to Emma. She couldn't get a read of what the audience was thinking because everyone was practically silent. Her thoughts raced, as usual, and she was quickly back to full-on stress mode.

The lights came back up, and suddenly, the room stood up in applause. Everyone was looking at her, smiling and clapping.

She was shocked, embarrassed, and then all of a sudden, proud. It took her a moment to realize that she had accomplished something great in her life. Thanks to her friends believing in her and due to her life-long passion for baking.

Emma took a moment as she let all of the adoration sweep over her. Maxwell was beaming at her, Gemma and Kiera were ecstatic, and she thought she saw Heather wipe a tear away from her eye.

After the applause subsided, music began to play while a dance floor appeared seemingly out of nowhere. Gemma and Kiera jumped out of their seats to have a little fun, and they wanted Emma to join them. As she got out of her seat, Heather stopped her.

"Emma, those videos are wonderful. We have struggled to breathe new life into my brand for so long, and you did it. You really did it. I am so thrilled that you have done this. Thank you. You're just amazing."

At first, Emma didn't know how to respond. Then she realized what she wanted to say, "Heather, thank you. Your words mean so very much. I have been so nervous about this. I am thrilled that you are happy with the outcome. I truly couldn't have done this without my friends and Maxwell. This is something that I never dreamed I would do. I just thought I would carry on with baking, as I always have. I love it, and that's why I did it."

Heather smiled at her honest response, "Well, your passion shows. Thank you for doing this for us."

And then she lifted a glass of champagne while handing Emma one. "Cheers to a wonderful new chapter for both of us. Thank you, Emma!"

The ladies clinked glasses, took sips, and smiled at each other. Something told Emma that this was the beginning of another great friendship.

Gemma and Kiera didn't take long to pull Emma onto the dance floor. The music was pumping. Considering how her day had started, she felt fantastic right now. Great things were happening with her career, which she felt immensely proud of, she was with her wonderful friends in an amazing city, and for the first time, she felt free.

She danced as if she had no care in the world while letting the music and dance beats wash over her. Every once in a while, she would have a fleeting thought that she wished Miles were here to celebrate this with her, but she quickly pushed that away. He would be here if he wanted to be.

The threesome danced for quite a long time. It felt exhilarating to all, as they had been so focused on the many aspects of this campaign for weeks and months. Soon Heather, Jonathan, and Maxwell joined them along with many others, filling the dance floor.

After a while, Maxwell danced to Emma and leaned in to tell her something in her ear, "I guess there's no need to dance on tables tonight, huh?"

She laughed and said, "Well, the night is still young!"

As they moved, the thin strap of Emma's dress slipped off her shoulder. Ever so subtly, Maxwell reached over and put it back in place. This sent a shiver down her spine. There was something about his touch that was so powerful to her.

Soon, the music turned a little slower. The sounds of a new song by John Mayer came over the speakers. It was one that Emma liked called *"Not Myself,"* which she had felt so often since her move to New York.

Maxwell moved in, and they began slow dancing to the song. The feeling in both of their bodies was immediately electric, but neither said anything. They just kept dancing and staring into each other's eyes.

The strains of the music and lyrics rang out, *"Would you want me when I'm not myself? Wait it out till I am someone else…In time, will come around. I always do for you."*

When the lyrics *"I always do for you"* sang out, Maxwell pulled her closer to him. He whispered into her ear, "I'll be here for you when you're ready. I know your heart is with him, but I'm here when you are ready."

Emma was stunned yet profoundly touched by his words. She was attracted to him, but this felt like so much more than that. She stared into his eyes and slowly nodded, "Yes."

Here, on the dance floor, amongst friends and co-workers, she felt she shouldn't say anything more. It wasn't the right time.

The song ended, and the beats turned back up. The floor was once again filled with dancers. They decided to take a break and grab a drink. After chatting with each other and a few others, Emma leaned into Maxwell and whispered, "Any chance you want to get out of here?"

She surprised herself as much as him, but he immediately said, "Yes."

Even at this late hour, it was quite a long drive from Central Park to Emma's apartment. Luckily, Maxwell had a driver for the night, so they slipped unnoticed into his car and were on their way quickly.

Emma leaned in and kissed Maxwell as soon as they were settled in the back seat. After quite a passionate moment, she said, "I thought I owed you a surprise kiss since you did that to me last night."

He laughed at her comment but welcomed her loving, eye-opening move.

He leaned in and kissed her back, "Well, that is the kind of surprise I could get used to." They made out with each other the whole car ride back to her apartment.

She was completely taken with Maxwell. He was strong, smart, patient, and so supportive of her. This turned her on immensely.

Was she thinking of Miles? Perhaps but every time he crept into her mind, she pushed it away because he had hurt her. Again.

This was her time to live without hanging onto the shadow of their love. If what his mother said was true, their relationship was truly over.

He was with Izzy, and now, she could be with Maxwell. For tonight at the very least.

They walked into her apartment, knowing where the night would likely lead.

Emma dropped her handbag, kissed Maxwell, and asked him if he would like some wine. He agreed and wandered into the living room.

She popped into the kitchen to grab a bottle of red and two glasses. As she did, the red light of their answering machine was blinking. It was late on a Saturday night, so she thought it was odd.

She pushed play on the message button and could only recall hearing her mother's voice saying, "Emma, you need to come home. Grammy's had another stroke."

The wine glasses slipped from Emma's hand and shattered onto the floor, just like her heart.

She had to go home. She had to be with her family. Now.

CHAPTER 22

HOME AGAIN

" Family always comes first."

The cold wind blowing into her face felt refreshing. After two very long flights from New York to Portland and one very long car ride to the coast, she needed to feel this. Tears of worry slowly fell down her cheeks.

Grammy was not yet conscious, and so they had reason to worry. This was her second stroke in less than two years. They didn't know yet if she would recover.

Emma's mother was a mess. Of course, she was. This was such a hard thing to watch your parent go through. Caroline couldn't bear to leave her mother's side.

Emma had come home to The Glass House for a quick shower. She had slept as much as she could on the flights, but adrenaline was still pumping through her body. She could only recall Maxwell running into the kitchen when he heard the sound of breaking glass.

It was impossible not to hear the message in the small apartment, but Emma's reaction still startled him. Tears immediately began streaming down her face, and he could easily see the devastation she was feeling.

He cleaned up the glass as best he could as Emma went to pack a bag and change her clothes. Miraculously, he could still get the hired car back to her apartment to rush her to the airport.

Before she knew it, she was on the first flight out of JFK, and she had Maxwell to thank for taking care of her. She was a mess, only thinking and worrying about her Grammy and mother.

He left her at the airline check-in while he made her promise to call him as soon as she arrived home. He would let her roommates know what happened. He also reassured her not to worry about work. Getting Emma home was the only thing that mattered right now.

So, here she was. Standing in the cold wind, allowing the ocean breeze to blow across her tear-stained face. With her eyes closed, facing the water, she let her sadness wash over her like the waves that were endlessly rolling in.

After a few moments, she opened her eyes and allowed herself to take in that she was here. She was home. A far cry from New York City but remarkable nonetheless. Emma turned and looked up at her home. Admiring its beauty and realizing how much she had missed being here.

Slowly, she made her way inside and into her old room. It felt the same, yet it also felt a little foreign to her. However,

Emma didn't have time to dwell on that for too long. She needed to get to the hospital to be with Grammy.

She was on her way after a quick shower and a fresh change of clothes. A wave of worry hit her as soon as she got to the hospital.

Emma was not prepared to see her grandmother when she walked into the hospital room. She was overwhelmed at the sight of so many wires and machines trying to help her Grammy stay alive. Even worse, she could tell that the stroke had impacted the left side of her body as her limbs lay eerily still yet, limp and drooping.

Her face was pale, and her facial features seemed so sallow. It was a far cry from the normal flushness of her face that always seemed so alive and vibrant.

Tears immediately stung Emma's eyes, and she caught her breath. The sound of her gasp made her mother look up from staring at Grammy.

Caroline quickly jumped out of her chair and took Emma into her arms.

Emma could see the heaviness of emotion in her mom's eyes, which scared her. Grammy wasn't ok this time. The longer she was unconscious, the more worrisome the impact of the stroke may be.

They hugged for a long time before her mother led her out into the hallway to chat.

"She has been like this for too long. The doctors say that she should have woken up by now. It's scaring me. This is the second stroke. I don't know if she will wake up this time," Caroline rambled through her worrisome thoughts. This scared Emma as she wasn't prepared for her mother to respond like this.

The last time Grammy had a stroke, her mom was full of hope and confident that everything would be fine.

Overall, she had been right, but this time her confidence had waned, and it was showing.

"Mom, where are the doctors? How often are they checking on her? What happened?" She knew she was asking too many questions at once, but she wanted answers.

Now that she was here, guilt washed over her for being so far away and not coming home as often as she should have. Asking questions seemed the only way she could show she cared.

They continued to walk down a long, endless hallway to a visitor seating area. Caroline explained that she found her mother in the hallway, just outside the kitchen. She had been baking bread and seemed to be improving each day, so Caroline had let her guard down a little. She ran to the store while Rosie baked some bread. It had been a good start to the day.

Then she came home to find her mother in the hallway, unconscious and barely breathing. Luckily, the ambulance arrived quickly and stabilized her with oxygen before whisking her to the hospital.

Emma could tell that her mother was racked with guilt for leaving Grammy alone.

"Mom, I can see that you feel bad about leaving her. Don't do that to yourself. It's not your fault. It likely would have happened even with you standing right next to her."

"Emma, I do feel guilty. I'm not leaving her side. I never should have in the first place. She would have never done that to me." her mother explained.

"Please don't say that, Mom," Emma said as she openly cried. "Grammy was always happy baking, and I'm sure she was happy right up until that happened. Please don't be so hard on yourself. And you do need a break. Why don't you go home and get some rest? I'm here now. I promise I won't leave."

At first, Caroline objected, but perhaps because of her relief at seeing her daughter, she suddenly realized she was extremely exhausted.

"Ok, I'll go home. But just for a few hours. And you call me the moment she wakes up or if anything changes, ok?" she spoke sternly to Emma.

"Mom, I will. Now go get some rest. You need it. I'm right here waiting for her to wake up. She'll be fine. I love you."

Suddenly, as Emma looked at her mother, she noticed how she had aged. It seemed like overnight, but it likely happened while she was exhaustingly caring for Grammy.

This also made Emma feel extremely guilty. Her mom never mentioned how tired she felt. Emma was so caught up in her own life that she probably wouldn't have even taken it to heart if her mom had been honest.

She wrapped her arms around her mother and held her tightly.

"Mom, I'm so sorry I haven't been here for you both. I wish I had known how hard this had been on you. But I'm here now, so that's going to change."

Caroline stood up to leave. "My dear Emma, there is nothing for you to feel bad about. You are living your life and fulfilling your dreams. That is what you are supposed to be doing right now. Yes, it is wonderful to have you home, but God as my witness, I will send you back to New York as soon as everything settles down here. No exceptions."

Emma laughed lightly through her tears and stood up next to her mother. They walked arm in arm as they returned to Grammy's room so Caroline could collect her things.

These three women had been through a lot, but they would get through this. Together.

CHAPTER 23

HEALING

"Wounds heal, but scars are forever."

Perhaps it was because Emma's body was now wired for east coast time, but over the coming weeks, she would stay overnight at the hospital while Caroline would sit with Grammy during the day.

Exhaustion was a silly word for how tired they felt. The doctors said very little about why Rosie wasn't waking up. They only mentioned that being unconscious for this long is sometimes how the body knows to heal.

Emma kept in touch with her roommates, and thankfully, there wasn't much she needed to do for the video campaign since filming had wrapped. It was more or less about marketing and PR now.

This was Gemma's new forte since leaving the fashion world behind, and she was all over it. Kiera just had to keep her in line and focused. They were a pretty powerful team.

Maxwell hadn't reached out except for a brief phone call when Emma first arrived. He knew she needed to be with her family and didn't push. He missed her, but this was so much more important.

So, day after endless day, Emma would watch her grandmother lay in stillness. She believed Grammy could hear her, so she talked to her quite a bit. She read to her, kept her updated on the latest Hollywood gossip, and talked to her about her life in New York. She also spoke endlessly about her fond memories of growing up with Grammy.

The nurses encouraged her to keep talking. They had limited scientific proof but believed patients in comas could hear what was happening around them. It was reassuring to hear that they recognized the voices of their loved ones.

Finally, one evening something changed. Just as Emma was dosing off in her chair beside Grammy's bedside, she thought she felt movement.

She had made it a habit to hold on to her grandmother's hand as she sat next to her. The stillness of her body was sometimes eerie.

So, when she thought she felt her hand move, Emma quickly opened her eyes. "Grammy, can you hear me? If you can, try to squeeze my hand."

Emma leaned in closer to her bedside, staring intently. Her eyes moved back and forth from her grandmother's face to her hand. Nothing.

Just when she thought it was her imagination, she felt a very slight, weak squeeze of her finger. This time, she definitely felt her grandmother move. "Grammy, it's Emma. Can you hear me?"

She was now standing next to the bed, willing some sort of movement or expression across Rosie's very still face.

"Grammy, can you hear me? I'm right here. I want to talk to you. I believe you can hear me. I just want you to wake up."

As if Emma couldn't believe what she was seeing, Grammy's eyelids began to flutter as if she was desperately trying to open her eyes. Emma also felt another weak squeeze in her hand. And then, nothing.

Almost as if those few movements exhausted all of her grandmother's energy. It still gave Emma hope. She waited a few moments longer and then pressed the call button for the nurse.

When the nurse came into the room and heard what had happened, they explained to Emma that it was a good sign. Sometimes even the slightest movement meant that the brain was healing. The nurse encouraged Emma to keep talking to her grandmother.

That night, Emma barely slept. She kept watching over Rosie, talking to her while always holding her hand. The hours passed, and she felt so weary.

Around 7 am, Caroline came in to relieve Emma so she could go home and rest. "Good morning, ladies. I think it's going to be a beautiful day to wake up, Mom!" she called out cheerfully.

Emma quickly told her mother what had happened that night. She explained that she had barely slept, hoping Grammy would wake up. Just as they were chatting, they looked over, and there was Rosie staring back at them.

Tears immediately came to their eyes, thankful that she was awake. Her mouth was dry, but she was trying to form words. Still so weak, she hadn't the strength to even whisper.

They ran over to either side of the bed, each taking a hand, and Emma began to speak first, "Oh, Grammy! You're awake. We have missed you so much."

Then Caroline began to chatter, "That was quite a scare you gave us. I've missed seeing your beautiful eyes. We are so happy to see you, Mom."

Emma had quickly hit the call button, and soon there was a flourish of activity in Grammy's room. They would run several tests to see the amount of brain activity and movement Grammy had. It would take some time, so Caroline encouraged Emma to go home and get some rest.

"We will need our energy to care for Grammy when she comes home. Now, go get some sleep. We will see you in a couple of hours. I'll call if anything changes."

Emma agreed and left to head home. The sun was shining brightly. It was a beautiful day on the coast. When she arrived back at the Glass House, she felt like walking the beach despite being exhausted.

She headed down the side path to the beach to enjoy the sand, breeze, and sunshine. It was still chilly, but the sun's warmth kept it from being too cold.

After a while, she sat on a piece of driftwood about half a mile from the house. She was silently praying and giving gratitude that her grandmother was awake. Feeling very emotional, Emma just let the tears fall down her cheeks.

For weeks, this was something she hadn't allowed herself to do. They were tears full of thankfulness and relief. She knew Grammy wouldn't live forever, but she didn't want her to go just yet.

Emma had been sitting there for quite a while when a little caramel-colored puppy came bounding down the beach and jumped in her lap. She was overcome with surprise and soon laughed as the pup covered her in happy licks. He was so full of energy and seemed to want to be friends.

"Well, where did you come from, little guy? You don't even have a collar on. Do you belong to someone?" she asked as she looked around her and far down the beach to see if anyone else was there.

At first, she saw no one. Then she continued staring down the coast, fighting through the glare of the sunshine blocking her view.

Then she heard his voice, "Jake! Jake! Jake! Where did you go?"

Emma saw Miles walking quickly down the beach with a leash dangling from his hands. The happy smiles from the puppy kisses quickly disappeared from her face. All she felt now was hurt.

The puppy had settled quite comfortably into her lap. He wasn't budging anytime soon, which made Emma laugh on the inside.

On the outside, her face was emotionless. Only her eyes showed the pain that she was feeling in her heart.

Miles knew this when he came up and saw her. He sat beside her, took a deep breath, and finally said, "Hi."

Emma continued to pet Jake, who had nuzzled closer into her while spontaneously licking her chin every few moments. His little tail wiggled as he looked back and forth from her to his master.

She wouldn't look directly at Miles, but she finally responded, "When did you get a dog?"

He knew she was upset. He was mad at himself too. "I got him about two weeks ago. I figured I needed something to keep me grounded since I got home. A dog seemed like a good answer. I don't know, though. We will see if he ends up liking me."

She continued to look out in the distance at the waves rolling in, refusing to face Miles.

"You didn't tell *me* that you were coming home. Why not?"

He reached over and petted Jake's chin as he answered, "I didn't want to have to tell you. I had hoped that I would be able to stay in the Navy, but I fucked up. Pretty bad. And they kicked me out."

She was stunned, "They kicked you out of the Navy? What in the hell happened?"

Now she was looking at him intensely. She wanted answers.

Miles hung his head low, running his fingers nervously through the sand beneath them. "I fucked up. I told you that. What else do you need to know?"

"Um, everything? When did this happen? Did you know when you were with me in New York?"

Jake tilted his head up and licked her face as she said this. She pushed him down but continued to pet the rambunctious pup.

He waited a moment before speaking, "I did know that I was in trouble when I was with you in New York. I didn't yet know that they would discharge me, though. Some procedures have to be followed. Right now, I'm considered to be Dishonorably Discharged, but if I don't fuck anything else up, they may change that in a year or so."

"Miles, what did you do?" Emma asked anxiously.

She not only felt hurt and confused but completely left out of his life. She loved him and thought he shared the same feelings. *Why wouldn't he come to her to explain what happened? Why wasn't he open with her?* It hurt immensely to feel shut out.

He continued to stare down at the sand, not wanting to meet the look of anger and confusion that he knew was in her eyes.

He decided to tell her everything.

"I was having a rough time out at sea. I missed home. I missed you more than I ever thought I would. I didn't feel like myself. I felt trapped on a ship, doing things I never wanted. We were docked for a few days in Italy, and I became a complete disaster. A few of the guys on the ship took me out to some bars where I drank a lot."

"One night, I just got rip-roaring drunk. I stumbled out of a bar. Only God knows where I was, and I ran into some shady guys. Before I knew it, we were yelling at each other, and then someone threw a punch. I beat some guys up pretty badly, and I got all messed up too. The guys I went out with tried to break up the fight, but it blew up in our faces. The cops came, we were thrown in jail for the night, and when we were released the next day, I was charged with disorderly conduct. That's a serious offense in the Navy. When I saw you in New York, I was on probation until my hearing."

Emma just stared at him in shock. She couldn't imagine Miles in a fight. He was always the one that had a level head. He didn't drink excessively and was never the guy to cause problems.

He continued to explain. "There were several times when we were together that I wanted to tell you. But I'm embarrassed. I thought maybe there was a chance that they would let this go. I've never been in trouble like this, before the Navy and during my time serving. When I left you that night, I thought I was going back out to sea. The next morning, I was told to go home. It sucks. I really fucked things up for myself, and I didn't want to drag you into it. So, I just came home."

She wanted to be mad at him. She wanted to tell him off, but she wasn't angry. She felt sorry for him. Emma reached out and took Miles's hand, "Look at me, please."

He slowly looked up and saw that she wasn't mad.

"I love you, Miles. That doesn't mean I love you only when things are going great. I love you no matter what we are going through. You should have told me. I want you to tell me these things. Instead, I was angry when I learned you were back home. I couldn't figure out, for the life of me, why you wouldn't share this with me."

He looked her deeply in the eyes, "I know. I am so sorry. I wanted to tell you. I wish I would have called you, but I felt so shitty, and the last thing I wanted to do was tell you how much I messed everything up."

Emma could feel herself getting angry again. "So, you just decided to shut me out? That doesn't feel like love to me. I was so hurt when I found out that you came home. And then I had to find out from your mom that you are dating Izzy! When I had to come out here to be with Grammy, in the back of my mind, I kept hoping that I wouldn't run into the two of you together."

Miles felt awful. He started reaching for Jake so that they could go. He just wanted to get away from her because he knew the pain he was causing. The dog wanted nothing to do with him. He pulled back and burrowed deeper into Emma's lap.

"He doesn't want to go with you. Why don't you want to talk to me about this?" she spat at him angrily.

The wind began to blow harder, and the warm sun faded quickly while they talked. Miles stood up, "Come on, Jake. Let's go."

The puppy looked up at him and hesitantly went with his master, who had been tugging on his leash.

"I do love you, Emma. I have since the day I met you and probably always will. You don't deserve to be with a fuck-up like me. You should be with someone like Maxwell, who knows what the hell they are doing with their life. You're on your way. You don't need me to get in the way of that."

He turned to walk away while Emma called after him, "You've got it all wrong! I love you, damn it! I want to help you through this! Please don't shut me out!"

Miles kept walking. By now, the puppy was excited to run down the beach. It was a good excuse not to turn back. Emma didn't know that walking away was the hardest thing for him to do. He had tears streaming down his face as he continued to move away from her.

What he said to her was true. She deserved better. She deserved someone who could love her, care for her, and know what the hell they were doing in life. That wasn't Miles. He didn't know what he was doing or where he was going. He only got the damn dog to give him a reason to get out of bed every morning.

He had shit to figure out, and he didn't want to make her suffer through that. Miles was in a shitty place in his life, so if he had to let her go to get through it, then that's what he would do.

CHAPTER 24

BRUISED

"But still in love."

The next several weeks were a blur. Emma spent every waking moment at the hospital, willing her grandmother to heal and get stronger.

She forced herself to push away thoughts of Miles. He just kept walking farther away from her as she called after him that day on the beach. She was just as hurt as before, yet the pain only cut deeper afterward.

Emma wanted to be there for him, to help him feel better about what happened. She couldn't imagine what he was going through. She loved him so much that she felt the hurt that he must have been experiencing.

However, he didn't believe that. It astonished her that he was trying to push her into Maxwell's arms. Maybe he didn't know what love was. She told herself she didn't have time to worry about those things. If he didn't want her, she would have to move on.

Well, that's what her head told her. Emma's heart told her differently. Her heart was broken, but she was still entirely in love with Miles. It was a sick twist of fate, full of pain.

Her solace was when she was with her Grammy. With her, she didn't think about what happened with Miles. She was determined to help her grandmother get better.

Emma only struggled with her feelings when she tried to sleep. Then the thoughts would swirl in her head, and she would have to fight the temptation to call him.

As the weeks passed, the urge of wanting to talk to him started to dwindle. She had concluded that she shouldn't want to be with someone that didn't want to confide in her.

The anger and hurt didn't fade as quickly. It was almost as if her heart had a little part permanently broken away. She knew she didn't want to carry the pain around, but she also couldn't let go of her love for him.

It was torture. A never-ending mind game of love vs. hurt and anger. She was so very frustrated.

In a way, it was a blessing that she had to focus so much time on her family. She was either with Grammy or taking care of the bakery while her mom helped at the hospital.

The encouragement that Rosie was receiving from her family was paying off. She now walked with a cane to assist with the weaker side of her body, and her one eye had limited vision due to complications from the stroke. Yet, she was regaining strength quickly, so she was determined to go home as soon as possible. Caroline and Emma were just as determined to push her toward that goal. Home is where they all felt they needed to be.

Late one evening, Emma was locking up the bakery and preparing to go to the hospital to relieve her mom. She was keenly aware that the local bar was just a few doors down.

This is where Miles's mother and Izzy worked. She hadn't stepped foot in there since she had been home. It hurt to realize that Miles was interested in her former friend. Why would she want to be around people who hurt her so much?

As she pulled the front door to the shop closed and turned the key to lock it, she heard Miles's voice behind her. A new feeling of fear mixed with anger shot through her body as he warmly said, "Hi."

Emma was still furious but didn't quite understand why she felt fear. Her instinct said to walk away from him.

She had only ever felt an attraction to him, but this time was very different. These new emotions were overwhelming any feeling of love that she had for him.

Miles kept glancing from Emma's face to the ground. His hands were shoved into his front jeans pockets, and he kept shifting the weight of his body from side to side. He was nervous.

Emma just looked at him, not knowing what to think. He could see the confusion on her face, so he continued to talk, "I know that I'm probably the last person you want to see right now, but I want to talk to you. I haven't been able to stop thinking about that last time I saw you."

Emma grimaced at this comment and shot back, "Funny because the only thing I keep replaying is watching you walk away from me as I called after you."

Miles nodded slowly at her words, "Well, you got me there. I can see that you're mad, and I don't blame you. I'm really mad at myself right now for many reasons. I'm not trying to make excuses. I couldn't talk to you anymore then, so I just walked away. I am sorry."

She shrugged and said, "Thanks for the apology. I should get going now."

Emma turned to walk down the street to her car, but Miles caught her arm as she walked by.

"Emma, please. Can we talk?" he pleaded.

This is where the fear that she was feeling intensified. Something was off. She just felt like she wanted to get away from him.

"Miles, I don't think now is a good time. I have a lot going on with Grammy. And you need time to figure stuff out for yourself. Really, thanks for the apology, but I have to go."

Hearing her painful, truthful words, his hand dropped from her arm. He could tell that she wanted to get away from him, and as much as it hurt, he knew how she was feeling.

Emma had been looking over her shoulder at Miles and turned quickly towards him to walk past him after she spoke.

She didn't realize that Izzy had come out of the bar and was barreling right toward them.

Emma bumped right into Izzy, which startled them both.

Izzy glared angry eyes at Emma as she suddenly snapped, "Watch where you're going!"

Emma just looked back and forth from Izzy to Miles and kept walking.

"Wait!" Izzy called after her with an evil smirk across her face, "I might as well tell you both at the same time. I'm pregnant."

Emma momentarily stopped in her tracks. She now understood the fear that she was feeling previously. She was simply crestfallen.

Miles was going to be the father to Izzy's baby.

She just turned and walked to her car. Emma had nothing to say.

CHAPTER 25

BROKEN

"Let that shit go."

To say Emma was stunned was putting it mildly. Actually, when she really stopped to think about it, of course, Izzy would be careless enough to get pregnant.

But Miles. How could he? She had given him more credit than that.

They were always careful when they had sex. It wasn't even a discussion. She was on birth control, and he used a condom.

What the actual fuck?

She didn't care.

Rephrase.

She couldn't care.

Emma had to focus on helping her grandmother regain her strength, and then she had to get back to New York. That was it. These were the two goals that she put in front of her.

She didn't realize it at the time, but her heart knew more than her head. The fear she felt after that day at the beach was a warning. Miles was no longer on the same path toward a future together. She needed to be focused on her life and her future. He had clearly made his choice when he slept with Izzy.

For the next month, she worked tirelessly at the bakery while making sure to help her Grammy however she could.

Her mother couldn't handle everything, especially when Rosie came home. So, Emma focused on setting up a daily nurse and physical therapist to come to the house.

Emma planned to come home to the Glass House as much as possible to help her family. As for Miles, her head and her heart were finally aligned.

She needed to return to the city to focus on her growing career. She was choosing to shut her heart down and protect it from any more pain from Miles. Anything she ever thought would happen with him was lost.

Emma needed to only think of where she would go next. She had faithful friends and someone that wanted her, and only her, in NYC.

On the day she left, she moved like a robot through the airport. She didn't even really remember saying goodbye to Caroline and Rosie. Emma felt like it was a good time to go back, and they didn't stop her. They knew little of the details, but it was obvious that she was suffering from a broken heart.

As she settled into her seat on the plane, she gazed out of the tiny window. It was an early flight, and she peered out at the low mountain range in the distance. It was a colorful view, covered in pink and orange from the sunrise yet mysteriously filtered by a white haze from the cold morning air.

Only, she really didn't see the beauty that was before her. She could only see Izzy's face in front of her, angrily, sarcastically, proudly pronouncing her physical status. Pregnant. She was pregnant with Miles's baby. What a moment it must have been for the two of them.

Not that she spent much time thinking about it, but she always imagined having babies with him. Boy or girl, it didn't matter. She just wanted to have a family with the love of her life. Emma knew now that was not to be.

Suddenly, it hit her like a bolt of lightning striking from a deep dark sky. The pain seared through her chest like fire, and the tears finally fell like a waterfall overflowing from heavy rain.

She was lost. They were no longer meant to be.

It didn't have to be this way. He could have been honest. He could have stayed with her in New York. She would have helped him. She would have listened and supported his pain.

But it wasn't to be. He chose to push her away when he likely needed her most. She had no way of knowing that. She only felt the distance that he put between them.

So, she was choosing to put a greater physical distance between them. She would be on the east coast while he, with his growing family, remained on the west coast.

As her plane soared into the sky, it jetted out over the Pacific Ocean. The jet soared quickly upward and then circled back to land to head eastward. She gazed down at the coastline with awe at its raw, undisturbed beauty.

Miles stood at the same time on that very beach and let the wind painfully whip into his face. It made the tears that streamed down his cheeks feel nonexistent.

He was going to be a father. A baby. He was going to have a family. Not the way that he had dreamed of, but he was going to be a dad. This was something he had always wanted. Of course, he always thought it would be with Emma, but that was ok.

Maybe he knew more than he thought. Miles had been pushing Emma away for a while now. Physically and in his head. Perhaps this was meant to be.

She deserved better than he could give her. Maxwell was who was best for her. He could see that when they were together in New York.

Izzy was quite a handful, but she would come around once the baby was here. She would calm down and be the best mother to their baby. He had to believe this to be true. Otherwise, why would this be happening to him now?

He looked up just as a jet plane zoomed overhead. For a moment, he thought that perhaps Emma was on that plane, but what were the chances? He thought she would still be here taking care of her family. He had time to smooth things over with her.

He just needed to focus on Izzy right now. He had to get his head together enough to figure out what they would do next.

His relationship with Emma would have to wait. He felt that letting her go months before was the right thing, and now he knew why. It didn't help the pain he felt in his heart, but that would just have to be ignored for now.

He needed to focus on his baby.

His life forever changed when the words poured out of Izzy's mouth, but now it was all that mattered. This baby was everything.

Emma would be ok. He would be ok. The baby would be what pushed him forward.

As the plane reached higher in the sky, she felt broken as she gazed down at the beach.

Feeling sad yet hopeful, he gazed up at the sky.

Both had tears streaming down their faces, not knowing that they were indirectly staring at one another from a distance.

Each of them had yet to truly realize just how much life would change forever as they knew it.

CHAPTER 26

NEW HORIZON

" Just keep looking ahead."

Maxwell was thrilled to know that Emma was coming back to New York. He hadn't wanted to pressure her, but he really missed having her around.

While working on the campaign for Heather's Bakery, she was constantly at his office since the video shoots took place there. She was the bright spot in his day, and he always made a point to interact with her somehow. Meeting her made him realize how long it had been since someone really intrigued him. He liked it.

The moment Emma landed back in New York, she met her roommates at the bar. Sam welcomed her with a huge hug and a large glass of Pinot Grigio. He also missed his friend.

Kiera and Gemma had updated him on her status when they came in, so he knew she had been through a lot.

The roommates squealed with delight while they jumped up and down as she walked towards their table. They had truly missed her.

As far as Miles was concerned, Kiera was surprised by his actions, and Gemma just wanted to kick his ass.

"All men are assholes, Emma. It just took him a little longer to show it," Gemma exclaimed as she took a long sip of her drink.

Kiera nodded along with this comment, "She's right. It's best to just stick with us."

And with that, their conversation was off and running. They had this way of bantering back and forth, holding three different conversations, yet never losing track of what each one was saying. Sometimes it hurt Sam's brain to try and keep up. He smiled at their chatter as he delivered another round. He had missed this, too.

Gemma was dating someone new at the office. It was a hot and steamy affair that she knew would likely not go anywhere, but she was having fun.

Kiera was unusually quiet about her current dating situation, making the other two even more suspicious about something bigger happening. And then there was Emma, sitting there with her heart completely and utterly shattered.

The drinks flowed along with their talking, and honestly, they didn't want to ruin the vibe, so Kiera changed the subject.

"So, Emma, you may not know this since you bolted right after the launch party, but your videos are a HUGE success! Heather is more than pleased with the results and wants you to continue to make more recipe videos. What do you think?"

Emma felt excited about something for the first time in a while. Her personal life had been so overwhelming that she forgot what it felt like to focus on her career.

She smiled, "That is fantastic news. I had no idea. I suppose I have been so absorbed in all my drama lately that I hadn't given it much thought. I mean, I guess I would be open to it."

Gemma jumped in, "Of course, you're open to it, darling! You have a budding career on TV or computers, or wherever they are putting these things. You have to do this! And I will be there with you every step of the way. I insist!"

This made everyone laugh, and Emma shot back, "Oh, I know you will!"

With that decided, they continued to chat about what they would do next and how soon Emma would be back at the agency.

Kiera also quickly explained a new opportunity, "So, speaking of TV, there has been quite a bit of buzz about a new cable network that is starting. It's called Culinary Television Network, or CTV for short. A producer friend of mine really liked your videos and thinks there may be a place for you there. We should talk about it once you're settled. I don't want to overwhelm you all at once, but I'm very excited about it."

Once again, Gemma piped up, "Excited about the show or the producer? Kiera, you two have been quite inseparable lately. So what do you have to share about Will?"

Kiera could feel the embarrassed heat rising in her cheeks, and she stumbled over her words at first, "I don't have anything to share. We work well together, ok? I can't help that I think he's hot. We work together so nothing can happen. Whatever. You're so nosy, Gem."

She was never so relieved to see Maxwell walk into the bar. She knew that all eyes would go back to Emma, and she was perfectly happy about that.

Even though Emma's heart was shattered and her head was full of thoughts of Miles, she was delighted to see Maxwell.

He quickly approached their table, his green eyes beaming directly at Emma. This made everyone smile as he began to speak, "Well, aren't you a sight for sore eyes? I have missed seeing you here, Emma. How are you?"

She stood up and gave him a rather long, intimate hug as she answered, "Well, hello there, stranger. I'm ok. How are you? Want to join us?"

He laughed at her question, "Like you even have to ask. Of course, I would. There's nothing better than sitting back and listening to the three of you banter back and forth."

Gemma chimed in, "Well, sit down and get comfy. We haven't been able to do this in months. We may be here for bloody days!"

The whole group broke out into laughter. The drinks and conversation flowed easily, and Maxwell beamed the entire time.

Sitting next to Emma, he casually put his hand in hers underneath the table as the night wore on. At first, surprised, she found that she was actually enjoying the simple gesture of comfort. She needed it now more than ever.

The evening wrapped up with everyone realizing that a workday lay quickly ahead of them.

While walking to the exit and waving goodbye to Sam, Maxwell gently took Emma by the arm and pulled her aside. "I don't want to pressure you at all because I know you have been through a lot. Yet, I have to admit that I haven't been able to stop thinking about you. We were in such a good place before you had to leave, and well, I hope you still feel the same. Can I take you on a proper date when you're ready?"

She couldn't help but smile at the ramble of words that he shared with her. Emma had realized that evening how much she had missed him, too.

"You sound so formal, Maxwell. You know that we will be working together again, so…I guess you should take me out before I start back. What about this weekend?"

That answer startled them both. Was she ready for that? It was just a date, so why not?

Maxwell smiled back at her, trying to contain the sheer happiness he felt hearing her answer, "This weekend it is. I'll call you with the details." She nodded her head in agreement and started to walk to the door.

"Emma," he whispered her name, "I really have missed you."

And then he took her hand, brought it to his lips, and gently kissed it. She felt a shiver up her spine, "Good night, Maxwell."

Saturday came along quickly. He promptly called and left a brief message on their machine that only said, "Dress elegantly and be prepared for a late night."

This sent the ladies into a frenzy of excitement. After several outfit changes and Gemma's help with hair and makeup, Emma was finally ready for their special evening.

Her hair fell in soft, chocolate waves that framed her face. She chose a simple black sleeveless sheath dress with a boat line neck. Kiera loaned her a beautiful pearl necklace that accentuated the elegance of the dress.

She felt like a princess because she came from a world where dressing up was wearing a button-down shirt with a pair of jeans. It was definitely a Breakfast At Tiffany's kind of moment for her.

When Maxwell arrived, looking at her literally took his breath away. He knew she was beautiful, but tonight, she was stunning.

A car was waiting for them on the street, and before they knew it, they were off into the New York night. They arrived at a restaurant in the West Village and took an elevator to the top floor of what seemed to be a very quiet building.

When the doors opened, Emma was overwhelmingly surprised at what was before her.

They stepped out onto an open courtyard filled with white lights, greenery, gorgeous, fragrant white flowers, and an expansive view of the city. She felt like she was in one giant twinkle light. It felt like a fairy tale.

As they walked forward, a single dining table was set at the edge of the rooftop patio, draped in gorgeous silver linen and accentuated with two simple, tall candlesticks. It was magical.

Soft music played in the background, and a lovely lady seemed to appear out of nowhere to lead them to their table. Maxwell had reserved the entire rooftop for their date. Emma was stunned.

As they settled into their seats, Emma noticed a patio seating area off to the side, complete with a glowing fire. He had thought of every detail for their first date.

She started feeling overwhelmed and out of place since she had never experienced anything quite like this before.

He sensed this and quickly put her at ease, "I know it may seem like a lot, but I thought I would treat you to a special way to see the city. I also wanted a night with you all to myself. Sounds selfish, I know, but I really have missed you, Emma."

She smiled at him as he continued to speak, "You were gone so long. While you were away, I realized how much I enjoyed having you in my life. I didn't expect it, but somehow you gently became the best part of my day. It was a gift, so tonight, I want to give you a little bit of that gift back. Cheers to what is hopefully the first of many nights together. I mean, unless I mess this up completely."

While talking, he had raised a glass of champagne, and she met his glass with a gentle clink.

This was unlike anything she had ever experienced. Being there with Maxwell made it even more special. As she took a sip, it was easy to begin to relax.

"Maxwell, this is spectacular. I highly doubt there is any way to mess up this evening. Thank you for doing this. I feel so special. Cheers." she happily responded as they clinked glasses again.

They enjoyed their dinner as the low patio lights gleamed and the fire gently burned off in the distance. Looking out onto the New York skyline from this height was mesmerizing.

Emma loved the beauty of the west coast, but there was nothing like this view. The city twinkled and glowed everywhere you looked, and on this particular evening, the moon shone brightly over their heads. It was a divine sight to take in.

After dinner, the server brought over Manhattans, and they casually walked over to the patio seating. This view highlighted midtown and the Empire State Building strikingly.

Emma gleamed and took a sip of her drink, "Cheers to enjoying Manhattans while looking at this gorgeous view of Manhattan. Well done, Mr. Clayton."

Maxwell couldn't help but smile back at her amusing comment, only to respond with a simple "Cheers."

Soon soft jazz music began playing in the background, and they sat quietly while the live band filled the floor with their sound.

After a few moments, Maxwell stood up and extended his hand to Emma. She accepted, and he led her to an open patio area. As the music continued to play, he took her in his arms, and they easily moved to the music.

She felt entranced. Her head rested on his shoulder as he led her in slow movements to the rhythm of the song. She felt happy. It surprised her how good this felt, and then she realized how long it had been since she felt this way.

The band played for quite a while, which they didn't mind since they were completely happy swaying along in each other's arms. When the music stopped, Emma saw Maxwell gazing down at her. He pulled her in just a little more as their lips met. They both finally gave in to a passionate kiss.

Emma swore that she saw stars as she continued to kiss Maxwell. It felt like a dream. They stood there and kissed for quite a long time as they enjoyed being in each other's arms.

He was so gentle, with one hand on her cheek and the other wrapped around her waist, pulling her into his body. She was suddenly feeling things she hadn't felt in quite a long time.

Finally, Maxwell backed away and said, "I'm sorry if this seems forward, but will you come back to my apartment with me? We don't have to do anything you don't want to. I can't bear for this night to end."

At first, she was taken aback because she hadn't planned on spending the night with him, but as she absorbed his words, she felt good about his suggestion. Maxwell was a friend, well, much more than a friend, and she was so happy to be with him tonight.

Emma hesitated at first, which made Maxwell feel like he had gone too far. He took a step back but didn't break eye contact with her.

She spoke softly, "Well, I didn't expect you to say that, but…yes, I would like to."

Going from the restaurant to Maxwell's apartment was a bit of a blur. She was completely enthralled with him and his kisses. She did recall how he held her close in the elevator and kissed her at every chance.

When they settled into the car waiting on the street, he pulled her close yet again, never letting go of her hand once. It wasn't overbearing, yet instead felt protective and loving.

They finally opened the door to his expansive apartment, which was modern, open, and had large windows overlooking the city. From this vantage point, the view was quite impressive, but Emma could care less. She was focused on every moment with Maxwell.

From what she could sense, he also enjoyed having her with him. He was standing across the room, watching her take in the view from the window as he poured each a glass of wine. He loved watching her genuine reactions to the city.

Maxwell had lived here his entire life, and while he appreciated the sites of the city, it came into vivid color when he saw Emma's response. This was very new to him. He was used to dating women that were only interested in him for his money, his name, or, well, mostly, his money.

With Emma, everything was different. He was drawn to her like a moth to a flame, and tonight, he wanted to capture that burning flame, even if it meant he would get burned. He realized she was madly in love with Miles, but he didn't care.

Emma was beautiful and talented, even if she wasn't yet aware of everything she was meant to be. He was determined to show her and enjoy himself along the way.

Maxwell walked over to her and handed her a glass of Pinot Noir. He took her petite hand into his, and they both looked out onto the city lights.

"You know, I have stood here thousands of times but tonight, the view is more beautiful than I ever recall." he said as he turned to her.

Emma kept staring out into the distance, hearing his words while also hearing her loud, racing heartbeat in her ears. He certainly knew how to make a woman feel important and beautiful.

She kept looking out the window as she sipped from her glass.

"It must be the wine."

He hesitantly released her hand and walked to the stereo to play music. She was surprised to see that it was an actual record turntable and not the ever-modern, trendy CD player that everyone had these days.

Soon she understood why as the beautiful strains of a trumpet and saxophone elegantly played through the speakers.

It was a gorgeous recording of Miles Davis and John Coltrane called *Kind of Blue.* Hauntingly beautiful and easy to dance to, Maxwell walked back to Emma and took her glass from her hands.

He gently set both glasses on a table and swiftly took her back into his arms. They began to dance just as they had on the rooftop, but this time, it was more magnetic and intense.

Maxwell gazed into her eyes, but his hands moved over her body. She felt the heat from his fingertips as they went from her waist and up her back to her dress zipper.

Gently, he opened the back of her dress and pulled it forward so the front fell to her waist. Never breaking eye contact while they continued to slow dance to the music, her dress fell to the floor. She willingly let herself step out of it.

She was dancing with Maxwell in a black lace bra and underwear, still in her patent black heels.

She should have felt exposed and naked, but looking back at him, she felt beautiful and seen. This time it was Emma that kissed Maxwell with deep intensity.

He took her hand and led her back to his bedroom. As he kissed her with a raw passion, she felt her head spin again. With one elegant move, he laid her back on his bed and then stood back to gaze at her body as she lay there.

Maxwell reached up, loosened his tie, and swiftly pulled it off his neck. He unbuttoned his shirt so that she could see his beautifully sculpted chest.

Just when she thought he would finish undressing, he leaned over her on the bed. With his tie in his hand, he straddled her on the bed and gently took both her hands in his. The tie was made of silk, so the cool feel of it was refreshing as he wrapped it around each of her wrists.

He leaned down and kissed her while grinding himself into her with a sexy passion that enthralled her.

As they continued to kiss, feeling the heat rising between them, he lifted her tied hands over her head and attached the rest of the tie to a bar on his headboard.

He could see the look of surprise cross her face as he did this and was quick to reassure her, "Do you trust me?" Emma slowly nodded yes.

He continued, "Then close your eyes and let me show you how to enjoy every moment we have together tonight. I know it won't be easy, but don't open your eyes. I promise that everything I do will only deepen with pleasure as long as you keep your eyes closed. Now, do you still trust me?"

At this point, her heart was beating wildly but in a very good way. She wanted Maxwell and was intrigued by what he was already doing to her.

She could only nod yes, as she closed her eyes and let her head fall back onto the soft pillow beneath her.

She felt Maxwell shift upward, but he was still straddling her. She imagined him taking off his shirt. Then she heard the gentle sound of his belt being removed. A quick shrill of his zipper, and she knew he was removing his pants. It was so amazing how intensified her other senses were just by being unable to see what was happening.

The music began to play a romantic ballad, and the light was low, so she wondered if she could tell what he was doing even if she had opened her eyes.

She didn't have to wonder for very long because all at once, Maxwell was hovering over her, his face very close to hers.

With one hand, he lifted himself just above her so she could feel the warmth of his body on hers. His other hand began to slowly graze from her left arm down to her shoulder to momentarily rest on her face, only to continue down her neck, chest, and breasts. He then allowed his hand to play and entice her ever so teasingly. This made her moan with pleasure as he then kissed her.

Just when she began to enjoy his tongue in her mouth, he moved to her breasts. He had this way of allowing just enough pain with his hands and then his mouth, only to be quickly followed by gentle kisses. It was sweetly torturous, and she was about to lose her mind.

Her hips had naturally begun to move in a motion of wanting. She knew he was naked because she could feel the warmth of his skin on hers. His hardness was impossible to ignore, and while his hands were working magic all over her body, she was showing him with her body how much she wanted him to enter her.

She couldn't tell, but he smiled with pleasure, knowing how much she enjoyed his touch.

At one point, he lifted himself off of her to take in the beauty of her body before him. "I'm not sure if you know this, but your body is amazing."

This made her almost want to open her eyes, but he stopped her, "No, don't open your eyes. Just listen to the sound of my voice. You, lovely Emma, are beautiful. You are sexy beyond anything I could ever imagine, and you have been driving me crazy with longing since the first time I laid eyes on you. I want to pleasure you and allow you to experience what I have felt for you for such a long time. "

And with that, he took his hand and removed her underwear. Gently, swiftly, and lovingly, he entered her, and she gasped with pleasure. Her hands were still tied to the headboard, making her writhe with even more pleasure, knowing she couldn't touch him the way she wanted to.

Knowing they were both ready to explode with pleasure, he reached high above her to release her hands. While he did this, she lifted her head to kiss his chest as she could feel it above her.

All at once, her hands were free to touch him, so she reached at first for his face to pull him in for a kiss and then down to his waist to encourage him to enter her again.

Slowly at first, a rhythmic motion moved them together before they passionately exploded in a moment of ultimate pleasure, which neither truly anticipated.

Out of breath, a little sweaty, and completely satisfied, Maxwell fell to Emma's side to lay beside her. They were both a little surprised by what had just happened.

Was it the drinks, the skyline, or something stronger developing between the two of them? Whatever it was, they both thoroughly enjoyed what had transpired.

They fell asleep easily in each other's arms, with Emma waking first the next morning.

When she opened her eyes, she only saw the back of his head. With one arm resting on his side, she pulled herself into his back and inhaled the scent of the man she loved so much. She closed her eyes, breathed deeply, nestled into the curve of his back, and began to relax. But wait. Something was different.

Her senses were triggered, and she realized that although everything around her was warm, welcoming, and full of sensuality, it was different. Very different.

Emma opened her eyes. It wasn't Miles.

It was Maxwell.

Her mind was sent racing, trying to figure out what she was feeling.

At that exact moment, Maxwell had awoken and embraced her arms still wrapped around him. He loved every moment, yet she was quietly trying not to freak out.

He took a deep breath and turned to face her, holding her gently in his arms, "Well, this is the best way I have woken up in a very long time."

Emma couldn't help but smile at his sweet words. She giggled lightly and leaned her head into his while responding, "Good morning to you, too."

Windows lined the length of the bedroom, and a warm stream of sunshine was just beginning to break through, giving a gentle morning glow to the room. Neither of them wanted to move out of the comfortable bed.

The brief, disorienting moment that Emma had earlier finally passed. She instantly recalled that she was with Maxwell and couldn't help but smile as she remembered the night before.

She was just fine where she was. She only briefly let her mind linger on her past with Miles, and it was only to wish the memory of their heartbreaking love a fond farewell.

He had stopped talking to her long ago, while she made the mistake of thinking he understood what it meant to love someone. He honestly didn't, and she knew that now more than ever.

So, she leaned into the warmth of Maxwell's body and let the morning unfold like the wrinkled sheets on his bed. This was where she was supposed to be.

Did she love Maxwell? She didn't yet know the answer, but she wouldn't stop herself from trying to find out.

Later in the day, she finally crawled out of his bed and stood in front of the immense windows looking out onto the New York horizon.

For a moment, it felt just like being at the Glass House. She felt a tinge of homesickness wash over her. Instead of seeing the gray mist of the ocean waves in front of her, she only saw skyscrapers and the bustling movement of cars below.

Emma suddenly let go of the sadness of missing home, and then with a confident step, she turned to Maxwell and said, "I feel like baking something. Want to join me in the kitchen?"

CHAPTER 27

EAST TO WEST

" Love travels."

From that night on, it seemed that Emma and Maxwell were inseparable. They loved being together, whether working, shooting new video content, having fun out on the town, or, especially, in his bed. There was no in-between.

The trajectory of Emma's career was skyrocketing. Of course, Heather's Bakery was interested in continuing its partnership with her. Contracts quickly followed for her to write a cookbook, a very attractive opportunity to host her own cooking show, and another show to travel around the world to find the most delicious bakeries.

There were times that her head would spin when she thought about how fast everything happened to her career.

Keira became her full-time business manager, and although still heavily tied to Maxwell's agency, Gemma negotiated all publicity events to her exact specifications.

They still shared their same apartment, but Emma was hardly ever there. She had all but officially moved into Maxwell's apartment.

There was this magnetic attraction to him that she could not resist. He was very open with her about how he enjoyed her company. Nights were always the worst for him, as he never liked sleeping alone.

Emma had to fly back to Oregon three months into their relationship to help her mother and grandmother. She would only be gone a week, but Maxwell made it clear that he wasn't happy about the temporary separation.

She offered to have him join her, but he had too many meetings and commitments to reschedule. It would be easier for her to go without him this time.

It wasn't lost on him that she would likely run into Miles. They never mentioned him or the details of what ended their relationship. Honestly, Maxwell didn't care. She was his now, and that's all that mattered.

Emma also refused to give Miles much thought. She had her career, wonderful friends, and an amazing man who pushed her daily to be her best.

She didn't need the small-town drama that her past offered her. Resolute in her clear thinking, she was going home to be with her family, that needed her.

It was early spring, so it was still cold on the coast. The only benefit was the longer days of light that had just shifted. She arrived home late Sunday evening and went straight to Grammy's room.

There was nothing like coming home. As soon as she walked in the door, it hit her how much she had missed being there.

Rosie had aged so much since her last stroke. However, her resilience had not changed at all. The television was ridiculously loud, with the sound of clapping and the booming voice of Pat Sajak projecting throughout the room.

Emma grabbed the remote and quickly turned the volume down before taking her grandmother's hand to say "Hello."

Grammy woke from her light nap and smiled at her beautiful granddaughter, "Oh, Emma. You're home. I have missed you so much."

This made them both smile as they looked at each other, happy to be in the same room as one another again.

"Hi, Grammy. I have missed you," Emma said as she leaned down to kiss her.

"What's with Pat Sajak? Are you thinking of asking him out on a date?" Emma joked as she sat in the chair beside Grammy's bed. They both laughed at the amusing question.

"Oh, honey, you know I only have eyes for one guy. Besides, I'm old enough to be his mother," Grammy said laughingly. "But maybe I could fix your mother up with him. She needs a date or two."

And just like that, their conversation was off and running. Emma filled her in on what was happening in New York, and Grammy let her know the latest gossip floating around town.

"That girl that used to come around here all the time is quite a handful. I guess she's getting ready to have a baby with Miles. She drags him around town like a lost puppy, and he just takes it like a dog. I can't quite understand what he sees in all that, but I guess it takes all kinds to make the world go 'round."

Emma wasn't paying attention initially but suddenly realized Grammy was talking about Izzy and Miles.

Something deep within her stirred, and it bothered her. She wasn't naive to think that Miles wouldn't appear somehow but not this quickly, especially in a conversation with her grandmother.

"I'm sorry, I missed the first part of what you said, Grammy. Are you talking about Izzy and Miles? You know they're having a baby, right?"

Grammy piped right back, "Oh, believe me, I know. She's as big as a house and loud about it, too. That girl has to make sure that every person within a five-mile radius knows that she is pregnant. It's ridiculous. I mean, I have had a baby, I know. She acts like the only one in the world who has been through this."

Another pang of jealousy and anger surged through Emma. "Well, that's not for us to worry about. I'm sure they are going to have their hands full soon enough. Now, tell me about what you have been up to."

And with that, they continued to catch up about Grammy's physical therapy, daily walks down to the beach, and her weekly visits to the bakery.

The following day, after Grammy's physical therapy, they journeyed downtown to the bakery to see how she could help her mother.

Caroline had already been there for hours when they arrived. Once again, the sweet smell of home hit Emma's senses the second she opened the door to enter.

The early day fog was still quite thick in town and would eventually burn off from the afternoon sun. But until this occurred, it was chilly and gray. It was something that you just got used to living on the coast.

Emma always found the fog comforting for some reason and was always slightly annoyed when the sun finally appeared later in the day.

As expected, the morning flew by with all three ladies working their magic in the kitchen.

It was just after lunchtime when Grammy's energy began to fade. Emma was first to notice and mentioned, "You know, Grammy, my jet lag is starting to take its toll. Want to go home and take a nap?"

It didn't take much more to convince Rosie it was time to go. They packed a couple of sandwiches to take back with them and headed out the front door.

Emma held the door as Grammy made her way slowly down the two front steps when a sudden push jolted Emma forward so that she had to grab onto her grandma for stability.

"What in the hell…" she started to say as she caught her balance, steadied her grandmother, and turned around to see Miles looking down at her.

He looked just as surprised as she did, "I'm sorry, babe, I…."

The words just spilled out of his mouth as naturally as the air that he had just breathed in.

As it turned out, his legs had gotten tangled in Jake's leash, and the dog had no interest in helping his master. The pup was only interested in sniffing and jumping on Emma. He liked her, remembering her scent from months ago on the beach.

She didn't hesitate as she pushed the dog down and grasped her grandmother's arm to steady her and help her to their car parked on the street.

Miles stood there as he and Jake watched her carefully help Grammy into the passenger seat. Slowly, she closed the door, dreading having to turn around to see him still standing there.

But she eventually did. She turned around and looked straight into those vividly clear blue eyes and felt a jolt of pure love shoot straight through her.

Of course, this was also the same time Jake decided to jump up on her again. She caught his front paws and pushed him down as both humans simultaneously yelled, "Jake, down!"

The dog cowered low to the ground and listened to his master's voice. They were oblivious to the dog as they both just stared at each other, lovingly having a whole conversation with only their eyes.

Emma was finally the first to speak, "I need to get Grammy home. It's been a long morning for her."

She started to walk around the back of the car to get into the driver's side when Miles caught her arm.

"I would love to talk to you if you are willing to listen," he said with a voice full of emotion.

At first, she didn't want to look up. It hurt too much as she heard his voice and suddenly realized how much she missed hearing it.

She finally gave in and looked at him, "I don't know if that's a good idea. We both have so much going on in our lives now."

He only nodded and pulled on Jake's leash to signal it was time to go. "Got it," he mumbled as he walked away with his adorable pooch.

She watched him walk away and felt tears instantly sting her eyes. She took a deep breath, walked around the car, got in, and started driving.

They were about five minutes into the drive before Grammy said anything. Emma was so distracted by what had just happened that she forgot someone else was in the car.

So it made her jump when Grammy finally spoke, "You love that boy, don't you?"

That same jolt of love Emma felt earlier came rushing back, "What? No. Why would you say such a thing?"

She felt her face flush instantly as she pretended she was focused on the road ahead.

"Emma, I may be old, but that only means I am wise and know when I see two people in love. I've been there. I know."

That was all that Grammy said for the remainder of the drive home.

The next morning, the sun shined brightly in Emma's bedroom. It was unusual for this time of year, but it instantly drew her to her windows and eventually onto the large patio overlooking the beach.

As much as she craved the gray, there was something so wonderful about feeling the warmth of the sun mixed with the brisk chill of the ocean air.

She grabbed a cup of coffee, wrapped herself in a blanket, and walked outside onto the upper patio. New York City had nothing on this kind of coastal morning.

She took a warm sip from her mug, leaned into the railing, raised her closed eyes to the sun, and took a deep breath. This felt good. She felt calm and peaceful with being at home.

As the warm sunshine filled her face, she heard footsteps behind her and the scrape of a chair against the patio floor.

Caroline was so happy to see her daughter enjoying a few moments of solace. "Good morning, sweetie. How did you sleep?"

Emma didn't turn around as she heard her mother's voice, "Good morning, Mom. I slept ok. This sunshine was motivation to get out of bed this morning." she said as she took another sip of her coffee.

Her mom joined her at the edge of the deck to take in the beach view. She also drank a hot mug of coffee. The ladies enjoyed a quiet moment, looking at the waves and a few people on the sand.

A running dog, the color of burnt caramel, came dashing toward them. Emma knew it was Jake from the moment she laid eyes on him. This meant that his master wasn't far behind.

It took her a moment to spot him since he wasn't running behind the pup, as she had expected. Instead, Miles was sitting very still on a piece of driftwood in the distance. It took her a moment to focus on him, but she quickly realized that he was staring up at her, not at the dog or the beautiful water.

She turned to her mom, feeling a bit uncomfortable. Caroline had spotted him quickly, too.

As she took another drink, her mom said, "He's there almost every morning. He lets Jake run wild cause that puppy seems to have endless energy. But, he always gazes up here. At first, I thought he was always watching us, but lately, I think he's focusing more on the house."

Emma listened to what her mom was saying but also felt very emotional.

She moved away from the edge of the patio and sat in one of the chairs as she finished her coffee. The sun's warmth and seeing him on the beach made her feel uncomfortably hot, so she shifted out of the blanket she had come outside with earlier.

"Emma, did you hear me?" Caroline said as she looked deeply at her daughter.

Quietly Emma responded, "I did, mama. I just don't know what to think."

From there, the two women sat and drank their coffee silently. Thoughts drifted for both of them, all while they enjoyed the cold chill of the air and the golden warmth of the sunshine.

After a while, Caroline went inside to check on Rosie. Slowly, Emma walked to the banister and looked to see if she could still see Miles or Jake. They were gone, so she descended the stairs to the sand below with a deep breath and a heavy, emotional heart. The waves called to her, and she walked briskly to the water's edge.

A strong wind would occasionally gust from the south, which made her close her eyes to brace for the intense breeze that met her face. She didn't mind because it helped calm the racing thoughts in her head.

"Love you…still."

The voice that she knew so very well startled her, even in the strong sunshine that was bright above them.

She turned quickly to see Miles standing behind her, with Jake patiently sitting beside him.

The pup didn't want to jump and interrupt with his unending energy for once.

She bowed her head and pressed it into Miles' chest as his lips met the top of her head.

In barely a whisper, she responded, "Love you. Always."

Tears stung their eyes as a strong gust of wind pressed them together into an embrace as they stood steadfast, trying not to fall into the sand beneath them.

Jake, ever wanting to move, ran circles around the two, enrobing them in the long leash that accidentally connected them all.

Slowly, Emma and Miles looked at each other and gently kissed each other. The kiss was almost a peace offering to calm the frustration that pulsed between them.

After a lengthy, healing embrace, they pulled apart, and at once both said, "Jake!" when they realized that they were entangled in the dog's leash.

Miles let the leather handle fall into the sand, and the two of them stepped back to release the cord's tension.

The dog jumped up on Emma as if to say a belated "Hello!" which was also met with licks of adoration. This made Emma step back and giggle.

"It's weird. He only does that with you. Most of the time, he is at my side and listens to me. You must trigger something in him." Miles said coyly.

Their eyes met as he finished speaking. And then silence. Until Emma said, "Miles, I have wanted to talk to you."

He turned abruptly as if something on the shoreline had caught his attention.

She wasn't going to let him go easily this time, "Please, listen to me. I want to talk to you."

"Emma, you don't need to explain. Look, I didn't tell you because I saw that you could do so much more without me. I know Maxwell loves you. He can give you so much more than I ever can."

She was enraged that he would ever assume that someone else could offer her more than he could.

Emma instantly yelled, "What in the hell gave you that idea? Did I not show you how much I loved you when you came back? Maxwell has nothing to do with this!"

He snapped angrily, "He has everything to do with this! He wants you and doesn't care who knows it! Especially me. And I don't have anything to offer you. I'm a Navy reject with no career direction and a baby on the way. You don't need that shit."

This pissed her off even more, "What in the actual fuck goes on in that head of yours? I just said I would love you forever, and all you can say is that someone else is better for me! That is the biggest piece of bullshit I have ever heard. So, then what? You just plant your ass right back here and end up fucking Izzy? You didn't call me. You didn't even consider leaning on the one person that loves you the most. And now, you're having HER baby. Not OUR baby. HER baby. What the FUCK?!"

Emma then let out a primal scream into the strong, cold wind that knocked them both on their butts into the sand. Jake came bounding over and landed in Emma's lap. The dog proceeded to lick the salty tears that streamed down her face.

This is the first strong emotion she had let out since finding out what was happening in Miles's life. She was overflowing with every emotion. Hurt, betrayal, and sadness, but mostly mourning the loss of love she thought would always be in her life.

She let Jake bounce all over her and kiss her tears away. It was a chaotic yet healing moment for her. The damn dog understood her more than the man she had loved forever.

He spoke quietly but firmly, "Jake, down. Emma, no. You've got it all wrong. I mean, right, but wrong at the same time. I love you. I always will. It was never supposed to be like this. We were going to build a life together, but then I fucked it all up. Jake, I said, "Down!" he finished as he angrily pulled the dog away from her.

She didn't want the puppy to get down. He was giving her more attention than Miles had in a long time. The dog showed her the unrestrained emotion that she wished he had, "Don't pull him away. He's just happy to be here with me! Unlike you."

With that, Miles yanked Jake away from her, "I said, 'Down, Boy!'

He started to walk away from her, but she wasn't going to let it end like that. He had walked away from her too many times.

"Miles, get back here! You are going to finish this conversation with me! I have had it with you walking away from me! Miles!" she screamed at him down the beach as tears streamed down her face and pain seared through her heart.

Suddenly, off in the distance, Emma saw her.

Izzy.

She was standing at the edge of the parking lot in the distance. "Miles! What the fuck? I am having your baby, and you are here with that whore?! What the actual fuck?!"

And then she dramatically grabbed her belly and fell to the ground as Miles ran after her.

Emma stopped in her tracks. This was it. This was what their relationship had come to. Chaotic love mixed with an unexpected baby from a so-called friend that had somehow become an enemy. It was earth-shatteringly painful.

She took a deep breath and watched as the love of her life ran up to the friend she no longer recognized.

This was it.

Emma would always love him, but not in the way she had ever imagined.

She slowly dried her tears, turned back, and walked towards the only true home she had ever known. Unsure of where her next steps would take her, she knew it was away from whatever mess Miles had made of his life.

The pain of this realization seared through her heart like a hot knife, but she didn't stop. She couldn't stop. She had to move on with her life without him. She didn't know how, but she felt he was no longer a part of her path.

Her idea of the perfect life with Miles was gone. So, she did the only thing she knew to do.

Go back to New York. Back to Maxwell.

CHAPTER 28

I DO.

"Move on."

Emma and Maxwell once again hit their stride when she returned to New York. They didn't speak about her trip to Oregon. Honestly, they didn't have the time because they were so focused on her career and the craziness of it all.

The deadline for her new cookbook was quickly approaching, so she spent most of her time working in her tiny apartment kitchen or the craft kitchen that Maxwell had built for her at the office.

What happened with Miles seemed to push her forward. Creativity easily poured from her, motivating her to see what she could do next.

She was also inspired by the memories of growing up with her Grammy. Emma easily took recipes that they had long enjoyed and added a modern twist to them.

That was it. The name of her new cookbook would be *"Modern Twist: Recipes for the Next Generation of Bakers."* She shared inspiring ways to cherish traditions and teach the reader to make it their own.

Maxwell and the team loved the idea. They even took her cookbook and quickly transformed it into a successful weekly cooking show on the cable network.

The days and months flew by, and before they knew it, fall was arriving. Maxwell always mentioned how much he loved this time of year. Emma felt the same way.

This season put her in a nostalgic mood, as it always reminded her of high school and, of course, Miles. Yet, she didn't want to be reminded of him this year.

If she allowed her mind to wander, she could only assume he was fully involved in caring for Izzy and their new baby. She didn't know this for sure, as her mom never mentioned him anymore. Caroline knew it would be too painful to share with her daughter, so she just didn't say anything.

Emma knew she would likely go home for the holidays to see her mom and Grammy. Yet, the lingering pain of seeing Miles with his new family made her reject thinking about it too much.

Maxwell's voice suddenly pulled her back to the present, "You're off in space somewhere. What are you thinking about, darling?"

Emma stared blankly at him for a moment before saying, "Oh, yes. You know me. Always thinking of what's next. Anyway, what's going on with you today?"

He had come to check on her in the kitchen studio to ask her a big question. He also noticed that she was deep in thought when he walked in. Now, he was happy to see that she was back to being entirely focused on him.

"Well, you see, I have something to ask you. The fall is the most spectacular time to visit the Hamptons, although the popular crowd will tell you otherwise. But I think it's time we went to my parent's place to spend some time at the beach."

Initially hesitant, Emma quickly responded, "Of course, that sounds amazing. When were you thinking?" She was back in work mode, reaching to check her calendar.

"Right away, darling. No time to waste. I've cleared your schedule, so all you need to do is pack, and we can be on our way." Maxwell said proudly.

This surprised Emma as she knew Gemma would be in a tizzy about having to rearrange their tight schedules.

Maxwell knew what was coming, "And not to worry, although she wasn't happy about it initially, Gemma finally conceded that everyone needs a long weekend to relax."

This made Emma smile and feel more than a little relieved. Those two ran her professional world, so she could completely relax if they were in agreement.

"Well, then. It sounds like you two have it all planned, so let me finish this recipe, and we can get going."

Within a few short hours, they were in the car and on their way to The Hamptons.

Two things were on Emma's mind: meeting Maxwell's parents and what the east coastline was like compared to where she grew up.

It didn't take long for her questions to be answered. It was dusk when they arrived at Maxwell's parent's house, a stately Cape Cod design. Draped in dark brown wood shingles, a warm glow emanated from the wrap-around porch and the lights from inside the house. The crunch of the gravel beneath the tires of the car as they pulled up gave a comforting feel to Emma, which helped put her at ease.

"Maxwell, this place is amazing. I can't wait to see inside." she said as they parked.

He smiled and gently took her hand, "I should have brought you here sooner, but I wanted to wait for just the perfect time." He lifted her hand to his lips and softly kissed it as they looked at each other warmly.

They were quickly greeted by Maxwell's mother, Julia, and his father, Joseph, as soon as they got out of the car. Emma instantly felt comfortable being here with his family.

After introductions, Julia led everyone inside their gorgeous home. It was large but had a welcoming feel, very similar to how Julia was treating Emma.

"Emma, it is such a pleasure to meet you. Maxwell has mentioned you quite a bit since you began working together. I had a feeling that he was interested in a little more than work after the first few hundred times he mentioned your name." Julia said in front of everyone.

Emma could feel the embarrassed heat rising in her cheeks, but Maxwell quickly reassured her by taking her hand in his.

"Now, Mom, it was probably only a hundred times. Let's not over-exaggerate," he said teasingly as they all laughed.

From there, the conversation flowed, and Emma began to enjoy being there.

There was a beautiful display of charcuterie and wine on the coffee table in the family room. The windows offered a stunning view of the beach, which Emma was instantly drawn to.

She took a glass of wine and wandered over to the expansive windows to take in the sights before them.

Emma spoke quietly at first, "This view is amazing. My home in Oregon is on the beach as well. It is truly spectacular to take in the differences between the two coasts."

Julia joined her at the windows as the gentlemen continued their conversation.

"I have never made it to the Pacific Northwest to know the difference. Tell me more, Emma."

They looked at each other and smiled while Emma began to share her thoughts.

"Well, I will say that one thing that is the same is the mesmerizing view of the ocean waves. That doesn't seem to change on either side of the country. Yet, what strikes me is the sheer natural beauty of each coastline. Where I live, the terrain is strong and rugged in its natural state. It seems to stoically stand ready for the great winds that roll in from the Pacific. Here, in only a few moments of watching, there seems to be more of a soothing ease and smoothness to the east coastline. Gosh, I don't even know if that makes sense, but there is a vast difference between the two. I do know that no matter the coastline, I could just stare out into the ocean all day, every day." she said with a smile.

As she spoke, she couldn't help but think of Miles vs. Maxwell and how her ocean description was similar to their personalities—except Miles hadn't been strong and stoic for her in quite a long time.

Lost in her thoughts and startled at where they took her, she missed part of what Julia had said.

Emma suddenly came back to the present when she heard her say, "Well, let me show you to your room. I hope you don't mind, but I did leave you a little something to wear for a party that we are having this evening."

This surprised Emma even more than her overpowering thoughts. *What did she say? She left me something to wear for a party I didn't know they were having. That seems odd that Maxwell wouldn't have mentioned anything about a party.*

They walked down a long hallway toward the far side of the house. The warm wood of the home continued throughout the house. The ladies finally made their way to the end of the hall to a closed door. Julia welcomely opened it and invited Emma inside.

She entered to find a soothingly calm interior with neutral tones that only complimented the vast glass wall of windows that showcased the beach view. Emma instantly felt at home.

"Julia, this is stunning. Are you sure you want me to stay in this room?"

Maxwell's mother smiled easily, "Of course, dear. This is our guest room, and we want you to enjoy the views as much as we do. Don't worry. We have a gorgeous view from our room, as well." This made the ladies giggle.

Julia led Emma into her en suite bathroom with a small walk-in closet. Inside hung an exquisite, almost ethereal light pink flowing dress.

"I truly hope you don't mind, but Maxwell said that he wanted me to pick a special dress for you to wear this evening." Julia said, slightly cautious.

Emma took in the dress from top to bottom, in awe of its simple beauty. As odd of a request as it seemed, she was ok with it. In fact, she was more than ok with the gorgeous design before her. This was unlike anything that she ever imagined that she would wear.

She gently ran her fingers along the dress as she responded, "Oh, I don't mind at all. Well, I had no idea there was a party this evening, so I certainly didn't prepare for it. Thank you for the thoughtful gesture and your amazing sense of style. It's absolutely gorgeous."

Emma's kind words touched Julia. She was a little anxious when Maxwell made the request. After all, they had never met, so she had to depend on what Maxwell had chosen to share about his new flame.

"Well, you are very welcome, Emma. I have to say that I was a bit nervous about doing this. Additionally, I was undecided about accessories and shoes, so there are a few options in the drawers," she said as she waved her hand to the rest of the closet.

"I will leave you to settle in and get ready for the evening. I also have more to do, so I will go."

She gently took Emma's hand and gave it a loving squeeze, "I have a feeling tonight is going to be memorable for us all."

Emma walked toward the windows to take a moment to admire the gorgeous view as Maxwell's mother left.

Her thoughts began to roll as she watched the endless waves reach the shore. This was surreal to her.

A fancy house with an even fancier dress to wear to a party where she would know no one except her boyfriend and his parents.

She felt a little uneasy, but she was determined to take it all in. She was spending the weekend with a wonderful man and his family. That couldn't be so bad. With renewed confidence, she walked into the bathroom to prepare for the evening.

Just a brief flicker of memories of Miles flashed through her mind, but she let them go as soon as she closed the door to get ready.

Emma emerged an hour later, looking elegant, gorgeous, and slightly nervous. Try as she might, the thoughts of what may come of this evening were beginning to stress her out.

On the other hand, this dress was nothing short of amazing. It was a lightly beaded, strapless gown fitted through the bodice and then flowed like the ocean down to the floor in a lightweight chiffon. It was truly stunning, and if she could let go of the nerves coursing through her, she would realize what a perfect dress this was for her.

She selected simple strap sandals that would work if they happened to venture onto the beach. Then she complimented the flowing dress with a single solitaire diamond necklace, which was a gift from Maxwell when she launched her first successful cooking show.

Emma glanced at herself in the mirror. Her hair was swept up in a loose twist, and natural, glowy makeup highlighted the soft sheerness of the dress. Then with a slow, deep breath, she wandered out of her room and into the main part of the house.

For a home that was preparing for a party, the house was unusually quiet. She looked around, poking her head into the main rooms until finally seeing Maxwell standing out on the back deck in front of a glowing fire.

She stood momentarily and admired how handsome he was, standing tall in a gorgeous, dark suit looking ever confident and handsome.

Emma opened the door and walked out to join him on the patio. The moment she appeared, he began to smile.

"Oh, Emma, you look stunning. That dress is amazing," he said immediately.

She blushed slightly yet felt happy enough to do a girlish twirl of the dress as she walked toward him. He smiled broadly and took her hands to guide her to the fire. As lovely as the beach was, a chill settled in quickly, so the bonfire was a welcome warmth for both.

"Where is everyone? I thought this was a party?" Emma teased.

Maxwell brought her into his arms and hugged her close. "Well, my dear, the party will begin soon, but first, there is something important that we must address."

She didn't know what to think, but before she could wonder anymore, he knelt on the ground, on bended knee, and pulled a black velvet box from his suit pocket.

"My dear Emma, I fell for you the moment I saw you. Then, we talked, and I knew we could be the best team that could conquer the world together. I love you and want to spend the rest of my life with you. Will you marry me?"

Emma was stunned. She was also touched, overwhelmed, shocked, but suddenly oh, so happy. This is what was meant to happen.

She wasn't supposed to marry the high school love from her small town. She was supposed to conquer the world with an amazingly handsome, driven, kind man. *She was supposed to marry Miles…er, Maxwell. What? Where did that come from? She was supposed to marry Maxwell. Maxwell. MAXWELL.*

With loving eyes, she could only muster one word. "Ok."

The party was nothing short of amazing. White twinkling lights seemed to appear out of the sky. Scattered down the beach were several bonfires glowing in the distance.

Endless bottles of champagne and the most delicious food Emma had ever experienced began to flow.

Julia and Joseph were the first to congratulate the newly engaged couple. And then it seemed as if the floodgates opened, and people appeared from every direction.

Emma was thankful for several quick sips of champagne, the warmth of Maxwell's hand, and then the surprise appearance of Kiera and Gemma.

Now, the party could really begin.

CHAPTER 29

EASIER SAID

"Than done."

The girls took no time to jump headfirst into wedding plans. Excitement filled each day with ideas for dresses, music, and location. Ah, the location.

At the engagement party, Maxwell and Emma stole a few moments away to call her family at the Glass House. Grammy wasn't able to make the trip due to her health. Yet, their love and happiness about the engagement could be felt 3,000 miles away.

So, this is why Emma felt it was so important to get married in her hometown. She had always dreamed of having the most important women in her life there to share in the joy of her wedding day.

Maxwell didn't object, and his mother loved the idea of a destination wedding for her friends and family.

That seemed to be the easiest decision to make. They would be married at the Glass House so that her family could be a part of their magical wedding day.

Soon after, Emma, Kiera, and Gemma traveled back home to work out the specific details of the ceremony.

Of course, they took it upon themselves to make as much fun of the trip as possible. Her mother and Grammy loved having the house full of their lively spirits. It had been too quiet for way too long.

One afternoon, as they were wrapping up menu planning, Emma wandered outside the bakery in the center of town. The sun was welcoming and warm as she walked toward the river.

She was just about to take a few steps down to the water when she saw Miles walking towards her, pushing a stroller. Emma felt a pang of love mixed with deep hurt but decided to say hello anyway.

After all, she was moving forward with her life, marrying Maxwell, and of course, Miles had made his choice to be with Izzy and the baby. The baby. Oh. She was about to meet the baby.

Taking a deep breath, she walked towards Miles with a gentle smile. She thought there was no harm in taking a peek at a precious new little one.

As she got closer, she could hear the baby crying. Miles stopped pushing the stroller, opened the canopy, and tried to soothe the infant.

"Hi, there," Emma said quietly as Miles lifted the tiny, sweet baby from its carrier.

"Hello. This is Isla. She is really making her presence known right now." he responded as he lifted her onto his shoulder and lightly bounced his baby girl.

She had petite features with a little mound of blondish-brown hair, just like her daddy. Emma immediately felt another strong pang of emotion but pushed it aside.

She walked behind Miles to see Isla a little closer as the baby rested on his shoulder. As she moved in, the baby stopped crying and peered with curious eyes at her new friend.

"Well, that was easy. You just need to keep looking at Isla. Then maybe she won't cry as much." Miles said with a slight laugh.

"She has been quite fussy this morning and is probably more than a little ready for a bottle. Would you mind holding her while I get it ready?"

Before Emma could hesitate, the baby was in her arms, as happy as could be, just like his puppy, Jake.

Miles bent down to grab a bottle of formula and mentioned as much, "You seem to have a way with those that are closest to me. First, Jake, and now Isla. You should come around more often."

He silently kicked himself for saying that last part, knowing that could never happen because of Izzy.

He handed Emma the bottle, and she began feeding Isla while naturally swaying back and forth. She really was a sweet baby, and it made Emma happy to see her.

"I have no idea what I'm doing, but if she's not crying, I suppose that's a good thing," she responded with a nervous laugh.

Emma was holding the bottle with her left hand, and the bright sunshine made her engagement ring glimmer dramatically in the light. "Whoa, sorry, your humongous rock temporarily blinded me!" Miles said as he pretended to cover his eyes.

This made Emma uncomfortable for obvious reasons, but she pushed the feeling away, "Yes, Maxwell proposed. It's why I am in town with the girls. Wedding planning is in full effect." she mumbled.

A pang of jealousy hit Miles straight in the chest, but he didn't let it show. All he could say was a quiet "Congratulations."

As he reached to take baby Isla back, he suddenly heard Izzy's loud, boisterous voice behind him. "That's right, take her back. That bitch has no business holding my baby!"

Emma looked beyond Miles and the baby to see Izzy making a beeline straight for her. She was bracing herself for the impact of more hurtful words from her former friend.

Izzy brushed right past Miles and immediately got in Emma's face, "That's my man, and that's my baby. Stay away, got it?" Her finger pointed right in Emma's face with a wave of unnecessary anger.

At this exact moment, Kiera and Gemma happened upon the altercation.

"Whoa, there, wild mare, I think you need to get your hoof away from my friend's face right now," shouted Gemma as she slid between the two women.

The two former friends never broke eye contact. Izzy's face was full of rage and jealousy, while Emma was just plain pissed. She was so confused at this situation and how two friends could now be this angry with each other.

While Kiera stepped to the other side of Emma and formed a wall of defense, the baby started wailing loudly. Miles tried his best to calm her, but the tension was too strong for the young one to ignore.

The loud crying broke Izzy's focus, and she turned abruptly around and grabbed Isla away from Miles.

"Give her to me. She needs her mama. You want your mama, don't you, baby." she said far too angrily as she glared at the group of ladies.

They stared back with a bold stance, silently saying, "Get the hell out of here."

Izzy turned back, grabbed the stroller, and angrily yelled, "Miles, come on!" as she stomped away.

The ladies were genuinely dumbfounded at this situation. Kiera was the first to speak, "What in the holy hell was that?"

Emma shook her head slowly from side to side as she responded, "That, my dear friends, is the infamous Izzy. Mother to my ex-boyfriend's child, former bestie of mine, and now just a plain, old angry person. Shall we find a bar and get a drink? I'll buy since you saved me from getting arrested for beating that girl's ass."

Gemma quickly chimed in, "Well, you don't have to offer me a drink more than once. Let's go, girls!"

CHAPTER 30

VENOM

"Oh, Izzy."

Emma decided to return to the bakery after the girls met for drinks. Her mom had so many things to take care of these days that she just wanted to make sure that everything was secure.

She unlocked the front door, clicked on the lights, and headed back into the kitchen. As suspected, she immediately noticed that eggs and milk were left on the counter.

After checking the milk to ensure it hadn't soured, she grabbed the items and headed back to the walk-in refrigerator to store them.

Just as she opened the heavy door, she heard the front door chime and called out, "Hey, ladies! I'm in the back, and I'll be out in a minute!"

She put everything on the shelf and shuffled quickly out to close the heavy door as she was getting chilly from the fridge's cool temperature.

It took both hands to close the door so her back was to the rest of the kitchen. After she heard the loud clank of the latched handle, she turned around to continue chatting with her ladies. Or so she thought.

Emma was shocked to see Izzy standing in the kitchen, playing with a long, steel-blade knife and staring back at her with a crazed look in her eyes.

"Izzy, we are closed. What are you doing here?" she said as calmly as possible.

Standing before her was a person that she no longer recognized.

Izzy was unsteady on her feet, her hair was disheveled, and she was either drunk, stoned, or possibly both. Clearly, she was in no state of mind to be standing there holding a very sharp knife.

Emma spoke again, more calmly, "Izzy, did you hear me? I was just getting ready to leave myself. Let's go out the front door, ok?"

But as Emma went to take a few steps toward the swinging door, Izzy stepped unsteadily in her path.

"You are not going anywhere unless I say you can. Got it, bitch?" Izzy practically shouted at Emma, which made her jump.

Taking a nervous step backward, Emma responded, "Yeah, sure. What do you want? To talk? Dessert?" The weak joke was her failing attempt to calm Izzy down. It didn't work.

"Stop with your bullshit, Emma. I know why you're here. You want my baby, and you want Miles back."

As Izzy spoke, she walked slightly closer toward Emma and threateningly waved the sharp knife out in front of her.

Emma's eyes continued to dart from the knife's sharp blade to Izzy's face. She was trying to figure out how to get out of there without getting hurt.

"Sorry, Iz. I was just trying to lighten the mood a bit. And I'm not trying to do that. I am here to plan my wedding to Maxwell, remember? We, you and me, we are good. Nothing to worry about from me, ok?" Emma nervously said.

For a moment, she was able to edge just a little closer to the door, but she was still stuck between Izzy and the knife. Beside them stood a large, heavy work table that was still covered with the day's remnants of baking.

Emma quickly glanced down to see if there was anything that she could defend herself with if needed. A whisk, a spatula, and a rolling pin. No. No. And definitely no. *I don't want to kill the girl. I just want out of here, away from this crazy bitch,* Emma thought. Then she spotted a heavy, stainless steel baking sheet. *That will do. But be patient.*

Izzy was rambling almost incoherently at times about Miles and the baby.

"They're mine, you bitch. That baby is what is going to keep him with me forever. That was the plan. Until you had to stick your claws into him when we were in high school. He was supposed to be mine, and then you *stole* him from me that night at the bonfire."

Emma was shocked to hear this, "Izzy, what are you talking about? You were drinking and having a great time that night. You had a boyfriend. How was I supposed to know you wanted to be with Miles?"

Izzy glared at Emma with an evil smirk, "Oh, listen to poor Emma. I had no idea that you wanted him," she said, mocking her former friend.

Then she continued, "Of course I wanted Miles. Don't you remember me kissing him after the football game? He was *mine*. Don't you understand? No, of course, you don't, Miss 'I'm So Innocent' and Miss 'I Don't Know What You're Talking About.' Stop your bullshit! You paraded around this town like your shit didn't stink because you had him right where you wanted him. You didn't care about anyone else but yourself. You think you're so great with your Glass House on the beach and your stupid cooking shows and cookbooks?"

The proximity to each other was much too close for Emma's comfort, so it forced her to take a step back. She tried to reach for the baking sheet but missed it.

Emma was trying to think quickly about what to do. So, she interjected to try and calm her down since it appeared that Izzy was getting crazier by the second.

"No, Iz. I don't think that at all. I'm in New York now, so that should show you that I'm over Miles. I have been for a long time. It's ok. As I said before, I'm getting married to someone else. It's ok…" Emma was trying to get Izzy to see that there was nothing to worry about, but this seemed to make Izzy even more irate.

She suddenly screamed, "SHUT UP! SHUT UP, YOU BITCH! I'm the one who is talking, not you, so shut the fuck up." Izzy walked even closer to Emma, putting the knife up to her face.

"I am the one that is talking, and if you interrupt me one more time, I will shut you up permanently. Got it, bitch?" Izzy was looking Emma dead in the eyes.

All Emma could muster was to fervently shake her head yes, in understanding.

Izzy smirked at Emma once again, "Good. Now listen closely because I'm only going to say this once. You stay the fuck away from my man and my baby. Got it? It took me and his mama way too long to get him on our side, and we ain't going to lose him again."

Emma was stunned. *What is Izzy talking about?*

She began to shake her head to say "No." but Izzy swiftly reminded her to keep her mouth shut by holding the knife dangerously close to her neck.

"No talking, remember?" Izzy said in an evil whisper. She was very close to Emma's face, and the smell of stale booze was wafting from her hot breath.

Izzy began to speak again, "Yeah. He just had to go and sign up for the Navy. I thought my chances were over, but then he went and fucked everything up for himself. Turns out that worked out great for me. It didn't take much to remind him of what a "high and mighty" bitch you had become with your *big* career in New York City. Between me and his mama, it was easy to show him that you weren't worth it. No need to go after you because you wouldn't have him anyway. So, yeah, it was easy to convince him not to call you and tell you shit."

Tears instantly stung Emma's eyes. *Oh my God. It wasn't Miles that stayed away. He listened to his mom and this crazy-ass girl, who convinced him I didn't love him. Are you fucking kidding me?*

Emma was instantly filled with defensive rage, "You did what?"

She forgot the rule. She didn't care.

She was pissed to find out that Izzy manipulated Miles into believing such awful things about her.

Izzy pushed Emma hard into the stove behind her.

"Are you fucking stupid? I said don't say a god-damn word!"

Emma was ablaze with anger but didn't move, knowing that the knife was resting on her throat.

Izzy began to confess even more. "Yeah, I told him that he was nothing and certainly nothing that you would want hanging around. Then I got him good and drunk, and then I fucked him. You weren't here to distract him, so I became his focus. It was easy to see him cause he visited his mama and me every night at the bar. It was a great routine. I'd serve him drinks, and then he'd serve me his cock. Every. Damn. Night."

The look of crazed obsession was all over Izzy's face as she said the last part of her sick confession.

Emma felt like she wanted to throw up out of disgust. The rage was simmering within her. Tears rolled down her cheeks as she began to shake with overwhelming anger.

Izzy still rambled on, "Yeah, the kid wasn't in the plan, but then I thought about it. The kid could keep him around forever, so in the end, that worked out in my favor." She smiled sadistically at her own words.

She continued, "That kid cries something fierce, but he takes her on. I'll put up with it so that he stays put. He knows that there's no baby Isla without me. So, yeah, I've got him right where I want 'em. And just to be clear. You stay the fuck away from my family. You got it, bitch?"

Izzy's disgustingly hot breath on Emma's face was making Emma more nauseated. She had to get out of there. This girl was insane. Izzy leaned in even closer, pushing the knife further into the skin of Emma's neck.

In a whisper, she repeated, "I said, you got it, bitch? You stay away from my fucking family."

A searing rage came deep from within Emma. With one swift move, she charged forward and knocked Izzy over the work table, grabbed the heavy baking sheet, and slammed it over her head. Izzy was instantly knocked out, and the knife fell to the floor.

Emma kicked away the knife and ran out of the kitchen through the swinging door to the front of the bakery. Just as she was about to reach for the door handle to go outside, she was knocked back by someone pushing open the door.

It was Miles.

CHAPTER 31

LOOK WHAT YOU DID

"Revenge is never a good idea."

Emma was trying to stand back up, so Miles reached down and took her hand to help her. As she stood, he noticed a thin trickle of blood running down her neck.

When Emma forced Izzy backward to escape, the sharp knife must have pierced her neck.

Miles was immediately concerned, "Emma, what happened to your neck?"

She reached up and touched it, only then realizing she had been cut.

The sight of her own blood on her fingertips, combined with the stress of what had just happened, made her lightheaded. Miles caught her just in time before she fell again.

Quickly remembering that Izzy was in the back and the fierceness of her words, Emma stepped away from Miles and stumbled toward the front door.

"Your crazy-ass girlfriend is in the back, so why don't you ask her while I go call the police."

She was on the phone with the police when Gemma and Kiera found her outside. The two women were shocked to see Emma bleeding as well.

Kiera blurted out, "Oh my god, Emma! What happened to you? You're bleeding."

Gemma thought she might kill whoever did this to her friend. It didn't take much to figure out who had hurt her. Fucking Izzy. That girl was bonkers.

Miles had found Izzy still unconscious in the bakery's kitchen, and honestly, it didn't surprise him. However, seeing the bloody knife and the overall mess of the room did shock him. He was trying to figure out what happened.

Earlier, he had gone to talk with someone on the other side of the bar, and when he returned, Izzy was gone. It took him way too long to figure out that she had fled the bar, making him wander down the main street searching for her.

Almost immediately, the police arrived, and soon the bakery was full of cops.

Miles had just got an ice pack to put on Izzy's head when she came to. Her eyes weren't even fully open, and she started wildly swinging her fists.

Miles caught her hands mid-punch, "Whoa! That's enough! Calm down. You've got quite a bump on your head, and I'm just trying to help you."

Izzy's eyes flew open at the sound of his voice, and she immediately became dramatic and teary-eyed.

"Oh, Miles! Thank goodness you are here. That bitch is crazy! She's the one that hit me!"

A tall police officer walked over just as he heard Izzy's voice, "Nice to see you conscious, Iz. Want to start telling me what happened here?"

Izzy shot her head up to look at the cop just as another officer with gloved hands picked up the bloody knife and put it in a plastic bag for evidence.

She started rambling on, "I don't know what that bitch told you, but she could have killed me and left my baby daughter without a mother! Look at what she did to me! You need to arrest her now!"

Miles and the officer exchanged a look of suspicion as the cop continued to press Izzy to explain what happened, "Izzy, I know you don't work here, and the bakery is closed. So, what were you doing here?"

This made her extremely mad, "What? Are you accusing me of breaking into this place? The door was unlocked. I did not break into this shitty bakery."

The officer looked at her closely and could see that she was intoxicated. He was also aware of the bloody knife and the cut on Emma's neck, "No, that's not what I said at all. In fact, I want you to tell me what happened."

Izzy was trying to stand up at this point, and once on her feet, she immediately got in the cop's face, "Now you listen here, asshole, she hit me and knocked me out. Go arrest that bitch for assault!"

Miles was trying to hold her back, but it was too late. One of the other police officers had already motioned for him to step to the side and began to place handcuffs on Izzy.

She immediately resisted, "What the hell is happening? You can't arrest me! That bitch knocked me out, but I'm the one getting arrested! This is bullshit! You can't do this! Miles! Tell them to stop this now!"

The officers dragged her outside and into a waiting cruiser.

Yes, Izzy was arrested, initially for verbally assaulting an officer and later for manslaughter. The investigation would show her fingerprints on the knife, and videotapes from the bakery's cameras would show the altercation from beginning to end.

Izzy would end up going to prison for the incident.

Emma thought about pressing additional charges but ultimately decided not to. The damage had been done. Now she knew the real truth. The love she previously knew with Miles felt like it was once again lost forever.

Izzy was a miserable person and had made Miles even more unhappy. Their one bright spot was Isla.

Emma and her friends left town as soon as they could without a single word to Miles. She knew everything she needed to know.

Plus, she had a wedding to attend. Her wedding.

CHAPTER 32

GHOSTED

"The feeling is mutual."

When they returned to New York, no one skipped a beat getting back into their routines. It was almost as if they couldn't get away from that disaster fast enough.

Maxwell was beside himself with anger over what had happened. He even went as far as to strongly suggest that the wedding be held on the east coast instead. Emma wouldn't hear of it. She quickly explained that Izzy was the problem and that she would be behind bars at the time of their nuptials.

This gave Maxwell a little sense of relief, and he was so happy that Emma was okay. He didn't even want to think about what would happen if she would have been seriously harmed. Or worse.

In these past few years, he had built his life and, more specifically, his livelihood around her. What would he have done?

As for Emma, she would sometimes be overwhelmed with anger and fury when she let herself think of that awful night. The intense hatred and fear overrode any other warm, loving thoughts of Miles. That was done. They were done. She was completely *undone*.

If she allowed herself to go there, she would begin to think about what their lives would be like now if Izzy and Sarah hadn't intervened as they had. Would Miles have come back to her? Would he have been open and honest with her about his issues in the Navy?

The manipulation and lies were just too much for her to take.

Miles was thinking very similar thoughts. He was furious with Izzy. He was livid with himself for not seeing her for who she truly was.

She made him lose the best person in his life. Well, second best. He thought of Isla, which always calmed him and helped keep his anger in check. She was the only good that came out of this mess.

Quite different than in the past, Miles had tried several times to reach out to Emma. She wasn't interested. Any other time before Izzy tried to kill her, she would ache to talk to him. This time, it had been way too much.

So, as Miles had done to her several times before, he turned into a ghost before her eyes.

There's such a funny, ironic thing about ghosting.

Its silence cuts like a knife.

It's a sword through the heart, severing the strongest of love's bonds.

It feels like a little razor twirling and weaving its way through thoughts and emotions, making one feel crazy, lost, confused, and unbelievably hurt all at the same time.

Silence is highly underrated yet so very powerful. It gains its power through the unknown thoughts and feelings of the one that can't be reached. This leads to imaginary conversations that turn into speculation, allowing the mind to run wild.

On both sides, ghosting brings out the worst in a person.

Being on the receiving end this time, Miles felt like he was quite literally going insane. Yet, he had to keep moving forward for Isla.

He just wanted to talk to Emma. His heart ached to hug her and reassure her that he had no idea what Izzy was capable of. Yet, he understood her silence. It meant she was hurting beyond what his words could do to console her. He knew that feeling all too well.

So, he finally gave up and stopped calling. She was relieved when the phone stopped ringing. Emma couldn't comprehend what he could say or why he wanted to talk now. Why wasn't he like this *before* he was lured into Izzy's trap?

As the weeks passed, she continued to push away the thoughts that made her heart ache, and her mind simmer with anger. Work was a good distraction, and Maxwell was an even better diversion.

So, like vapor in a cloud, Miles and Emma disappeared from each other's lives. The only problem was that their hearts didn't quite know this.

CHAPTER 33

WE FOUND TONIGHT

"Tomorrow? Who knows."

The weeks leading up to the wedding were unbelievably busy. Emma and the girls were constantly finalizing all of the details. In addition, it seemed like Maxwell was presenting Emma with a new project opportunity every day.

As much as she loved what she did, it was starting to get more than a little overwhelming.

The night before she was due to fly back to the Glass House for the wedding, he again outlined more upcoming projects.

The anger over Izzy and Miles was constantly simmering just below the surface within Emma's emotions. This time,

Maxwell's insistent pushing was just enough to make her snap at him.

"Maxwell, I know you aren't flying out until later in the week, but can you please stop with these projects until after the wedding? I honestly can't take on anything else right now." she spouted at him.

He was taken aback by her words. All he ever thought of was her career and how they would make an empire out of her amazing talents. *No,* he thought, *this couldn't wait until after the party.*

His bright, green eyes shot tiny, little daggers of anger back at her. This surprised her.

"Good god, Emma, I cannot wait for this thing to be over. We have *so much* work to do. The producers aren't going to wait forever for you to decide what's next," he scowled back at her.

She immediately went on the defense to angrily remind him, "What did you just say? Did you just say that you can't wait for our wedding day to be over so that you and I can get back to work? This is the biggest day of our lives, and you want it over with? What the hell, Maxwell?"

He had triggered her. Emma's emotions were ready to boil over, and oh, how they did.

Even she was surprised by the words that came out of her mouth next.

"Maybe we should reconsider? I wouldn't want our little party to get in the way of our next career move, right, Maxwell? I mean, fuck love, and that 'to have and to hold' bullshit! We have work to do! Fuck you, Miles! ...I mean, Maxwell. Fuck you! I thought you wanted to marry me. I thought this meant just as much to you. I suppose I was very wrong!"

She had not meant to say the name Miles. They were both very uncomfortable with this mistake. Yet, Emma's frustration and seething anger were taking over her logic.

"I have to finish packing, and whether or not we get married, I'm going home for the week." She glared steely at him as she continued, "Everything else can wait until I get back. That is final. I love you, Maxwell, and I take this commitment very seriously. Please don't make it seem like an inconvenience for your career."

And with those final words, she left his place to go home and pack.

Emma was so angry that she barely recalled anything leading up to landing in Oregon. She drove the familiar curvy roads from the airport to the Glass House. It was dusk and a beautifully clear evening. Her mom had sent her a text earlier explaining that she would have the place to herself for the night because she and Grammy were staying the night in Portland.

This was a relief. Emma wouldn't be much of a happy, blushing bride this evening. She needed time to think and process everything she was feeling.

After settling in her old room, she decided to walk down the beach since her mind was still swirling.

She hit the sand with a firm determination, almost as if she wanted to throw her anger and emotions into the wind.

Emma walked for a very long time. It was at least two miles before she realized how far she had gone. The sun was going down, which made it quite chilly.

As she turned to go back, she noticed someone in the distance. It was Miles. He was staring out at the horizon with Isla in a baby carrier strapped to his chest. His dog, Jake, was calmly lying at his feet. Miles must have been standing there for quite a while.

Emma initially hesitated, but then she decided to go see them. Perhaps it was the baby, the sunset, or that she finally had burned off her anger during the walk, but she felt calmer at that moment.

She spoke first, "Hi, Miles."

He looked over at her, but it appeared that he didn't really see her. He seemed tired, and his expression was empty and distracted.

He could only muster a short "Hey."

They stood at a distance for a few moments, each looking at the constant waves rolling onto shore.

Isla broke the silence as she made a sleepy gurgle while nestling a little closer into her daddy's chest. She seemed so peaceful lying there as Miles looked down and kissed the top of her head.

"She seems to love it out here. That's why we have been camped out on the beach for the last few weeks. We needed a change, didn't we, baby girl?" Miles said. He talked to Emma and Isla simultaneously but still seemed so distant with his words.

Emma turned and looked behind her to discover an RV camper parked in a lot as close to the beach as possible.

"You've been living here with the baby?" she asked.

Miles also turned back to look at their temporary home and shook his head up and down.

He then began walking toward the lot, "She's going to get cold quickly now that the sun is down. Want to come back for a few minutes to warm up?"

Emma was confused yet a little comforted by the invitation, so she said, "Ok, maybe for a minute."

They arrived at the camper, and Miles held open the door long enough to let Jake and Emma enter. He then silently walked to the back and laid the sleeping baby down in her travel crib. Jake lay down protectively at the foot of the bed, watching over Isla.

Once she was settled, Miles returned and invited Emma to sit at the little table at the front of the RV.

For a long time, they just stared at each other. Neither knew what to say or do.

Finally, Miles stood up, walked to the freezer, and pulled out an ice-cold bottle of tequila.

He spoke over his shoulder as he opened a kitchen cupboard, "I only have one shot glass, so we will have to share. You ok with that?"

Emma smiled gently and said, "Sure." He sat back down, filled the glass, and took a small sip. Then he slid it across the table to her without breaking eye contact.

She took a nervous sip as he finally began to talk. "Emma, I don't know exactly what to say. I mean, I am so sorry for everything that you have gone through with Izzy. I'm to blame for a lot of it, but you have to know that I had no idea she would do that to you."

Trying to be as understanding as possible, Emma looked at Miles and said abruptly, "How could you not see that she was capable of such a thing? Her anger towards me just continued to grow once you two started hooking up. I didn't think she would try to kill me, but I knew she was trouble. How could you not see that?"

She unconsciously reached up and touched the scar on her neck. Miles noticed, and he felt the guilt deep in his gut.

Both uncomfortable, they reached for the glass to take a gulp at the same time. Miles let Emma go first. She winced as she downed the last of the tequila in the shot glass, "This shit needs some lime. Damn, that's strong." She was trying to break the tension.

He got a lime from the fridge and sliced a wedge for their shared drink to give them some space. It was apparent she was still mad.

"I get that you are angry. I can't imagine what that was like. It had to be so scary." He continued, "She convinced me you were better off without me. You were some rich, spoiled famous person who no longer wanted to be with a Navy drop-out. That's all I could see. And then, once she got pregnant, things really changed. I mean, Isla changed my life in the best way. That kid is my world. But things with Izzy were awful."

These are the details that Emma had been wanting to hear directly from Miles all this time. She knew that he would be an incredible father. It's just that she didn't think that Izzy would be the mother. In her mind, it was supposed to be her.

Miles continued to explain, "As soon as she had the baby, she couldn't get back to the bar fast enough. She claimed that we needed the money, but honestly, it was so she could drink and flirt with the tourists that came in. Before the baby, I could go and keep an eye on her at the bar. But now, I'm with Isla all the time. So, I didn't realize Izzy was obsessing over you. I thought she knew I was dedicated and trying to have a family with her."

He had such a hurt, pained look on his face. It brought tears to Emma's eyes as she continued to listen.

Miles explained, "I've been in school, so I can't be with them all the time, but I am with Isla as much as possible. Well, now that Izzy is in jail, it's all me. It's ok. We have a routine, and it's so much calmer with her not here. I'm just sad that Isla doesn't have a mom. She only has me."

Emma felt emotion rising in her throat and took another small sip to push it down. Quietly she said, "Maybe you are the best thing for Isla. You know, there's nothing like the love of a father."

He glanced at her with a small smile, "Thanks. I think we do ok for the most part. It's just not how I thought things would be."

Emma shook her head in understanding but decided to change the subject. "So, what are you going to school for?"

Miles shifted in his seat as if he was uncomfortable talking more about himself. Still, he finally responded, "You know, ever since I can remember walking on the beach, I was always mesmerized by the design of the Glass House. Even before us. The scale of the windows, the position of the house, and how it perfectly captures the water's light always drew me in each time I saw it."

This surprised her to hear, but she continued to listen intently.

"When I came back home from the service, I really struggled with what I was going to do. I walked this beach every day like it would somehow give me an answer. And it finally did. One day I found myself staring at the house yet again, and then I thought, well, why don't I build my own? That's when I decided I would go to architecture school. So now, I work for a design office in town and go to school at night."

This made Emma so happy to hear. "Miles, that is wonderful. I am so glad to hear that you are doing this. It's going to be fantastic for you and Isla."

Miles smiled back at her, "I have less than a year left, and the company I work for said they would hire me permanently. I'm trying my best to make this work."

She grinned widely, picked up the shot glass, and said, "Well, cheers to that!"

They each took a drink and then continued to chat easily for a long time. It felt good to talk and reconnect with one another.

Eventually, Miles had stretched out on the small couch across from the table while they chatted. At one point, when Emma came out from the bathroom, she found that he had fallen asleep. She found a blanket to cover him.

Just as she was deciding whether to stay or go, the baby began to stir. She thought Miles could use the rest, so she quietly picked up the baby to soothe her.

Isla looked up at Emma and smiled sweetly at her. They watched each other for a long time while Emma walked back and forth. For some odd reason, they felt a connection to each other.

Miles awoke to find Emma snuggling with Isla on the back bed. He smiled at the sweetness of the moment. He warmed a bottle quickly and handed it to Emma to feed the baby.

He sat on the edge of the bed and watched them with loving eyes. He couldn't help but think this was how it should have been from the beginning. It just seemed to make sense to have the three of them here together.

Isla quickly fell back asleep, so Miles laid her back in the crib.

Emma stayed on the bed quietly, as she didn't want to wake the baby. She watched Miles take care of Isla.

He came back in and laid down beside her. It felt natural to be there with her. They both turned on their backs and stared at the ceiling, unsure what to do. Of course, they knew what they wanted to do. The physical attraction could not be denied.

Yet, their circumstances had significantly changed. She was engaged to be married in just a few days, and he was trapped in a relationship with someone that was not about to let him go. Even prison wouldn't stop that.

A gentle rain had begun to fall outside, and the wet drops echoing on top of the camper created a soothing calm.

They both fell asleep within moments. Sometime during the night, their bodies found each other to intertwine into a comfortable embrace.

When the early morning came, they awoke facing each other, holding hands. Miles bent down before they were fully awake and gently kissed Emma on the forehead.

For a brief moment, they forgot their individual situations and were happy to be there close together. Emma looked up, and they immediately began to kiss. It was a gentle, soft kiss at first, and then the passion within them was instantly ignited.

Miles was quick to move on top of Emma without breaking their kiss. Then suddenly, Isla began to cry, which pulled them both out of the momentary glitch that had reignited what they knew had never really been lost.

He rose from the bed to get the baby. Emma lay there and wondered what had just happened.

One thing was certain. Their feelings were still very real for each other, and neither knew what to do.

CHAPTER 34

I SHOULD GO

"Always in my head."

The baby was ravenously hungry when she awoke, and her cries were a big indication of her appetite. Emma quickly took the baby and held her close while Miles warmed a new bottle.

The angry cries seemed to calm just a bit when Emma bounced her back and forth down the tiny hallway of the RV.

As soon as she had her bottle, she returned to her usual smiley self, which was a relief for Emma. She was not used to being around babies and didn't know if something was really wrong. By the sound of the loud cries, she wasn't sure.

"I think she gets her anger issues from her mother," Miles said lightly as they both watched Isla play with Emma's hair while drinking from her bottle.

This made Emma smile but also triggered worry in her head about Izzy. The girl may be locked up now, but she wouldn't be forever.

It was as if Miles could once again read Emma's mind, "I don't think Isla will know Izzy when she gets out. Hard to imagine that this little baby will be walking and talking by the time her mom gets out of prison two years from now."

A shadow crossed Emma's eyes with this realization. The comfortable, happy feelings of this morning's embrace were completely gone. That happiness was not to be as long as Izzy was around. And she always would be because of the baby.

Emma suddenly felt that familiar urgent feeling to get away. She gently but abruptly handed the baby back to Miles.

"I should go. Mom and Grammy will be back soon," she announced.

Miles could sense that she was uncomfortable.

"I get it, Emma. I fucked up. I mean, I really fucked things up for us. I don't think I can ever forgive myself for that. I'm so sorry."

Tears once again stung Emma's eyes at the realization that things would never be the same between them.

She touched his arm, looked into his blue eyes, and then down at baby Isla.

"You're right. Things got completely messed up. But you have Isla now. She needs to be your everything. You're on the right track with what you are doing. Don't stop. Keep moving forward for her." Then she paused and looked deeply into his eyes, "I suppose we just weren't meant to be."

With those words, Emma kissed baby Isla on top of her head and then gently kissed Miles on the lips one last time before beginning her walk back to the Glass House.

As she turned to leave, she looked back one more time at the two of them, "I will always love you. Take care of your daughter."

When she arrived home, an overwhelmingly large bouquet of all-white flowers awaited her at the front door. They were from Maxwell, of course.

The card attached read, *"My lovely Emma, I cannot wait to marry you and celebrate our life together. I'm sorry. All my love, Maxwell."*

What was a girl to do? She was supposed to get married in just a few days. It was too late to call it off. And honestly, there really wasn't a need.

She had to marry Maxwell. He was her life now. She had a very successful career because of him and an amazing life with him. Of course, she would marry Maxwell as planned.

As the day went on, she didn't have time to think of her night with Miles and Isla. Her mom and Grammy returned home, and soon after, Gemma and Kiera arrived.

When Maxwell and his parents showed up later that night, all was forgiven and almost completely forgotten. He hugged and kissed her with the passion of any groom getting ready to marry a bride.

She could do this. She could marry Maxwell and be happy. They loved each other, and they really did make a great team.

So, a few days later, that is precisely what they did. They exchanged their vows at the newly opened five-star resort built into the ocean cliffside about five miles away from her home.

Everything was white, crisp, and bright, from the flowers to the tent where the reception was held. The guests were also encouraged to wear white. Emma thought the wedding planner wanted to distract from the possibility of a gray day, which was common in the Pacific Northwest.

Surprisingly, she was right. It was a misty gray day, but luckily the rain held off in time for the newly married couple to take a few photos on the beach.

The photographer encouraged them to kiss in the wind, smile at each other and then run and jump in the air with all the wedded bliss they could muster.

From a distance, they appeared to be in love and happier than ever.

This is exactly what Miles could see from where he stood farther down the beach as he watched the love of his life in a beautiful gown frolic on the beach with her new husband. He let one small tear fall as he held Isla a little tighter and then began to walk in the opposite direction.

What appeared to be a joyous, happy day was only on the outside. The entire day, Emma could only think of Miles and how this should be their wedding.

Her wedding day was filled with tears of what others assumed was happiness, but she was really emotional about not marrying the true love of her life.

She shared none of her feelings with anyone as she didn't feel like she could. Being with Miles felt impossible, so she had no choice but to move forward.

The reception was decadent and full of east coast glam. Everyone danced, ate, and drank to their heart's content. Even Grammy did a little shimmy on the dance floor with Gemma.

This made Emma truly smile. For the first time that day, her heart was happy.

The evening ended with a grand display of fireworks and the couple driving off in a beautiful, gleaming white Rolls Royce to begin their perfect life together.

CHAPTER 35

THE IDEA OF YOU

"It's all an illusion."

Emma knew exactly when Izzy got out of jail.

The phone calls were increasing in frequency now. It was always an unlisted number, and words were never spoken in return to Emma's constant questioning.

"Hello? Is anyone there?"

"Hello? Please stop calling me. I don't know who this is, but I really don't have time for this."

Frequently, she would let the unknown caller roll into her voicemail, but they would stay on the line. Even on the recording, they wouldn't say anything.

It took several times for Emma to start piecing the details together. After one of her weekly calls with her mom and Grammy, she finally figured it out.

It was casually mentioned that Izzy was released early due to good behavior and the fact that the local prison had too many inmates for the space.

Miles and Emma had not spoken since the night at the beach. Clearly, they could not have a relationship, even a friendship, so why would they bother to contact each other?

Life had been quite hectic for Emma since the extravagant honeymoon that she went on with Maxwell. They enjoyed almost three weeks of sunshine and blue waters in Fiji. Maxwell certainly knew how to enjoy the rewards of their hardworking life.

The constant attention, lovemaking, and frolicking fun were quickly put aside as soon as they returned to their day-to-day life. Which is why the annoying phone calls were so irritating to Emma. She honestly didn't have time to deal with such an annoyance.

One afternoon, she was having lunch with Gemma when she received another silent phone call, "Ugh. This is just getting ridiculous."

Gemma looked at Emma with curiosity, "What's up? Wrong number?"

Emma responded with a sarcastic response, "More like wrong life. It may be coincidental, but ever since Izzy got out of jail, I keep getting these phone calls. No one ever says anything. It's just silence."

Gemma was distracted by digging her lipstick out of her purse, "Well, then don't bloody answer it."

"That's the thing," Emma explained, "Even if I don't answer it, I get a voicemail message of nothing but silence.

It's happening practically every day now, and what used to be annoying is now starting to get creepy."

Gemma always loved a bit of tea, in and outside her cup, "Do you think that crazy bitch is stalking you from the west coast? Good god, enough, already. I mean, you'd think she would want nothing to do with you since she spent time in jail for almost killing you."

This got the attention of the surrounding tables in the restaurant, and Emma quietly whispered, "Shh. The whole place doesn't need to know about my ex's crazy girlfriend." The absurdity of the whole conversation made them laugh, and they moved on with their lunch.

As they were saying goodbye on the busy street, Gemma mentioned it again, "Just be careful. That woman is crazy, so I would steer clear of her path no matter where you are."

Emma nodded in agreement, "Well, wish me luck. I have to go back home tomorrow for Grammy's birthday. Maxwell can't make it, of course, so let's just hope I can make it there and back without any drama."

She returned to the Glass House late the following evening and went straight to bed. The next morning, Emma was greeted with a day full of sunshine and the welcoming smiles of her two favorite ladies.

All three enjoyed a leisurely breakfast before heading to the bakery to put the finishing touches on Grammy's birthday celebration.

It was to be held the next night at the Glass House. The party would be a casual dinner with some of Grammy's closest friends. The main detail was, of course, the cake.

Grammy's only request was a decadent chocolate cake baked by her favorite granddaughter. This brought a smile to

Emma's face, and she was thrilled to be able to be there to bake it.

"So, Grammy, what about a Black Forest cake for your special party?" Emma asked while sipping her coffee after their breakfast.

Her grandmother quickly smiled and responded, "That sounds magnificent, Emma. Are you going to bake it today or tomorrow? I'd love to help if I could."

After a bit more coffee and discussion, they decided that tomorrow morning would be the best time to assemble the main birthday attraction.

"So, with that decided, Mom, do you need any help at the bakery today?"

Caroline seemed quieter than usual but perked up at Emma's question, "Well, if you could spare a little time later today, it would be wonderful to have the extra hands to help with tomorrow's orders."

Emma didn't hesitate, "Of course, Mom, I would love to help. So, I will get dressed, and we can head into town. Sound good?"

Caroline and Emma worked hard to fulfill the bakery orders for the next day, along with the delicious goodies for Grammy's birthday.

It was refreshing and motivating for the ladies to work in sync and with such efficiency. They hadn't spent time in the bakery together since the wedding, and it felt so good.

There is such beauty in working so closely with someone. When no words are needed, there is a symphonic connection that cannot be mistaken.

The exhilaration that Emma felt from being with her mother that day continued late into the early evening. It was still summer, so the sun was shining brightly. She didn't yet want to go home and decided to go for a drive down the coast.

She had heard that Big Reggie had opened an oceanside bar and wanted to check it out. By the time she arrived, the sun was just getting ready to set. It was a gorgeous evening, and there were bonfires set up randomly on the beach.

Emma grabbed a beer from the bar and headed to an Adirondack chair on the outer deck. The ocean and sun had choreographed a beautiful scene, so she didn't want to miss a moment.

A familiar voice called out behind her as she settled into her chair. It was Big Reg, and he happily called out, "Well, hello there, beautiful."

Smiling as she turned around, Emma stood up quickly. Before she knew what was happening, he had swept her up off of her feet into a huge, welcoming hug.

He spoke first, "You are more gorgeous than I remember. How are you, darling?"

His voice was much deeper, almost sensuous than she remembered. She began to blush, "Big Reg, how are you? Gosh, I have missed you."

He quickly responded as he set her back down, and they both settled into the chairs on the deck, "Well, you've been a little busy getting married and becoming a TV star and all." He said this with a chuckle that brought back their memories of high school.

She giggled and waved her hand up in the air, "Hey, now! Look what you're doing! I'd say your days have been busy, too. This place is amazing, Reg!"

It was Big Reg, that now looked a little uncomfortable, "Ah, what else was I going to do? I'm a born-and-bred coastie, and I love beer. So, it only made sense to open a bar on the beach, babe!"

She smiled broadly at his words, "Now that you mention it, that makes perfect sense. You've got your own piece of heaven right here, so thank you for sharing it with the rest of us."

He looked at her directly and explained, "You know, it's not just me that came up with this place. Miles had the vision, and I just came up with the cash."

Emma was intrigued, "What are you talking about? I didn't know Miles was a part of this?"

Reg continued to explain, "Yeah, we spent many nights at the bar in town talking about how we could make a better place. He sketched this out from top to bottom on the back of a drink napkin. It's hanging above the bar in there if you want to check it out."

He waved his hand towards the large glass windows that perfectly framed the ocean view.

Emma couldn't help but suddenly see Miles's vision for this place. Similar to The Glass House, no view was obstructed. The classic wooden frame of the bar was only there to offer protection from the windy, wet elements of the Pacific Northwest.

Otherwise, the beauty of the coastline was the star of the show at this place. Making this connection made her smile, and Big Reg knew she was thinking of him.

Just as they were chatting, the unmistakable roar of a Harley Davidson came closer to the deck. They looked over to immediately recognize Miles stepping off his bike and removing his helmet. He looked at the two of them with his familiar, shy smile and headed inside to get a drink.

After a few minutes, Miles came out, joined them, and said, "Well, this is a sight for sore eyes. I can't even remember a time beyond high school when the three of us were in the same place." They all smiled at this memory.

Emma and Big Reg had the last two chairs on the deck, so Reggie suggested they head down to one of the open bonfires on the beach. "For old times' sake."

As they walked into the sand, memories of the old days began rushing back for all of them, including thoughts of Izzy.

Emma didn't hesitate to speak up, "You know, if this is uncomfortable, I can go. I don't want to cause any issues, Miles."

The glow of the fire made her look even more gorgeous than he remembered, and for a moment, it took his breath away.

Some things never change, he thought. Miles gave her a sideways glance as he said, "No worries. She's with the baby and doesn't need to know about anything that I do tonight. I needed a break, and she knows that. I'm good. It will be great for us to catch up with Reg."

Emma didn't want to push anything even though she felt uneasy. She just nodded in response and settled into a beach chair close to the fire.

They all took a moment to take in their surroundings. There was a magical glow from the fire, and as they gazed upward, the unending amount of stars in the sky was simply stunning.

Big Reggie was the first to mention the stars, "Not a building on earth that could compare to the beauty of that there sky. But, ya know, Miles gave it his best shot."

He waved his beer high in the air as if offering a blessing to the planets and stars above, and they all laughed at his observation.

In true high school style, Miles flicked his beer cap at Reg as if to get him to stop talking.

Reg hit it back to him, "Don't act like you didn't do some stellar shit of your own with this place, man. You're talented, and I'm gonna tell her about it.

Miles just nodded and looked into the flames of the fire. Soon the three of them fell into a familiar banter about high school memories and tried to catch each other up on their lives.

At last, Big Reg stood up, "Well, this has been great and all, but I got a bar to run. Y'all stay out here as long as you like, but I gotta get back in there."

Emma immediately stood up and wrapped herself in a giant bear hug from Reg.

She spoke softly, "Thank you for tonight, Reg. I have missed you."

He picked her up and gave her a jovial spin around the sand, "Well, just don't stay away so long next time, chef." With that, he saluted goodnight to Miles and headed back inside.

A very uncomfortable silence fell between Miles and Emma as Reg walked away.

They were both lost in their thoughts about the risks they took by being alone on the beach. Yet, the beauty of the fire, the slow-burning glow on the ocean's horizon combined with the view of Haystack Rock, was too much to resist.

Very few people understood the magical shadows of the last glow of a sunset on the horizon. It can create a vision and a feeling that cannot be experienced anywhere else.

So, they sat in silence for quite a long time until Emma began to speak quietly.

"You know, now that I have my place in New York, I've begun to decorate it. I picked out this artwork that's a reproduction of a painting called Haystacks by Monet. It's real haystacks in an open field as the sun is setting or maybe rising. I'm not sure. But I didn't realize why I was drawn to that painting until right now. It reminds me of this view."

Miles looked over at Emma, completely drawn into her words as she continued, "They are both mesmerizing and beautiful in different ways. And they both capture the beauty of light based on the time of day. I think I was drawn to that painting because it drew me home, to the Glass House."

She caught herself as she was thinking out loud and was momentarily embarrassed, "I'm sorry. I think I am rambling."

Smiling easily, Miles glanced at Emma, "You're not rambling. I was just enjoying your thoughts. I've missed hearing them. And it is so refreshing to hear versus the constant complaining that Izzy does all day, every day."

A shadow crossed Emma's eyes momentarily, and Miles immediately noticed, "Listen, she can rant all she wants about you. There's something that pulls me to you, whether you are physically here or not. No one can stop that. Not Iz, not me, not you." He moved closer to her at that moment, and she looked at him deeply.

"It's like the light that is reflected onto those Haystacks. Sometimes it's so dark and can barely be seen with the naked eye, but it's always there. Then there are the days when the sun shines so brightly and magically on them that it's inescapable. Something always reminds me of you, and it draws me back to you."

Miles knew he couldn't kiss her like he achingly wanted to, so he reached for her hand.

The simple gesture of touching each other's hands was a deep connection that only the two of them could feel.

Mesmerized by the glow of the fire and the warmth of each other's hand, held them there for what seemed like hours.

Finally, it was time to go. They wanted to stay there forever but knew that they couldn't.

Miles slowly walked Emma to her car, and when they arrived, he spoke quietly, "I carry your light with me all the time. I like the idea of you being with me. It pushes me forward, kind of like those haystacks in the distance. I don't always see you, but I know you are there. That's something no one can take away from me."

He leaned down and pressed an emotion-filled kiss on the top of her head. Emma stood there with her heart aching for more. But she knew she couldn't. They couldn't. Life really sucks sometimes.

CHAPTER 36

LAST WASTED EVENING

"Take me away."

Grammy's birthday party was nothing short of perfect. Emma couldn't remember when she last saw her grandmother happier except for her early memories of when Grandpa was still alive.

The ladies of the Glass House were happy and content for the first time since the wedding. The night was clear, a little chilly, but perfect for sitting by the fire out on the deck.

After the last of the guests left, they retreated to their favorite outdoor chairs and sipped on some champagne.

Caroline raised her glass and looked lovingly at her mother, "Cheers to the best woman, mother, and friend I could ever ask for. I love you, Mom."

Through the glow of the fire, they could see the tears glistening in Rosie's eyes.

She held her glass high in the air and said, "To my beautiful ladies. You are my light and the reason that I get up every morning. Thank you for such a lovely evening."

Emma was just about to say a few words when they were all jolted by a searing sound of a dog howling and a woman's voice screaming in the distance.

Caroline and Emma jumped up from their seats and raced to the deck railing to peer into the distance. It was very dark except for the reflection of the quarter moon shining over the water.

Emma immediately recognized the voice. It was Izzy.

"Mom, I think we should go inside. That's Izzy with Jake. I don't want to deal with her, so let's go inside, and maybe she will just go away."

Izzy's voice was getting louder, and they could see she was making a beeline for the Glass House. Leaving their drinks and the fire behind, they all moved as quickly as possible into the living room, locking the doors behind them.

Emma kept her cell phone in her hand, ready to call 911 if needed.

The peaceful, festive evening was long forgotten as they all watched from inside as Izzy staggered up the steps and onto the deck.

"Get your fucking ass out here, bitch! I told you to stay away from my family, but apparently, you don't listen very well!" Izzy screamed.

She was visibly drunk and unstable. Jake was at her side, begrudgingly attached to the leash that she held in her hand.

He was whining and kept trying to jump up on her, which only irritated Izzy further, "Get off me, you little fucker!"

The champagne glasses had temporarily captured her attention, and she dragged the puppy with her to drink from the three glasses.

As she took the last swig from one of the glasses, she peered into a large window of the house to notice that she had a captive audience.

"Oh, well, hello there, bitches! All three of you are here for the show, huh? Do you want to watch me beat your precious Emma's ass? Ok, let's get going then!" she yelled as she threw the crystal glass against the window, shattering it into a million little pieces.

Grammy jumped from the sound of the crash and automatically leaned into Caroline. This infuriated Emma.

She immediately handed her phone to Caroline, told her to call the police, and grabbed one of the fireplace pokers from the mantle.

She shouted through the door before opening it in a rage, "Izzy, what the fuck? That is enough! You can threaten me all you want but leave my family out of this!"

This made Jake bark, and Izzy lunged forward at Emma. Jake jumped on Izzy, making her lose her balance.

She immediately screamed, "I hate this fucking dog!" and kicked him in the backside.

He lunged at her again, which caused her to drop the leash. Jake ran beside Emma, putting him in full-on protection mode.

Izzy sneered, "Oh, of course, he runs to you. Fucking traitor."

Jake barked at her continuously, and Emma yelled, "Oh, come on, Izzy, it's a dog. A great dog that loves your daughter. He just hates you because you are so fucking mean."

Izzy screamed out wildly and lunged at them both. Jake jumped up and knocked her to the ground. She tried to push him off her, but he growled at her long enough that she finally submitted to his fury.

Emma swiftly grabbed the leash, keeping the poker securely in her other hand, "Izzy, this is your last chance. Get the fuck away from my house."

With an unexpected strength, Izzy kicked her feet upwards with all her might. One leg sent Jake flying backward, and the other forced Emma to fall back as well.

She came to her feet instantly, "The fuck I will! You can't tell me to stay away from your family when you get your goddamn hands on my man every chance you get!"

Her rant continued as Emma tried to figure out what to do to calm her down, "See, the problem with living in a small town is that you can't go anywhere without someone seeing you. And you and Miles weren't even shy about hiding your stupid shit. Sitting by the fire, holding hands, leaning close to each other. How did you not think that someone would see? How could you not think that I have people to tell me what Miles does every moment? Do you think I don't know about the night in the trailer? I know shit. I know you're a fucking slut! I know you want my family, you goddamn bitch! And now you're going to pay!"

Now it was Izzy standing over Emma. The poker was still firmly in Emma's grip, but the dog's incessant barking distracted them both.

At the same time, both women screamed, "Jake, STOP!" but he was relentless. Innately, he was trying to protect Emma and lunged at Izzy again. This time, he bit her in the leg, again making her fall to the ground.

"Fucking asshole dog! Damn it! He bit me!" Izzy screamed.

Emma got to her feet, waving the poker over Izzy's body, "I'll say it one last time. Get the fuck out of here, you crazy bitch!"

Crying, bleeding, and slightly scared, Izzy tried to limp down the stairs. Emma and Jake stood back to make sure that she would indeed leave when Izzy lost her balance and fell violently down the remainder of the stairs, landing in the sand at the very bottom.

This scared Emma. She dropped the leash and ran down the stairs, screaming, "IZZY!"

Emma ran so fast down the stairs she didn't see that Izzy had purposely stuck her arm out so that Emma would trip and land hard on the sand beside her.

Hurt and bleeding, the exhilaration of her anger overtook all pain, and Izzy flipped on top of Emma. Fury was in her eyes, and she trapped Emma beneath her grip, "You motherfucking bitch. Now I can finally kill you."

Izzy began choking Emma with every ounce of strength she had. Jake had bounded down the stairs and started yanking at Izzy's arms and pantlegs, trying to pull her off Emma while growling madly and barking.

Poker still in hand, Emma swung wildly, first hitting Izzy in the hip, then one more time in the shoulder. Gasping for air, she was afraid of losing consciousness.

All at once, through tear-filled, squinted eyes, Emma saw Miles towering over them both.

"God damn it, Izzy! Get off of her!" he screamed.

Miles yanked Izzy by the back of the head, pulling her hair and shoving her into the sand.

Suddenly, he had both of her arms pinned over her head, and he sat on her to try to contain her rage.

"What in the actual fuck, Izzy?" he continued to scream. "Emma did nothing wrong. You are trying to kill her, AGAIN?"

Lights and sirens began wailing in the street. Jake continued to bark and jump from Miles to Emma. Meanwhile, Emma grabbed her throat, struggling to sit up to catch her breath.

For a brief moment, she thought of taking the fireplace poker and striking Izzy with it while Miles had her pinned to the ground. Rage seared through every ounce of her being.

At that exact moment, Jake jumped on her, and Miles was able to free one hand to touch her leg.

Her sanity returned enough for her to take a deep breath, drop the poker to the ground, and scream for dear life.

The cops arrived on the scene to a petrified Emma, Jake barking wildly while bearing his teeth, and Miles still trying to restrain Izzy.

There was no question about what had occurred in the moments before. Izzy was promptly handcuffed and taken to jail.

Emma lay in the sand, still gripping the fireplace poker and scared out of her mind. Jake found a protective place at her feet while Miles just peered down at them both in a bewildered stupor.

The mother of his child had once again been dragged off to jail, while the love of his life looked war-ravaged and scared.

What a fucking worthless evening.

CHAPTER 37

GOODBYE, IZZY

"Goodbye."

An ambulance arrived immediately after the police and checked out Emma. Besides being in shock and having mild bruises around her neck, she was ok.

Wordlessly, Miles walked Emma up the stairs to the deck and into the house, where Caroline and Rosie were pensively waiting.

Her mother ran over to her when she saw her daughter, "Oh my god, Emma, what happened to you?"

"Mom, it's ok. The cops took Izzy into custody a few minutes ago. She tried to choke me, but she didn't kill me, thanks to Jake and Miles. Again." Emma explained in a hoarse voice.

The worn-out pup had easily settled down in front of the warm fireplace. He knew his master and friend were ok, so he could rest.

Miles finally spoke up, still bewildered, "Thank god for Jake. I ran down the beach following the sound of his barking. I had no idea where Izzy had gone when I woke up."

Rosie spoke quietly, "Miles, this has to stop. This is no way for you to live, and Emma can't keep getting attacked by that girl."

He hung his head heavily as she spoke, feeling every ounce of the weight of her words. All he could do was slowly shake his head in agreement.

As Grammy spoke, tears once again stung Emma's eyes. It was all too much to take in. How could a person want to do so much harm to another? She would never quite understand.

She also immediately recalled the rage she felt as Izzy attacked her and when Miles had her restrained on the beach. Emma had never felt like that before, yet she instantly felt it returning at this moment. Izzy could have hurt her family.

Caroline was standing with her arm around Emma, and suddenly, Emma stepped away from her to speak.

"Miles, I love you. I will probably always love you. You are a part of me that I don't completely understand, but this can't happen again. Izzy has now tried to kill me twice, but this time was the worst. She could have hurt my mom and Grammy."

A wave of emotion physically overtook her just at the mere thought of what could have happened.

"We cannot do this anymore. As long as Izzy is in your life, this will always be a problem. You have a daughter with her.

She will never let you and I forget it. I hope and pray that she goes to prison and stays there for a very long time, but I will always be wondering and fearing when she may try to attack me again."

She looked over at Miles and saw tears streaming down his face. He just quietly said, "I know. You're right. I know."

Just as Emma was going to step toward him, Grammy collapsed into unconsciousness onto the floor.

Caroline screamed, "Mom!" Emma shouted, 'Grammy!" Jake barked, and Miles ran to Rosie.

Grammy had another stroke. The stress of the evening was just too much on her body, and she collapsed. She spent a month in the hospital, and Emma refused to leave her side.

Once she came home, Caroline all but ordered Emma to get back to her life in New York.

"You have a husband and a career to focus on. We are fine. You need to go back," her mother pleaded.

They had been down this road before, and her mom knew what to do. There would be a constant influx of nurses and physical therapists to help Rosie recover. There was nothing for her daughter to do.

At the end of a very long conversation, Emma, full of guilt, finally agreed. She had been filled with anger, remorse, and unending sadness since that night. How had her life turned into this nightmare?

She couldn't sleep because she only dreamt of Izzy continuously attacking her. Emma felt a constant sense of dread knowing that she was forced to stay away from Miles, even though Izzy was locked behind bars.

Izzy was being arraigned in court in the next few weeks, but until then, she was spending her time in a jail cell not far from downtown. Emma still didn't feel safe, but her worry about Grammy overrode her fear most days.

Miles had tried to apologize to the ladies several times, and Caroline sent him away every time. He was at a loss. So, he just continued to focus on Isla and school.

Emma went back to New York, but something was just off. Maxwell seemed annoyed that she had been gone for so long, yet his schedule didn't allow them to spend much time together outside of work.

In the past, this would have made Emma angry. This time around, she didn't have enough energy to care. She was fine when she was working, but as soon as the day was done, she was exhausted and unmotivated.

Thankfully, she had her friends. Gemma kept her schedule full and was always ready to share a drink or two with Emma. Kiera was just a constant source of comfort. She was the one that would offer a kind smile or gentle squeeze of her hand when she could see Emma getting overwhelmed. They were her rocks.

It was late on a Friday night, and the girls sat in Emma's expansive living room. Maxwell was traveling again, so it was another girl's night in, with takeout food and wine.

Emma had been typically quiet all week, and the other two were determined to get her to vent about what was going on with her. They knew about the traumatic experience at the beach and were trying their best to get her to move forward.

Kiera spoke first, "Em, I've really missed talking to you."

Emma smiled and glanced at her friend, "I talk to you more than I talk to my husband. What are you saying?"

Gemma spoke up, "Oh bloody hell, Emma, you know what we are talking about. Tell us what is going on with you?"

There was a long pause as they all waited for a response. Finally, Emma began to quietly explain, "It's complicated. To say I feel guilty about what happened to Grammy is an understatement. But then I get angry because it really wasn't my fault. Izzy is to blame. No, Miles is to blame. Fuck! They're both to blame. But I am the one left dealing with the impact of their mess."

The two other friends exchanged a look of understanding, then looked back at Emma as she continued, "And Maxwell is no help whatsoever. He's been traveling a lot and never has any time to spend with me, yet he's mad that I was gone for so long. We're both so frustrated."

Emma thought back to the conversation that they had just had that morning.

Maxwell was angrily shoving clothes in his suitcase to leave as Emma followed him around the bedroom, trying to confront their unhappiness.

He swiftly turned around to her and spoke, "It's getting to be too much. If I don't make you happy, I can hop on a plane and leave you alone. I'll be gone, and you'll have to deal with what that feels like for once."

He was referring to her sleepless nights and depression over the last several weeks because Emma just wasn't getting over that she was attacked again by her former friend. He also told her he hated when she left him to go home.

His words cut her like a knife. She needed comfort, support, and love from her husband. Instead, she was met with defense and another packed suitcase that he carried out the door, along with her heart.

Emma continued to talk to her friends, "It hurts. It pisses me off. Is this what marriage is supposed to be? It doesn't feel like it."

Gemma was annoyed, grabbed the open bottle of wine, and refilled all their glasses, "He's a mother-fucking asshole. How can he not see what you have been through?"

Kiera spoke up, "That's just it. He can't. He wasn't there both times and never understood why they let Izzy out of prison early the first time.

Emma nodded in agreement, "I know he's mad about that. Believe me. But what about our marriage? Why does work come before us? Is this how it's always going to be?"

The three of them fell into silence, thinking about her questions.

After a long time, Emma spoke again in a way that seemed that she was talking out loud to herself as much as she was saying it to her friends, "Does it have to be this way? I'm not sure, but here we are. And there he goes. This isn't how it used to be. I'm not sure who we were, but it wasn't this. How long do I hold on? Or do I hold on because I'm in such a bad place?"

The girls took each other's hands as Emma began to cry.

Kiera spoke again, "Those are good questions. Sometimes we hold on until we can better see where we are headed. But promise me that you won't lose any more of yourself. It's too hard to watch you slip into this sad person that I don't know. Hold on to us if you have to."

This startled Emma, and she looked at her friend with tear-filled eyes, "Have I been that bad?"

She looked back at forth from Gemma to Kiera. Slowly, they both nodded their heads in agreement.

Gemma squeezed Emma's hand a little tighter, "Love, you always have us. Just don't leave yourself behind in the process. You don't have to decide right now. I know you'll figure it out. And maybe when the dust settles, Maxwell will come back around."

Emma let the tears roll down her cheeks as she squeezed both her friend's hands in her own and quietly said, "Maybe."

They finished up their wine, and the friends headed back to their place. Emma poured herself one more glass after they were gone and found herself gazing out the big windows overlooking the city.

Suddenly, the front door opened, and Maxwell stood there with his suitcase. He simply said, "Hi."

Emma was so relieved that she dissolved into tears and fell into his arms.

Maxwell squeezed her back, "Hey, what's going on? I thought you'd be happy to see me?"

She laughed through her tears, "Oh, I am so happy to see you. Thank you for coming home."

He dropped his suitcase, slammed the door closed, and swept her up in his arms. Maxwell carried Emma to the bedroom and made love to her with the passion they hadn't felt in months. It was exactly what Emma needed to feel.

Afterward, they lay there holding each other in silence for a long time.

Finally, Emma found the words she wanted to say to her husband for several weeks, "Maxwell, I'm sorry. I know I haven't been here, and now that I'm back, I know I haven't been myself. It's been hard, but I am so glad you are here now."

Maxwell pulled his wife closer to him, "I get it. Things haven't been the same. And I have been mad as hell about what happened to you. But I feel helpless, too. It's like you have a whole different life when you are out there, and I'm not a part of it."

Emma better understood where he came from now, "I'm sorry. I didn't know you felt that way. Let's find a way to fix that. Come home with me next time. You haven't been there since the wedding. Mom and Grammy would love to see you."

She felt Maxwell tense slightly when she invited him back to the Glass House.

"What's wrong?" she asked.

He took a long deep breath and hesitated, "Nothing. Let's plan a trip home soon."

They fell asleep in each other's arms that night, something that hadn't happened in a long time. As she drifted off, Emma thought hopefully that maybe they would get through this bump in their marriage.

It was the middle of the night, and they awoke to a phone endlessly ringing.

Amid their passion, they had left their cell phones in the living room, so it took some time to figure out what was happening.

Emma stumbled in the dark, following the ringtone and the glow of her phone. She found it under the coffee table and quickly recognized the number.

It was Miles.

She answered, "Hello? Miles?"

Silence.

Not again.

"Hello? Izzy? Miles? Who's there?" she repeated.

At this point, Maxwell had entered the room and was listening intently.

After an endless pause, Emma heard his voice.

It was Miles. His voice sounded hoarse and full of shock, "Em. Emma. She's dead. Izzy's dead."

CHAPTER 38

BREAK MY HEART

"Not my soul."

She looks up, and there he is. She doesn't believe it at first, but before her are his brilliant blue eyes staring back at her.

He gently smiles and quietly says, "I love you. I've wanted to say that to you for so long."

She is shocked. How is this happening? Before she can answer, they have left an outdoor table at a restaurant and are wandering down the street, chatting about how they feel and the details of what happened to keep them apart.

Then she remembers that he is still with her. Wait, she can't go with him. Suddenly, the dangerous woman is standing in front of them with hurt and anger all over her face. The woman begins to speak, and as she does, her face changes dark and then morphs into a skeleton face, with her skin dripping off her skull.

"Do you think you can have him? Do you think that this is ok? He's going to hurt you just like he hurt me. It won't work. He will leave you and come back to me. Again." Emma is scared but also feels the hurt and anger return, flooding over her like a wave that can't be conquered. She feels her emotions being taken under like a giant ocean wave.

Suddenly everything is gone. She awoke in a searingly hot sweat. It was still dark outside, and Maxwell was sleeping soundly beside her. She had an undeniable urge to get up and move, so she wandered into the kitchen. Her thoughts became a little clearer, and it didn't take long for her to remember the phone call from the previous night.

Izzy's dead.

Miles called in shock and in a condition that she didn't recognize.

From what she could gather from his explanation, Izzy got out of jail and went on a crazy rampage to try to find him and the baby.

It turned out that Izzy's old high school boyfriend, Andy, had just been promoted to assistant Sheriff at the local police station, where she was being held until her arraignment.

Through a series of flirtatious and manipulative conversations, Izzy convinced Andy to "just let her out for a few hours to see her baby."

He finally agreed to let her see the baby. Nervously, he drove her late that night after the other officers had left. He made sure to keep her handcuffed until they got to the trailer at the beach, but then she took off.

Initially, she went straight to the RV, but this was just long enough for Andy to let his guard down.

The night was pitch black, with a powerful wind blowing in off the ocean. When she discovered no one was there, she flew into a rage, smashing everything in her path.

According to Andy, she kept screaming Miles and Isla's names. He didn't think much of it at first, and then he realized she was walking, then running down the beach.

He knew he was taking a huge chance by letting her come out here, but she gave him a false sense of trust, combined with a lot of "mom guilt" about not being able to see her baby.

It took Andy way too long to figure out where she was going, and by the time he went after her, it was too late. As he went running down the beach after her in the ravaging wind, he could hear bits and pieces of her wild rant.

"You stupid, fucking bitch! I'm coming after you!"

"You have my baby and my man!"

"Emma, I am going to kill you!"

And on and on it went until…silence.

Andy had his flashlight out, trying to keep track of her in the distance, but he was too far behind. He only had her footprints in the sand to go on.

The wind was out of control and spinning the sand in his face, which made it even harder to keep up. When he lost track of her footprints, he immediately understood why.

In her angry rant on that black night, she lost her way and walked right into the angry waves of the ocean. She likely got pulled under by a strong undertow and couldn't fight the strength of the water.

Andy had already called for backup, but it was too late. An extensive search party, including Miles, tried desperately to find her. The Coast Guard brought in their best rescue team to try and save her.

By the time sunrise came, her lifeless body had washed up on shore about two miles away, somewhere in between the RV and the Glass House.

Izzy was dead.

The sun was just beginning to rise over the city skyline, and although exhaustion coursed through Emma's body, she didn't want to sleep. She felt a little numb and, dare she think it, a little relieved to hear that Izzy was truly gone.

She was sad for her former friend realizing there was something within Izzy that would never change about her feelings for Emma. That was a very scary realization.

Emma also felt horrible for Miles and Isla. She would never wish that someone would have to grow up without their mother, but then again, maybe that would be the best in the long run for them both.

The sun's glow continued to cascade brilliant colors across the cityscape as the early morning hours ticked forward. Soon, a soft light of sunshine warmed Emma as she lay on the couch in the living room. She gently closed her eyes and finally drifted off to sleep.

Awakened a few hours later by the doorbell, Emma was a little startled but lay back down on the couch when she heard Maxwell answer the door. He was talking in a hushed voice to the other person, but Emma was too exhausted to care.

She closed her eyes and tried to relax when she heard Maxwell enter the room. Emma opened her eyes to see her husband standing before her with a large white box topped with a giant red silk bow.

He gently smiled down at her, "I promise this was planned before the surprising events of last night, but I still think it might help."

Just as he finished speaking, she heard a small whine come from the box. This made her smile broadly, "Give me the box! I have to see what's inside!"

To her delight, as she lifted the top, a beautiful silver-gray Labrador puppy with gorgeous sky-blue eyes bounded onto her lap.

Emma giggled at this as she quickly scooped the dog into her arms, "Now, who is this adorable little one?"

Maxwell was relieved to see his wife smiling, "Well, that's for you to decide. What would you like to name this sweet little girl?"

They had talked recently about getting a dog, but as much as they worked and Maxwell constantly traveled, they had decided it wasn't the right time.

She looked at Maxwell inquisitively, "I thought we decided to wait until we could be home more before we got a dog."

He sat beside her and began petting the excited pup, "Well, that's the thing. The way things are going and expanding, I don't think we are going to slow down anytime soon. So, why not get a friend to keep you company while I'm gone? We own the office, so you can take her with you."

Emma's face fell at his words, "What do you mean when you say 'while I'm gone'? Why are you telling me this now?"

Maxwell started to feel uncomfortable, so he stood back up and paced in front of the couch, "Look, the network loves everything that we are doing. They want more shows as fast as we can produce them. There's a fantastic new chef in England that will bring in a new demographic, so I have to go there." He hesitated before he continued, "I'll be gone for a month or so."

There was no doubt she was upset at this news. She gently pushed the puppy aside so that she could stand directly in front of Maxwell.

Angrily she said, "So, this is how you handle it? You get me another responsibility to keep me busy so I won't be so sad that my husband is leaving, yet again? Maxwell, I need you here. Not only for work but I'm not ok. Especially after last night." Tears instantly came to her eyes as she saw the intense annoyance that crossed his face.

He angrily responded, "Oh, here we go again. Emma. When are you going to leave that shit with Miles behind? Enough already!"

His words shocked Emma, "What are you talking about? You don't think that Izzy dying isn't a big deal? That I'm just supposed to get over it? That's a big part of my life. And it just happened a few hours ago! I can't believe you, Maxwell!"

She stormed off to the bedroom, only to discover two large, packed suitcases. Emma was incensed. He was leaving and seemed to manipulate this entire situation.

The puppy came bounding in and pounced on the bed excitedly while Maxwell casually walked in behind her.

"Emma, no, that's not what I mean. I just meant that we have a life to live. We have a great business together, and you know what a great team we are." he tried to explain.

She was full-on crying now with a multitude of emotions coursing through her. Exhausted and mentally drained from the news about Izzy, she wasn't in a good place to deal with Maxwell's blow about leaving her alone. Again.

She couldn't help but think that if he truly loved her, the only place that he would want to be was by her side, especially when she was in this much pain. Yet, Maxwell seemed like he couldn't leave fast enough. He wanted to leave, or else he wouldn't have put all these details in place just to announce his lengthy travels. He had to have known how upset she would be.

He tried to hug her, and she immediately pushed him away. This made the puppy bark, thinking it was playtime. Emma scooped up the dog to avoid having to deal with her husband.

"I'm going to take this little girl for a walk. I assume you will be gone when I get back?" she snapped.

Hanging his head low, Maxwell just nodded his head in agreement as she walked away.

She closed the door to their apartment and waited until the door to the elevator completely closed before she sank to the floor and sobbed. The sweet little puppy could only jump on her lap and lick away her salty tears.

Emma knew at that moment that her marriage was over, and her heart was broken once again.

CHAPTER 39

THE SPACE BETWEEN

"Pulling me back to you."

Emma laughed lightly as Brayley gently tugged her forward as they walked in the sunshine on their way to the office.

She was thinking about the last six months and how much things had changed in such a short period of time.

With the help of Gemma and Kiera, they decided that the puppy's name should be Brayley.

The dog had become her constant companion. Maxwell was right that she needed her newest best friend.

The divorce was finalized the month before, as it was an easy dissolution. As it turned out, Maxwell and Emma were excellent business partners but lousy as a married couple.

He quickly went back to dating when he was in town but traveled almost constantly.

She moved back in with her dear friends, although now they had a bigger place with a proper kitchen and plenty of closet space. This was a necessity for Gemma.

The decision not to attend Izzy's funeral was relatively easy for Emma. She didn't want to add unnecessary drama to a very tragic situation.

Miles seemed to be ok but kept his distance. They talked once more right after the funeral. He sounded numb and even more broken.

Isla was crying in the background, so the conversation was brief, with no promises of talking again. Emma didn't want to push, and honestly, she was hurting too.

The whole situation was sad. It just seemed to be too much. She thought of Miles often, but the gravitational pull to him seemed less frequent. If she was truly honest with herself, she was still afraid.

The biggest threat to their relationship, Izzy, was gone, but a relationship with Miles still seemed too risky. She felt very fragile, so she didn't reach out.

Work, her friends, and Brayley kept her busy. She couldn't say for sure that she was happy, but she was relieved now that the divorce was final. She felt at peace with where she was in her life.

Maxwell would invite her to dinner whenever he was in town. He always found his way to Sam's bar to have a drink every once in a while. It seemed like he was happiest single, almost longing for the past.

Sometimes Emma would entertain the idea of getting back together with him, but lately, she just wanted to move forward.

The latest big project was opening a chain of boutique-style bakeries across the US called Emma's Family Bakery.

The shops were purposely small, with homemade, fresh baked goods offered daily. They were a huge success and often had a line down the block before the doors opened early in the morning.

Emma was astounded by their success, whereas Maxwell seemed to expect it. He was always true to his belief in her success, and she knew that was what helped push her forward.

The next store openings were scheduled for San Francisco, LA, Seattle, and Portland. It would be a lengthy trip, so Emma decided to bring Brayley along this time. She planned to spend the weekends at the Glass House. The dog would be some much-needed entertainment for Grammy and her mom.

Grammy hadn't been feeling as strong lately, and Caroline was getting increasingly worried. Emma tried to reassure her but was distracted by the recent bakery openings.

Just as she was boarding her flight from LA to Seattle, her mom called. Emma doesn't remember much after her mom announced that Grammy had passed.

It was so unexpected. Caroline and Emma were in shock. In a teary-eyed blur, Emma somehow managed to change her flight and find her way back to Oregon.

How could she have missed this? How could she not know that Grammy was so ill?

Emma's grief was overwhelming, and she just wanted to go home to be with her mom.

When she finally arrived at the Glass House, it was eerily quiet. Usually, the stillness of the house was peaceful and comforting. Yet, today, it was heartbreaking.

As she walked through the door, the realization that Grammy wasn't there hit her squarely in the heart. Caroline met her daughter there, and the two women hugged each other tightly while the tears of grief poured from them both.

After a while, they made their way to the living room and settled onto the couch to chat. Her mom always knew a fresh pot of tea and fresh-baked cookies would comfort her daughter.

Emma smiled for the first time all day when she saw the treats, and Brayley curled up in front of the fireplace.

Caroline shared how much Grammy had grown to love the sweet dog in the last several weeks, "She is truly a special dog. Brayley was lying outside Grammy's door the morning that she passed. She wouldn't move until I went in to check on Mom. It's like she knew Grammy was gone."

This made Emma tear up again, but this time, she was comforted knowing that Brayley had protected her grandmother.

They sipped their tea late into the afternoon, and then Emma decided to walk on the beach. So she bundled up, grabbed Brayley's leash, and off they went.

CHAPTER 40

BEGIN AGAIN

"The heart just knows."

There they were on the beach. Jake and Brayley were making friends while Miles and Emma stood staring at each other, feeling almost like strangers.

Miles shuffled his feet awkwardly in the sand, initially unsure what to say, "Your dog is beautiful. Is she a silver-gray Lab?"

Emma looked at her constantly growing puppy, "Yes, Brayley is a silver-gray Lab. She's quite a handful, but I love it."

He smiled at her comment, "Puppies will do that to you." Then he took a deep breath before he spoke again, "Look, Emma, I know that I have been distant. These last several months have been a lot."

The hurt returned to her eyes as she recalled that horrible night, along with flashbacks of everything they had both been through.

She only nodded in response. He didn't know how to take that, but he kept talking now that he gained some courage. "Emma, will you look at me, please? I've been thinking a lot, and some things need to be said."

A lump of emotion began to rise in her throat. She just couldn't handle any more pain on top of losing Grammy, plus the divorce and the haunting ghost of Izzy hanging in the air.

She decided to push down the tears and steel herself against the hurt she was preparing to hear with Miles' words.

Slowly, she raised her head to look into his brilliant blue eyes. His next words truly shocked her.

"With all the crazy thoughts running through my mind, they always come back to you. Emma, I still love you."

Those words made her catch her breath, and she looked deeper into his eyes as he continued, "I messed up bad. I should have trusted you and our love for each other when I got kicked out of the Navy. It was my fault that all of this happened. But then I think about Isla and how I wouldn't have her. Maybe we were supposed to be apart so I could figure out what to do with my life. Perhaps I had to be without you to realize that I don't want to live my life *without you.*"

Overwhelmed with emotion, tears flooded down both of their cheeks. Miles continued to share what he was feeling, "Something always brings me back to you and your life. When I was young, the Glass House was an obsession of mine. I loved looking at it, admiring its light, shape, and angles that effortlessly matched the coastline. I never imagined that I would fall in love with the girl that lived in the house that I admired from a distance."

He took both of her hands in his and pulled her closer, "Emma, I'm tired of loving you from a distance. I want a life with you in it. I'm not living if I don't have you here with me. Please forgive my stupidity and say you want to be with me, too."

She couldn't believe what she was hearing. It was a lot to take in, yet so much of what he said was also true for her. As she thought more about it, she was just going through the motions of her life but not really living.

It was the right choice to divorce Maxwell, so she thought that made her happier but was she truly happy?

Emma took a long time to speak, making Miles nervous, and he began to think she would reject him. It made sense since he had been such an ass for so long, but God, he loved her so much and just wanted to be with her.

Tears were still falling on her cheeks, and he automatically reached up to brush them away, "Tell me what you're thinking. I can take it."

She reached up and gently touched his cheek to bring him closer so she could kiss him. Very lightly, their lips touched. It was like a match igniting the fire of their love.

The soft kiss quickly turned into a passion that they never truly lost.

Emma broke away just long enough to say, "I love you, too. I never stopped and probably never will. I made mistakes, too, you know. Loving you scares me, but being without you is unimaginable. It's like you are ingrained within the tapestry of me. I can't let it go. I love you so much, Miles."

They embraced for a long time, feeling the love they thought was lost forever. By the time they tried to pull away, they realized the dogs had wrapped their leashes around them, and they were stuck.

Jake and Brayley sensed their love and happiness. The pups began jumping up on their masters and barking in unison. They laughed as Miles and Emma fell into the sand and awkwardly untangled themselves from the intertwined leashes.

Once they were untangled, Miles fell back into the cold sand and amusingly said, "I thought you were stuck with me for a minute."

Emma rolled over to lay on top of Miles with a huge smile and responded, "Oh, you are stuck with me forever, buddy."

They kissed endlessly as the dogs ran and played beside them.

BACK TO THE GLASS HOUSE

EPILOGUE

CAN WE GET TO THE GOOD PART?

"From here on out."

It felt like summer, even if it was just for a day. See, it is never hot at the beach in Oregon. Like ever.

On this day, of all days, it is California hot. The breeze offered a little sweet relief, but the sun was so intensely bright. It heated the sand, which brought out everyone that craved its warmth.

This was their wedding day. A day that they had waited fifteen years for.

They had planned a simple, quick ceremony at the beach. Typically they had cold, windy weather, so they wanted a place where everyone could take cover in the welcome warmth of Pelican Cove, Big Reggie's beachfront pub.

This was the perfect spot for Emma and Miles to finally say, "I do." But damn, it was hot. No one planned for that.

She had chosen a simple, white satin body-skimming dress. She decided on no veil, and her hair hung in soft waves down her back.

Miles was dressed in dark jeans and a crisp, white button-down, opened at the top. A simple red rose was pinned to the pocket of his shirt.

Little Isla was also in a simple white dress with a puffy chiffon bow tied in the back. She giggled down the outdoor aisle, holding black velvet leashes while Brayley and Jake led her to meet her daddy.

Miles grinned widely as he watched his little girl toddle toward him.

Then he saw Emma. He beamed brightly and was completely transfixed on her as he watched his lovely bride walk towards him on the arm of Caroline.

He had never seen anyone more beautiful, and he was still astonished that she was marrying him.

The ceremony was emotionally charged with all the love these two held for each other.

While they chose traditional vows, Miles took a moment to speak from his heart as he placed the ring on Emma's finger.

"My dear Emma, I have loved you since the moment I met you. We thought it may have been too soon, but honestly, I kept thinking, "It's about time that I found someone to love." Although we found each other when we were young, it has been quite a journey to get to this day. I place this ring on your finger as a promise to love you, respect you, protect you, and be your partner forever. I put some of those scars on your heart, and I promise to spend the rest of my life trying to heal them."

As he said those words, he reached up and gently touched the scar on her neck. This time, she didn't feel the pain of the past. She only felt the love that they had for one another.

Emma beamed back at Miles as he spoke. They had found their way back to each other.

Then he asked her the most important question of all, "Emma, can I finally call you mine? Forever?"

Tears sprang to her eyes as she looked deep into his blue eyes and emphatically shook her head up and down as she confidently said one simple word, "Yes."

Everyone was emotional from the words that Miles spoke to his soon-to-be wife. There was no doubt that this marriage was going to last forever.

The sun was beginning to set when the reception started. Emma quickly changed into a flowing white top and jeans, which she paired with bare feet. She was born for jeans and no shoes. It was the beach girl within her.

During the toasts, it was Emma that surprised everyone when she stood to speak.

"My lovely friends and family, thank you for being here today. We certainly did take our time getting to this point, didn't we, my love?"

This was met with small chuckles from the guests at the surrounding tables.

Emma raised her glass and looked down with endless love for her husband, "To Miles, thank you for not giving up on us but most importantly on yourself. The only thing missing from this day is my lovely grandmother, Rosie. I know she is here because why else is this day as hot as the sun!"

More laughs were heard from the group as she continued, "But in all seriousness, my grandfather built the Glass House as a symbol of his love for Grammy. It shines like a beacon as bright as any lighthouse on the coast, and I know that you, Miles, realize this because you have spent years of your life staring at it in just as much wonder. May our love continue to shine as bright as the Glass House and forever be a symbol of our endless love story. I love you. Cheers!"

Hearts were full as those they loved raised their glasses in adoration for the beautiful union they witnessed.

Just as the sun set on the beach, Miles, Emma, and Isla wandered to the water's edge while the dogs played and jumped in the waves.

They turned and gazed down the coast at the Glass House as it shined brightly against the reflection of the last moments of the day's light.

This was a home that was originally built to illuminate one couple's love, and on this special day, there was no doubt that another great love would be carried on indefinitely by Miles and Emma.

ABOUT THE AUTHOR

This is the author's debut novel. Bridgette works full-time in marketing and writes whenever she gets a moment. She lives in the Midwest with her family. Writing this book fulfills one of her life's dreams, and it has been her biggest accomplishment, aside from having her children.

More books coming soon.